Praise for the *Perspective* Series

"Give Amanda Giasson and Julie B. Campbell a chance and they'll draw you into a world of intrigue…It's a place where beauty and horror live side by side."
- Susan Doolan
Special Arts & Life Reporter to the Barrie Examiner

"Amanda Giasson and Julie B. Campbell have crafted the perfect combination of strength and vulnerability in Megan Wynters and Irys Godeleva, the female dynamic duo that resides within the fantastical world of Qarradune. We are whisked away with our delightful female protagonists where there are twists and turns and nothing is as it seems in this mesmerizing tale of chivalry, bravery, and honor."
- John Darryl Winston
Author of the IA Series (www.johndarrylwinston.com)

"I instantly fell in love with the writing and the characters in Love at First Plight. Right from the start, the plot draws you in and I appreciated the great deal of care that went into writing this novel - the expertly crafted sentences and subtle details made for a very satisfying reading experience."
- Kat Stiles
Author of *Connected* (www.katstiles.com)

"Julie B. Campbell and Amanda Giasson easily bring you into the world of Megan and Irys, and once you are in their world you never want to leave. From the first page, to that last moment you are left wanting more."
- Diane Hodgson
Elementary Teacher

"J.Campbell and A. Giasson do a brilliant job of weaving their two writing styles together to create well developed characters and a captivating storyline that had my daughter and I struggling to share the book! We are eagerly awaiting the next novel in the the series!"
- J.Tauskela
Avid Reader

"Diving into a debut book proved exciting and extremely rewarding – especially when the book ends up blowing away my expectations and surprisingly, it left me hanging."
- Sandy Pestill
Nautica Book Club coordinator

Third Time's a Charmer

Book 3 of the Perspective Series

Amanda Giasson
&
Julie B. Campbell

Qarradune Books
Ontario, Canada

Copyediting by John Campbell and Donna Campbell

ISBN: 9781729466506

First Printing: 2018

www.PerspectiveBookSeries.com

Love the Perspective book series?

Check out the official website at
http://www.PerspectiveBookSeries.com

Follow us on social media:

Facebook (@PerspectiveBooks)
http://facebook.com/perspectivebooks

Instagram (@PerspectiveBooks)
https://www.instagram.com/perspectivebooks/

Twitter (@QarraduneBooks)
https://twitter.com/QarraduneBooks

YouTube (Perspective Books)
https://www.youtube.com/channel/UC9Sx6EXyP_oQ5pVQFxdk_Dg

Acknowledgements

The road to Third Time's a Charmer was as much of an adventure story for us as it was for our characters. Surgeries, new homes, new puppies, new "real jobs" were only the start. We're thrilled the third novel is finally here and couldn't have done it alone.

Incredibly, amazingly, astoundingly, and dream-come-true-ingly, you, our readers, have become such a beautiful part of this experience! You're out there to share in a favourite part of our life with us – this series.

Thank you to those of you who have left reviews on Goodreads, Amazon, iBooks, and anywhere else you've picked up a copy. Thank you for the likes and comments on social media. Thank you also for coming to see us at Comic Cons and events! It means the world to us – this one and Qarradune – and we hope to see more of you soon.

We did things differently this time and are more than thrilled with how it went. We're unbelievably grateful to everyone who came through for us to get it done. Our new unbelievably dedicated editing team, Donna Campbell and John Campbell, absolutely blew us away. Thank you, forever and ever, for your mastery of English grammar, your respect for Irys and Megan's voices, your eye for even the sneakiest typos, and your willingness to drop absolutely everything in your lives to (competitively!) complete every stage of editing. Wow!

To our team of beta readers, Sean Evans, Linda Evans, Bill Evans, Pat Giasson, Donna Campbell and John Campbell, thank you for your impeccable feedback. You've made sure our story – the one we really want to tell – is being told. Laura Campbell and Jason Giasson, thank you so much for trying even during the busiest months of your year (lives?!).

We'd also like to give a special oh-my-goodness-you're-a-lifesaver thanks to Elizabeth Rogers, who found a new software for us to use when the legacy version of AIM (with see-as-you-type real-time) we'd depended on for our unique writing and story creation style, finally shut down its servers. Elizabeth, we wish you a lifetime of sparkles for coming to our rescue. We're not sure how we would have completed this book – or the rest of the series – without your tech wisdom.

Now, it's on to the fourth book. Can't wait!

Chapter 1

Megan

This can't be happening to me. Not again. Not after everything I've been through on this cursed world. It isn't fair.

I had been so careful. I had made friends with some of my enemies, and I had followed all the rules. I did what had been asked of me, and I had been so close to escaping Kavylak's capital with Thayn that we should have been on our way back to Syliza by now. I shouldn't be stuck with Amarogq's fiancée, Amorette, locked in a carriage heading to who-knows-where.

I'd been kidnapped; snatched right off the military compound in the Capital City along with Amorette and possibly the two other women who had been in the underground bunker with us. I had no idea who our captors were. Amorette had said that they were rebels but that meant nothing to me. Still, the fear I saw on her face told me that we were in serious trouble.

Between the benches of the carriage, Amorette was sitting on the floor next to me, facing the door and hugging herself. She had previously tried to open the door, but it was locked. We were trapped for the time being, but I couldn't give up hope. I had to find my way back to Thayn, somehow, and find out if Pounce was alive. The only way I could do that was if I learned more about these rebels.

Focusing my gaze on Amorette, I asked, "Who are the rebels, Amorette, and why would they want to take us?"

"They're likely from one of the new states. This has happened before – not to me – but to the loved ones of top officials," she explained quietly, looking at me with sad eyes.

She gasped suddenly, when the carriage made an unpleasant noise as it went over a large lump in the road, jostling us around. Tensing at the feeling and the sound, I braced myself for anything. I was just as jumpy as she was.

"So, are they taking us for ransom or something?" I asked once I was able to work up the nerve to speak again.

"Ransom." She nodded and added, "Or they want something back. They might want an exchange."

I frowned at her words, wondering what they could possibly want to trade us for. These rebels either had a death wish, or they wanted something or someone badly enough that they would risk invoking the wrath of the Warriors. An uneasy feeling slithered up my spine.

"Will people come for us?" I asked Amorette, even though I already know what her response would be.

"Yes," she said with certainty. "Amarogq will. He'll bring Warriors with him. They were stupid to take us."

I nodded in agreement. While the Warriors were still a mystery to me, the one thing I knew for certain was that I wouldn't want to tick one of them off. I doubted that the tolerance and friendliness they had shown me would extend to anyone they saw as a threat. Both Irys' handkerchief and Rral's ring, still tucked in my pocket, were proof enough of that. One way or another, I knew Amorette would be just fine. Amorogq would come for her, and these rebels had better watch out when he did.

Reaching out, I took Amorette's hand and held it in a firm and friendly way. "It's going to be alright," I assured her. "I've seen Amarogq in action with his wolves. You're his fiancée. He'll find you and bring you back."

I didn't know Amorette very well but from what I did know of her, I liked her. She was kind and seemed decent. I wanted to bring her comfort. Regardless of my opinions on the Warriors, and regardless of the fact that she was from Kavylak – and I saw Kavylak as my enemy – no one deserved to be taken away from their home and from the people they loved. I knew all too well what that felt like, and I didn't wish that feeling on anyone. I knew then that I was on her side, at least until this was over. We were in this together.

She looked relieved when I took her hand, holding mine in return. "I just hope they find us soon. We could be going very far, Megan," she warned me.

I didn't want to think about how far we might be traveling. With any luck, we were heading closer to Syliza.

"Do you think they've taken the other two women as well?" I asked.

"I didn't see," she replied honestly. "Did you see anything? Was there more than one carriage?"

I shook my head. "I didn't see anything. Everything happened so fast. I knew only that they had grabbed you."

She nodded. "We should do as they say. If we get the chance to escape, we should try. Otherwise, we should do as they say," she repeated.

I agreed, completely on board with her logic. I had no interest in angering these guys. I didn't know who they were or what they were after, and I certainly had no quarrel with them. Based on what Amorette believed, they were definitely enemies of Kavylak but considering I was an enemy of Kavylak, too, I certainly wasn't about to judge without knowing the facts.

"I won't do anything stupid," I assured her. "I want to stay alive and in one piece. We need to be smart about this."

"They might think you're related to one of the Warriors or that you're one of their girlfriends. If they do, let them think that. Otherwise, you're worthless to them. If they don't know who you are, make up a relationship with one of the Warriors," she advised.

"Alright. Thanks. I'll do that," I said, taking her words to heart. "I guess I'll pretend to be Mez' girlfriend. You thought I was. I could sell that."

Truth was, I knew next to nothing about Mez, but for some reason I felt like I could better sell a lie about being his girlfriend than being Keavren's, even though Keavren was technically the male Warrior I knew best. I think part of the reason I felt this way was that if these rebels knew anything about the Warriors and their skills, they might think twice about messing with the girlfriend of the mind-warping Warrior.

Amorette nodded. "They won't want to mess with Mez."

Exactly.

"Yeah," I agreed and looked at her thoughtfully. "Have you ever been kidnapped before?"

She shook her head. "No. I'm scared," she confessed.

I understood. "It's..." I trailed off, catching myself before I could reveal that the Warriors had kidnapped *me* from Syliza. While it was relevant to the situation, I realized that I shouldn't divulge that information to her because that could open up a whole unnecessary can of worms. The less Amorette knew about my past, the better. "It's going to be okay. You're strong. We both are," I finished.

She gave me a strange look before answering, "We are."

Without speaking another word, I shifted to sit closer to her on the carriage floor, still holding her hand. We both needed as much comfort as we could get and, at this point, words of encouragement weren't going to do the trick. I rested my head back on the side wall of the carriage, wondering where we were headed and how long our journey would be.

*   *   *   *   *

We rode in the carriage for a long time. Amorette and I dozed off and on. As time dragged on, I was finding it hard to keep my eyes open. It was more from sheer boredom than exhaustion. I had no way of knowing how much time had passed, but I would guess that it had been at least three or four hours since we'd been abducted.

I was hungry and desperately thirsty. My mouth was as dry as dirt, and my tongue felt like sandpaper. I'd had nothing solid to eat since the day before, and I hadn't had anything to drink for hours. My body ached all over, and my head had begun to throb. I was growing less concerned about who had captured us and where we were headed and was more concerned about whether or not we'd be given food and water.

Abruptly, the carriage came to a halt, jerking us forward.

I looked at her with wide eyes. Her expression mirrored my own. We could hear men and a woman talking. Their voices grew louder as they approached the carriage. Amorette's grip tightened on my hand, and I gripped back, ready for anything.

The door to the carriage was thrown open. We both jumped, and Amorette pushed herself back against the wall of the carriage.

A man and a woman, each dressed in a Kavylak soldier's uniform, stood before us.

"Get out," the woman barked at us.

Wow! Someone's not interested in being friends...

Amorette glanced in my direction and gave a tiny nod of her head, clearly indicating to me that we should follow the order. I couldn't have agreed more. This wasn't the time for revolt.

We both slowly moved forward and climbed down from the carriage. We kept our hands locked together the whole time. We were both prepared to do as we were told, and at the same time, neither one of us had any intention of letting each other go. Together, we would face whatever these people had in store for us.

Chapter 2

Irys

From under the pale glow of the moonlight, the fields appeared to extend until forever – or at least until the darkness swallowed them. Screaming would not bring me a rescuer. The only person who would hear me was the man who had brought me here in the first place: Rimoth.

He had been working at the inn where I had stopped with Sir Dynan Fhirell, the second-in-command of the Knights of Freyss as well as Desda, my maid and chaperone, and the dozens of others who made up the group that was journeying with us. We were headed to the Sylizan province of Gbat Rher in order to lend our assistance in rebuilding, following a difficult take-over. More importantly, Rimoth was a Traveller; a man who could disappear from one place and reappear in another.

A moment ago, I had been in my room at the inn. Now I was here, standing in an empty field, enveloped in darkness while wearing only my nightgown and dressing gown. The chill from the damp grass under my bare feet trembled its way throughout the rest of my body. It was in part from the cold, but my fear was only worsening it.

Hugging my arms around myself, I begged my mind to understand this situation and overcome my denial. Before me stood Rimoth, looking pleased with himself. The expression could have been a trick of the pale light, of course, but I doubted it.

"I can't be here," I insisted to him. "Please bring me back. I cannot be here alone and without my escorts and belongings."

"I'm aware of that," he replied with amusement. "I don't plan to abandon you here." He chuckled quite merrily.

I did not share his mirth. "Thank you. Please bring me back to the inn."

Shaking his head, he continued to smile. "I won't bring you back, but I will bring you one person who can stay with you until the

6

rest of your entourage arrives. Consider this a head-start. Who would you like me to bring you?"

"I don't want anyone to join me. I want to go back. Please. What must I do to convince you?" My teeth were beginning to chatter.

Rimoth sighed as though my response was not only disappointing to him but also boring. "Alright, alright. I'll take you back, but I want to know one thing first: why was the Sefaline after you?"

"I don't know," I replied honestly. "He asked about a book that belonged to a friend of mine. It didn't make sense to me that he would go to such great lengths for so simple an object."

I was fairly certain that I could see a brow raising, unless my imagination was playing tricks on me. His face was very pale, and his hair and brows were the colour of polished pewter. It was enough of a contrast that I might have been right about my assumption.

"That is a little hard to believe," he said in agreement with me.

"Yes," I responded and was fairly certain that the Traveller had resigned himself to bringing me back. He was beginning to move toward me, but he halted quite suddenly. If there had been anything else I'd wanted to say, I was never given the chance to utter it.

As quickly as a blink, someone else appeared between us. It was a woman who was, I supposed, another Traveller. Never in my life had I seen one of these creatures and yet now I was meeting two of them in a span of minutes. Still, I was barely able to consider the thought before the woman forcefully grabbed hold of me and brought the blade of a dagger to my throat. I could feel the point of it grazing my skin, and prayed that it would not press any harder against me.

Barely moving, barely breathing, I stood as still as I could, terrified that even the slightest shift would cause the knife to cut into me.

Rimoth, for his part, looked just as shocked as I felt. He stood where he was, arms at his sides, and watched us.

"Who are you, and what do you want?" he demanded.

"I want the Sefaline Warrior. What did you do with him?" the woman retorted with an intensity that mirrored Rimoth's.

"I put him in a place where he won't be bothering anyone. This woman isn't a threat to you. Let her go." His voice was just as stern, but he was certainly the calmer of the two Travellers.

"No," the woman replied flatly. "You're going to bring me the Warrior, *then* I will let her go." Her tone made it clear that this was the only action she was willing to accept. I had no doubt that she would kill me if Rimoth failed to comply. Whether or not Rimoth believed the same thing, I couldn't tell.

Without responding, Rimoth disappeared, reappearing immediately next to me. He placed his hand on my arm, only to look surprised yet again. It appeared as though he had expected to be able to take me with him but that he had been unable to travel.

The woman confirmed my hypothesis by pressing the blade more firmly against my throat. It was no longer just brushing against my skin. I could feel the sharpness of the metal and gasped as it bit into my flesh. I imagined that at least a small amount of blood must have been drawn.

Great Goddess, save me.

"As long as I have her, you can't travel her," the woman said with impatience. "Bring me the Warrior, Traveller."

Rimoth's expression turned to anger. I could see him much more clearly now that we were this close.

"Fine." He spat the word with distaste. "Don't hurt her. It may take me some time to find him."

"You have five minutes, or she's a corpse," was all the woman said. Again, I believed her.

"Please..." I whispered, unsure of to whom I was directing the plea.

"It will be alright, Miss Godeleva," Rimoth said and without another word, was gone.

"Please don't hurt me. I promise not to fight you," I begged of the woman whose stance and hold on me had not changed.

"Shut up," she said coldly.

I did. There was nothing else for me to do.

The wait stretched into an eternity. Five minutes must have come and gone several times over. My muscles were starting to ache from the tension in which I held them in order to remain still.

Great Goddess, please hear me. I am terrified and alone, and yet I know you are with me. Please guide this woman to your Light and show her that she should not cause me harm. I wish only to return to my people and continue my mission of mercy. Please show me that I am following your Path and that you do not want this woman to stop me here.

I was shocked that I didn't scream when Rimoth reappeared with the Sefaline Warrior. The Warrior was in a vicious rage. As soon as they arrived, Rimoth released the Sefaline and turned to escape him, but he was not fast enough.

The Sefaline lunged at him, using a slashing motion with his hands held in the shape of claws. At the same time, he forced his body weight forward and slammed into Rimoth, knocking him to the ground.

Rimoth didn't move. The Sefaline turned his attention toward me and the woman holding me. His fangs were bared as he panted from the exertion. There were dark smudges on his face and hands. My stomach turned as I realized they were likely blood.

"Lieutenant Fhurrk," the woman addressed him sternly. "Calm yourself. You're no longer in danger."

Lieutenant Fhurrk appeared to lose much of his anger. In a matter of seconds, his stance had completely altered. Still, though the aggression appeared to have subsided, he did not look calm or well.

On the ground, Rimoth twitched. My heart leapt at the thought that he was alive, but that thrill was short-lived when he disappeared only a moment later.

"No!" I cried out, receiving a huff of displeasure from the woman.

"You must leave this area, Lieutenant," she commanded the Warrior. "Travel east toward the sea. Zayset will collect you from there. I will make sure the other Traveller will not be able to track you."

At that, she shoved me forward, and I fell to my hands and knees. It hurt, but I pushed myself back to my feet to create some distance from these two enemies. Moving through the darkness was easier said than done.

"How injured are you?" I heard her ask Lieutenant Fhurrk.

"I will survive," he replied and allowed his glowing cat-like eyes to fall on me. I froze. He seemed to recognize me for the first time. "Why is she here?"

"I don't know," the woman answered, uninterested. "The other Traveller likes her, I suppose."

"Where are we?"

"Best I can tell, we're precisely in the middle of nowhere."

The thought did occur to me that I should attempt to get away from them but as neither of them appeared to be interested in me any longer, and as I didn't know which way to travel, I remained where I was – out of reach, but very lost. I considered waiting until the sunrise. At least that way, I could try to make my way south, toward the rest of Syliza. Hopefully, I would find someone who would help me. I wouldn't be going far in bare feet and my nightwear.

With a plan like that, my odds of survival were slim, and I couldn't pretend otherwise.

"I will tell you where we are if you will tell me which way is south," I said before I could think about what I was doing. I forced my voice to sound braver than I felt. My hope was to be able to begin my journey southward now, since it wouldn't benefit me to stand here in a field for the entire night.

"We're in Gbat Rher," the woman huffed as they both stared at me.

I frowned. That was the only thing I knew, and it was useless.

The woman turned back to Lieutenant Fhurrk. "Go," she commanded and disappeared before he could acknowledge her words.

Lieutenant Fhurrk, hadn't any intention of responding. His gaze hadn't budged from me. The fierce glowing violet orbs of his eyes cut through the darkness like a predator preparing to spring on his prey.

I looked back, wide-eyed and unmoving.

Great Goddess, I need you again...

Chapter 3

Megan

"There's an outhouse. Do either of you need it?" the woman rebel asked.

"I do," I said immediately, jumping at the chance to use the facilities and also hoping that we'd be able to see more of where we were. While nothing looked familiar to me, maybe it would to Amorette, giving us an advantage somehow.

Amorette nodded and without a word in reply, the female rebel grabbed hold of the back of my shirt and the back of Amorette's jacket. She shoved us forward in the direction I assumed would lead us to an outhouse.

I didn't resist. This woman clearly wasn't interested in making friends, and I had a feeling she'd more than shove us forward if we gave her any trouble. Amorette and I stepped forward hand-in-hand.

As we walked, I took a better look at our surroundings. We appeared to be in some type of small woodland clearing. I noticed a few other rebels around, all of whom were dressed as Kavylak soldiers. They were hanging around a lone rundown building that looked like it must have been a small house once but was now missing some of its walls. The trees surrounding the clearing were tall and so dense that even if we were surrounded by other structures, I'd never be able to tell.

She stopped us in front of the house and waited as Amorette and I took our turns using the outhouse. I was thankful it still functioned considering the dilapidated conditions of the structure. While I would have killed for some hand sanitizer, there was at least a working water pump that let us wet our hands. This helped me to feel a little cleaner.

The water only reminded me of how terribly thirsty I was. While I debated taking a drink, the run-down condition of the building made me doubt the safety of the water. It wasn't worth the risk. These rebels had to give us water at some point, right?

Deciding we were done, the woman grabbed us again, shoving us toward a different carriage that was nearly a mirror image of our first one.

The door to the carriage was open and as we drew closer to it, I could see that it wasn't empty. There was a very odd-looking and very tattooed bald man sitting on one of the benches. My eyes shifted back to the bald man but before I could take in any more of his appearance, Amorette and I were given a final rough shove toward the carriage, and the female rebel released her hold on us.

We both stumbled from the unexpected force of the woman's push. Amorette nearly fell, sharply pulling my arm as our held hands kept her upright. My anger spiked, winning out over my fear, and it took everything in me not to turn back to the rebel woman and scream in her face. I didn't know what the hell her problem was, but she certainly wasn't getting any sympathy from me. I hoped all the rebels weren't like this.

Wow! Never thought I'd miss being the prisoner of the Warriors...

I released Amorette's hand so she could climb into the carriage, and I followed her. I was barely inside when the door slammed shut, causing me to jump and gasp. I whipped my head around to glare at the door just as I heard the bolt slide across on the other side.

Calm yourself, Megan. Think about a nice stone cottage by a river. Don't think about punching a certain rebel woman in the face.

I knew that the violent anger I was feeling toward the woman was entirely overblown. I was hungry, dehydrated, exhausted, and beyond afraid. This was not a good recipe for positive thinking.

"Was that really necessary?" The bald man in the carriage asked.

I looked at him, wondering if he was commenting on my reaction but saw that his inquiring gaze was directed at the door. As if in response to his words, the door was brusquely unbolted and bolted again as if to tell him her slamming actions were indeed necessary.

Gotta say, I'm liking Mr. Bald-Tattooed-Man.

He was easily one of the most interesting-looking men I'd ever seen in my life. If I were home, I'd have assumed he was of South-Asian descent; perhaps from Nepal, or even Northern India or Tibet. He wore what could best be described as a medium blue Tibetan-ish-style monk robe with long sleeves. I also noticed he was wearing a bright yellow fabric that was barely visible behind the blue cloth that covered his torso.

Although I'd never seen anyone else dressed like him on Qarradune, his attire wasn't what drew the eye. It was the numerous tattoos that decorated just about every visible inch of his skin that were truly remarkable. Diverse intricate patterns and images in blue ink marked his head, neck, hands, and even his face. There were so many, in fact, that at first glance his skin itself almost looked blue.

From what I could see, no two tattoos were the same. While I didn't know it for certain, I had a feeling that this man was covered in tattoos literally from head to toe.

Taking a seat next to Amorette on the bench opposite the bald man, I took her hand again. Only then did I notice that the man wasn't alone. Beside him, sitting perfectly calmly and serenely, was the woman whom Amorette had identified to me as Fiffine Wintheare; the wife of Captain Aaro Wintheare.

Unlike Amorette and I, who were starting to look like we'd been dragged backwards through a hedge, Fiffine appeared entirely un-rumpled. The only thing that betrayed her pristine appearance was the dark circles forming under her eyes, revealing she was just as exhausted as we were. I was glad to see that she was alright but realized that the other woman from the bunker wasn't with us: the one dressed all in white and with the connection to Aésha, whom Amorette had called Ihleah.

What did they do with her?

"Good morning. I'm Rakej." The bald man introduced himself. "I think you've both met Fiffine."

He spoke in a warm and friendly way as if he were hosting some gathering. Considering the actual situation, this seemed bizarre, to say the least.

"Fiffine, are you alright?" Amorette asked her. I could hear the worry in her voice as much as I could see it in her face.

"Yes. I have been treated well," she answered placidly.

I had no idea how she was that calm. Did they drug her or something?

"Ihleah?" Amorette asked.

I looked from her to Fiffine, who shook her head.

"She was not taken," Fiffine revealed. "They wouldn't take a Robe."

They wouldn't take a Robe?

I assumed she was referring to Ihleah and not to an article of clothing. This had me curious. I didn't know why they wouldn't kidnap a Robe, but I had to find out more about these Robes and see if I could become one while I was stuck on Qarradune. That might help reduce my chances of future kidnappings.

"I'm sure she'll tell the Warriors what happened," Fiffine concluded.

Finally, some good news!

"We're counting on it." The Rakej guy nodded.

Um, wait. What? They're counting on it? These rebels actually want the Warriors to know what happened? Okay...they're a lot crazier than I initially thought.

I looked at him incredulously. "You're counting on it?"

"Yes," he replied simply. "How are we going to arrange everything we want if nobody knows where you went? We needed someone to be a witness."

I stared at him blankly for a moment. I was too surprised to talk. It didn't make sense to me that these rebels would kidnap us only to tell the Warriors they had done it. I supposed it was possible that there could be a peaceful negotiation once they had found us, but I couldn't ignore the uneasy feeling that this was going to end in anything but a nonviolent resolution.

"I'm going to have something to eat. Does anyone else want to share?" he asked.

"Yes, please," I responded immediately, suddenly no longer caring about peaceful resolutions. With the offer of food, I could only think about feeding my empty stomach.

He nodded and picked up a wooden box that had been resting on the bench beside him, setting it on his lap. He opened the small box and extracted four square-shaped objects wrapped in an opaque wax-like paper. He handed a random square to each of us before taking one for himself.

"Thank you," I said, and he nodded to me.

Amorette took one of the squares but just held on to it, not acknowledging Rakej. Fiffine nodded her thanks and lifted her free hand in the air toward him and made a deliberate and fluid movement with her fingers. He returned the movements, though not as smoothly as she had done.

Um, weird. Maybe that was "thank you" in Qarradune's equivalent to sign language. They do remember that they can talk, right?

Not interested in wasting another brain cell on the silent code lingo, I unwrapped my square-shaped food and discovered what looked like a granola bar.

Briefly looking it over, I surmised it was composed of a bunch of grains and seeds that had been pressed together. I bit into it and as I chewed, I found that the bar had a slightly sweet flavour that reminded me of honey. It was like eating a homemade granola bar.

I ate the entire square. I did debate saving it, but I decided it would be better to eat it, just in case the food was taken away. Rakej ate his as well. Amorette only nibbled at hers, and Fiffine was able to manage only a few bites. I hoped she was feeling alright.

"Water?" Rakej asked us, first drinking out of a canteen and then holding it out to us.

I looked eagerly at the canteen, but waited for the others to take it first.

"Go ahead. I'll have it after you," Amorette said to me. I looked to Fiffine, and she nodded.

I didn't need to be told twice. I nodded to them in return and took the offered canteen and had a generous drink of water. I couldn't recall another time in my life when drinking water felt so utterly satisfying and amazing. The only thing that stopped me from drinking it all was that I knew I wasn't the only one who needed it.

"Thank you," I said to Rakej and handed the canteen to Amorette, who also take a generous drink, before she held it out to Fiffine.

"No, thank you," she said softly to Amorette, declining the canteen.

Amorette's brow furrowed. "Go on, Fiffine. Have a little, at least," Amorette encouraged.

"She's had a few sips," Rakej said, gently taking the canteen from Amorette. "She's still trying to take it easy to keep everything down," he added, and Fiffine nodded to confirm his words. It was as if he and Fiffine were old friends, and he knew exactly what she needed.

Amorette wasn't appeased by his words or by Fiffine's nod. She frowned. "Try when you can," she said.

"I will," Fiffine promised.

I watched them all, a little perplexed. I felt like everyone in that carriage knew something about Fiffine that I didn't. Amorette looked at me and gave my hand a squeeze. I squeezed back, hoping to bring her some comfort.

Oh, no! Is Fiffine sick?

"Are either of you in the family way, or is it only Mrs. Wintheare?" Rakej asked.

I blinked in surprise, both at his question and at what he had revealed: Fiffine was pregnant.

Amorette shook her head, and I did, too. I looked at Fiffine and felt just awful for her. I didn't want to imagine what she was feeling or how terrified she was for her baby.

Rakej nodded. "Just wanted to make sure," he said. "I'd have switched benches with you, if you were. It's easier to face forward in a carriage than backward."

That was nice of him to say and all, but if he really wanted to make things easier for us, he could let us go or, at the very least, let Fiffine go.

"Is it not possible to take Mrs. Wintheare somewhere safe, where she can return to her family? Surely you didn't mean to kidnap her," I said, keeping my voice as gentle as possible. I was hoping to appeal to his good nature.

"We didn't," Rakej agreed, shaking his head. "But we don't intend to cause any harm, so as long as your Warriors come to find you, and as long as they are willing to meet our demands, there won't be anything to worry about."

I frowned, not liking his answer. Honestly, they wouldn't take the other woman because she was a "Robe," but they'd kidnap a pregnant woman? These rebels didn't make the slightest bit of sense to me.

I looked at Fiffine, who appeared as calm as ever, willing to wait this out for as long as she must.

"Your intentions toward us are peaceful, then?" I asked, turning my attention back to him.

"Toward you, personally?" He nodded. "Yes. As long as you behave, we'll feed you and treat you as comfortably as the rest of us. The point isn't to hurt you. It's to keep you until we can trade you for what we want."

Amorette had been right. This was a trade. It was my turn to give her hand a squeeze. She returned it.

We had to be strong for Fiffine. We might all be in the same circumstance, but neither Amorette nor I had an unborn child to worry about. I had to keep my focus. I had to learn more about these rebels.

Fixing my gaze on Rakej, I asked with curiosity: "Where are you from?"

"I'm originally from Lhador," he answered easily before adding, "but I'm fighting with the Dsumot resistance."

Well that's good to know, and I'm sure that will mean something to me one day. I should start carrying a map of Qarradune at all times.

Amorette shifted and out of the corner of my eye, I saw her face contort in slight disgust when he mentioned the resistance.

Okay, so she's not a fan. Also good to know.

"The Dsumot resistance?" I asked, "From whom or what are you resisting?" I saw no reason to hide my ignorance, though I had a feeling I might already have known the answer.

"Kavylak. They've already taken Sorcheena, and we know they're eyeing our border. We're not interested in a similar fate."

I listened and forced a small nod to indicate only that I understood but not that I was on their side. That said, I didn't honestly blame them for resisting. Who wouldn't want to protect their home from being swallowed up by invaders? I didn't agree with their whole kidnapping thing, but oddly, I also felt that I couldn't judge them too harshly for it. I had reached some pretty desperate points since winding up on this crazy world. I wanted to believe that I would always do the right thing, but I also knew that I couldn't be certain of what I would or wouldn't do unless I was living and breathing their exact situation.

Since being on this crazy world, I had already been brought to a desperate point in which I felt that I had nothing to lose. In that moment I chose to enslave myself to a madman to save someone else. What would I do if I felt this way again – or worse – what would I do if I felt I had everything to lose? How far was I prepared to go to escape from these rebels when the opportunity came? Thinking about it made my stomach swirl.

I leaned my head back against the wall of the carriage and shut my eyes, hoping that the Warriors would find us soon, before desperation drove any of us to a breaking point.

Chapter 4

Irys

I froze for a long time as we watched each other through the darkness. While I could see his cat-like eyes, I imagined that he could see a great deal more. Slowly, I slid one bare foot backward on the cold grassy ground, pausing sharply when he suddenly spoke.

"I'm not going to hurt you," he said flatly.

It was the last thing I would have expected him to say. Thinking back though, I realized that I was likely the least of his concerns. Why ever would I have mattered to him now? His situation was only slightly better than mine, in that we were both alone in this dark field without any help or supplies. He, however, had a direction to take. Then again, he was also wounded.

"Are you badly injured?" I asked, feeling obligated to speak as he had not stopped looking at me. "Will you make it to your checkpoint?"

He began to walk, though without any great speed to his stride.

"I should make it. I have been stabbed, but it is not too deep."

Great Goddess, please save this man from perishing before he meets the people who will bring him home. It is my fault – at least in part – that he came to harm. Please don't place his death upon my conscience.

"Is your wound bandaged?" I couldn't help but ask him. He was a Warrior, a Sefaline, and quite terrifying, but at the moment he was not a threat to me. He was merely a man, and he was wounded.

"No. I will have a better look at it when I am farther from here and when there is more light. I have to keep moving."

I realized only now that I had been following him. When had my feet decided to take this path? Before I could give it any further consideration, he turned and looked at me again.

"Why are you dressed like that," he asked with disapproval in his tone.

"Because I was taken from my room at the inn shortly after you were. I was not given the chance to dress," I replied curtly.

"You will freeze in what you are wearing."

"Then I'd best keep moving and find some shelter." I hoped my words came with some semblance of confidence. I did not want to appear weak in front of this Warrior. He returned his gaze to me frequently, and I would not tolerate his judgment of me. Neither his predicament nor mine was my choice.

"If we can find a tree, I will climb it and see if there is anything around that might provide you with some shelter," he said after a long stretch of silence.

"No disrespect, Lieutenant as that is very generous of you but is that wise? You're bleeding."

"I will survive." He brushed off my concern. "My chances are better than yours."

"I needn't be reminded of that, thank you," I attempted to keep the chill out of my voice. "Why would you risk your life for me?"

The Warrior fixed his eyes on me as though pondering the answer to my question. "Because you will die without my help. I am not that kind of killer."

I nodded, uncertain as to how to reply. "If you do climb a tree, will you allow me to look at your wound afterward? Perhaps I can help you to treat it to improve your own chances."

"Yes," he agreed flatly. "Come this way. The air smells better this way."

Without another word, I followed him in the direction that he seemed to think was more appealing. As there wasn't any way for me to know whether or not this was the right way, I felt as though I hadn't anything to lose.

I was more than aware of how slowly I was walking. Every step was a careful examination of the ground with my bare toes as I desperately hoped to avoid treading upon something sharp or otherwise harmful. Lieutenant Fhurrk didn't seem to mind that we were moving at a rather glacial pace. I suspected that he might not have been able to travel any faster than I could.

After a while in utter silence, I could hear him fussing with his jacket. I imagined that he was searching for something in one of his pockets, but I was taken utterly off guard when the jacket to his

Warrior's uniform was offered to me. At nearly any other moment, I would have politely refused, but the warmth that would come from slipping its leather sleeves over my light dressing gown was something I simply could not decline.

As my fingers wrapped around the collar to accept the gift, I was astounded at just how warm the jacket truly was. The man must have been feverish to have been giving off such heat. Sighing with relief, I allowed the warmth to sink into me. Upon an inhale, I drew in the unique spicy scent of the Sefaline man before me. It was somewhat soothing at first, but my stomach flipped as I detected the lingering odor of blood on the jacket as well.

"You won't become cold without your jacket?" I asked, feeling somewhat foolish and yet still obligated to pose the question. He was wearing what appeared to be only a thin long-sleeved shirt. Little more than what I'd worn prior to donning his jacket.

"No."

"I recognize the scent on your jacket. Could you tell that I had detected it along the road while I was travelling with my group?" It was a strange question, but it felt better to talk than to walk in silence.

I couldn't tell if he was actually smiling or if it was merely my imagination playing tricks on me in the darkness. I could have sworn I caught sight of a fanged tooth. At the same time, his spicy sweet fragrance seemed to intensify for only the briefest instant. It was deliberate, I realized.

"Fascinating," I replied to his wordless answer to my question.

"I am Sefaline."

"Yes. I noticed your eyes and teeth when we first met."

To that, he looked rather proud, but his attention was caught by something farther into the darkness than I was able to see.

"There is a tree," he said, indicating toward something beyond the obscurity. It took less time to walk to it than I had expected; a solid reminder that I was little better than blind until the sun should decide to rise.

When we arrived at the base of the tree, he grabbed the lowest branches and deftly brought himself upward until I could no longer see him for the leaves – or possibly the darkness. I could tell by the occasional sounds of struggle that this was not as easy for him as it usually would be.

He wasn't up there long before he descended once again, catching his breath for slightly longer than a well man would.

"There is a shelter of some kind. That way." He indicated to the right of whatever direction we had been travelling. If we were indeed headed east, then I assumed that the structure was to the south of us.

"Thank you. I will go directly there," I assured him, slipping his jacket off with the intention of returning it to him.

"Keep it. You will need it," he said with a brief shake to his head.

"It's a Warrior's uniform," I replied respectfully but to explain why I didn't feel I could continue to wear the piece. "The people here will already detest me for being from Lorammel."

He received the jacket without any sign of insult. "You'd likely be hated more for being from Lorammel than you would for being a Warrior. Your people were thorough in destroying this place. The air here still remembers the stink of death."

"I was on my way here to help in the rebuilding. I've been doing all I can to assist these people since I learned about what happened here," I said more defensively than had been my intention. My country's treatment of the people of Gbat Rher shamed me more deeply than I was willing to admit, and it hurt to have it rubbed in my face as directly as Lieutenant Fhurrk was doing now.

"Safe journey, Irys Godeleva." His voice was gentler than it had previously been. Under other circumstances, I might have been able to convince myself that we were kind acquaintances and not on opposite sides of enemy nations.

"Wait..." I called out quickly before he could leave. "I promised to look at your wound."

His glowing eyes narrowed and rounded again. "The shelter I saw was not far from here. You can look at it there."

"Thank you," I replied, genuinely feeling that this was somehow as much a favour to me as it was to him.

This time, he walked next to me. His pace was slower than before, and his feet were nearly dragging.

Great Goddess, please save this man. In his heart, there is a place of goodness. He did not need to strain his already wounded body in order to assist me and yet this is what he has done. Please, I beg of you, let him be strong enough or give me the wisdom to help him so that he can reach his people.

As we approached what appeared to be a run down and badly damaged farmhouse, Lieutenant Fhurrk drew a long inhale through his nose.

"It's abandoned," he concluded, based on whatever he had – or had not – scented.

"It will be enough to stay warm until morning. Perhaps there is something inside for warmth and light."

"Careful where you step," he cautioned.

The ground was rutted and crunchy as though it had been pummeled by horses' hooves and wagon wheels before it had been scorched. I slowed my speed and used my toes to test every place before stepping down upon it.

Quite suddenly and with a deep grunt, Lieutenant Fhurrk lifted me up and into his arms.

"Stay still," he demanded, removing any potential for softness from the gesture. I brought my arm around his shoulders to hold on and did as I was instructed. As soon as we arrived on the doorstep of the house, he set me down, taking an extra moment to rise to his full height, which as it turned out, was not much taller than me.

Once he was upright again, he was able to shove the stiff door open and step into the empty structure. I followed and pushed the door closed behind us.

I may not have been a Sefaline but even I was able to smell that this house had been abandoned for some time. The dust and mustiness filled my nostrils as soon as I was fully inside. I hesitated to touch anything and remained standing just inside the entrance, looking through the darkness of the damp and chilly wooden building.

"Do you think there are any candles?" I asked, hoping for some light.

"I will look for some."

I could hear him opening cupboards and rummaging around. Soon enough, a match was struck and the glorious little yellow flame was transferred to the wick of a stubby homemade candle. From the scent of it, I'd say it was tallow, but I certainly wasn't about to complain. It was the first light I'd seen since I'd arrived in Gbat Rher.

As Lieutenant Fhurrk lit a second candle, I looked about the room, stepping carefully. Even dressed in his black Warrior uniform, he remained the most vibrant part of the room. His bright orange hair in long messy spikes picked up the light from the little flames.

There were still possessions throughout the space. Items on shelves, dishes in cupboards. This home was left in a hurry.

After an initial moment to look around, I recalled that Lieutenant Fhurrk was here for a purpose. I was supposed to be looking at his wound. Fishing through the kitchen, I found some folded tea towels in a drawer. It was fortunate that they had been stored there and not where they would have been covered in the same dust that coated everything else I had seen so far.

When I turned around again, the Sefaline Warrior had seated himself on a chair and had pulled his shirt up to his chest. I was inclined to turn away until I realized that there really wasn't any other way for me to check his wounds.

I stepped boldly toward him, kneeling down on the floor in front of the chair in order to better examine his injury through the dim light of two candles and to be able to reach him.

The sight of his skin was unexpectedly fascinating. It appeared as though his entire body was covered in designs and patterns that were several shades darker than the rest of his skin. These markings swooped gracefully to harsh points in ways that looked too appropriate on him to be anything but natural.

I would have obsessed over them further if it were not for the large bruises that were forming beneath them as well as the considerable gash on the right side of his body, directly over his ribs, which seemed to be oozing blood. It looked painful, but I could only pray it was not dangerously deep.

My heart sank at the look of him. How could Rimoth have done this to him? Lieutenant Fhurrk hadn't deserved these wounds. If Rimoth had wanted to remove him from my room at the inn, he could have dropped this Warrior anywhere in the world. Instead, he placed him in Korth, where barbarian clansmen still fought to the death over a single footstep into their territories. I dared not imagine what he must have faced there to have received such wounds in such a short time.

Folding one of the tea towels, I held it onto the laceration. He didn't even wince. Removing the belt from my dressing gown, I tied it around him to hold the tea towel bandage in place. At first, my fingers automatically began tying the belt into a bow as that was how I always fastened it around myself, but it looked rather silly on Lieutenant Fhurrk, so I untied it and made it a regular knot, instead, tucking the ends out of the way.

He watched me the entire time. It was impossible to ignore his glowing eyes.

"Are you used to caring for injured people?" he asked.

"I have done it before, but I wouldn't say that I am used to it."

He nodded and said nothing more on the subject.

I stood and took that opportunity to pick up one of the candles and head into the only adjoining room: a bedroom. The drawers were partially empty, but there was a woman's dress and several pairs of men's socks, which I rapidly collected. The dress was the type of plain design a farmer's wife would wear, and which I imagined would usually be worn under an apron. What mattered most was that it was made of a tightly woven wool that was far heavier than my nightgown.

Taking off my dressing gown, I pulled the dress on over my head and replaced the dressing gown on top of it. I wished I could have washed my feet before pushing them into the socks but told myself to stop being silly and be glad that I had any footwear at all. I pulled on two pairs of the large socks and folded them over to help them to stay in place.

Feeling slightly warmer and better protected against the cold, I walked back to check on the Warrior. I'd half expected to find that he had left. He did, after all, have somewhere to be.

He hadn't left. It looked as though he'd only recently stood up as he was just now pulling his shirt down over the newly bandaged wound. Stepping up to him, I picked up his jacket and tucked another tea towel into the pocket.

"In case you need a clean bandage," I explained as I handed him his jacket.

He merely nodded. "You should not be friends with a Traveller," he said as though that were the logical response to what I'd just told him.

"I'm not," I replied. "I didn't even know he was a Traveller until he took you away. Then he reappeared and brought me to that field. It all happened very quickly."

"They are broken in the mind."

"Many say the same thing about Warriors," I replied quickly, immediately regretting that I'd spoken without thinking first.

"They are right," he responded quite simply, to my utter and complete surprise. Taking the jacket from me, he slipped it on over his shoulders, his arms in the sleeves. He didn't fasten it, leaving it open. He stared at me for a very long time. I felt as though he expected me to do something, but I hadn't any idea what it could be.

"Will you stay here until dawn?" he asked.

"Yes. I haven't any real choice about it. I cannot see outside and I don't know where I'm going."

"That is wise," he said decidedly.

"What about you? Why don't you stay as well? You were slowing down out there. We both know it. Rest a little and regain your strength before you go out." My concern for him was genuine, if not entirely rational.

"I will go find a tree and will rest there for a while before moving on. I should not stay here."

"Why?"

"I don't trust what you might do if I sleep."

That certainly surprised me. It never crossed my mind that he might view me as a threat.

"I just bandaged your wound. Had I had any intentions to harm you, I could have done so then. I was in the kitchen, after all. There could have been something sharp in there. I have no reason to cause you harm. You have been helping me. I've been assuming that we would peacefully go our separate ways when the time comes."

He watched me in silence, narrowing his eyes.

Finally, I sighed. "Thank you for your help. Enjoy your tree," I said softly.

"I will stay."

"There is only one bedroom. You sleep out here, and I will sleep in there."

"If you find it too cold, you can sleep beside me."

It made me proud that I did not allow even a twitch of my face to reveal my thoughts on that offer. "I'm sure I will manage. There must be blankets, and the morning cannot be long off," was all I could think to say.

He simply nodded and lowered himself back into his chair.

Heading into the bedroom, I decided to investigate the available bedding. Looking through the drawers and the cupboard, I discovered that the only blankets available were what was already on the bed, and I was fairly certain that the bed was the source of the musty smell I had first detected upon entering this house.

After standing and staring at the offending furniture for a ridiculous amount of time – as though I would somehow be able to clean it with my gaze – I decided to swallow my pride and go back out and face the Warrior. I would not sleep next to him as he had suggested, but I would need to share a room with him.

Lieutenant Fhurrk was busying himself by attempting to make a fire in the hearth.

"It seems that the bedroom is not at all suitable. I will sleep in here if you are able to light the fire."

"I could smell the room from here," he agreed, watching me with his blue cat-like eyes. "See if you can find something to spread on the floor so you can sleep on it."

I hadn't any intention of sleeping on the floor but if he wanted to rest there, I didn't mind busying myself by finding something to spread beneath him. After a few minutes, I decided that the best I would find was a tablecloth that had been folded in the same drawer as the tea towels. I spread it out on the floor where he had indicated, before I took a seat in the chair he had vacated and where I intended to spend the remainder of the night.

Lieutenant Fhurrk, for his part, was able to build quite a nice little fire, which crackled beautifully and drank the moisture from the air. It left behind the delicious scent of wood smoke, which masked the home's original odor quite effectively. Seating himself on the tablecloth, he lay back, turning onto his uninjured side.

I respected his unspoken request for silence and watched the fire, the shadows dancing on the wall, and the Warrior curled on the floor. Before long, he was snoring softly; a sound that reminded me of a purr in its gentle rhythm.

Though longing for sleep, I could not seem to let go of consciousness. Over-exhausted, I remained settled there until the sun began to rise. I decided not to move quite yet as I did not wish to disturb Lieutenant Fhurrk, who needed his sleep and who had risked his health and his life in order to help me. I would head out when he was ready to rise on his own.

That time came sooner than I'd expected.

From what appeared to be a sound sleep, the Warrior lifted his head.

"Someone is coming."

Chapter 5

Megan

We drove in silence for what must have been hours. None of us were interested in making conversation. I think I must have nodded off at one point because I was suddenly startled awake when the carriage slowed to a halt.

"We'll stop here before we continue our journey," Rakej told us. "I'd say I'm looking forward to stretching my legs, but I'm not sure they're mine anymore," he joked.

I looked at him and nodded with understanding. I couldn't remember the last time my legs felt this bad. They were cramped, sore, and tingling from lack of use. I never thought I'd hate sitting so much in my entire life!

The door was thrown open from the outside, and I was willing to bet it was Miss Sunshine who had done it. To keep myself calm around the hateful rebel woman, I decided I'd secretly give her a ridiculous nickname that was the least suited to her personality, for my own amusement and sanity.

"Ah, we've been summoned," Rakej said with a hint of a smile on his lips and a touch of sarcasm in his voice.

I almost laughed at his remark, and I watched him step out of the carriage.

"Does anyone need help getting down?" he offered.

I looked at Fiffine. "Did you want our help, Fiffine?"

Fiffine smiled at me in her gentle way and said softly, "I'll take his help. I'm alright, thank you."

I nodded, accepting her choice. She seemed to be a woman who knew what she was doing.

Amorette and I waited for Fiffine to exit the carriage. Both of us watched her like a hawk as she gently took Rakej's offered hand and stepped out of the carriage. Amorette went next. She gave my hand a meaningful squeeze before standing. If she were in any discomfort from sitting for so long, she never showed it. She stepped out of the carriage, purposely not taking Rakej's help.

Unlike Amorette, when it was my turn to exit, I moved to the door on shaky legs. Each step was a new adventure of discomfort as my muscles raged at me for keeping my body locked in the same position for so long. This feeling was definitely worse than having the horse-legs I'd had from the long-distance ride with Keavren. I gladly took Rakej's offered hand and gave him a small smile when he helped me down. He warmly returned the smile.

"Please don't try to escape here," Rakej cautioned in a friendly way. "There are far too many of us. We genuinely don't want to hurt you. Don't take the risk."

He made it sound more like brotherly advice than a warning with a promise behind it. Fiffine nodded calmly to his words, but Amorette still made no effort to acknowledge him. It was apparent she'd heard him, but she wasn't going to give him the satisfaction of a nod.

"We're not going anywhere," I said, feeling the need to assure him with words and not just a nod. I felt it was important to keep up the friendliness with this guy, mostly because at the moment, I knew that escape was impossible. Plus, he did give us food and water and wasn't physically pushing us around like Miss Sunshine had. He deserved good friend points for that.

"Stretch your legs and stay in the clearing here," he said, indicating the open space in a forested area. There were a few other rebels - at least I guessed they were rebels – around, but there was no building this time.

I walked forward a few steps before finally deciding to give my legs a good stretch. Amorette followed. She was looking around, scoping out the situation. I could tell that she wasn't planning an escape, she was simply assessing the scene.

"Do you know where we are?" I asked her quietly.

"We've been travelling north," she whispered. "I think we might be heading to Dsumot."

I nodded, wondering if she was right, and how long it would take us to get there. I didn't think I could handle much more of sitting in that carriage.

"They will know by now," Fiffine said. Her gentle voice invaded my head, pulling me from my thoughts. I turned to look at her as she stepped up to us. "Men will have been dispatched to find us," she added with soft reassurance.

I nodded and smiled at her and secretly wished one of those men would be Thayn, but I knew that wasn't going to happen. In all honesty, I wouldn't actually have blamed him if he had gotten away and had decided to return to Syliza without me. It might not have been my fault for being kidnapped, but even I had to admit I had rotten luck on Qarradune. Would he really want a girlfriend who was turning out to be as much of a hassle as I was, when there were already dozens of pretty Sylizan women who would likely jump at the chance of a courtship with him?

Face it, Megan. You never really had a shot with Thayn.

I frowned.

"We aren't like other hostages," Fiffine told me, likely misinterpreting the reason for my frown. "We have Warriors after us. We won't be gone long." She said this with such certainty, I couldn't help but believe her.

"Do exactly as you're told," she instructed quietly. "Try to stay with Amorette and me. We should stay together and keep out of trouble. That way, when they arrive, they can find us all."

"That's pretty much what I told her, too." Amorette said with a smile.

I nodded to them both. "Do you think they'll send a lot of them?" I asked.

"At least three, with soldiers to back them up," Amorette replied.

I turned my attention to Fiffine and said, "Until then, if you need anything…" I paused looking at Amorette for a brief moment, "We'll help you in any way we can." I felt confident talking for Amorette. I knew she felt the same way I did, and I caught her nod out of the corner of my eye.

"Don't worry about me." Fiffine smiled at me like she thought I was genuinely sweet to offer.

"Fiffine is tougher than the two of us put together," Amorette said quietly but with confidence.

I didn't doubt Fiffine's toughness. She'd been amazingly calm and collected so far, and she was married to a Warrior. But the fact remained that she was pregnant and, tough or not, that made her more vulnerable than Amorette and me, because she had to protect the life of her unborn child.

"How far along are you, Fiffine?" I asked.

"Only a season."

Uh, right. Season...season...how many days did Mez say were in a season? Right! Sixty! So, that would make her about two months along.

I smiled at her. "Is it your first?" I asked.

"Yes," she said. "I think it will be a boy. My husband thinks the opposite."

"Your husband is Captain Wintheare," I stated, more as confirmation than a question.

"Yes. Aaro Wintheare." Fiffine nodded.

I was inclined to ask what his "skill" was as I knew each Warrior had some sort of magic or super-power, but I decided against it for a few good reasons.

Firstly, I thought it would be rude to ask, given the situation. Secondly, I didn't want to reveal to the other two women just how ignorant I was about the Warriors, Kavylak, and all of Qarradune, for that matter. Lastly, part of me kind of didn't want to know.

So far, I'd met a guy who could brainwash people, a guy who could muscle-up quickly, a dude who could walk on water, a guy who could control ghost-wolves, and two Warriors who could pretty much make you fall in love with them whenever they wanted. To top it all off, the only other Warrior with the rank of Captain whom I'd met was Galnar, and the last time I'd laid eyes on him, he was lighting stuff on fire with his bare hands! If it turned out that their so-called skills got freakier with their rank, who knew what Fiffine's husband could do...

"Which Warrior is yours?" Fiffine asked me. I had been so lost in my head, I almost jumped when she spoke.

Oh! I know the answer to this one!

"Mez."

Fiffine nodded her approval. "He's a good man," she said smoothly, never letting on whether she could tell I was lying.

"He is," I agreed genuinely. He had given me a kitten and good snacks after all. He also pretty much saved my life...

"I'm sure he'll come for you," she said, making her voice just slightly louder, so a passing rebel dressed in a Kavylak soldier's uniform would be able to hear.

"I don't actually think he will," I said in a hushed voice. "He was injured."

Concern washed over the faces of both women when they heard the news.

"Injured? How? What happened?" Amorette asked, her brow furrowing.

"He pushed me out of the way of flying debris," I explained with a frown. "I'm pretty sure a chunk of building struck him in the back."

Amorette raised a hand to her mouth and murmured, "Oh Goddess! Poor Mez."

Fiffine made that sign in the air I'd seen her previously make to Rakej, when we were in the carriage. I really had to find out what it meant, but now wasn't the time to inquire. I spotted Rakej walking toward us.

"It's time to go back to the carriage," he said.

I nodded to him and as much as the thought of sitting in that carriage was making me desperately want to run away, the three of us followed him to that cursed mode of transportation.

Like before, he offered his assistance to us. Both Fiffine and I took it, and Amorette refused it. We all took seats.

Rakej climbed in last and looked back out toward someone I couldn't see at first, but then saw that it was Miss Sunshine, who must have shown up to slam our door.

"It's alright. I've got it," Rakej assured her in a super-positive way, reached out for the door and slammed it far harder than was necessary. I heard the lock jam into place immediately afterward, and I could just imagine the scowl on her face from having lost her door-slamming rage-filled fun.

A laugh burst from my throat. I couldn't help it. That really tickled me, and I was in a place.

Amorette looked at me in surprise, and I forced my laugh down. I tried to look more serious for her but couldn't suppress my smile. That's when I noticed that Fiffine was smiling, too, and so was Rakej, which made me feel better.

"Just a few more hours of travel today," Rakej promised us as he drew up his legs to sit cross-legged on the bench, resting his palms on his knees and shutting his eyes.

Um, is he meditating?

I decided not to think on that for too long, because I didn't actually care if he was or not. I had to work on finding my own comfortable position.

Shifting slightly on the bench, I leaned my head against the back of the carriage, closing my eyes and hoping for sleep. I felt Amorette rest her head against my shoulder a few moments later. I found her hand and held it.

Only a few more hours...

Chapter 6

Irys

My eyes widened, and I stood on legs that were weakened from having been seated in the chair for most of the night. Slowly, Lieutenant Fhurrk rose to a sitting position releasing a groan that I could only assume was involuntary.

After a moment, I heard a voice calling. I was prepared to help Lieutenant Fhurrk to hide, when I heard my name. It was a man's voice, not yet immediately outside this cottage.

"I won't tell them you're here," I promised rapidly as I rushed toward the door. Rimoth must have brought people to look for me, and I was not about to miss them.

Pausing just inside the door, I glanced back at Lieutenant Fhurrk, who merely nodded to me. In the daylight, I could tell he was pale. I'd never seen him in full light before, but it was clear he had lost a great deal of blood, and his wound was a serious one.

"You're not going to make it to your checkpoint, are you?" I asked him hesitantly, my hand on the doorknob.

"Don't worry about me. Forget you ever met me. Go let your people find you," he replied. His voice was hoarse and dry.

"What if my people can help you? Will you let me get them for you?"

"No. I don't trust them. You travel with Knights. I don't trust Knights."

"Irys Godeleva!" called the voice from outside.

I couldn't wait much longer. I stepped up to Lieutenant Fhurrk and touched his face very gently with my fingers.

"Thank you," I said meaningfully, before I turned and threw open the door. "I'm here!"

It was Sir Dynan Fhirell. He was walking toward the house with an unlit lantern and a bag in his hand. As soon as he spotted me, he quickened his pace, nearly running.

"Miss Godeleva! Thank the Goddess. Are you hurt?" he asked with relief written all over his face. He was carrying a messenger bag across his body that I hadn't initially seen and was wearing his Knights uniform.

"I'm merely cold and tired. Thank you, Sir Fhirell. Goddess, it's good to see you."

"Let's go inside. It's cold out here. I have clothes and shoes for you. I'll explain everything else to you once you're dressed and more comfortable."

"Thank you. I'll go in and dress. There is only one proper room. The rest of the rooms have been abandoned and have mildewed. I will make haste and call you in as soon as I'm proper."

"Of course," he replied and held the bag out for me to take.

I took it and stepped back inside, determined to dress quickly so that he would not be required to wait in the cold for long. Still, before I could do that, I needed to know that Lieutenant Fhurrk would be safely hidden or would be able to make his exit without being noticed.

I searched every part of the house into which a man of his size could conceal himself. I even attempted to scent him out. After very little time, I came to the conclusion that he had already taken care of the matter for himself. He was gone. Oddly, I felt disappointed, but more potent was the concern I felt for his wellbeing. With the injuries he had sustained, the odds were not with him, and it strained my conscience to think that I would now turn my back on him and go about rescuing myself as though we had never met.

Please don't forget about him, Great Goddess. Let him lean on your immeasurable strength so that he may find his way to those who will give him the care he needs to heal. Please, let him live.

I felt my heart ease at the belief that the Goddess would somehow hear me and see to it that Lieutenant Fhurrk would successfully reach his destination. Turning my attention to the bag and its contents, I discovered a complete change of outfit and my pair of riding boots as well as a few other small personal items.

I dressed as rapidly as I could, glad to be done with the borrowed clothing. I ran my brush through my hair and drew my cloak over my shoulders, fastening it under my chin. It took some willpower to overcome the inclination to snuggle with the cloak around myself as one would with a particularly beloved blanket on a snowy night.

Plaiting my hair into a simple braid behind me, I gave the house a final glance and picked up the bag and the remainder of its contents, to which I'd added my nightgown and dressing gown. It now looked mostly empty.

When I stepped back outside, Sir Fhirell was there with a smile on his face. "Feel better?" he asked in a voice that sounded warmer than the fire had been last night.

"Much. Will we be going now?"

"If this place isn't too unbearable, we might do well to stay here for another hour or so to give the sun some time to warm the air and burn off the dew. It will be easier to move with more warmth and light and without wet feet," he replied calmly.

"Is anyone else coming? Will there be horses?" I asked hopefully, turning back to enter the house once again.

"No," he replied with a shake of his head. He followed me inside and took my bag, folding it around the few remaining contents and tucking it inside his messenger bag, which he placed on the floor next to a chair he intended to claim.

The fire had burned down to the point that it was merely embers, but he added a bit more wood to give us more warmth.

"You managed to get a fire started, at least," he commented, sounding rather impressed.

It felt wrong to lie to him, but I could think of no other way to reply to his comment than to accept the credit for Lieutenant Fhurrk's resourcefulness.

"It was terribly dark when I first arrived. I found that I couldn't get enough of the light," I said in as much of an indirect response as I could muster.

"It was fortunate that you found your way here at all. It was a very dark night."

"The Goddess blessed me and showed me the way here through the darkness."

"Rimoth said the Sefaline Warrior was here. He didn't cause you any grief? He didn't bother you at all?"

"No. He didn't bother me. In fact, I find myself worrying about him. He was badly wounded and showed me no aggression. He helped me to find my way to this house when I would otherwise have been lost in the cold."

I could see certain truths clicking into place in his mind after the initial surprise faded. "Where is he now?"

"I don't know," I replied, glad to be able to give him an honest answer.

"When was the last time you saw him?"

I paused in my moment of guilt. "A few seconds before I stepped out to greet you when you were calling out for me," I confessed. "He left while we spoke outside."

"Can you detect his scent at all?"

"No. As far as I can tell, he's not in the house. Otherwise, I likely wouldn't have agreed to return inside with you. He doesn't trust you, and I don't want to cause any more problems."

"I don't trust him either. I understand why that would have been your choice." His calm and acceptance both surprised and impressed me.

"I only hope he is well enough to make it to his destination."

"We will keep watch for him as we walk. If we should cross paths with him and if he requires help, we will offer it."

My heart skipped a little at his words. What a good man Sir Fhirell was. Though I wondered if he would approach the Warrior with the same offer of assistance if he were travelling without me, I appreciated the fact that he would help in order to ease my worry.

"Are we headed to the nearest town?" I asked, wondering if Sir Fhirell was equipped with a map or some other way of knowing how to find civilization.

"Rimoth told me to travel to the east, toward the sea. He said the closest town is in that direction."

This must be the same location to which Lieutenant Fhurrk is headed. Perhaps we will be able to offer our assistance after all.

I chose not to share this thought with Sir Fhirell, regardless of how willing he may have been to help the Sefaline Warrior. Instead, I decided to focus on other topics.

"Is Rimoth very injured?" I asked with genuine concern. "Is that why he has not returned with you?"

"He is. When he arrived at the inn, he was unable to stand. He told me that he hadn't meant to leave you where you were, but he wasn't able to return to retrieve you because another Traveller was holding you and threatening you. He believed that he had the ability to bring me to find you but would be unable to help in any other way until he could heal and regain his strength," Sir Fhirell explained. "Desda packed the bag for you, and I left with Rimoth right away."

I hoped that Rimoth had found his way to a doctor or someone else who could properly care for him.

Great Goddess, please let these be the last of the injuries for this journey. Please keep everyone else safe from harm.

"Will Desda stay with the group and continue the journey toward us?" I asked, suddenly realizing that my poor loyal maid was now alone and possibly only slightly less frightened than I currently was.

"Yes. She will continue with everyone else. I have spoken with Sir Breese, who has promised to keep watch over her and ensure that she does not become too lonely. She will be well looked after," he reassured me.

"Thank you. You have a way of assuaging all my fears, Sir Fhirell."

He smiled and even that simple expression was calming to me. "When we reach the nearest town, I will find out where the Knights are stationed. We can rest overnight, then head back to our group with the assistance of a guide, if needed."

As I raised my trembling hands to the fire to warm them, I realized that my shaking had nothing to do with the temperature. It was the strain of the last few hours and of the uncertainty that lay before me. The warmth of the fire was soothing, but it did not serve me as I wished it would.

"I will be ready to leave the moment you feel it is safe enough to do so," I said, hoping my words were true. I wanted them to be. I wanted to be ready. Nothing left in this room would help me to prepare myself any more than I already was.

As I watched the low flames before me, his hands slipped over mine, pressing my palms together. I felt a warmth from them that the fire could never have offered. Somehow, in this terrible place and in this terrifying circumstance, this was quite possibly the most romantic moment of my life. I was struck with a sudden bout of shyness and tilted my head down, sneaking a peek at him through my lashes.

"I promised Lord Godeleva that I would keep you safe. I intend to keep that promise, Miss Godeleva," he said gently. It reassured me but simultaneously disintegrated every hint of romance.

"Thank you," I replied more formally than I'd intended. "I will be certain to tell Lord Godeleva of the great lengths to which you went in order to ensure that your promise was kept."

Softening, he shook his head. "You needn't tell him. I didn't say what I did for his sake. I only wanted you to know that I take my promises seriously and that I won't let any harm come to you. Not if it is within my power to prevent it."

"Sir Varda chose the perfect second," I said. I couldn't smooth the stiffness from my voice. I'd enjoyed my romantic little daydream, but it had been far too short-lived. "I do feel much safer now that you're here."

Instead of speaking, he swept his thumb over my hand. I allowed my gaze to linger over the gesture before watching his face in the flickering firelight.

"You're a very brave woman," he commented easily in a tone that did not require me to reply. He smiled at me for a moment and shifted the way he was seated so he could reach his bag and open it. "Are you hungry? I don't have much, but there are a few things here to sustain us."

"I should probably have a little something," I agreed, forcing my mind to think practically. "I'm too tired to be hungry, but I know it would be foolish to go without."

He withdrew a few little bundles and unwrapped one of them, extending a cookie in my direction. I received it and found that it was heavier than it looked. It was made from a dense grain and dried fruits. It certainly wouldn't have been my choice if we were having a morning tea, but for this meal, it suited me perfectly.

As this would need to do for a while, I took care to take small bites and chew them carefully. I wasn't trying to be dainty. The intention was to fool my stomach into thinking I was having a bigger meal, since I was taking so long to eat it.

"No one will blame you if you decide that you would rather return home than continue with our mission once we have been reunited with our group, Miss Godeleva." Sir Fhirell broke the silence. "I will not blame you," he added.

I looked him directly in the eyes as I responded. "Sir Fhirell, at the moment it is safer for me to be in this cabin here with you than it would be to be back in Lorammel, even when surrounded by the gates of the Godeleva Estate." I spoke deliberately and with meaning.

"Why do you say this? Is it the Sefaline Warrior? Did he threaten you?" His words were serious and concern laced his expression.

"No. He said nothing threatening to me. I was not his target. In fact, I believe he placed my wellbeing ahead of his own." I delayed before I continued, but the confusion on Sir Fhirell's face obliged me to speak the truth to him. "It is Emperor Gevalen. He has taken more than a slight interest in me," I confessed. I felt shame wash over me as though it was my fault the emperor's eye had fallen upon me.

I watched his expression with great care. It was clear that he had not initially caught on to what I was suggesting. Perhaps it was because he was still thinking of threats in terms of violence or abduction, such as those I could potentially have faced from the Warrior or one of the Travellers. Soon enough, realization crept into his eyes. It was evident with the subtle green tinge his complexion had adopted.

"I see," he said with a hard swallow.

"I would have liked to remain home so that I would be there when Miss Wynters returns," I admitted. "Still, I consider it a blessing to have been offered such a worthy alternative, when I suddenly found myself in need of a reason to leave the city. The Goddess brought us together to speak at the Knights' Headquarters, Sir Fhirell. I feel as though She was showing me the way to remain safe by giving me the chance to spread Her Light."

My hand was once again nestled into his as he slipped his fingers around mine.

"I'm grateful to the Goddess for her Wisdom," he said, and for a moment, he appeared to be debating something in his mind. "The dawn seems to be fully upon us. Shall we begin our journey?"

I nodded daintily to him, unable to take my gaze from his. I felt nearly certain that he had been considering something other than the timing for leaving this cottage. Still, he gave no other indication that he intended to pursue whatever thought had come to him.

He rose, keeping my hand in his to help me to stand as well. I accepted his assistance and found the strength to release him once I was upright.

Taking a moment to look through the drawers and cupboards one more time, I acquired a few small items such as matches and tea towels that I thought might be of use to us along the way. I tucked them into Sir Fhirell's bag, which he promptly slung over his shoulder to carry.

With no further reason to delay, we stepped outside and turned toward the east. Facing into the sunlight, I looked around to discover that we had been staying on a ruined farm with fields that stretched in every direction.

It took only a few steps to fall into a steady rhythm with Sir Fhirell as we walked through the tall green remains of a partially harvested crop. It appeared to have been scorched in places, though long enough ago that the rains had washed much of the char away, allowing healthy green sprouts to hide the evidence beneath.

"I don't imagine you've ever needed to walk a great distance before," Sir Fhirell commented, when the farmhouse was still in sight but looked quite small in the distance.

"No. Not where there haven't been sidewalks," I admitted. Certainly, I'd walked from my home to the dockyards when I'd run away, and I'd run through the streets of Fort Picogeal in an escape from the fires there, but this was a different type of journey altogether.

"Should you need to stop and rest, only say."

"I will," I promised, looking off at the horizon instead of staring down at the path in front of me. I was paying attention to where I was stepping, but I'd once read that looking out toward the distance would help to make a journey seem shorter than focusing on each individual step. I welcomed all the help available to me in what would easily be the most difficult expedition of my life.

Our progress wasn't fast as we were continually avoiding holes and other obstacles, but before I could reach the point at which I would request my first break, I spotted it. It was precisely what I'd hoped we would not see.

In the distance ahead of us was a lump on the ground. It was neither a rock nor the stump of a long-ago felled tree. It was a body. My heart told me that we would soon be upon the Sefaline Warrior.

Chapter 7

Megan

I gasped awake. It took a moment for me to realize the reason why. The road beneath us had changed and had become extremely bumpy. To keep from bouncing out of the seat, I braced myself, hoping this wild ride would soon end. Thankfully, it did. The carriage slowed and came to a stop.

"What do you know? There was an end to this journey after all." Rakej smiled.

Neither Amorette nor Fiffine said anything in response, so I jumped in to ask the burning question: "You mean, we don't have to ride in this carriage anymore?"

He looked at me and said, "I mean you don't have to...and there is bathing water here, too." His smile grew warmer with the last part of his statement.

I perked up at his words, feeling my exhaustion slip away for a moment. Amorette seemed interested, too, acknowledging Rakej's existence for the first time. I think we were more thrilled at the prospect of bathing than we were about getting out of this box on wheels.

The door was thrown open and instead of bright sunlight, I was met by darkness.

What do you know? It's night time.

"Thank you, Lida," Rakej said to Miss Sunshine, in his calm and pleasant tone. "We'll join you when our legs all work."

He didn't receive a response in return, but I could hear footsteps walking away. That woman was such a sweetie!

Rakej stepped out first and turned to offer us each a hand when we were ready to get out. I went first, taking his hand and exiting the carriage on wobbly legs. I took in our latest surroundings.

A few feet from where I stood, was an entrance to a cave. I stared at it as if I were expecting it to magically turn into a stone cottage.

They didn't expect us to go in there, did they?

"Please head on into the cave," Rakej said. "I promise it's nicer than it looks from the outside."

I guess they did. God, I hope there aren't any bats in there!

I waited for Amorette and Fiffine to be ready. I wasn't going anywhere without them. They were both out of the carriage, by this point, and Amorette had a supportive arm around Fiffine, who was looking more nauseated by the second. Amorette gave me a small nod, and I nodded back before walking forward into the mouth of the cave.

To my surprise and relief, the interior of the cave was not what I had expected. After walking through a short dark passage, the cave opened into a large and well-lit cavern. There were several sections in the space that were shielded by makeshift curtains hanging from wooden frames. I assumed they were set up this way to create "private" rooms. Considering it was a cave, I had to give the rebels credit. They did their best to make this place look as cozy as it could get. Even the dampness was tolerable.

A woman approached us. She had chin-length platinum blond hair with a deep brick-red streak running straight down the middle of it. Although she appeared fit and ready for action like Miss Sunshine, her expression wasn't unkind or sour. Instead, her pleasant round face bore a welcoming smile. I didn't know if it was because I liked her nifty hair or her friendly features, but I had a good feeling about this woman. I guessed she was in her early twenties.

"Hello," she said. "You must be so sore after that ride. I've got hot water boiling for your bath. Until then, can I interest you in some tea? I've also got some stew on, but I imagine you'll want that after you've cleaned up," she added warmly.

Okay, I loved this woman.

"Thank you," I said appreciatively to her, taking the initiative to speak on behalf of us all. I couldn't tell what Fiffine or Amorette thought of this woman, based on their weary expressions, but she couldn't have made a better first impression on me, and I really wanted everything to stay friendly for as long as possible.

"I'm Sabear," the woman introduced herself, smiling at the three of us. "Follow me. Everything you need is this way."

She turned, clearly expecting us to follow her. I put my arm around Fiffine to help Amorette support her. It was the least I could do for her, because as much as I didn't want to be me right now, I really wouldn't want to be Fiffine.

"Thank you," Fiffine said softly to me.

I smiled at her in response before sharing the expression with Amorette, who returned it weakly. We moved forward, following Sabear past several of the curtained "rooms" until we reached a small area where four bowl-shaped wooden tubs sat waiting for us. They looked big enough for a single person to sit in and soak, but they certainly weren't as large as a regular sized bathtub. I could see steam rising from each one and as we drew closer, I noticed that they were half-filled with water.

"I was told that there would be four of you," Sabear told us. "It seems there was a sneaky one in your group." She smiled. "But that's alright. I plan to treat you all well. Try to think of yourselves as guests of honour on an unplanned vacation, if you can." She was obviously trying to be as welcoming and comforting as she could.

In response, Fiffine lifted her right hand and made the same sign language-like motions with it that I had previously seen her make to Rakej.

"Thank you," she said to Sabear, who gave her a deep nod.

I smiled and nodded my thanks, too. Amorette, however, purposely chose not to make a comment. I got the feeling she wasn't as taken with Sabear or her hospitality as Fiffine and I were.

Sabear walked up to a fire over which a large metal kettle was hanging from a hook secured to a metal frame under a hole in the cave's ceiling. She picked up the kettle by its handle, struggling with it for a moment – a clear indication that it was heavy – and brought it over to one of the baths, pouring the boiling water into the tub.

"That's one done," she declared. "I'll start on the other two. You can use the last one for your laundry if you'd like. While your clothing dries, I can give each of you something to wear."

Sabear added more water to the kettle, from some source I couldn't see behind the curtain, and heaved it back onto the hook over the fire to heat it up again.

"Thank you," I said, hoping that she could hear the gratitude in my voice.

Honestly, this woman was providing us with everything I could have wanted. If she'd said there was also a bed with a pillow somewhere, she would officially have been my new favourite person on Qarradune.

Amorette began to help Fiffine undress. Wearing only her underwear, Fiffine carefully climbed into the readied tub, and with Amorette's assistance, she slowly sat down, looking relieved as the warm water embraced her body. She picked up a bar of beige soap and began to wash.

Not wanting to stand idly while I waited for the other tubs to fill, I stepped up to Fiffine's clothes and gathered them up.

"Would you like your clothes washed Fiffine?" I asked her.

"Thank you very much," she said, nodding to me with a tired smile. "That's very kind of you."

I returned her smile and took her clothes over to the "laundry tub" where Sabear was adding some soap to the water. Once finished, she returned to the kettle. I dumped Fiffine's clothes in, to let them soak. I wasn't quite ready to sink my hands under the water. The last time I'd plunged my hands into water for cleaning purposes, I'd burned them with the corrosive cleaning chemicals I'd had to use. I knew this makeshift laundry tub wouldn't be the same flesh-burning experience as washing Galnar's floors had been, but the memory still left my hands with a phantom sting.

"Would you like some tea?" Amorette asked, drawing me out of my thoughts.

I turned and saw she was holding two wooden cups that reminded me of handle-less Japanese-style tea cups. I took one from her.

"Thanks," I said.

"It smells strange," she commented quietly to me. "I've never had tea before."

I smelled the tea. It smelled different from the tea I'd had in Syliza. This one smelled more like green tea than black tea and looked more like green tea, too. That said, I knew that it wouldn't taste like any tea I previously experienced on Earth. I was surprised that Amorette had never tried tea before.

Does Kavylak not have tea?

"If you've never had tea before, you might find it tastes strange at first, but most of the teas I've tried have been pretty good."

She nodded and said, "At least it's warm."

I took a nice long sip of tea and let the liquid warm me. I didn't mind the taste. It had a mild earthy flavour with just a small hint of whatever Qarradune's answer to honey was. I liked it.

"You look like you're holding up better than I am," Amorette said after taking a sip of her tea.

'It's not the first time I've been in an unpleasant situation beyond my control," I replied.

She nodded. "You handle it well."

I smiled a little. "To be honest, it helps that I'm not alone," I said.

She reached out and took my free hand in hers, giving it a gentle squeeze of friendly support.

"It won't be long. There are lots of noses to sniff us out."

I nodded to her. I knew what noses she was talking about: spirit wolf noses. Having already had the experience of being tracked by Amarogq's spirit pack before, I knew firsthand just how well those wolves could track. A small shiver crawled up my spine as I remembered when they chased down Rral and me in the woods. While it was an unpleasant memory, to say the least, I knew they would find us. I shuddered to think of what would happen to these people. I shuddered to think of what had happened to Thayn. Had he gotten away? I hoped he had.

As I sipped away at the beverage, I glanced over in Fiffine's direction. I saw that she was now washing her hair and that Sabear had set out three brown belted bathrobes; one at each of the bathing tubs. It was obvious that this is what we would wear after our baths, while we were waiting for our clothes to dry.

"Ready for the next lucky bather!" Sabear announced as she heaved the kettle over to one of the tubs and poured out the steaming water.

"You go," I encouraged Amorette.

"Are you sure?"

I nodded. "I'm sure. Give me your clothes, and I'll start washing them for you."

She nodded, not needing a second offer, and removed her shoes and clothing, keeping on her under things before heading off to the waiting tub.

Finishing my tea, I set the cup down and decided I'd start washing my clothes, too, since it wouldn't be long until my bath. I took Rral's ring from my pocket, and for safe keeping, I placed it on the chain I wore around my neck. It was much too large for me to wear on any of my fingers. Also, not wanting to accidentally misplace Irys' handkerchief, I removed that from my pocket and tucked it into the side of my bra. It wasn't the most ideal place to store it but, hey, desperate times call for desperate measures. Pssh, besides, now Irys was closer to my heart.

Satisfied, I stripped down to my underwear as Fiffine and Amorette had done, tossing my own dirty clothes in with the rest.

Getting over my stupid fear of submerging my hands in water, I started to scrub at our clothing.

"Mind if I help? Or would you rather I didn't touch your things?" Sabear asked, stepping up beside me and kneeling down.

"I don't mind at all," I replied honestly.

She nodded and began to help me wash the clothes.

"Are you a girlfriend or a wife?" she asked as we worked.

"A girlfriend," I replied.

And a liar...a big liar.

"He'll come for you," she assured me. "We just want to trade for some of the people we're missing."

This woman had no idea how much I was hoping it would work out that way, but I really didn't think it would. Not with Warriors coming.

"People were taken from you?" I asked, to distract myself from worrying about Warriors showing up and wreaking havoc.

She nodded. "We just want to make an exchange. It can be peaceful, if they allow it. That's why we chose people with high value for better odds of peace."

Um...

"Have you ever taken people of value from the Warriors before?" I asked carefully, not sure if I really wanted to know the answer.

"I haven't, but I know others who have taken wives of military high-ups."

"But not Warriors?" I confirmed.

"No, not Warriors. We got lucky this time. We didn't know specifically who would be in that bunker," she admitted.

Oh my god! She thinks they got lucky? Do I tell her that Amorette's fiancé's pack of wolves are going to shred everyone here once they find us?

I swallowed hard in silent response and watched as Sabear – who was apparently entirely oblivious to the danger that she and her group had invited to their doorstep – carefully, but thoroughly, wrung out some of the clothing before hanging it to dry.

I shook my head a little to clear my dark thoughts as I wrung out my own clothes. No, maybe I was wrong. Maybe I was assuming the worst. Maybe Sabear and the rebels did know what they were doing. Maybe this wouldn't end badly...

Yeah, right.

"Are you from Dsumot?" I asked her, feeling the need to change the topic.

"Yes. I'm a teacher there. So is my husband."

I looked at her in surprise, not expecting her to say that. I was expecting more of a response like, "Yes, I'm from there, and Kavylak burned down my town. Now it's payback time!" I really wasn't expecting: "I'm a teacher."

Why the heck is a married teacher part of a rebellion?

"How did you get involved in the resistance?"

"It's something a lot of us have done," Sabear said. "It's all we have left to keep our borders intact. Kavylak has been breathing on us ever since they took Sorcheena."

"I guess that makes sense," I told her. When I really thought about it, it did.

Sure, I was supposed to be pretending to be pro-Kavylak for the time being, but how would I feel if I thought my country, my home, or my family was threatened? Wouldn't I want to get involved somehow, to help protect and defend what I loved? To defend my freedom? Could I really blame these rebels for doing what they felt was necessary for their survival? I still couldn't say I agreed with the whole kidnapping thing, but at the same time, what would I do if push came to shove? Would I be above kidnapping if I'd thought it could keep me, my home, and the people I loved safe? I didn't know the answer and that left me with an uneasy feeling.

At that moment, I would have given anything to go back to being troubled by what once seemed so important but that was now so trivial: worrying if I'd get into university. Such concerns seemed like a lifetime ago.

"Thank you," Sabear said in response to my understanding her plight. "I've never been a part of the actual fighting. I'm too much of a coward. But, I help to run stations like this one, for washing, food, and for medical care."

"I don't think I'd ever want to be a part of the fighting either," I told her honestly.

"I have a lot of respect for those who do, though," she said seriously.

I nodded in agreement with her statement.

"What do you do when you're at home?" she asked, changing gears on me.

Uh...I don't think my amnesia lie will work here.

"I'm a translator."

'Cause that's as good a lie as any.

"Oh, interesting." She smiled as we hung more clothes to dry. "What languages?"

Uh...all of them?

"I know several. Sylizan, Kavylak, Gbat Rher," I told her, listing off all the ones I've heard others say I could speak.

She smiled, looking impressed. "Sounds like an interesting job."

Yeah. I bet it will be...

"Yes," I forced myself to reply as I glanced down at the military chain I wore around my neck with the tag that proved to Kavylak I wasn't a criminal.

"Your water is boiling," Sabear said. "I'll get it and fill up the rest of your tub. It was nice talking with you."

I looked at the woman smiling at me, and I felt myself warm a little, because I knew she meant what she said. I smiled back at her.

"It was nice talking to you, too, Sabear. By the way, I'm Megan."

"Hi, Megan," she said cutely before getting up to tend to my bath.

Standing, I hung a few more articles of clothing, then headed to my bath. I glanced at Fiffine and Amorette to make sure they were still doing alright. Amorette was washing her long black hair. Fiffine looked serene as she drank her tea.

Without wasting another moment, I stepped into the tub. I was immediately greeted with cozy warm water. I sat down and hunched a little so the water would cover as much of me as possible. It wasn't perfect, but after such a long travel without bathing, this feeling was beyond heavenly.

I picked up the bar of soap from the edge of the tub and smelled it. It didn't really have a fragrance, and I was fine with that. As long as it could clean my skin and hair, this soap was aces in my book.

I got to scrubbing myself clean. I was thorough and took my time, washing ever inch of skin and every strand of hair on my head. I probably would have stayed in the tub all night long if I could, but as the water began to cool, it started to lose its cozy effect. The last thing I wanted was to ruin the magic of this bathing experience with old chilly bath water.

I stepped out, grabbing the waiting towel to dry off. Once my body was as dry as it was going to get, I wrapped my hair in a turban-like style with the towel. Picking up the robe and putting it on, I took off my wet undergarments and tucked Irys' handkerchief into the robe's pocket. Tying the robe closed with the belt, I walked over to the laundry tub, washed my under things, and added them to the line.

I noticed Fiffine had retired to a pile of straw. She was curled on her side with her eyes closed. A soft blanket covered her small form. Frowning slightly, I turned, looking for Amorette. I spotted her, seated close to the fire. She was wearing a robe like mine and also had her hair up in a towel. I sat next to her and opened my mouth to speak, but Sabear spoke first.

"Stew?" She offered. "And bread?"

"Thank you," I said appreciatively, smiling at her. I was hungry and warm food sounded sooo appealing.

"The stew, I've mastered," she told me with a smile as she handed me a bowl and a piece of bread. "But my fireside bread leaves something to be desired. It's good for dipping, at least." She grinned and then handed the same meal to Amorette.

Amorette accepted it with a curt nod and began to eat slowly as she stared at the flames. If Sabear was at all bothered by Amoertte's cold response, she didn't show it. She simply smiled and nodded to us before she left to tend to more laundry.

In truth, the way Amorette was acting didn't bother me either. These were her kidnappers, *our* kidnappers. They didn't deserve her smiles or gratitude. Still, I couldn't help but like Sabear and be nice to her. The difference between Amorette and me was that Kavylak was her people and her home. To me, Kavylak and the Warriors were just as much my kidnappers as these rebels. Kavylak had snatched me from where I had wanted to stay and where I wanted to be right now: in Syliza's capital, Lorammel. I wanted to be with Irys in her beautiful home, and tell her how excited I was to be courting Thayn.

....*Thayn.*

I desperately hoped that he was safe, unharmed, and un-captured. I also desperately hoped that, wherever he was, he hadn't given up on me. Clinging to my dreams of a fairytale ending with him – for however long I might be on this crazy world – was getting me through every minute of this insane situation.

As I sat in front of the fire, mechanically eating my stew, I allowed my thoughts to drift to him and to Pounce. It saddened me that I might never see my kitten again, but it broke my heart to think she could be dead. I wouldn't accept that. I had to believe she was alright and was being pampered by someone who adored her as much as I did.

I set down my empty bowl and looked at Amorette. She was still eating, just as robotically as I had been, looking zoned-out at the fire. I frowned, and my heart ached for her. If I had been thinking about Thayn, she had to have been thinking about Amarogq. While I was looking forward to being Thayn's girlfriend, Amarogq was something much more to Amorette. He was her fiancé. I would probably be less smiley at these people, too, if they had yanked me away from an actual life.

I reached over and gave Amorette's knee a gentle squeeze. She blinked away from the fire and met my gaze.

"He's going to bring you home, Amorette," I assured her.

"All of us," she corrected quietly. "He'll bring all of us." Her tone betrayed her true feelings. She was uncertain, and she was scared.

"He will," I told her with confidence I definitely felt. "One way or another, Amarogq will. He really loves you, Amorette. When Amarogq first told me about you, his eyes lit up. It was obvious to me how much you mean to him."

She nodded and smiled, looking calmer. "I love him, too. I can't wait to marry him. We've been engaged forever."

"Have you set a date?"

"No." She shook her head. I raised an eyebrow. "But I have a dress," she added.

"If we get the chance, you'll have to show me!" I smiled, because I did want to see her dress, and I was curious to see what a Kavylak wedding dress looked like.

"I will. As soon as we get home," she promised.

"Great! You know, I also think that the next time you see Amarogq, the first thing you should do is set a date." I smiled.

She chuckled at my statement. "You tell him that. I've tried."

Hmm...so it's Amarogq who has the cold feet. I wonder why?

"Alright, I'll tell him."

And, ya know, if I do see him, I am going to tell him. I mean, dude, your fiancée just got kidnapped. What are you waiting for? Set a freakin' date!

She smiled and finished the last of her stew, setting the bowl down with its spoon.

"I really hope they come soon. I want to bring Fiffine home. I'm worried about her," she said.

"I am, too," I confessed, stealing a glance at Fiffine. "We'll take care of her as best we can until Amarogq or another Warrior arrives."

I felt confident saying that. I knew they'd find us. Aside from Thayn, I'd never met a more tenacious group of people.

"I hope she's sleeping. Maybe she'll be able to eat in the morning." Amorette sounded hopeful. "I'm going to go lie down with her," she told me.

I nodded. "Alright. I'll stay up for a little longer. If anything weird happens, I'll wake you."

"Thanks," she said and then whispered: "Just so you're aware, I have a knife in my shoe. You never know."

I nodded seriously. Under other circumstances, I would have been shocked but right now, all I could think was that hiding a knife in her shoe was very sensible. Once I returned to Kavylak, if I'd be staying there much longer, before I could escape with Thayn, I just might start concealing a knife in my shoe, too. After all, like Amorette had said: "You never know."

Amorette gave me a small hug, which I returned. She drew away, stood, and walked over to where Fiffine was lying down. She lay down next to her and snuggled in close.

Watching them, I found myself missing Aésha. I had spent several nights on the Warrior's ship, travelling back to the Kavylak capital, snuggled in the same bed as her. If it hadn't been for Aésha's company during those first few nights after I had witnessed the death of Rral, I don't know how I would have mentally survived. She had been my safety and my comfort.

My friend.

"More tea?" Sabear asked, nearly causing me to jump out of my skin. I hadn't realized I'd been so lost in thought.

"Yes, thank you."

Sabear filled up my cup and sat down beside me, setting the pot of tea aside.

"Do you plan to stay up all night?"

"No." I shook my head. "I'm tired, and I will sleep eventually, but my mind is a little too active for rest."

"I'll stay up with you, so you're not alone, if you'd like."

Aww, she was such a nice lady!

"Thanks," I said to her.

"If I nod off, just push me. I'll wake up," she joked.

I chuckled at the mental image but abruptly stopped when a tall man walked into the space and bowed to us. His dark, shoulder-length brown hair flowed freely.

"I'm just here for a cup of tea. I don't mean to interrupt," he said respectfully.

I couldn't have been more unprepared for his presence. It wasn't his appearance that shocked me. It was the uniform he wore that captured my full attention. The dark green doublet was worn, and its edges were tattered, and his pants and boots were weathered, but there was no mistaking what he was.

"You're a Knight of Freyss!" I blurted, unable to hold my tongue or mask my surprise.

The Knight smiled, un-phased by my outburst.

"Are you a fan?" he asked, first pouring himself a cup of tea and then sitting in front of us.

You have no idea, Buddy...

"I just recognized the uniform," I lied. I really didn't like how telling lies was becoming an increasingly natural state of affairs for me.

He nodded. "It has seen better days."

I had to agree with him. I deduced that, either he was one of the rebels and had been roughing it in his uniform, or he needed to stop washing the poor thing in whatever low-grade detergent he was using.

"You're part of the Dsumot resistance?"

"Yes. I've seen too many people lose their homelands and cultures. I've decided to be on the right side of the battle, this time. The side that lets me sleep at night. I'm Uori Hafel," he introduced himself.

Woah! That's a loaded statement. What does he mean by that? Did he just badmouth Syliza? No, I must have misunderstood. He's a Knight, isn't he?

"Are you not a Knight anymore?" I asked tentatively, not sure I was going to like his answer.

"I'm still in the books, though I haven't been back to see those books in a very long time. I'm sure they think I'm dead by now."

Um?

"So, you're helping the people here because you didn't like what you did as a Knight?"

I hoped I was guessing wrong.

"That's right."

I frowned. Damn. I had really wanted to be wrong.

An uneasy truth crept over me, and the stew in my stomach suddenly wasn't sitting well anymore as I looked at the rebel-Knight in front of me. I mulled over his words and just like that, I realized that I didn't really know anything about Syliza. I had merely assumed that country was the "good guy" based on Irys' kindness, my crush on Thayn, and my fear of Kavylak.

Still, I wanted to believe that Syliza was better than Kavylak. It had to be. But if it was, why would a Knight be driven to abandon his post and his people? I could never imagine Thayn doing that. Maybe this guy wasn't cut out to be a Knight.

Or, maybe he's a liar.

"Are you saying that Syliza's just like Kavylak?" I asked carefully, unsure if he'd take offence to my question.

To my relief, he chuckled.

"They're nothing alike."

Yes! I knew it!

"And yet, they're exactly the same."

Aw, fiddlesticks!

"I don't understand."

Seriously, could he be more cryptic?

"You'll live a happier life if it stays that way."

What the hell's that supposed to mean?

"I doubt it," I said, not bothering to hide the irritation in my voice. I was beyond fed up with having no clue as to what was happening on crazy, dysfunctional Qarradune.

Uori nodded with solemn understanding. "In that case, when you return home, find yourself a history book and look at the way the maps of Syliza and Kavylak have changed over the cycles. Then, think about the people who used to live in the places that were taken over. None of them have been allowed to remain as they were. They're now either citizens of Syliza or Kavylak. There may still be people in those same places, but they're not the same people."

My brow furrowed as I listened. His explanation made me think of Rral and what I had read in his journal.

"Like Gbat Rher." I heard myself say out loud.

Uori raised a brow when I spoke. "Yes. Exactly like Gbat Rher."

"He saw it as it was falling," Sabear added.

I looked at her and then at Uori, who nodded to confirm what she had said.

"I knew a Paladin and learned his story," I said with as much sadness as I felt and found that I had subconsciously raised my left hand to touch the ring that was concealed underneath my robe.

"You met a Paladin?"

I looked at Uori. He was staring at me intently and with a new respect as if he had suddenly realized we were on the same side.

"How did you come to be so fortunate?"

I stared at him for a moment as I considered what to say. I didn't want to tell lies when it came to Rral. It felt wrong to include such an honourable person, who had lost everything, in any lie.

"I was in a bad place, and he saved my life." That was the gist of it and the truth, at least.

"That sounds just like a Paladin," Uori agreed. "There are lots of them, you know," he continued, and I listened with interest. "They have land between Syliza and the Great Northern Ocean. Syliza walked into their land and took it from them. They didn't ask. They didn't negotiate. They burned their homes and barns. They burned everything until those men had lost what was worth fighting for." Uori's voice rose slightly higher with raw emotion as he told his tale, in a way that only a person who had witnessed it firsthand could.

I released a shaky breath I didn't know I'd been holding and clutched at Rral's ring.

"Uori," Sabear interjected softly. "We're trying to be calm. How is anyone supposed to sleep with your bedtime stories?" She gently rubbed my back to comfort me, likely seeing the horror on my face.

"Is this what Syliza has done with every nation they've taken for their own?" I had to know.

"It's what Syliza and Kavylak both do," he stated firmly. "That's why I'm here. Dsumot could be next, and I'll be one more man standing in the way."

I nodded to his bold statement. Whether I liked it or not and whether I agreed with their methods or not, these rebels made more sense to me than Kavylak and Syliza did. The rebels were fighting to keep their homes and their country from being consumed by two powerhouses and were resorting to desperate measures to keep their freedom.

"For what it's worth, I hope you're successful and maintain your independence. No one should have to lose their country or their home," I said with greater understanding than either of them would ever realize.

They both looked at me with very respectful expressions, letting me know that my words were welcome and appreciated.

"For now, we just want some of the prisoners returned to us. Then, we'll fight again," Uori said.

I focused my attention on the once-Knight, looking deeply into his soft brown eyes.

"Have you ever encountered the Warriors before?"

He gave a slow nod. "A very long time ago. Before most of the current Warriors had joined."

That was an interesting response. I wondered how long the Warriors had been around. I'd have to ask Amorette when I got the chance.

"So, you know that they're not like other soldiers?" I clarified, heavily implying that the Warriors had freaky powers.

"Yes," he replied solidly. "We're prepared for that."

"I don't think you are," I disagreed, and I had to be blunt about it. It wasn't because I thought Uori specifically was unprepared, it was because I believed anyone would be. Every Warrior I had encountered had a different skill and each skill gave them a considerable advantage beyond their supreme fighting abilities as soldiers. If Aésha and Amarogq could easily take down a giant of Gbat Rher, what chance would Uori have against them? What chance would any of them have against Galnar? The last time I saw that psycho, he was literally lighting fires with his hands! Then, there was Mez. With his supposed mind manipulation, which I thankfully hadn't yet seen in action, I still didn't know what he could do.

"I guess we'll soon see," Uori said, brushing off my warning as if I was trying to spook him. "We're not about to return you now, without trying to bring our friends home."

I looked at him for a long moment and then frowned. I knew then that any warning I gave would fall on deaf ears. They were determined to see their plan through, no matter the cost. I just hoped the price they would pay wouldn't be their lives.

"I think I'm going to try to sleep," I spoke quietly. With the way I felt now, I knew that sleep was unlikely, but I couldn't have this conversation anymore.

"Sleep well," Uori said. "Things will feel better after you've had some rest."

No, they wouldn't. Only when I woke up on Earth would things feel better.

Sabear gave my back another supportive rub. "I'll have breakfast for you in the morning, and your clothes will be dry."

"Thank you, Sabear." I did appreciate her kindness.

She smiled at me and continued to sip her tea with Uori. I left my unfinished tea on the floor of the cave, stood up, and walked over to where Amorette and Fiffine were sleeping.

I sat down on the pile of straw next to Amorette and removed my damp hair from the towel. I placed the towel where I intended to rest my head and lay down with my back to Amorette. I pushed all my hair above my head so it could finish drying while I slept, and pulled the waiting blanket up over my shoulders.

Shutting my eyes, I pleaded for sleep to find me. I knew things wouldn't be better when I woke up, but I didn't want to be conscious anymore. Emptying my mind of all my worries, my fears, and my hopes, I focused on memories of happy times that I'd spent growing up with Aunt Vera. Tears brimmed behind my eyelids.

I miss you, Aunt Vera.

I'll find my way back to you.

I love you.

Chapter 8

Irys

Raising my hand to shield my eyes from the sun, I squinted at a shape in the distance. With every step we took, it became more evident that it was indeed the figure of a man lying on the ground. Finally, I could no longer stand the silence. Sir Fhirell had said nothing, though he must have spotted the figure by then.

"Someone is there," I said quietly, indicating the direction of the person.

"Yes," Sir Fhirell confirmed. "I see it."

I tried to guess at what he might be thinking, based on his tone and his expression, but I couldn't. At first, I thought his intention was to ignore the person and continue on our path, but then he changed our direction, so we were aimed directly at it.

"It's Lieutenant Fhurrk," I whispered when we were close enough to identify the Warrior with certainty. My heart sank. I simultaneously did and did not want to see Lieutenant Fhurrk again. I was relieved not to be left wondering over his condition but, at the same time, I was saddened to see that he had made it only this far and was now lying in a field.

Great Goddess, please give me a sign that he lives. Please, tell me that he is alive and that he can be saved. I do not wish him to suffer, but I do not want to live with the guilt from thinking that he has perished here as a result of having rescued me last night.

Summoning my courage, I quickened my pace, stepping rapidly ahead of Sir Fhirell toward the fallen Warrior.

"Please be cautious, Miss Godeleva," Sir Fhirell warned as he lengthened his stride to keep up with me.

"I will," I assured him. "Lieutenant Fhurrk?" I asked the Warrior as I approached.

When he did not reply, I closed the distance between us and saw that he was not merely lying down as one would do if one were to exhaust oneself and choose to lie down for some rest. Lieutenant Fhurrk was crumpled forward in the long grass in an uncomfortable and unnatural way. His face was pressed against the ground, and one of his arms was bent underneath him.

Sir Fhirell was immediately at my side, watching the Warrior but scanning the area for others as well.

"He's breathing," he assured me as I sank to my knees and very gently rolled Lieutenant Fhurrk off his arm and onto his back. I dusted the dirt from his cheek.

It occurred to me that I could not detect the unique spiced scent that usually followed this Warrior. With him unconscious and lying on his back, I took the opportunity to open his jacket and lift his shirt to check on the bandage I had fashioned for him a few hours ago.

To my surprise and relief, though there was some blood showing on the fabric, the bandage was not saturated. However, the comfort that discovery brought me was short-lived as I realized that this might mean he had sustained injuries far beyond those I was able to treat. The wound wasn't limited to what could be seen. He was likely dehydrated, but I could not ignore the nagging thought that he might have suffered internal harm that we would be entirely unable to remedy.

"I think he must have internal wounds," I told Sir Fhirell, frowning deeply.

Sir Fhirell reached down and pressed on the side of the Warrior's neck with two of his fingers. "His pulse could be stronger, and he is running a temperature."

"He's naturally warmer than we are," I told him, not divulging where I came upon this knowledge.

"Should he be this warm?"

"I don't know," I admitted. "I know only that the healthy body temperature of a Sefaline is warmer than that of someone like us."

"I know nothing of Sefaline health, but I would imagine that this temperature must be feverish. He's very warm," he concluded.

"May I try to give him some water?"

"It couldn't hurt. Do you know of any injuries other than that wound on his body?" he asked as he passed me a water bladder.

"I don't believe so," I replied as I brought the opening of the vessel to Lieutenant Fhurrk's lips. It struck me that this felt rather natural to me after having done it many times for Sir Vorel on a ship not so long ago.

"He won't survive if we leave him. I will carry him. We can only pray that we are close to an inhabited farmhouse."

"I will help," I agreed and stroked the poor Sefaline Warrior's face. "Lieutenant Fhurrk? Can you hear me?" I asked hopefully.

His only response was a snuffing of air through his nose, followed by a rumbling sound in his throat that resembled a growl. He didn't appear to awaken. I remained quiet with him for a moment but just as I had given up hope that he would regain consciousness, his eyes started to open, and he muttered something I could not understand.

"Shhh," I said gently. "We're going to help you. You collapsed in a field and we came upon you."

His eyes narrowed, and he snarled something at me, but I couldn't tell if it was merely noises or if there were words embedded within the sounds.

"Please be calm. We're going to bring you to someone who can help you. We aren't near to civilization here."

"East," he finally spoke in words. "I must get to the east."

"We will go to the east. If you hold onto both of us, will you be able to walk at all?"

His thoughts were visibly clearing. Through the sheer intensity of his eyes, I could see the various components of our situation all slipping into their positions in his mind. Unfortunately, that included the realization that he and I were not alone. Quite suddenly, his gaze flicked to Sir Fhirell. For the briefest moment, his spicy scent filled the air but just as quickly, it was gone.

"We only want to help you. We want to repay you for keeping me safe last night," I assured him.

Sir Fhirell nodded in agreement. "We only want to help," he repeated, to my relief. It both honoured me and bolstered my confidence that Sir Fhirell was respecting the tack I had taken with this Warrior.

Lieutenant Fhurrk nodded. I wasn't sure whether it was out of trust or whether it was an acknowledgement that he hadn't any real choice in the matter. He was at our mercy. He was in no position to fight.

"I will walk," he said firmly.

"Please hold onto us while you do," I said as though he would be doing us a favour in allowing us to support him as he walked. In truth, I desperately hoped he would let us help. It was upsetting to think that he believed we would seek him out and wake him, only to lead him to harm. "You collapsed and have had very little water. Should you lose consciousness again, it will be more difficult for us to carry you."

"Yes," he grumbled. " I will walk with your help."

Sir Fhirell, for his part, had been standing back throughout my rather awkward negotiation with the Warrior. However, he took Lieutenant Fhurrk's acceptance of our help as his cue to step forward.

Though I offered my hand to the Sefaline, he did not take it and rose to his feet under his own power. It was a slow movement accompanied by a growl that graduated into a pained whine.

"Put an arm around my shoulders. You can hold onto Sir Fhirell and me. We will keep you up." I spoke as softly as I could so I would harm neither his calm nor his pride.

After a moment of what looked like an assessment, he nodded and brought an arm around my shoulders. I could tell that he was not putting a great deal of his weight on me. I wasn't sure whether it was because we weren't yet moving or because he didn't trust my strength.

On Lieutenant Fhurrk's other side, Sir Fhirell moved very predictably. He ducked under the Sefaline's arm, providing his own support.

"I will take the majority of the weight, Miss Godeleva," he assured me as he secured his own arm around the other man's back. I could tell by his expression that he did not imagine Lieutenant Fhurrk would remain conscious very long. It was likely that we would be carrying him soon enough.

"We will work together," I replied, suddenly noticing the warmth that was making its way through my cloak. I'd never worn a scarf as cozy as this Warrior's arm. "We all need to make it to the town. I will do my part."

Lieutenant Fhurrk was stone-faced and looked as though he was possibly nauseated. Still, as we started moving, he managed to keep up a steady pace.

It took a few steps before we could all align our strides and cross the land more smoothly. I found that when our steps were taken together, there was less bumping about and colliding with one another.

Unfortunately, as successful as we were as we set off, it was not long at all before Lieutenant Fhurrk started leaning increasingly heavily on Sir Fhirell and I. This made it much more difficult to continue forward, particularly while maintaining a stride with each other.

"Lieutenant Fhurrk, shall we rest?" I asked when he was most definitely beginning to slump. His feet were barely lifting off the ground as he stepped.

The Warrior appeared startled as though sharply woken from sleep. "Yes," he agreed.

With a glance to Sir Fhirell, we lowered ourselves to our knees to ease the Warrior to the ground.

"I think I am injured inside," Lieutenant Fhurrk confessed.

"I am afraid you might be right. I wish I knew more about medicine. I don't know what to do about such a wound", I told him honestly.

"In the east, there is someone who can help me."

"We will do everything we can to bring you there."

"Would you allow us to carry you? This will allow you to conserve your strength and may be more comfortable for you," asked Sir Fhirell.

Lieutenant Fhurrk's lip curled at the sound of Sir Fhirell's voice. As the offer was made, the Sefaline's expression worsened to the point that he was baring his fangs.

"Lieutenant Fhurrk, this proposal has been made out of kindness in the hopes of saving your life. We've barely moved since we started walking together. Please consider Sir Fhirell's suggestion. If we continue at this pace, it will be many days before you reach your checkpoint."

As I spoke, the Sefaline's gaze moved sharply to meet mine. "I know this," he snapped but then took a breath and released it in a deliberate attempt to calm himself. "I'm going to kill that Traveller," he muttered before turning to Sir Fhirell. "Can you carry me on your back? I will hold on as best I can."

Sir Fhirell nodded confidently.

"I will carry the bag," I decided. If Sir Fhirell was going to carry another man across these fields, then certainly he should not be our porter as well.

"Thank you, Miss Godeleva," said the Knight as he held out the strap of the bag to me. I nearly smiled at the thought that he did not attempt to deny me the burden of the bag. It made sense that I should carry it and while he may never have asked me to do it, I felt a deep respect from him when he did not decline my request.

I decided to wear the bag under my cloak so the strap would not bunch the fabric. It was heavier than I'd expected, but I was determined to do my part. If Sir Fhirell could carry a Warrior, then I could manage a satchel.

By the time I'd sorted out the bag and my clothing, the two men had decided on the best way for Lieutenant Fhurrk to be carried. Sir Fhirell crouched partway, and the Warrior approached him from behind, climbing onto his back as I'd seen boys do in play. The Knight rose to his full height and started to walk. I rapidly caught up with him, deciding never to be the reason that he would have to slow down. His journey would be hard enough as it was. He didn't need me to make it any longer than necessary.

We were moving. We weren't going as quickly as we had been when we first left the old farmhouse, but this was much faster than when Lieutenant Fhurrk was trying to walk on his own feet.

After a while, the strap of the bag caused my shoulder to ache. I allowed it to remind me of the far greater struggle these two men were facing.

To distract us all from the pain of our bodies and the strain of our thoughts, I started humming. I remembered the difference it had made in soothing Sir Vorel on the ship during our return to Lorammel from Fort Picogeal. It had earned the notice of the entire ship's crew. My hope was that my little hums would do the same for our own little ragtag traveling group.

As I hummed, Lieutenant Fhurrk turned his head toward me. In response, I changed my hum into a song with pleasant, poetic lyrics. His face was calm, and I basked in this sweet little victory.

Sir Fhirell's expression remained stern. I imagined it was a reflection of his determination to continue forward while bearing his load and not an indication of his opinion on my singing. I wondered if any music could penetrate such a barrier.

After a while, I lost count of the number of tunes I'd quietly sung. A final note silenced on my lips as we all seemed to simultaneously notice a man walking in the distance. It didn't take long to realize he was a Paladin. He was far larger than any typical man.

"Should I approach him first?" I asked, attempting to look confident as I did so. I hoped Sir Fhirell would understand my offer. A young woman would pose a far smaller threat to a Paladin than a Knight or a Sefaline Warrior from Kavylak.

To my surprise, and even relief, Sir Fhirell nodded. "He's a Paladin. He will not place you in any danger."

"Yes," I agreed. "I assumed the same."

Glancing to Sir Fhirell and Lieutenant Fhurrk, I nodded to them and picked up my pace to allow me to walk well ahead of them. As the Paladin seemed to glance in our direction, I raised my arm to wave and catch his attention.

The Paladin looked surprised to see us and called out something in the language of the Gbat Rher people. I could tell by the tone that it was a greeting of some kind. It was friendly at the very least.

"I am sorry," I called in return, speaking in the Simple Tongue. I gave the man a gentle smile to improve the dreadful limitations of the common language. "I do not speak Gbat. I need help. Will you help me? I am friend to Kolfi Ingmardr."

I decided not to wait before dropping the name of the only person I knew from the province, and who still lived there. This Paladin was about to meet my travelling companions. It was vital that he think of us as friends, before he could be allowed to see who they were.

The man was as large as Sir Radone but appeared far more rugged. Where Sir Radone was well groomed and had his large body tucked neatly into a Knight's uniform, this man had long, wild reddish/brown hair and a fuzzy beard with braids worked into it. He wore a beige homespun tunic, loose leather trousers, and soft leather boots. Over the tunic was a sleeveless leather jacket long enough to dust his knees and that was drawn in at the waist by a wide belt with a heavy buckle.

"I do not know your friend, but his name is a good one," he replied, joining me in the Simple Tongue. Looking past me, he let his eyes fall on Sir Fhirell and Lieutenant Fhurrk. "They are your friends?"

"Yes," I replied. "One man is hurt. He needs medicine."

The Paladin nodded more seriously, taking in the situation. "I am Drudvis. My house is there," he pointed in a direction where a rooftop was just visible from behind a large hill. I likely wouldn't have seen it if I hadn't been told where to look. "I will help."

"Thank you. I am Irys Godeleva." I turned to indicate Sir Fhirell, who continued to walk toward us. "He is a Knight. He likes Paladins and is a friend."

An intensity entered Drudvis' gaze, but it left just as quickly. "If he does not make trouble, he will not get trouble."

"None of us want any trouble," I said, hoping he would understand that I was genuine and that I did indeed speak on behalf of my entire party.

He seemed to accept my answer and began to walk toward Sir Fhirell and Lieutenant Fhurrk.

"The Knight's name is Sir Dynan Fhirell," I said, trying to share more information so it would appear that we were not trying to hide anything from him. "The hurt man's name is Fhurrk."

Drudvis nodded. "Why are you here?"

"We are friends to Gbat Rher. We are a part of a larger group that travelled here to rebuild homes and farms and help the sick." I explained in the Simple Tongue. I loathed speaking in the Simple Tongue. I would have loved to have explained our presence and intentions in greater detail, but the limited number of adjectives kept my thoughts and concepts in a permanent cage.

I was distracted from my struggles in expressing myself when we reached the men. Lieutenant Fhurrk looked tense but was only just clinging to consciousness.

I made the introductions and explained that Drudvis had offered to help us. Sir Fhirell looked to Drudvis and gave him a deep nod of gratitude.

"I am the friend of the Paladin Rral Radone," Sir Fhirell said. "I have fought by his side. I think of all Paladins as friends." His tone clearly expressed the respect he felt for Sir Radone and for the man in front of us.

Drudvis nodded to Sir Fhirell. While he was clearly feeling more suspicious of Sir Fhirell than he had been of me, it was Lieutenant Fhurrk who drew the majority of his attention.

To try to calm the situation, I approached Lieutenant Fhurrk and spoke softly to him. "It will be easier for you soon. This man's home is nearby. I won't leave you." I gave his arm a gentle touch.

Lieutenant Fhurrk started to nod to me, but his eyes rolled back in his head, and he lost consciousness.

Sir Fhirell looked to me and then the Paladin. "He is hurt both outside and inside and is bleeding both outside and inside." If Sir Fhirell was feeling as frustrated by the Simple Tongue as I was, he didn't let on.

Drudvis' expression turned grave. "We will help," he said firmly.

"Thank you," Sir Fhirell and I replied in unison.

"I will carry Fhurrk," Drudvis said, stepping up to Sir Fhirell to take the Sefaline from him.

To Sir Fhirell's credit, he nodded and released Lieutenant Fhurrk into the Paladin's arms. As much as Sir Fhirell may have been glad to ease his own physical burden, he was also showing Drudvis that we trusted him enough to carry our injured friend.

"He is hurt here," I explained to Drudvis, indicating Lieutenant Fhurrk's front, just below his ribcage.

To that, Drudvis nodded and gently adjusted the way he was carrying the Sefaline, keeping pressure away from the wounded area.

I decided to walk quite closely with the Paladin. It concerned me that Lieutenant Fhurrk might wake and feel threatened by this large stranger. Though I'd hardly call us close, it seemed that we would all be safest if I was to be the first person Lieutenant Fhurrk would see upon waking.

Lieutenant Fhurrk didn't wake. As much as this made the situation calmer, it worried me that he continued to remain unconscious. I glanced to Sir Fhirell for reassurance. In return, he took the bag from me and lightly placed a hand on my back for a moment. His expression was a comforting one. It was just what I'd needed.

I gave him a small smile in gratitude and turned to face forward.

Thank you, Great Goddess. Your gift of this Paladin, and the honour and goodness by which he guides his life, are everything we could have asked of you on Lieutenant Fhurrk's behalf. Your greatness and love for us is beyond measure.

As we approached the house, it was clear that Drudvis' farm had either not been harmed by the conflict between Syliza and Gbat Rher, or it was among those to have recovered very quickly. The farmhouse looked neat and very well maintained. Behind it was a sizeable barn that was also in fine condition and which had recently received a fresh coat of grass-green paint.

Beyond were rolling fields. The variety of colours among the plants suggested that there were many types of crop growing on Drudvis' land. As far as I could tell, the farm was a healthy one.

Drudvis stepped up to the farmhouse and pushed open the door, walking in.

"Elika, I have a wounded man here. Bring bandages," he said, speaking the Simple Tongue, so we would know he was not saying anything he did not wish us to understand.

Sir Fhirell and I entered the house behind Drudvis and found ourselves in a simple but very clean cottage. A woman, whom I could only assume was Elika, stepped out of the kitchen and rested her hands on her hips.

Elika, unlike Drudvis, was not nearly as concerned with making us feel at home. She spoke sharply to him in the Gbat language and did nothing to hide her displeasure.

I stood inside the door next to Sir Fhirell, unmoving and hoping not to incur Elika's wrath. The Paladin may have been twice her bulk, but it was clear that Elika was the most powerful person in this house.

Drudvis walked to the hearth where a small fire was burning, and set Lieutenant Fhurrk down on the rug in front of it. Elika followed and looked him over, turning a disapproving gaze on Drudvis.

He spoke gently to her, this time in the Gbat language. His tone was kind but firm. She stared at him in annoyance but finally nodded and walked back into the kitchen to fetch what would be needed.

I took this opportunity to step up to Lieutenant Fhurrk and kneel next to him. I intended to stay out of the way of whatever assistance was to be provided, but at the same time, I felt that it was my responsibility to ensure that he would remain calm upon waking.

Drudvis worked on removing the clothing from Lieutenant Fhurrk's upper half, while Elika prepared the items she planned to use for healing.

"How was your friend injured?" Drudvis asked, taking a closer look at the wound I'd bandaged.

"I do not know," I replied honestly, stroking the Sefaline's hair.

Drudvis took great care in examining Lieutenant Fhurrk. "Elika knows medicine. She will heal him if he can be healed."

Sir Fhirell stepped up behind me and rested a hand on my shoulder.

"We are grateful to both you and Elika," he said to Drudvis, who nodded in acceptance of the gratitude.

His wife returned with some bandages and a few other items in her hands. Directing her attention to me, she spoke in a commanding tone. "Boil water."

"Yes ma'am," I replied obediently. I had never boiled water in my life. Giving the Sefaline a glance as I left him, just to be certain that he wouldn't imminently wake, I headed to the kitchen. I shuddered to think of his rather less-than-agreeable response if he were to wake while I was away from him.

Stepping into the kitchen, I was relieved to see that the kettle was already on the stove. I heaved the large cast iron kettle off the woodstove with a kitchen towel wrapped around the handle. Setting it into the basin, I pumped water into the opening and carried it back to the stove, only just barely strong enough to lift it once it was full. As I set it back on the surface of the stove, I stepped back to watch it warm. I wanted to be ready the moment it began to boil.

"Be ready to hold him down," I heard Elika's voice command.

"Yes, ma'am," replied Sir Fhirell. My stomach flipped at the thought of what Elika's instruction implied. Lieutenant Fhurrk was about to experience something very painful. Suddenly, the water seemed far less important than making sure I was with the Warrior through what was certain to be a very difficult time. I abandoned the kettle to its own devices and returned to be near the Warrior.

"Drudvis, go out and get yegdrodid," Elika said sternly as I approached. Drudvis went immediately out the door to find whatever it was that Elika had requested.

"Bring me some towels," ordered Elika. This time, the demand was directed at me again. "They are in the room on the right. You will find them in a cupboard."

Nodding, I turned to the room and was glad to see that there was only one cupboard, and it did indeed contain towels. I quickly rifled through them, selecting the towels that appeared to be in the worst condition. I didn't want to think that my time here would spoil Elika's best towels.

Jogging back into the main room of the house, I was about to offer the towels to Elika when I heard a sharp hiss from Lieutenant Fhurrk. He was awake and was clearly confused and in pain.

I rushed to his side, kneeling down so he could see me and not only strangers.

"It's alright, Lieutenant Fhurrk. It's me, Irys Godeleva. This is Elika. She is healing you." I stroked his hair and looked reassuringly into his eyes. "I'll stay with you. I won't leave."

His gaze fixed on me. Though his confusion remained, what had been aggression became a wince as Elika continued to check him over. She muttered something under her breath that I could only imagine was a curse.

"What is it?" asked Sir Fhirell.

"He has broken ribs," she stated solidly. "I can help him with healing broken bones but if he is hurt on the inside, I can do nothing for him. I will treat what I can treat, but fate will determine the rest."

Sir Fhirell and I exchanged a look. I knew my expression was as grim as his.

At that moment, Drudvis returned, carrying a plant, which he brought into the kitchen.

I kept my attention on Lieutenant Fhurrk to keep him from focusing on the giant in the room.

"You have broken ribs," I informed the Sefaline. "The bleeding seems to be under control. Elika will make sure you heal the way you should." I hoped he believed my words more than I did.

He nodded, and I found myself wondering whether he was convinced or simply wanted me to stop talking.

"You go to Drudvis and help him prepare the elixir," Elika suddenly instructed me. "Crush the leaves into a paste in the large bowl, then add hot water to it. Do you understand?"

Dear Goddess, please guide my hands in the kitchen as they have had no guidance from experience. Please, don't let my inadequacies lead to Lieutenant Fhurrk's demise.

"Yes, ma'am," I replied obediently to Elika, confirming that I had understood her instructions. "I will crush the leaves into a paste within a large bowl before I pour hot water into the bowl with the paste."

In reply, she directed a very stern nod to me before turning back to look at the Sefaline.

"I'm going to help make your medicine," I informed Lieutenant Fhurrk in the hopes of keeping everything predictable and calm. "I will return to your side after it is ready."

He nodded to me and locked his gaze upon me as I rose to leave. I could feel his intense, watchful cat-eyes as they followed me into the kitchen where I would hopefully be preparing the medicines to make him well again. Sir Fhirell gave me a reassuring look. I hoped I could live up to the confidence he appeared to have in my abilities to follow Elika's instructions.

"May I help you to prepare the elixir for Mrs. Elika?" I asked Drudvis as I approached him.

I could hear Elika instructing Sir Fhirell to assist her in lifting Lieutenant Fhurrk to a sitting position so he could be better bandaged. I tried to focus on my conversation with Drudvis as I knew this would be painful for the Warrior. Still, I winced as Lieutenant Fhurrk hissed and snarled before releasing the high pitched sound of a wounded animal.

It surprised me that this was not followed by the sounds of a fight between the two men but when I glanced over at them, Lieutenant Fhurrk was keeping control of himself. It wasn't an easy effort. He'd bitten his lip hard enough with his fang that a drop of blood had run halfway down his chin. Sir Fhirell was holding him up while Elika was efficiently bandaging him.

Returning my focus to Drudvis, I asked "Do you know how I am to crush the leaves? I've never done such a thing before."

"I can do it," Drudvis replied calmly. "You take the kettle off the stove so the water will no longer be boiling by the time we pour it in."

"May the Goddess bless you," I said, relieved beyond expression that Drudvis knew how to brew this potion and that my possibly badly crushed leaves would not be the deciding factor between the Lieutenant's life or death.

Drudvis seemed unaffected by my words and instead went about using a pestle on a handful of small leaves in a mortar, grinding them down until they were a fine but thick paste. He scraped the paste into a clay bowl.

For my part, I used a potholder to move the kettle off the stove and waited calmly for Drudvis to need it. It was heavy, but I tried to appear composed so I would seem as useful as I could.

"Shall I pour, Mr. Drudvis?" I asked, hoping I would be able to follow through with the offer.

"You pour, and I will tell you when you have poured enough," he instructed. As direct as his words were, his tone was far softer than Elika's. It seemed to me that his patience for this silly woman from Lorammel was also greater than that of his wife.

Lifting the heavy iron kettle by its handle, which I clutched in both my hands with the potholder to protect them, I angled my entire upper body until the spout started to dribble hot water. Most of it went into the bowl, though a shameful puddle formed on the table at the bowl's base.

"That is good. That is enough," Drudvis said. I hoped he was telling me this because the medicine now contained enough hot water and not just that he wanted me to stop ruining his table. Heaving the kettle out of the way, I rested it back down onto the stove.

Thank you for making me useful to this effort, Great Goddess, but please let that be my last opportunity to heave an iron kettle full of hot water. It is only through your great mercy that none of us were scalded.

"Bring this to your friend," said Drudvis, handing me the bowl.

"Thank you very much for your help, Mr. Drudvis. I wouldn't have known how to do any of this on my own." I took the bowl from him and received his kind nod at the same time. With an appreciative smile to the man, I brought the bowl back to his wife, who continued to care for Lieutenant Fhurrk.

The Sefaline Warrior was still lying down on the floor, though now he was propped up with rolled towels behind his upper back and shoulders. This allowed him to recline slightly instead of lying flat.

I knelt down near Lieutenant Fhurrk where I felt it was my best position to stay out of the way, and I set the bowl down next to Elika.

"Good," she said in gruff approval, after having examined my work with a critical eye. I was relatively sure I had just received the highest praise this woman could issue. "You make sure he drinks all of that. I will make our meal."

My stomach flipped, both at the thought of Lieutenant Fhurrk having to drink this odd green liquid and at the thought of having to eat the type of breakfast this woman would prepare. I was confident that fresh fruit and poached eggs on a light toast would not be available on this morning's menu.

"Yes, ma'am," I replied obediently. I was determined to be a gracious guest. After everything Elika and Drudvis were doing for our little group, the least I could do was complete my task and eat my breakfast.

Holding the bowl in one hand, I stroked Lieutenant Fhurrk's hair with the other.

"Lieutenant Fhurrk," I spoke softly to him. "I have medicine for you, and you will need to drink it."

He looked at me from behind heavily lidded eyes. It was then that I noticed that the blood had been cleaned from his lips. His face had been carefully washed. In fact, much of his exposed skin had been wiped down.

"No," he said, shaking his head as he looked at the bowl with a curled lip. "…smells bad."

I raised the bowl to bring it closer to my own face, inhaling. It wasn't a pleasant smell, but I wouldn't have called it offensive.

"Come now. It's not so bad. I will plug your nose for you if you'd like. I know it doesn't smell like your favourite meal, but it is medicine, and it will help the wounds inside your body to heal. It will help to stop an illness from taking hold." In truth, I hadn't any idea what the medicine was meant to do, but Elika had said that it was an elixir and that Lieutenant Fhurrk was meant to drink it. I was determined to achieve my objective.

With an unhappy look on his face, the Warrior slowly nodded.

"Thank you," I said, acknowledging that he was doing this because I asked him to and not necessarily because he believed it would be of any use to him. I gently stroked his face, sliding my index finger across the space between his nose and upper lip. It looked a little silly as though I was trying to give the man the look of a moustache, but I hoped it would help to reduce the smell of the elixir.

He seemed to understand my meaning and inhaled a little at the presence of my hand. Once he had done so, I brought the bowl to his lips and sang to him quietly. It was a song mothers often sing to soothe their children, and it was soft enough to be just for him. Even Sir Fhirell, though seated nearby, may not have been able to hear me well enough to recognize the tune.

Tilting the bowl, I slowly brought the contents toward Lieutenant Fhurrk's lips. He sipped at it, clearly battling through what looked like quite the unpleasant flavour. It took several minutes, but he did manage to swallow everything that was offered to him. I set down the empty bowl, keeping it well away from him so any lingering odour would not disturb him. Picking up one of the towels, I lifted a corner to his lips to wipe away any residual taste.

Lieutenant Fhurrk watched me with heavy eyes, and when he spoke, his speech was slurred. "Be..." he began, blinking his eyes very slowly. Once they were open again, he completed his statement. "...careful, Irys." At that, he appeared to lose consciousness.

"Sleep well, Lieutenant Fhurrk," I replied quietly, watching his body ease into sleep. When I was certain he had entered into a deep sleep, I released my contact with him and drew away, seeking out Sir Fhirell's company instead.

Sir Fhirell smiled as I approached. I slipped my hand into his and felt stronger when his fingers closed around mine, giving it a gentle squeeze.

"How are you holding up?" he asked quietly.

"To be honest, I don't quite know. I haven't allowed myself to think about it," I confessed with a touch of a smile. "Thank you for allowing this, Sir Fhirell."

"You don't need to thank me, Miss Godeleva. I wouldn't have left him out there. It is not the way of the Knights, and it is not my way."

With a quick motion of my fingers, I made the sign of the Goddess in reply. He nodded and mirrored the sign.

"Elika was right, Miss Godeleva," he said after a quiet moment. "His fate is in the hands of the Goddess now. The medicine will help him sleep, and the sleep will help him heal, but whatever happens, you are not to blame. We have done all we can for him."

"Then I will pray all the harder for him," I replied. "If it is in the hands of the Goddess, I will do all I can to make sure She doesn't let him go."

"I will join you. She will not let him go before his time."

Sir Fhirell had never been more handsome to me than he was at that moment. His caring words and gentle heart showed a kindness in his very soul. I could have spent the entire day watching him. The depth of his eyes as he pondered our situation, the stubble that had formed across his jaw line, and the way his mouth twitched just a little before he moved his gaze to look upon me. His every feature, expression, and gesture was fascinating and entrancing to me.

"Come and have something to eat. You need to be strong for yourselves and your friend," demanded Elika's voice. The caring nature of her words was a stark contrast to the harshness of her tone.

I glanced over at Lieutenant Fhurrk, who appeared to be sleeping soundly. He looked quite peaceful, and I was relieved for him.

With a little smile to Sir Fhirell, I rose and washed my hands at the sink before obediently sitting at the table as Elika had instructed. Sir Fhirell followed, washing up before taking his own seat across from me.

"Thank you for this meal and for the help you're giving us," I said, looking at the proud woman. Her self-sufficiency and usefulness were a clear illustration to me of how little practical knowledge I had accumulated, despite the library of books I'd studied.

The meal consisted of a thick porridge with some fresh berries as well as a slice of warm, soft, buttered bread with dried fruits in it. Were I not as hungry as I currently was, I may not even have tried the contents of the bowl. This was nothing like what I was used to eating at home, and I wasn't typically accustomed to such dense foods. However, I was surprised at how well the simple flavours and textures suited me, and I ate hungrily.

"Are you married?" Elika asked me quite suddenly, looking from me to Sir Fhirell. I was relieved that I'd already swallowed my most recent bite of food. Still, I could feel the blush rising to my cheeks as I shook my head.

"No, ma'am," I answered simply.

"He is your family then?" she persisted.

I shook my head again. "No, ma'am. I was a part of a mission to bring help and supplies to Gbat Rher. I was separated from the group and was lost. Sir Fhirell is a part of the same group, and he came to find me to bring me back again."

"And the man with the marks? Is he a part of your group?" she asked, nodding toward Lieutenant Fhurrk, whose fascinating skin markings were easily visible in his current state.

"He is not a part of the group, but I crossed paths with him while I was lost. He helped me to find shelter for a night. We went our separate ways when Sir Fhirell found me, but as Sir Fhirell and I journeyed together, we found the man collapsed in a field."

"Where did he get those injuries? Those are not from falling down in a field, and they are fresh."

"I don't know, ma'am. He insisted he was fine when we were at the house we used for shelter that night, though he was already wounded then. I made a bandage for him out of some towels and fabric I found, but we barely spoke."

Elika narrowed her eyes and studied me intensely as though trying to find a secret meaning to my words. Suddenly, she darted her gaze at Sir Fhirell.

"Did you hurt him?" she demanded accusingly.

Drudvis said something to her in the Gbat language, but she ignored him as though he hadn't spoken.

"Oh, no, ma'am," I interjected before Sir Fhirell could have the chance to reply. "Sir Fhirell wasn't there yet when Lieutenant Fhurrk helped me to find that shelter, and he was already injured then. Sir Fhirell didn't arrive until the dawn."

"I came upon them in the morning, just as Miss Godeleva said," Sir Fhirell added, speaking calmly. "In fact, by the time I arrived, Lieutenant Fhurrk was just leaving. We didn't even converse, let alone get into any kind of scuffle. It would have been foolish of me even to try. That man is a strong fighter."

Elika responded with a curt nod, but it was clear that she was unsatisfied with the details we were providing.

"You may stay with us until your friend is well enough to travel," Drudvis said decidedly. "I could use a hand on the farm."

"Thank you, Drudvis," I said to him with a genuine little smile.

"Thank you," Sir Fhirell mirrored my gratitude. "I would be honoured to help."

Elika didn't hide her displeasure with her husband's decision, but she didn't object to it, either. I was glad for her acceptance of the large man's generosity.

"What help does your mission bring to Gbat?" she then asked or, rather, demanded.

"Building supplies, food, medicines," I replied directly. "We also brought assistance in the form of many men, women, and robes."

"She knows one of us. A man named Kolfi Ingmardr," Drudvis stated, quite suddenly.

"Yes, I met him a couple of times. He's a young man, though a tall one like you, Drudvis," I confirmed, willing to follow this topic of discussion with the assumption that Drudvis had selected it to ease Elika's tension.

Elika, for her part, was mulling over the name. "Ingmardr," she said as though it sounded familiar to her, but she couldn't quite place it. "I do not know a Kolfi Ingmardr, though his family name is known to me. I think there are Ingmardrs to the southwest. Paladins," she concluded. "Several days' journey from here."

"I don't know where he and his family reside, but he once travelled all the way to Lorammel. That was where I met him. I'd had no concept of the plight of Gbat Rher. He shared his story with me, and I wrote about it so that others would also learn the truth. I was honoured that he was willing to tell me of the struggles you faced and that you continue to face here."

She nodded to me but frowned. "Your support comes too late."

"Elika," Drudvis said with disapproval in his low tone.

"You're right," I replied. "This is late. However, it is the earliest that I was able to offer this help. I didn't know of your needs before now. It is my hope that while I am tardy with my assistance, I am not too late to make a difference. My group has not arrived at the time when you most needed our help, but help is still needed, and we want to offer it. Sir Fhirell went to great care to arrange this assistance, and it meant the world to me that I was welcomed and permitted to join. I left everything I had to come here. Late or not, I want this to mean something."

Regardless of my having poured out my heart, Elika looked unmoved. Still, if she'd had any nasty remarks, she kept them to herself.

"You will have your wish. The more you see of Gbat, the more you will see of need," she said flatly.

"I don't want to see such need, but I know I must. When I do, I will do all I can to help. Once I can help no further, I will go home and tell people what I saw here with my own eyes. Perhaps this will lead to more help – more people who want to make a difference. Then more after that when they bring their stories home."

Elika fixed her gaze on me for a nearly unbearable length of time. She remained expressionless until she finally stood.

"You can clean up breakfast while I attend to other chores." She turned her back to me and walked into a room with a door consisting of a curtain hanging from a rod with dull metal rings.

"Yes ma'am," I replied without any confidence in my ability to comply with her wishes.

Before I could exchange even the slightest glance with Sir Fhirell, Drudvis addressed him.

"You may accompany me in the fields," he said, and Sir Fhirell nodded in reply.

Finally, he caught my eye. It was as though he knew how much I needed his glance. I needed that tiny, wordless communication that told me all would be well. I needed his confident expression to tell me that I wouldn't somehow burn down this house by trying to wash the breakfast dishes.

"You'll be alright, Miss Godeleva," Sir Fhirell said with a friendly smile, punctuating the discussion we'd already had with our eyes. From that moment, I was able rise above my doubts and fears. He wouldn't leave me in the house if he felt I would be unable to manage on my own.

"Yes. Of course. Thank you," I said, liking how certain I sounded.

At that, I began collecting the dishes and bringing them to the basin, setting them gently inside. I had very little idea of how to proceed, but I was determined to live up to Sir Fhirell's belief in me. I nodded to him as he rose from his chair and followed Drudvis outside.

Elika buzzed around the house as I painstakingly slowly scrubbed each dish and found a new place to set it aside to dry. I wondered how the staff at home managed to find the space to dry all our dishes after a large party. I knew the laundry had places to hang clothing and linens to dry, but dishes could not be strung up on a line. I did my best to find places for each plate, cup and utensil while keeping the kitchen as neat as was possible.

Occasionally, Elika shot strange glances in my direction but overall, she continued about her business. Clearly, she did not approve of my methods for doing the dishes but would tolerate them as long as I stayed out of her way.

Every now and again, I would glance over at Lieutenant Fhurrk, to be certain he was still sleeping. Blessedly, that situation hadn't changed.

"You look like you have never done dishes in your life," Elika observed quite suddenly during her most recent high-velocity trip past me. My shoulders fell. I had been starting to fool myself into thinking I was getting the hang of my task.

"I haven't," I said without shame or pride.

"What do you know how to do well?" she asked. "What chores do you complete in your day when you are at home?"

I prepared myself for the judgment I knew was coming. "I study and research. I write academic articles. I also play the harp, and I sing." These were all very respectable pass times for a young woman of my status, of course, but I knew she was hoping to hear a list of far more domestic activities.

Her brows knit and lips pursed. "You said that you were travelling to Gbat Rher with others who intended to help us here. How is it that you planned to do this with your harp playing?"

"The main reason for my journey here was to see the truth for myself, so I could write about it and tell the people in Lorammel. I wanted to observe the situation in Gbat Rher so that I may encourage others to lend their support.

"I also intended to make myself useful wherever else I could. For example, I imagined that I would assist some of the nurses who were travelling with us. I have a bit of experience in tending to those who have been wounded," I explained. I had hoped at least the last point would allow me a touch of relief from her hard, disapproving stare.

"You are likely to find people with many kinds of needs for assistance," she said with a solid nod.

"Yes. My group is mainly prepared to help with certain types of rebuilding projects and to offer medical assistance. I planned to do as I was told and follow the directions of those with more experience and specialty. Certainly, the medics and the builders can always do with the help of someone willing to organize things, fetch things, or to run notes from one person to another."

"As long as you are here to help. The last thing we need is another Sylizan with eyes on our resources."

"What harm could someone like me possibly do to your province?"

"Eat our food, need our help, or go home and tell others how much fertile land there is up here," she said with an accusatory expression. "Where does your group intend to stay while you're here? What do you plan to eat?"

I boldly returned her gaze. I would not be cowed by this woman who so persistently belittled me, the group, and our intentions to help.

"Please accept my apologies for the drain I have already been to your home. These were extenuating circumstances, and I take the blame for them entirely," I shook my head. "I don't know where the group will stay or what they will eat. Sir Fhirell has that information. That said, I'd been warned before our departure that there might be camping involved during this trip and if I must sleep in a tent, then that's what I must do."

Elika nodded but maintained her stern expression, watching me and judging me.

Instead of standing there and waiting for her to finish deciding on her next criticism or question, I crossed the room to where Lieutenant Fhurrk was lying. Quietly, I checked him over, making sure his condition didn't appear to have changed. He seemed the same, so I stroked his hair, hoping he would feel comforted, even while unconscious.

"Do you know how to do the washing?" Elika asked, quite out of the blue.

Preparing for another disapproval, I shook my head. "No," I said softly so I wouldn't disturb Lieutenant Fhurrk.

"Would you like to learn? This skill may be useful if you will be helping nurses and the wounded."

This surprised me. I hadn't expected her to lend her support to someone she thought was all but useless in the effort to help her people. However, I was not about to reject this attempt at peace or to miss the opportunity to learn. She was right. That might be a useful skill.

"Thank you. I think you're right. I may be far more helpful if I am able to complete tasks like the washing," I agreed, continuing to stroke the Sefaline's hair.

"We will do it outside. Follow me," she said, leaving the room before returning a moment later with a basket full of laundry.

I rose and quickly followed her. She was feeling generous toward me, and I didn't want that to change.

Outside, Elika proceeded to set up an astounding number of wash stations. I became keenly aware that I neither had any idea of what went into the washing of clothes, nor was I going to enjoy the discovery.

I watched, learned, and obeyed at each step of the laundry process as we agitated each piece of fabric in large soapy tubs of water, scrubbed it against washboards, rinsed the clothing, boiled it, and rinsed it again, wringing it out at each step until I thought my fingers would no longer respond to my will. Finally, we hung the cleaned items on clotheslines. My shoulders ached from being raised. Elika looked as though she could have repeated the whole thing a dozen more times.

Certainly, this was a useful skill, and I was grateful to have learned it in case it came in handy. That said, I prayed that the Great Goddess would choose never to make me do laundry again.

The one part of the chore I did enjoy was the chance to observe Sir Fhirell as he worked with Drudvis. By the time the laundry was finished, Sir Fhirell's shirt sleeves were rolled to his elbows to cool him from the relentless sun.

I enjoyed that same sun and the fresh air that came with it. The breeze just seemed to know when the temperature was becoming uncomfortably warm as it always chose those moments to flutter by and whisk the heat away.

"I must say. I do like hanging the laundry far more than washing it. I would hang them twice if I thought I wouldn't have to wash them," I said jovially, breaking a stretch of silence.

Elika's stern expression broke, and she smiled rather warmly at me. "Yes. It is a shame that clothing cannot be cleaned just by hanging it." She wiped her brow with the back of her sleeve and placed her hands on her hips, observing our work. "You can help me make lunch for the men. They will be hungry after their work this morning."

"I don't know how to cook, but I will be happy to learn and help where I can."

Though I'd expected another look of disapproval, Elika simply nodded. "You will learn. You are smart and understand things quickly."

"Thank you. That's one of the finest compliments I've ever received, if only because I know you wouldn't give it just to make me feel good about myself." I chuckled.

"I'm not inclined to give compliments to those who don't deserve them," she replied. Her words were stern, but there was amusement in her expression.

"I believe you." I certainly did.

She turned and walked inside without another word. Following her in, I glanced over at Sir Fhirell and gave him a small wave when he looked up at me. He replied with a smile and a nod but continued working at his task.

Back inside again, I washed my face, hands, and arms and returned to the main living space where I checked on Lieutenant Fhurrk. He was still asleep.

"Do you think he will be able to eat some of our lunch?" I asked with doubt in my voice.

Elika was already dashing about the kitchen, preparing to make the meal.

"No," she said with an evaluating glance at the Sefaline. "I might try him on something if he wakes, but he'll be in a deep sleep for a while. I don't want him to be disturbed from that. The sleep will do him good."

"Should he eat when he wakes? Will he be able to?"

"He can try. Any food he puts in his body will help him to heal."

I approached her and helped out where I could. I assumed that the tasks she was assigning me would have been the same ones given to a child in her culture. I set the table and poured the water while she put together the rest of the meal.

"Is there a town or anything else nearby?" I asked with curiosity.

"There is a small town two hours' walk from here if you keep up a good pace. Do you need to be in a town?"

"I was only wondering what Sir Fhirell, Lieutenant Fhurrk, and I might pass as we keep up our journey. The more towns we pass, the easier it will be for us, particularly if there are inns."

"If you head to the town, you may be fortunate enough to see one of your Knights. He passes through there from time to time," she said with distaste. It was evident that while this may be fortunate for us, she did not find the presence of Knights to be at all fortuitous for her own people.

Still, I was overjoyed at the thought that we might come across another Knight. "That's very good news. Thank you!"

"If your friend does not recover so that he can walk on his own, I will have Drudvis hook up the horse and wagon and take you all to the town so you can wait for a Knight to help you."

"Oh, Mrs. Elika, that's the best news I've heard since I've been lost," I said with relief.

Her expression gentled, and she rested a hand lightly on my shoulder in a supportive gesture. She took the hand away again as quickly as she had placed it there. Still, the warmth of it remained, and it felt wonderful.

"Go ahead and call the men in. I'll finish the rest here," she instructed me when everything was nearly ready.

Obediently, I stepped outside to fetch the men from their work on the farm. Although I assumed that Elika would have shouted for them from the door, I simply couldn't imagine myself bellowing at them that way. Instead, as briskly as I could, I crossed the distance from the house to where they were working and waited until there was a pause in their task before speaking.

"Lunch," I said simply with a smile.

Drudvis smiled even more widely than I had, looking keen to take his break and satisfy his hunger with a good meal.

Sir Fhirell set aside the tool he'd been using and looked surprised as Drudvis gave him an enthusiastic clap on the back that forced him to take a step forward.

"You've done well," declared Drudvis. "You work hard. Come, and we'll enjoy good food and some mijols."

I felt deeply proud of Sir Fhirell's accomplishment. Clearly he'd been much more prepared for his tasks than I had been for mine. I wondered what "mijols" could be and if I'd played any role in making it with Elika.

Together, we all returned to the house as I gave Sir Fhirell what little update I had on Lieutenant Fhurrk's condition.

I led the men inside and though I was allowed to pass unscathed, both Sir Fhirell and Drudvis received a thorough scolding for stepping past the threshold in their boots. Both men obediently removed their footwear before going to wash up for the meal. I wasn't sure why, but it warmed me to see this average-sized woman barking out orders to a giant and a Knight, only to have them both do as they were told without argument.

I looked at the food laid out on the table and my stomach growled. It surprised me that I'd felt as hungry as I did, but the hard work I'd done all day certainly justified it.

We all took a seat at the table and began our meal. I said grace with Sir Fhirell, but though Drudvis and Elika remained quiet for the prayer, they did not seem to take part in it.

I sipped my water at the same time Sir Fhirell drank from a large mug that was placed in front of him. Both he and Drudvis had one of these mugs. Elika and I had cups of water. When I saw Sir Fhirell's reaction to the beverage, I was rather glad the water was all I had. At first, he looked as though he'd been stuck by a pin and then his cheeks turned slightly ruddier. Whatever that drink was, it was powerful.

Drudvis, Sir Fhirell, and I chatted as we ate, never speaking of anything too profound. The meal was a friendly one. It was pleasant to feel that way.

After we'd had the chance to satisfy the worst of our hunger, I brought up the topic of the nearby town and that Elika had mentioned that a Knight often visited there. Sir Fhirell's interest piqued quite visibly.

"Do you know the name of the Knight who visits the town? Is it always the same one?" he asked.

"His name is Fasido," said Drudvis. It was more than evident from the expression on the giant's face that Sir Fasido was not well liked. At least not in this house.

I'd never heard the name before and glanced at Sir Fhirell who didn't show any more recognition than I had.

"I do not know his name," Sir Fhirell said, confirming my suspicion. "Has he been in Gbat Rher long?"

"Yes. For at least a cycle," Drudvis replied.

Sir Fhirell's look of surprise mirrored the expression I must have had on my own face.

"I look forward to meeting him. Is he the only one?"

"Yes. He lives here. He has taken a local woman as a wife."

Again, we were surprised. It worried me that Sir Fhirell had not heard of this man. Would he not have been informed of a Knight who had been stationed here in Gbat as he was travelling to this province? Was the Knight's post here not an official one?

We finished our lunch without saying much else. Each of us was lost in our own thoughts. Drudvis rose and kissed his wife's cheek before heading back outside again. Sir Fhirell gave me a resigned look accompanied by a pleasant smile.

"It looks like it's time to get back to work," he said with a chuckle.

I nodded. "See you soon."

He gave a short bow to Elika and me and followed Drudvis outside.

Without asking, I stepped up to the sink and prepared to wash the dishes, accepting the fact that my fingertips were to be wrinkled for as long as we would be staying in this house.

Chapter 9

Megan

The sound of men yelling and running feet pulled me from sleep.

"We have to hide now," Sabear whispered with urgency, giving my shoulder a shake and shoving my clothes toward me. "Take your clothes and get up."

I slowly sat up. My body felt stiff and as though it had been hit by a truck. I knew I was in need of more sleep, but now wasn't the time to complain about it. Glancing at Fiffine and Amorette, I saw that they looked just as out-of-it as I was and had been given their clothes, too.

"Hurry! Come with us," Uori urged.

I looked toward the sound of his voice and noticed that Rakej was standing beside him. The three rebels appeared to be on edge. Their expressions, coupled with the sounds of yelling and running, pierced my confusion.

The Warriors are here.

I flew into action, hauling on my clothes and whipping off my robe as quickly as I could. I stuffed my feet into my boots and was dressed in record time. I was pretty sure Amorette and Fiffine had the same realization I did, because they were dressed and ready to go, too.

Sabear put a supportive arm around Fiffine and said, "This way." She gestured for us to follow her.

Looking stern, determined, and ready for anything, Amorette took my hand, and I held hers back tightly. I had no intention of losing her. We moved forward with Rakej and Uori close behind.

There were branches of other tunnels that veered off the main one through which we were travelling. I felt like we were in a maze as we made our way deeper into the cave. The path we traveled grew colder, narrower, quieter, and ever darker as we walked. The ceiling became lower until it was maybe seven feet high, and the walls closed in to the point that by walking side-by-side with Amorette, I could easily touch the rocky surface of the wall. I wasn't claustrophobic by nature, but I could feel my panic rising as the tunnel became narrower and darker.

The only light came from the lit torches on the walls but there weren't many of them. Their dancing flames cast eerie shadows, which did nothing to ease my nerves.

Sabear reached out at one point and took a lit torch from the wall, the last one along our path. Now, our only light was the one Sabear held. Outside that meagre illumination, it was pitch black. This was the darkest place I had ever been. I drew even closer to Amorette and used my free hand to slide it along the wall as I walked, so I could follow it and make sure I wouldn't walk into it, in case it happened to curve.

Occasionally, I could hear the faint echo of people yelling. I didn't know where they were or why they were yelling, but I didn't imagine anything good was happening.

Finally, Sabear led us into a very small "room" filled with rocks and dust.

"We'll be safe here," she whispered quietly and set the torch she had carried into a nook in the wall.

I looked at Sabear like she was a few bricks short of a load.

Is she kidding? Safe? In a tiny, dark dead-end space with only one exit? We aren't safe, we're sitting ducks!

Fiffine looked around the room for a brief moment and then slid down to her knees, crossing her hands over her chest, mouthing the words of a prayer.

I watched her pray.

Now, she *had the right idea! What we need is divine intervention to get us out of this mess.*

Amorette knelt down beside Fiffine, and I joined her. She wrapped her arms around me, and I held her back.

"It's going to be alright," she whispered in a tiny terrified voice.

"No matter what," I agreed in an equally terrified voice, "We'll stick together."

"We'll protect Fiffine." Amorette nodded.

"Yes." Regardless of how scared I was at this moment, I was prepared to protect the lives of these women with my own. It didn't matter that I barely knew either one of them. We'd been through so much in the past while that it just felt right.

We huddled in silence for what felt like an exceptionally long time and then we heard the sound of heavy footfalls approaching in the distance. This was soon followed by a man's loud voice.

"There's light at the end," he called to someone else. "Try this way!"

I knew the owner of the voice, but adrenaline was coursing too heavily in my veins for me to figure out who it was.

I heard the sharp sound of a sword being drawn from its sheath and saw that Uori had armed himself, ready for a fight. Rakej was also standing, braced for a fight, and Sabear crouched in front of me, Amorette, and Fiffine like a human shield.

I appreciated that they wanted to protect us but honestly, I felt like these rebels should have been hiding behind us. I knew now that most of my fear wasn't fear for our lives, but for theirs. I desperately hoped that what was coming was negotiations and not an attack from ghost-wolves.

What happened next, I wasn't expecting. A man's silhouette appeared in front of the room's entrance. A second later, the lit torch on the wall revealed it was Keavren.

I knew I recognized the voice!

Even though I had expected the Warriors to show up, I was still shocked to see him all the same. Uori didn't share my surprise and struck quickly with his sword. Keavren reacted fast, using the gauntlet portion of his fighting gloves to block the blade. He took a swing at Uori, his fist connecting with Uori's gut. At the same time, Rakej kicked Keavren in the side.

Okay, so I guess it's a "no" for the verbal negotiations.

"They're here!" Keavren bellowed back down the cave's passage as he simultaneously fought both Uori and Rakej.

The fight was dizzying and horrible to watch, but I also couldn't deny that a part of me was fascinated with watching Keavren in action. Yeah, he was definitely taking his fair share of hits to his face and body. Still, he was blocking every one of Uori's sword attacks and battling off Rakej while managing to land some of his own kicks and punches, too. He was gradually advancing into the room, successfully holding his own against the two men in our tight dimly lit area. It was amazing that he hadn't been stabbed!

I glanced at Amorette and Fiffine to make sure they were alright. Fiffine was still praying. Amorette, on the other hand, was staring intently at the battle, clutching a small knife in her hand. It must have been the one she had told me she had hidden in her shoe. She didn't look like she was about to join the fight, but it was very clear by her expression and the way she held the small blade, that if anyone tried anything near us, she was going to get stabby.

Suddenly, Sabear rose from her crouched position and walked, trance-like, toward the torch on the wall. It was as though she was completely oblivious to the fight happening right in front of her. Everything about her movements seemed strange and unnatural. Then, for no logical reason I could decipher, she picked up the torch and snuffed it out.

I gasped when everything went dark. Panic and fear exploded inside me, and the immediate silence that followed didn't help.

What in the heck is Sabear thinking? Has she lost her mind? She just made this situation ten times worse for everyone, especially her own people!

I held tighter to Amorette and Fiffine.

"What's happening?"Amorette whispered. In spite of the freaky silence that surrounded us, I still struggled to hear her over my pounding heart.

"I don't know," I whispered back.

The quiet was broken a moment later with the sound of Sabear's crying. It didn't sound like she was afraid or sad, it sounded like she was seeing something horrible happening – life-shatteringly horrible.

I had no idea what was happening to her, and I debated calling out to her, but before I could process another thought, Sabear cried out again. This time it was a wail, one that could only be caused by physical pain.

Did someone hurt her? Was it Keavren?

"Sabear!" Uori called urgently.

Sabear didn't respond to him. She didn't make a sound.

Dread filled me.

Several footsteps stumbled awkwardly in her direction. I could only assume that both Uori and Rakej were attempting to reach her to see if she was alright. Abruptly, there was a hard thud as one of the men collapsed to the dirt floor. This was immediately followed by his loud grunt of pain as if he'd been hit with something hard in the gut. There was another thud and he was silent.

I wanted to scream in fear from being blinded and bombarded by all the horrifying sounds, but I was much too terrified. Like Amorette and Fiffine, I was shaking with fright and had no intention of moving from where I was. We clung to each other, holding on for dear life. None of us wanted to get in the way of whatever was happening.

More footsteps shuffled in the darkness, the sound of a sword blade hit the stone wall, and a man roared in anger and in pain. Then, he went silent, too.

A tiny light pierced the darkness.

"Amorette? Mrs. Wintheare? Megan?" Keavren asked.

"We're here," Amorette replied in a mixture of terror and relief.

I was glad she spoke. Fright still clung to my vocal chords. Any bravery I'd had earlier, had long since left me.

"It's going to be alright," Keavren assured us. "Come on. All of you follow me. Follow my light," he encouraged. "Just come straight to me so you won't trip or slip."

I slowly stood with the two other women. My legs felt like noodles as if there were no bones in them. I realized as I took a step forward, that my whole body was shaking, and I wasn't able to make it stop. Amorette held my hand tightly, and Fiffine held on to us, too, but Fiffine's touch was calmer. Even though it was still too dark for me to see her, it didn't seem that she was as worked up as Amorette and I.

We slowly shuffled our way toward Keavren's small light. I had no idea what device he was using to make the flame. A lighter maybe? I had never seen a lighter on Qarradune before but that didn't mean they didn't have them.

When we reached him, I could see his relieved smile.

"Just keep following me, and we'll make it out of the caves. We have horses for you outside. We're going home," he said. He wasted no more time talking and started to walk ahead of us.

When I stepped forward, my foot came in contact with a lump on the floor. I looked down to see what it was, and to my shock, I saw a leg. The leg wasn't clothed in a Knight's uniform or a monk's robe, so I knew it belonged to Sabear. With Keavren's retreating light as my only source of illumination, I couldn't see beyond her middle. I had no idea whether she was simply unconscious...or worse. Even though I knew they probably needed help, I was too afraid to find out what had happened to her or to Uori and Rakej.

A good person would have stopped to make sure they were okay, but I wasn't a good person right now. I was a scared one. The only person I wanted to help and save was myself. I stepped over Sabear's leg and didn't look back, knowing that the guilt would haunt me later.

It felt like an eternity before we finally reached the area of the cavern where we had originally been held. The place was now a disaster. It was void of people, but all the remaining items had been destroyed. Screens were toppled over and curtains torn down. The place had been ransacked. Feeling numb, I looked past it all.

Not long after, we reached the mouth of the cave. Daylight was waiting just outside. As I drew closer to the light, I squinted. After being in darkness for so long, my eyes weren't ready for the assault of the morning sun's radiance. It stung.

When I was able to open my eyes again, I turned toward Amorette and Fiffine. Amorette looked shaken and pale, which was how I imagined I looked. Fiffine looked like her usual serene self, only with dark circles of exhaustion under her eyes. All three of us looked dishevelled.

Suddenly, there was barking, and a pack of wolves appeared from out of nowhere, running toward us as we exited the cave.

"Amarogq!" Amorette called out.

When they reached us, the wolves sniffed and inspected us. It still blew my mind that Amargq's ghost-wolves – or, spirit wolves as he called them – could feel so real, even though I had seen them appear and disappear on more than one occasion.

A few moments later, Amarogq ran into view and bee-lined for Amorette. She released my hand and threw herself into his arms, holding him tightly. She burst into tears, and he kissed her head, fiercely clutching her to him as if he had no intention of letting her go again, *ever*.

Something soft brushed my face. I turned and saw that Fiffine had dabbed my cheek with a handkerchief and was looking at me with understanding.

Touching my face, I discovered it was wet. I had been crying without realizing it. I had no idea when the tears had started or for how long they had flowed.

"It's over," Fiffine told me softly. "Now we go back and heal." She gave my hand a gentle squeeze of reassurance.

How in the world is this woman so calm?

I nodded out of respect, but I knew it wasn't over. It would never be over until I was free from Qarradune.

"You're both alright, right?" Keavren asked, stepping up to us.

Fiffine and I nodded to him. Now, in the light, I could see him clearly for the first time. His face was swelling from the hits he had taken, and it was evident that bruises would soon form.

"We've got the horses and will turn back now," Amarogq spoke, drawing my attention away from Keavren. I noticed Amarogq was still holding Amorette in his I'm-never-letting-you-go-again-ever-for-as-long-as-I-live embrace.

"I'm going to head to the first town with Amorette and Fiffine. They're sure to have a midwife there, just so we can be safe," Amarogq said.

I nodded. That made sense to me.

"You'll ride on ahead with Keavren and Mez," he told me.

I was about to nod my head again but then my brain clued in to the second name in his statement, and my eyebrows rose.

"Mez is here? Where?" I looked around and couldn't see anyone else but the five of us and the wolves.

"This way," Keavren replied, gesturing for me to follow him toward the trees, where I now noticed there was movement, likely from waiting horses and a waiting Mez.

I turned to Fiffine and Amorette to say goodbye. Fiffine stepped forward and kissed me on my cheek, and I returned the parting gesture.

"We'll have a meal together when we're both home again. Be safe," she said.

I smiled to her. "I will. You be safe, too."

I turned to Amorette. She released Amarogq and flung her arms around me. I returned her tight hug.

"You were great. Be safe." I told her.

"You were, too. I'll see you very soon. We won't be far behind you, I'm sure. Be safe."

I withdrew from her embrace and headed off with Keavren.

"Did you want to try riding on your own or did you want to ride with me or Mez?" he asked as we walked toward the trees.

I shook my head. Now wasn't the time for riding lessons. I wanted to get back to Capital City as quickly as possible and in one piece.

"I'll ride with you," I decided.

I'd already been Keavren's passenger once before, and I had no idea what condition Mez was in. I mean, the last time I'd seen the guy, he'd literally been clobbered in the back with flying concrete and was injured enough that he'd had blood in his mouth.

How is he even okay enough to be here?

Keavren smiled and winced at the same time, and it occurred to me that riding with him might not be the best idea either. He'd just been in a fight with two men. Who knew how many other bruises he had on his body that I couldn't see.

"On second thought, maybe if Mez is in a little bit less pain than you are, I should ride with him," I said, changing my plan.

"It's up to you, Megan. I'm sore, but I don't mind."

I nodded with a small sigh. I guess I'd have to see which guy was less injured and ride with him.

Darn it! I seriously have to make a priority of learning how to ride a horse. Why can't Qarradune have cars? Would that be too much to ask?

I'd gotten my license when I was seventeen, so I knew how to handle one of those.

But, noooo. Qarradune had to be all about horses, horses, horses. I hate horses. Okay, all horses except Chivarly.

As soon as we stepped through the woods, Mez was there waiting for us, standing next to three dark brown horses. He was wearing his full black Warrior's uniform, identical to what Keavren and Amarogq wore. Stupidly, I found this surprising, only because I had grown accustomed to seeing Mez with his jacket casually open, or off, during our previous talking-sessions on the ship. This was the most "Warrior" I had seen him look.

Still, what was far more surprising was that, aside from appearing to be exhausted, he seemed completely fine. I was expecting him to look pretty beaten up, but the only signs that he had suffered any pervious injury at all were the two small white butterfly-closure bandages on the right side of his forehead.

I couldn't have been more confused. How could someone who had been hit by a ton of bricks only have a couple of tiny bandages on his forehead? Dude looked like he only got a bad scratch when he should have been in a body cast!

"I'm glad to see you're alright, Megan." Mez greeted me with a tired smile.

"Thanks. I'm glad to see that you're alright, too."

It's true that I didn't understand how he could be as alright as he was, but I was still happy that he had healed, regardless. The man had pretty much save my life, after all.

"I'm surprised you came," I added because, happy or not, he was one of the last people I'd expected to be a part of the rescue team.

"I mean, the last time I saw you, you looked like you got hurt pretty badly."

"I had a rough night," he nodded in agreement. "Nothing a few stitches and a lot of riding couldn't fix." He grinned.

I gave a half-hearted smile back. I didn't believe what he'd said, and I had a feeling he didn't expect me to, but now wasn't the time to play the twenty-questions game with Mez.

"Which one of you is in the least amount of pain? I'll ride with whoever that is."

"I am." Keavren chuckled. "Mez has got to feel like his head is splitting open by now."

What? Why? Did a rebel hit him in the head, or something?

I looked curiously at Mez, waiting for the big reveal, but he was giving Keavren a disappointed look, like he couldn't believe how much of an idiot Keavren was.

Uh?

"Are you going to be alright to ride?" Mez asked Keavren as if he hadn't even heard what Keavren had previously said about his head. "Or do you want to stop in the town, too? Don't forget we're headed back through the Northerners' territory, and it's daylight now. You may need to be at your best."

Northerners' territory? Should I be worried?

"I'm fine." Keavren shrugged, and Mez nodded.

I guess not.

"Why don't you just start with one of us then switch," Mez suggested to me with an exhausted smile. "We'll need to change horses anyway."

"Okay," I agreed. "I'll ride with you first," I told Mez. "I know you've got bruises I can't see," I said to Keavren.

"Alright. Fair enough," Keavren said.

He then proceeded to climb up onto one of the horses. Once he was settled, he took the reins of the vacant horse to keep it with us on our journey.

Sorry Vacant Horse. You have no idea how much I wish I could ride you.

Turning to Mez, ready to get going, I saw that he was unwrapping a small piece of paper. He popped whatever the paper had contained into his mouth. Based on his expression, I knew that whatever he had just eaten wasn't a breath mint. It had to have been of the painkiller variety. I guessed Keavren was right. Mez must have had one terrible headache. I didn't envy him. I hated headaches.

Mez mounted the remaining horse and reached down to help pull me up onto it behind him.

Under other circumstances, I would have made a comment to Mez about his long silver hair, which still somehow managed to look perfect, but I was too exhausted and upset from what happened in the cave to be playful. That said, I did notice for the first time, that he wore two sheathed matching swords that were crossed diagonally on his back. I must have been seriously out of it if it took me that long to notice he was armed with twin blades. They weren't exactly small. *Whatever.* At this point I was lucky I was still conscious.

I gently placed my arms loosely around Mez' waist to feel more secure as we rode. He took that as the sign to start our journey and encouraged the horse to get moving. Keavren followed with Vacant Horse in tow.

We travelled at a steady pace, but we were far from a gallop. We wove our way around the trees and away from the cave until we reached a dirt road. Being in the open air and the movement of the horse was soothing. I could feel myself growing more relaxed, and I closed my eyes.

*　*　*　*　*

"Halt! Kavylak Swine!"

My eyes flew open, and I jolted to attention. I hadn't realized I'd fallen asleep, but by the sun's position in the sky, I knew it had to be sometime in the late morning. Dazed, I turned my head toward the sound of the speaker. Although I couldn't see her, the strong commanding voice belonged to a woman, and she had a strange accent that was new to my ears.

Oh, no.

"Northerner," Mez said quietly to Keavren.

Keavren nodded in agreement, and they stopped the horses.

Um, do we like Northerners?

A woman strode confidently out from among the trees. She was tall and tan skinned with long, glossy black hair drawn into a high ponytail by a strip of leather. She was dressed in a leather tunic with a flattering cut, over darker leather leggings, both decorated with intricate stitching and lacing. Everything about this woman was bold and strong. Her forest green eyes were solidly fixed on us. As interesting as this woman looked, she was carrying a bow with an arrow pointing threateningly at Keavren.

I guessed she wasn't a friend. Maybe she was another rebel.

Wonderful.

Keavren raised his hands in surrender and said, "We leave in peace. We do not want fighting."

I looked at Keavren oddly. He had spoken in very basic words in yet another new accent that sounded nothing like hers or like any other accent with which I was familiar. I didn't get why he did that.

Is this his attempt at speaking her language?

Much to my dismay, the woman didn't seem impressed.

"I don't speak filth," she spat back in disgust in the accent she had used before, which I was now assuming must be Northerner.

I glanced at Mez and Keavren, waiting for either one of them to respond, but my gut told me that they didn't understand her anymore than she understood them.

"Uh, what's the problem ma'am?" I asked, desperately hoping she would understand me in the same way that everyone else who spoke different languages on this planet were somehow able to do.

Mez looked back at me in surprise. His expression helped to boost my confidence that I had at least spoken something other than Kavylak.

The woman turned her attention to me. "My people have claimed these lands. You have walked upon them. Give us your horses," she demanded.

The arrow she kept trained on Keavren told me she wasn't kidding.

"What is she saying?" Mez whispered.

"She said that these lands belong to her people and she wants our horses," I paraphrased.

Mez nodded. "Tell her we are lost, hungry, and were just attacked by rebels. We only want to get home, and we mean no harm."

I nodded to him and looked back at the woman, whose narrowed eyes were now suspiciously fixed on Mez, and relayed his message to her.

Her gazed flicked to me when I spoke, and she took a step closer to me, though her arrow never stopped pointing at Keavren.

"How is it you speak my language? Have you lived among us?"

That's an excellent question, lady, and boy, do I wish I had the answer for you.

"No. I have not lived among you, but I know many languages." That, at least, was the truth.

She nodded, seeming to accept my answer and appearing interested.

"Your man does not speak the languages you do?" she asked, nodding toward Mez.

Hmm...do I keep up the lie that he's my boyfriend? Meh, it seemed to have been the best road to take so far, and I'd grown comfortable with the lie. Why over-complicate things now?

"He does not," I confirmed and realized that I'd have to let Mez in on my little relationship falsehood when I got the chance. I hoped he wouldn't mind.

She nodded, studying both Mez and Keavren until a man, casually stepped out of the woods with a knife in his hand.

His presence startled me because there had been no indication that there was anyone else there. Tensing, I wondered how many more people were there that we couldn't see.

The man was only just slightly taller than the woman. His black hair was cut into many different lengths in such a random way that it had to have been deliberate. The longest pieces were dyed a rich earthy brown. He wore a taupe leather vest, which hung open to reveal a number of decorative necklaces on leather thongs, not to mention a well-muscled chest. It was well-muscled enough that I couldn't help but notice it despite the tribal-style tattoos he had both there and on his upper arm. Shaking myself from my well-muscled daze, I took a closer look at the man and the woman that stood before us. In a certain way, they reminded me of Amarogq.

"She speaks like the People. We should feed them before we send them off," he said to the woman.

She considered what he'd said for a moment and then looked at me. "You need food and shelter. We will give it to you until tomorrow when you will be taken off our lands," she decided, adding, "Then, you will not return."

Um, what if we want to go now?

"That's very generous of you, but we would really just like to get home. We promise to leave your lands immediately and not return," I vowed.

"We insist," she said without anger or insult but without room for argument, either. "It is our custom, and it will allow us to discuss the situation that brought you onto our land."

Her arrow remained locked on Keavren. It was clear that we would not be allowed to leave without a fight. Since I didn't know how many of these people were around, and with Keavren and Mez being injured, it would be too much of a risk for us to take our chances and try to leave. We'd have to go with them.

"Thank you. We accept."

"What's happening?" Mez whispered. It was obvious by his tone and expression he was wondering if I'd just agreed to something.

"They're going to give us food and shelter until tomorrow when we will be taken off their lands. After that, we can't come back. I tried politely asking if we could just leave peacefully now, but she more than insisted we should stay. I don't think we have a choice in the matter if we want to be safe, so I thanked her and agreed."

Mez asked: "Did they say what they would do if we didn't go?"

"No." I shook my head. "But I don't think we want to find out."

He looked thoughtful for a moment, no doubt debating our best course of action, before nodding in agreement.

"Tell your man and this boy to give their weapons to Rain Traveller," the woman instructed me. "They will get them back when you leave our village."

I gave her a single nod and turned to Mez and Keavren.

"She wants your weapons. You'll get them back when we leave," I told them.

Keavren looked at me as if I was nuts and for a second, I thought I'd spoken in Northern, but Mez nodded to me and reached behind himself to unclasp the leather double back scabbard that held his swords. He handed it and a concealed dagger to Rain Traveller, who accepted the weapons, looking at them with fascination.

Keavren begrudgingly handed over only a dagger, because his other weapons were his fists. Now, holding all the weapons, Rain Traveller looked very pleased, like a boy who had just discovered awesome new toys. He even smiled at me.

Wow! I knew what his family could get him for his birthday.

"Are your man and the boy too injured to walk?" the woman asked me.

I had no idea why she kept referring to Keavren as "the boy". I mean, none of us really looked any older than he was. I couldn't figure out if it was a deliberate insult or if something was maybe getting lost in translation.

"I think they want us to walk. Are you both okay to walk?" I asked Mez and Keavren.

The two men nodded and proceeded to dismount. I followed suit and slipped down to the ground.

Mez moved with a stiffness that wasn't usually there. His head, his body, or both, were certainly causing him massive discomfort. I felt bad for him and was now annoyed that the Northerners were making us walk.

Keavren took the reins of the horse he'd been riding, and the one he'd been leading, looking ready to walk. I observed him curiously. Was he actually not in a lot of pain from the beating he'd taken or was he just trying to look tough in front of our new "friends".

No longer seeming to see us as a threat – for now, at least – the woman lowered her bow and arrow, turned and walked away from us.

"This way," Rain Traveller said to me with a friendly smile. He beckoned for us to follow before turning and walking ahead with the woman.

Mez took the reins of the horse we'd been riding and looked at me. I nodded and started to walk with him, trailing the Northerners. Keavren followed close behind us with the other two horses.

I glanced up at Mez and decided that now would be as good a time as any to fill him in on my little relationship lie.

"Um, Mez? I hope you don't mind, but the woman kind of thinks you're my "man" or boyfriend or whatever, and I've just let her think that's the truth."

He raised a brow.

Well, at least he isn't upset.

"If they think I'm your man, they think we're married," he informed me.

What? Married!

My mouth dropped open in shock, but I shut it quickly to regain some of my dignity.

"Um? Married. Okay. Wow. I'm sorry I didn't realize it was that serious. I just thought it meant we were together like a boyfriend-girlfriend thing. That's what I had the rebels who captured me believing, because they already assumed that I was the girlfriend of one of the Warriors, because I was in the bunker with another Warrior's girlfriend and another Warrior's wife..." I trailed off with a nervous giggle, realizing I was babbling to this poor guy.

Oh, how I wished I would wake up from a bad dream right now.

Both his brows now raised, but he still didn't look upset. In fact, I felt pretty confident that if this were another situation, he might have even looked amused.

"This is quite the headache," he said. "I don't remember most of our relationship."

I did my best to hold in a laugh at his response. I knew that what would burst from my throat would be a loud, mad cackle because the threads of my sanity were thin. I was worried that if I got started, I wouldn't be able to stop laughing.

When I felt a little more under control, I said, "Yeah, I don't remember much of our relationship, either." I then added more seriously: "sorry about all this." I did feel bad. I knew I was using him to feel safer.

He nodded and then took my hand, surprising me, making it clear that he was on board with the ruse. I smiled and bit down hard on my tongue as I felt another surge of mad laughter threatening to erupt.

I took a few calming breaths, relaxed my hand in his, and decided to focus on another topic to help calm my case of the crazies.

"Did anyone find Pounce?" I asked hopefully.

"I don't know," Mez spoke with honesty. "I left shortly after it was discovered you were missing. I'd been in Medical until then."

I frowned, but I could tell by the tone in his voice, and by the way he looked at me that he wished he could have told me better news.

"The base is filled with people, and it's in the city. Pounce was likely picked up by someone and is drinking milk as we speak," Mez added, doing his best to cheer me up.

"Yeah, you're probably right," I agreed, accepting that there was no way for me to know, and I just had to hope for the best for my little kitten, even if I'd never see her again.

Mez squeezed my hand a little in an effort to comfort me.

"I'm sorry you ended up where you did. We had no idea the rebels would take that opportunity to strike."

"I know." I squeezed his hand back. "It's not your fault," I told him, because I never blamed him for my having been kidnapped.

"I felt like it was. I put you in that hole," he said

"I get it," I said. "But, you should have stayed back and healed."

"I promise you, I'm fine, Megan."

"He really is fine," Keavren chimed in. "The rock didn't get him as much as his skill did."

I turned to look at Keavren and saw the smirk on his face.

His skill? Wait a minute...

I looked curiously at Mez. "Were you in the cave?" I asked him.

He looked at me for a brief moment, and I could see the debate warring behind his ice-blue eyes.

"Yes," he spoke finally.

I nodded. My gut told me he'd answered honestly, even though I hadn't seen him in the cave. Still, I was having a hard time making sense of it all.

"Did you injure your head while you were in the cave fighting?"

He shook his head. "No. This cut," he indicated the bandage on the side of his forehead, "was from the shrapnel that hit me back at the base. My headache is from overusing my skill."

When had he used his skill? I'd seen only Keavren fighting Uori and Rakej...

Sabear.

Realization hit me like a truck, and I stopped breathing for a moment. That's why Sabear had acted so weird. Mez must have somehow messed with her mind.

"You...Did you make Sabear snuff out the light," I said, keeping my gaze on the ground.

"Yes," Mez admitted. "The cave was too tight for Keavren to fight properly."

I nodded, processing what he was saying, but I couldn't stop my mind from spinning with thoughts and questions: Why had Sabear started crying? Why did she scream? What had he done to her mind? What could he do to mine? Why did his head hurt from using his skill?

"I'm sorry I scared you. It was safer for you, Fiffine, and Amorette."

I nodded and swallowed hard. "You were protecting us and rescuing us from the rebels," I said, more to convince myself than to respond to him.

"I was. There was a sword fight going on in a tiny, dark space. One of you would have been hurt if the fighting had continued."

He was right. I knew he was, but it was a hard truth to swallow, especially when I understood so very little about the Warriors and their skills. It also didn't help that I had no idea if Sabear would be alright.

"Did you try to negotiate with them at all?" I looked at Mez hopefully. "They told me they wanted prisoners you have."

"No," he replied simply. "We just came to get what was ours. When they try again to claim what they're after, they'll have learned to leave the Warriors out of it."

I nodded. I was pretty confident that the rebels wouldn't try messing with the Warriors again after what had happened in the cave. I did try to warn them, and I wished they had listened.

I looked ahead to the Northerners in front of us and saw that we were heading toward a village. I wondered if the Northerners would listen if I ever felt it necessary to warn them about the Warriors. For now, I intended to keep what I knew to myself. Currently, Mez and Keavren were my allies, not my enemies. They were the best hope I had of making it back to Thayn.

Chapter 10

Irys

After a long and busy afternoon and a well earned hearty meal, I checked on Lieutenant Fhurrk once again. He had slept for nearly the entire day and stirred only occasionally. I hoped that was a good sign.

Seated on the floor next to him, I gently stroked his hair. Taking his hand, I held it securely, hoping it would reassure him even in his unconscious state. I wanted him to know someone was there with him.

I couldn't but recall my time with Sir Vorel as we travelled home on the ship from Fort Picogeal. The Knight had been badly burned and found my presence to be soothing, particularly when I sang to him. I could only hope that Lieutenant Fhurrk would feel the same.

Softly, I sang lullabies to the Sefaline Warrior, this vicious predator who looked as vulnerable as a baby.

Quite some time passed in this way. The remainder of the afternoon and the evening drifted along as I sang to him, spoke to him, or stroked his hair and face. I was lost in the routine of it when a hand rested on my shoulder. Pausing my latest song, I looked up at Sir Fhirell. He was smiling at me with an understanding tenderness.

Drudvis and Elika walked through a curtained door into their bedroom without a word of goodnight. It was for the best. I was exhausted, and my mind could barely spare any more attention beyond what was already thinly stretched between my wounded Warrior and my handsome Knight.

"When you're tired, you can take the loft. I will remain below," Sir Fhirell offered.

"Thank you, Sir Fhirell, but I'd like to stay with him until he wakes. I don't want him to awaken confused and alone. I'm afraid that would be dangerous to us all," I replied, appreciative of his attempt to provide me with some privacy overnight.

"You're a good woman, Miss Godeleva," he said respectfully as he took a seat next to me, looking over the Warrior's unconscious form. "Many people wouldn't do what you're doing for a man from an enemy nation."

"It is my duty to watch over him. He rescued me, first. The Goddess placed us together to keep each other alive. Right now, he isn't an enemy soldier. He is an injured man who helped keep me alive."

"Perhaps, but I continue to be impressed with the extent to which you care about the wellbeing of others. You stowed away on my ship to help with Miss Wynters' rescue, and you comforted Sir Vorel through his injuries upon our return."

"Indeed but, again, Miss Wynters and Sir Vorel had both ensured my safety and survival. The Goddess expected me to look out for each of them in return...and I wanted to. The Goddess has granted me the opportunity to reach out to these good people and to comfort them when they are in pain. This is my opportunity to show Her and to show them that I have not failed to be grateful for their acts of selflessness."

Sir Fhirell listened to me as I explained myself and nodded in acceptance of what I had said. Finally, after a moment of contemplative silence, he said, "You're a good woman, Irys."

I smiled, and a blush climbed into my cheeks as he repeated his earlier compliment with a much greater familiarity. "I only hope that when I repay the kindnesses you have shown me, you are in far better condition to receive it," I said playfully.

He grinned, an expression that was nearly boyish. "I'd like that. In fact, it would be my preference," he chuckled.

Lieutenant Fhurrk shifted, groaning through the discomfort he clearly still felt, even in sleep.

"When we take him to the town tomorrow, I want you to know that I have no intention of remaining there with him. We need to make our way back to where we can meet our group."

I looked at the injured Warrior, then back to Sir Fhirell.

"I understand," I said. "If Sir Fasido is in the town, will he give Lieutenant Fhurrk the chance to heal before deciding whether to imprison him or release him to return to his people?"

"I'm not sure what Sir Fasido will do. To be honest, I'm not entirely sure who he is. As far as I know, he has not been stationed here in Gbat Rher. If he was, it isn't something that happened recently. I look forward to speaking to him to find out what it means that he is present here."

"Why would he be here if not on an official assignment?"

"I don't know, but I find it suspicious that a Knight has been here for over a cycle, living with a wife, without reporting back to the Headquarters about his position. I looked over every report from the Knights in preparation for this mission. I never came across his name."

"Perhaps he has sent reports that never made it to Lorammel."

"It is possible. If we meet him tomorrow, we will find out," he turned his focus on Lieutenant Fhurrk, and my gaze followed his.

I reached over to a bowl of water resting on the floor near to where the Sefaline was lying, and I withdrew from it a soft flannel cloth, wringing it out and using it to wipe his face.

"Have you ever thought of volunteering at a hospital or a care facility? You seem to have a natural predisposition for helping the injured," he asked with curiosity.

"No," I replied honestly. "It isn't something young ladies do."

"It isn't something they typically do, but there isn't any reason that they couldn't start if they wanted to. Certainly, it would not be frowned upon."

"It would be frowned upon by some," I replied, knowing that Lord Imery would most definitely object if I should take on such an activity. "There would be enough who would disapprove that I can't imagine ever being permitted to try."

"It is a skill that seems to come quite naturally to you. If you enjoy it, I hope you find a way to continue with it in some way."

"Thank you," I smiled appreciatively to him. "We shall see how well I fare as we rejoin our group, before I decide whether or not I'd like to play at being a nurse back home."

"You'll manage just fine. I haven't any doubt," he replied with a confidence I could only take as complimentary.

"Thank you for your faith in me." I felt a flutter of excitement at how sure he seemed that I could take on such important responsibilities.

"How could I not? Not many women successfully stow away on my ship. None, in fact, other than you," he chuckled.

I could barely meet his eyes as I giggled at his tease. He was so very handsome as he laughed in the firelight. "No, I suppose I would be alone in that," I smiled widely as my heart raced.

Quite casually, he lifted his hand and tucked a loose lock of hair behind my ear, returning his hand to his side. How I managed not to swoon at that moment, I'm not entirely certain. It was such a simple gesture and yet it was done with such comfort and tenderness that I was flattered and overwhelmed all at once. I looked down at my hands, taking the moment to steady myself before I could look back up at him again.

"I'm glad you came on this mission, Irys," he said, clearly not facing the same struggle with eye contact that was currently challenging me.

"As am I, I confess," I replied, looking at him through my lashes. It was the best I could do, particularly as the fingers of one of his hands slipped around mine.

"I have my own confession to make." He did indeed look as though he had a secret to share.

I wasn't sure whether I should be thrilled or terrified, but the feeling of his warm hand eased my uncertainty. "What confession could you possibly have?"

"My reasons for asking you to join this mission to Gbat were not entirely unselfish."

I furrowed my brow a little, failing to understand his meaning. "Do you mean you were hoping that I would be able to write my article so more people would be willing to send funds and assistance to your mission? Might my presence help your chances of success here?"

His smile betrayed his belief that my query was sweet but naïve. "No. I was hoping to be able to spend more time with you. I've wanted to know you better."

My mind emptied of all rational thought as romance flooded into the fire-lit space between us.

"Oh," I said quite unintelligently. "What a fine compliment, Sir Fhirell. You were very patient and kind with me when we travelled on your ship. I certainly welcome the chance to know you better as well." How I wished my words could have been more delicate and poetic. Somehow, though my heart was filled with song and wonder, I sounded as if I were writing a letter of recommendation for a tradesman.

"I'm glad to hear you feel this way," he said. "My hope is that if you come to know and like me well enough while we're here, you might be willing to consider a courtship with me upon our return to Lorammel."

How he was able to speak with such calm confidence, while my mind was drowning in a scrambled thought deluge, I would never know.

"I..." I began without direction. "Oh," I added with meaningless punctuation. I scoured my brain for words that would provide me with even some hint of intellect or, at least, some of the feeling I would like to express. "I think I'd like that very much, should Lord Godeleva approve, of course." I replied after what must have been a painfully long stretch of time. "I can't imagine any reason that he would not."

Again, my words belonged in a tradesman's letter of recommendation, not in an acceptance to a proposal of future courtship. Where was the sweetness this Knight deserved and that I longed to share with him? Why was it that I had been reading poetry for nearly every cycle of my life if I was to remember none of it at a moment such as this one?

Had a moment such as this one ever even existed? I couldn't imagine that it had. I'd always thought that if a man were to ask to court me, he would already have discussed it with Lord Imery. He would have planned the moment and had a romantic speech prepared. I'd dreamed of such a moment. Yet this was immeasurably more meaningful, more wonderful, more romantic.

Despite all those feelings, I couldn't possibly have been falling in love with a man who had just blurted out his intentions without even having first spoken to my family.

Could I, Great Goddess? Is this why my heart feels as though it is too large to be contained within my body? Is it possible to feel more from a frank discussion while seated on a farmhouse floor than one could from having all my former dreams come true?

His handsome smile took the opportunity to make its appearance. I wasn't certain if the relief I was seeing in his eyes belonged to him or if it was a reflection of my own.

"It will be up to Lord Godeleva," he agreed, "but my first concern was for your feelings on the matter."

"I'm very pleased. More than pleased. I don't know what to say." My words were accompanied by, what I could only imagine was a very deep blush, based on the rising temperature of my face. Still, I smiled genuinely and honestly. If I could not share with him the song he'd brought to my spirit, I could at least share with him the joy I was feeling as a result of it. "I'm very happy, Dynan." I paused and my smile broadened to a wide grin. "You mustn't speak of this in front of Desda. She will only tease me the entire time we're here and all the way home," I laughed happily.

He chuckled with genuine amusement. "It will be our little secret." Raising the hand he was holding, he kissed the back of my fingers. My heart raced as though it were trying to leave me to be closer to him. I used my free hand in a futile attempt to fan the warmth from my face. This only seemed to please him more.

Giving myself the moment to feel genuinely blissful, I sighed away the tensions of the day and lightly squeezed his hand. Lost in the moment, I was startled back to reality as Lieutenant Fhurrk grumbled in his sleep.

Turning my attention to the Sefaline, I wiped his face and neck, hoping to keep him comfortable as he slept. I knew his survival over the next few days was dependent on the sleep he would obtain that night.

"Do you intend to stay up with him all night, even if he does not wake?"

"I may not be able to stop myself from nodding off," I admitted. "But I want to be here with him."

He nodded without showing any doubt in my choice.

"Please, take the loft. If I become too tired, I will curl up on the sofa," I told him. It seemed silly for us both to be sleepless when it made sense for him to rest.

"I won't insist that you sleep in a proper bed tonight. I know you won't do it anyway," he smiled knowingly at me. "Wherever we stay in the town tomorrow, you can take the bed."

I grinned and nodded in agreement. "Thank you. After a night this long, I believe I'd be willing to drag you out of the bed by your feet if you did not."

He laughed, and the thrill of having caused it filled me.

"Goodnight, Irys. Sleep well. I'm sure your patient will wake you if he needs you."

"Goodnight, Dynan," I said, smiling to myself, enjoying the opportunity to address him by his giving name again before he could leave. "Sleep well."

He kissed my hand as he rose to his feet, then bowed to me before heading up into the loft.

For a long moment, I watched the place where he had last been before stepping out of sight. Turning back to the Warrior, I stroked his hair, cooled his face with the cloth, and sang to him for a while, until I finally pulled a pillow and throw blanket off the sofa and lay down next to him on the floor.

Reaching out, I took his hand and held it. If he should wake before I did, I wanted him to know I was there for him. Equally, if he should try to make his escape, I wanted to be made aware of it. Shutting my eyes, I let my mind swirl and wander over the memory of my freshly kissed hand and the affection I felt for the man who had kissed it. I cradled it closely until I was finally able to sleep.

I slept until the growling started. My eyes flew open in the darkness.

Chapter 11

Megan

We followed the Northerners into a clearing where there was a large corral for horses. Behind it, there were several buildings that looked somewhat like plus-sign-shaped longhouses.

Rain Traveller continued into the village, but the woman stopped, halting us.

"Leave your horses here. They will be cared for and returned to you," she said.

I turned to Mez and Keavren and passed on the message. Keavren looked to Mez, and Mez nodded. Keavren took the reins for all the horses and guided them into the corral.

"Bring your man and the boy," the woman commanded. "You can eat at my hearth."

She spoke with such authority that I had to resist the urge to say, "Yes, ma'am" or drop into a curtsy or stand at attention.

Instead, I settled with a simple, "Thank you."

She nodded. "I am Dawn Seer," she introduced herself and turned, walking toward one of the houses.

I nodded to Mez and Keavren, indicating that we should follow her and walked forward, still holding on to Mez' hand. I was grateful for the contact.

We headed across the open space of the village, and I allowed my eyes to wander a little as we went. From where we were, I could see three of the large plus sign-shaped structures, though I suspected that there were likely several more beyond those right in front of us. The buildings were made entirely of wood with perfectly straight walls under curved roofs. From the ground, it looked like they had shingles made of bark. Plumes of smoke rose from what had to be holes or chimneys of some kind. Each building had more than one of these smoke-releasers.

A small river ran along the edge of the village and there were a few implements here and there at what looked like various work stations. Everything looked orderly and organized but very natural, too.

A large man wearing leathers and a lot of weapons, walked up to Dawn Seer. They briefly discussed something too quietly for me to hear, before he stepped up to the entrance of the house, which was covered by a thick leather flap. He stood there like a sentinel. It was more than obvious that this man was on guard duty. He looked at each one of us, watching us stone faced as though he were waiting for us to commit a crime.

Yikes! Remind me not to get on his bad side.

Dawn Seer pushed aside the hanging leather "door" and walked into the house. Mez went next and held the flap open for me. I released his hand and entered. The guys followed behind me, and we stayed close.

The smell and slight presence of wood smoke greeted us inside the home, which looked more like a shelter to me than what I would classify as a traditional house. The walls of the immediate portion of the structure had pallet-style beds along their length as well as shelves and hooks where belongings and supplies were stored.

Dawn Seer walked up to one of the smouldering fire pits in the center of the floor and added a bit of wood to it to build up the fire. A few clay pots rested at the edge of the fire, and from a spit above the flames, hung a big sack-thing that I guessed contained food.

We approached Dawn Seer.

"Sit," she said. "We will eat, soon. There is water," she added and poured steaming water into stubby pottery cups.

"Thank you," I said with gratitude, taking a seat.

The men took the hint to sit down when I did, and one sat on either side of me. I had to admit that I was glad to be sandwiched between two Warriors. Each of us reached for one of the offered cups.

Keavren smelled the cup's contents, looking at it questioningly, then whispered to me: "What is this?"

"Water," I told him.

"It smells like something," Keavren said, looking at his cup as if it might contain poison.

I smelled the water and noted that it had a fresh and sweet earthy scent, like pine. I took a sip of it.

Yup, tastes like hot water that has pine needles boiled into it.

"Tastes kind of like pine needles." I shrugged.

Keavren didn't look comforted by my deduction, but he drank the water anyway, even though I could tell he was fighting the urge to scrunch his nose. Mez didn't seem to be as fussy about his water as Keavren and sipped it calmly as he looked around the space.

"Dawn Seer said that she's going to have something for us to eat soon." I informed them.

"This is kind of her," Mez said. "Please thank her for me and Keavren...who loves the tea."

My lips twitched nearly into a smile at Mez' tea comment and from the "you're a jerk" look Keavren shot at Mez, but I composed myself and looked at Dawn Seer.

"Thank you, Dawn Seer."

She nodded and asked, "Are these soldier-men?" She gestured with her head toward the guys.

"Yes," I confirmed, but I didn't elaborate. I had a strong feeling that revealing that these two men were Warriors would be a bad idea for all of us.

"Are you a soldier-woman?"

"No." I shook my head. "I'm not a soldier or any kind of fighter."

Dawn Seer nodded, seeming to have no problem accepting my answers.

"Have you been married long?"

Oh, goody. Time to lie. Make it good, Megan. Your life and Keavren and Mez' may literally depend on it.

"No." I smiled a little. "Only for about a season."

Oh, yeah! Look at me go remembering to use the word season instead of month. Feeling emboldened by my Qarradune word-usage victory, I rested my hand on Mez' knee as a sign of affection. Without missing a beat, he very naturally rested his hand on top of mine as if this was something we always did.

Boy, did I pick the right Warrior to be fake-married to. I so want to high-five him right now!

"Is he a Demvjekyan soldier?" Dawn Seer asked, sipping her tea.

Uh, what the heck is a Dmevjekyan soldier?

I hoped to god that wasn't Northern for "Warrior". I really wished I knew more about Mez beyond the fact the he once had a dog.

"Did she ask if I am from Dmevjekya?" Mez asked.

I looked at him and nodded with a smile as if everything in life was wonderful, because I didn't want Dawn Seer to think I was learning something about my "husband" for the first time.

"Yes." I said, hoping Mez knew what she was talking about.

He smiled and said, "I moved away from there many cycles ago. That is where I was born," he informed me.

Wow. The things you learn about people when you're telling bold-faced lies to survive.

"Yes, he is." I informed Dawn Seer. "He was born there. He was surprised that you knew of his home," I lied.

She scoffed. "It's not far from here. We have traded with them. He is ignorant," she said looking unimpressed at Mez.

Okay, so she doesn't like Dmevjekyans, good to know. I'd have to remember to ask Mez about Dmevjekya later.

"That other one: the boy," Dawn Seer said, now focusing her attention on Keavren, who suddenly paused mid-sip of his tea, realizing he was now the topic of discussion. "He is not from Dmevjekya," she observed. "They are both Kavylak soldiers now?"

"They are both Kavylak soldiers now," I confirmed. She didn't look happy about that, but she seemed to accept it anyway. I looked from Keavren to Mez, wondering how she could tell Mez was from Dmevjekya and Keavren was not. I guessed the only logical reason had to be that people from Dmevjekya had features similar to Mez'.

I returned my attention to Dawn Seer and instantly felt a little rude and embarrassed when it occurred to me that I had never told her my name when she had shared hers with me.

"I am Megan." I told her.

"Megan," she repeated with a nod. "This is your adult name?" she asked..

Her question threw me, and I stared at her for a brief moment before answering, "It's the only name I've ever been given."

"What does it mean?"

"Um, I think it means 'pearl'," I said, scrambling to come up with one of the many different name meanings I remembered discovering for my name when that sort of thing mattered to me.

"Just 'pearl'?" Dawn Seer asked, not masking the confusion on her face. "Not a kind of pearl or a finder of a pearl?"

I nodded. "Just 'pearl'. I think it might mean something else, too, but I only remember that one," I added, feeling the need to give her a better explanation, since she seemed so deflated by my definition.

"The People give names with pleasant sounds to the children. When we become adults, we earn names with meaning. These are good names. We live by them. Your names don't have such meaning?" She asked, and I knew by her tone that she expected the answer to be: "no".

"I can't speak for everyone, but for me, personally, my name is just my name. It doesn't have the same meaning that yours does."

She nodded to me, accepting what I said and then began to tend to the hearth.

I watched her as I sipped my tea and wondered when she had said "The People" if "The People" was how the Northerners referred to themselves. I had to admit that what she said about names with meaning sounded very interesting, and I didn't have the heart to tell her that, where I came from, there were a million and one girls named Megan. I understood then, that while I was perfectly happy with my name, it didn't hold the same importance and meaning to me as hers did to her and to her people. I was curious to know what her name meant and if she was linked to a spirit animal like Amarogq. Maybe she was some sort of visionary who could see the future or new beginnings, or something? If that was the case, I wouldn't be surprised, considering Amarogq controlled a pack of ghost-wolves, and I was pretending to be married to a guy who could manipulate minds. The supernatural were no strangers to Qarradune.

Before I could inquire about Dawn Seer's name, Mez spoke. "What are you talking about?" he asked with calm interest.

I slid my gaze to his. "We're talking about names. She's telling me how the names of their people have different meanings, important meanings. I was explaining to her that I only have one name."

"Cool," he said with a bit of a smile.

I smiled back, knowing that he'd said that as a comfort to me.

"If she asks, what do I say your name is?"

I wanted to know what I should be calling him and Keavren, to make sure I didn't cause any unnecessary problems due to my ignorance.

"Mez." He grinned. "It's alright, Megan. It's short. Easy to forget," he teased me.

I laughed a little and squeezed his knee slightly in response with my fingers, since I didn't have a free hand at the moment to give him the playful arm slap that I felt inclined to deliver for his "helpful" comments.

"I have told her that you and Keavren are Kavylak soldiers."

He nodded, maintaining his smile. "I'm sure she guessed that, anyway. Don't volunteer more than you have to," he cautioned gently. "Our particular brand of soldiering doesn't necessarily have a lot of fans up here, and my skill doesn't work on the People of the North," He confided in me.

Aha! That's what they're called: The People of the North. It all makes sense...wait a minute. Did he just say his skill doesn't work on these people?

"What?" I couldn't hide my surprise that time. "What do you mean it doesn't work on them? Why not?"

"I don't know," he confessed. "I don't know why it works in the first place, so I don't know why it doesn't work in this case." In spite of admitting that he was pretty much defenceless against a group of people whose language he couldn't understand, and who wouldn't be happy if they found out who he really was, he still looked entirely calm.

I didn't know what to think about what he'd said. How could someone who had a skill like his not know how it worked? I would have guessed that he'd had it all his life or that maybe it surfaced when he went through puberty or something, like in the superhero comics Cole used to read back on Earth. In spite of my lack of understanding regarding his skill, I couldn't deny that as much as the idea of Mez' mind powers freaked me out, I would have rather he'd had them right now.

There was something about the People of the North that left me feeling uncertain and unsafe. At least with the rebels, I felt like I knew what they were after. With the People, I felt like there was something going on that they weren't telling us, and I worried that the longer we stayed among them, the worse that feeling would grow. I could only hope that they would allow us to leave without a fight as they had promised.

I focused my attention back on Dawn Seer, realizing it might not have been the best idea to have a conversation with Mez in front of her when she couldn't understand us. I didn't want her to think we were rude or plotting our escape.

She was in the process of taking down the weird food-sack and cutting into it. The contents were brown and looked like a thick stew. It had to have been afternoon by now, and the smell of the food made me hungry.

"That looks amazing," Keavren murmured.

I glanced at Keavren out of the corner of my eye. Clearly he liked the idea of the food better than the tea.

"That looks good," I complimented her food. "Did you hunt it?"

She shook her head. "No. I will be going on the next hunt. This is from the last one. Rain Traveller brought this for my hearth."

Ouuu. Does Rain Traveller have a crush on Dawn Seer?

I nodded and decided to ask, "Are you connected to a spirit animal?"

Dawn Seer looked up from scooping the stew into the pottery bowls. Her brow furrowed.

"Yes. I have a leaning toward a spirit, if that is what you mean. This was part of earning my name."

I nodded with interest. "So then, your adult name is linked to the spirit with which you identify?" I asked to clarify.

"I earned it at the same time that I met her," she explained, handing me a bowl of stew, with a small utensil that was shaped more like an oar than a spoon. She then served Mez and Keavren.

"Can you share what your spirit is or is that something you keep to yourself?" I asked. I did want to know, but equally I wanted her to know that I completely understood if it was a private thing.

"I am proud of my bond. She is a Skydasher bird. The first to see the dawn."

"That's amazing," I said genuinely.

I had no idea what a Skydasher bird looked like, but now Dawn Seer's name made a lot more sense to me. I kind of wished I had a spirit name, too. The only animal I had really bonded with was Pounce. Other than being utterly adorable and pouncing on fluffs, I hadn't noticed any trait she had that would give me a name with a cool meaning. Oh, well, guess I was sticking with Megan.

"Am I allowed to start eating?" Keavren asked, interrupting my silly thoughts.

In response to his question, I took a bite of my own food and was surprised that it didn't taste as I thought it would. I was still pleased with the overall flavour. Keavren smiled and followed suit. I smiled back at him and watched him look happier with each chew.

"Oh, yeah! This is really good," He said and smiled at Dawn Seer, rubbing his belly.

At first she looked at Keavren like he was a moron, but then her expression softened, finding his reaction cute.

"He really likes your stew," I told her.

"Yes. I can see that. He has no belly. It must fill up his arms."

I laughed.

"Are you two laughing at me?" Keavren asked, looking like he wasn't too happy to be the butt of a joke.

"Yes," I said but threw Keavren a winning smile, because I did think he was great.

"One day, his woman will wonder if she will run out of food to feed such a man," Dawn Seer said.

"Probably," I agreed with her. "Do you have a man?"

She shook her head. "Rain Traveller wants me, but I am not ready to ask him. He needs to work harder for me." She spoke with confidence that made me glad I wasn't Rain Traveller.

I glanced at Mez to see how he was doing. He had been quiet for a while. He was eating slowly, not in a savouring-his-food way, but in an I'm-focusing-on-chewing-my-food-and-not-throwing-up-from-the-pain-in-my-head way. I hoped whatever pain medicine he'd taken before would start working soon.

Holding onto my bowl with one hand, I reached out with my other and gave his leg a light and supportive rub.

He turned his head and smiled at me. Still chewing, he leaned toward me and affectionately bumped his nose against my temple. He made it look as though he had wanted to kiss me in front of Dawn Seer, who hadn't stopped watching our every move, but his mouth was full, so he settled for this sweet, brief and tender gesture instead. He straightened up, smiling at me as he continued eating. My response was nowhere near as cool as his. He had taken me entirely off guard, and I was blushing from ear to ear like an idiot fan-girl.

Dawn Seer's raised eyebrow only made my embarrassment worse, and I jammed more food in my mouth to try to get my blush under control.

"You're not yet pregnant?"

I coughed in shock from Dawn Seer's question, nearly choking on the food I was swallowing. So much for getting my blush under control and now my dignity was gone, too.

Mez and Keavren immediately abandoned their bowls of food, coming to my aid.

"Megan, what did she say?" Mez asked with genuine concern, rubbing my back. "Are you alright?"

Oh, great, now I've made them think I am dying.

I forced my food down and nodded. "I'm okay," I promised giving him a reassuring smile, and giving the same smile to Keavren who was staring at Dawn Seer like he was ready to send her into next week.

Dawn Seer picked up the knife she'd used to cut the sack of food, holding Keavren's menacing gaze.

"Get back to your dinner, boy," she told Keavren in a warning tone.

The stone-faced guard who had been outside, stepped into the house, no doubt hearing Dawn Seer's threatening tone. He remained there, watching all of us with his intense eyes.

Wow, way to turn everything south for no good reason, Megan. Pull yourself together!

"Everything's alright," I said quickly to Mez and Keavren. "She asked me a question while I was swallowing my food, and it surprised me. That's all."

Mez looked at me carefully but then nodded, giving my back another rub and looked at Keavren.

"It's alright, Keavren. Go back to your meal."

Keavren picked up his bowl, but he didn't take his gaze from Dawn Seer.

I released a sigh. "No, I'm not pregnant." I finally answered.

"Uh, good."

I froze when it was Mez who responded. I whipped my head around to look at him in horror, realizing that from being so flustered, I must have spoken Kavylak instead of Northern.

Oh. My. God. Kill me now.

My blush was going to be permanent. I giggled nervously and looked back at Dawn Seer.

"I'm not pregnant," I said again, hoping this time I had said it in the correct language.

She nodded, but it was clear that she thought I was a little nuts. I couldn't blame her. I was acting like a crazy person. Thankfully, she decided not to continue the line of conversation, and neither one of the guys spoke, which allowed me to finish my food and calm down a little.

Just as I was setting my bowl down, two children ran into the house, followed by an old woman. The woman walked past us and gave Dawn Seer's shoulder a squeeze as she did. She moved further into the house and sat down at another hearth. The two children, a boy and a girl, who looked to be the same age, maybe four or five, stopped when they reached us.

The boy was soft and healthy-looking, with round cheeks and two braids to keep his hair neat and out of his way. He was dressed in a shirt and pants set of matching natural leather. The girl looked bright and athletic. Her long, dark brown hair was down, but looked freshly brushed, with a decorative braid coronet crowning her head. Her outfit was similar to his, only with little shells decorating her neckline.

The boy plunked down next to Dawn Seer and snuggled up against her as if he could go to sleep. The girl climbed directly into Mez' lap.

Wow! She's a bold little thing.

I could tell Mez thought so as well, by the surprised look on his face, but his surprise was short-lived. He smiled easily at the girl and placed a gentle arm around her, holding his bowl of food in his other hand. I was amazed at how natural he looked with her.

The girl looked up at Mez, smiling. "Are you a ghost? she asked him brightly.

Mez smiled at the girl but then looked at me, because he had no idea what she'd just asked him.

"He's not a ghost," I told her.

She looked at me, confused. "Why can't he talk? Did a ghost take his voice?"

I smiled. I loved child-logic.

"He can talk. He just doesn't know your language," I explained.

Her expression faded to disappointment, and she looked back at Mez with a scowl. "Are you stupid?"

Mez, having no idea he'd been insulted, set down his bowl and stroked the girl's hair in a gentle and friendly gesture.

"No, he lives somewhere that doesn't speak your language. Just as he doesn't understand you, you wouldn't be able to understand him."

She nodded and reached up to pet his hair. Mez just patiently accepted her attention. He was so comfortable with her, like he was her big brother. It made me think that he must have spent a lot of time with younger kids in his life, maybe siblings, cousins, nieces, or nephews.

"What's your name?" I asked her. "Mine's Megan."

"Ehsaig," she said proudly. "What does Megan mean?"

Oh, geeze. Not this again.

"It just means 'pearl'. It doesn't have a special meaning like Dawn Seer's."

Ehsaig nodded, accepting my explanation and started to braid a section of Mez' hair. He didn't stop her or seem to care. He just resumed eating. I smiled and almost laughed at the bizarreness of it all. It was strange to watch such a cute and normal scene in what was a very uncomfortable and awkward situation that, at times, almost felt hostile.

"Why are you here?" The boy inquired. "Do you live here now?"

I looked at him with a friendly smile and shook my head. "No. We're only here for the night. We lost our way, and Dawn Seer invited us to join her at her hearth."

"Want me to show you how to get home?" the boy asked eagerly. "I'm really good at finding my way."

"Sure."

Because whatever and why not? I mean, who doesn't need a five-year-old GPS, right?

"Tomorrow, I'll guide you," he stated proudly.

"Thank you." I smiled.

"I'm Bediagq"

"Nice to meet you Bediagq."

He nodded and looked at Dawn Seer. "Is Ash Dancer coming back soon?"

"Your mother has mourned enough for the day. She will eat with us now," Dawn Seer responded.

I instantly liked the name Ash Dancer and wondered what it meant, but the fact that she was mourning quickly sucked the fun out of my curiosity.

I looked at Mez. He was still eating and having his hair braided. Keavren, on the other hand, was looking eagerly for second helpings of food. Dawn Seer noticed and obliged. I was about to say something to Keavren but was distracted when a woman entered the house and nodded to us. When Bediagq saw her, he got up and ran over to her. She heaved him up into her arms, carried him back to where we were sitting, and joined us.

I didn't need any introductions. I assumed this was Ash Dancer.

Ash Dancer was as graceful and elegant as she was fit and strong-looking. She was that rare balance of lean muscle with feminine curves. Even the touch of sadness in her amber eyes didn't stop the tiny upward twist at the corners of her mouth. Her long hair hung perfectly down her back. She wore a form following knee-length duster-type tunic of nearly white leather, with dark brown leggings underneath. As she moved, gorgeous beads hanging from decorative fringe along her neckline and sleeves made a gentle clacking sound like the crackling of a fire.

"This is Megan, Dark Silver, and Hungry Boy," Dawn Seer informed Ash Dancer.

I was glad I wasn't still eating, because I would have choked again, this time from laughter, when she called Mez "Dark Silver" and Keavren "Hungry Boy".

"They will stay at our hearth until they can find their own way tomorrow," she added simply.

The woman, I'd assumed was Ash Dancer, nodded to Dawn Seer and turned to face me.

"I am Ash Dancer," she said, confirming my assumption to be true. "These are my children," she said, nodding to Bediagq and Ehsaig, "And my once-sister," she concluded, referring to Dawn Seer.

"It is good to meet you and your children, Ash Dancer," I told her genuinely. "I'm sorry, I don't know what you mean by Dawn Seer being your 'once-sister'."

In all honesty, I had a guess of what it might mean, but in this case, I felt it was just better to ask.

"I am the sister of the one who was her man." Dawn Seer said.

I nodded solemnly, realizing that it was probably Dawn Seer's brother whom Ash Dancer was mourning.

The door flap opened again, and an extremely fit, confident-looking man strode up to us. He had a very neat, together, and no-nonsense way about him, and he looked directly at me.

"You speak our language," he said.

I looked at Captain Uber-Confidence, trying not to show how intimidated I felt, and nodded.

"I will speak with you when you have done your meal. I will wait outside," he informed me.

"Just me?" I asked, surprised.

He nodded. "They don't speak the language, and they are men. Just you," he said like these were the reasons that made sense.

Um. Okay. I get the "they don't speak the language" thing but what does the fact that they're men have anything to do with it?

It was odd to suddenly feel like I needed to stand up for men's rights. Yet another reason I needed to head back to Syliza. Standing up for women's rights felt much more natural to me.

Focus on equal rights later, Megan. Right now, focus on Captain Uber-Confidence and on not saying something stupid. You need to get out of here alive.

"I'll join you soon," I told him.

He nodded and headed out of the house without ceremony.

"What did he say?" Mez asked.

I looked at him, and if I wasn't feeling so nervous about taking to Captain Uber-Confidence, I would have laughed at how silly he looked with his hair all braided.

"The man who just entered wants to speak with me alone."

"Why?"

"I don't know. Apparently because I speak the language, and I'm a woman."

He nodded not looking at all surprised by that. "Women lead here. Do you want me to come with you?"

Ohhhh. This is a matriarchal society! Well, I guess that makes a little more sense.

I thought about Mez' question for a moment and then I shook my head. "No. I think it may be better if I go alone. If I talk to him about something serious, I don't want to accidentally goof up the language if I feel that I need to translate something to you. I don't want them to become more suspicious of us than they probably already are," I reasoned.

He nodded and raised the hand that wasn't around Eshaig, who still sat in his lap, and gently stroked the side of my face, resting his hand on my shoulder. I shut my eyes briefly at the contact and then looked at him. My heart instantly began to beat faster.

"Keavren and I will be here," he spoke gently. "Call if you need anything, and we will find you."

His words were protective, but his tone was soft. I knew that he was reassuring me while making it look to everyone else like he was saying, "I'll miss you, honey." Even though I knew it was an act, it didn't stop my heart from racing or my face from flushing. I couldn't help it. Freaky mind powers aside, Mez was a handsome man, and my instincts told me that he was a good one, too.

I lifted my hand and rested it over his on my shoulder, gently curling my fingers around it.

"I will," I promised him.

"I will be listening for you. Don't worry," he said, holding my gaze steadily, "I won't get wrapped up in a conversation." He smiled then, and I smiled back, because we both knew that the only person he could talk to was Keavren. Just like that, his tiny little joke made me feel more at ease.

"I'll be back."

He nodded with a soft expression and watched me stand. I took a breath and walked out of the house in search of Captain Uber-

Confidence. It didn't take me long to find him. He was standing directly outside the door, waiting for me.

Chapter 12

Irys

"Go back to sleep," Lieutenant Fhurrk said as his growl came to an end, looking directly at me through the dim remainder of the firelight. "You need your rest. There isn't anything you can do for me." His voice softened substantially. He looked just the same as he had before I'd shut my eyes. He was still lying down, but his eyes were open.

"I can stay here with you. We're going to travel more in the morning. We're going east, toward your destination. We will have a wagon, so you won't need to walk or be carried."

"I won't make it to my destination. My body is dying. I can tell," he said with a striking calm.

"You're healing. I've been caring for you, as has the woman who lives here. You've had medicine, and you've slept for hours."

"I need better medicine than what you have."

"There will be more in town. I'm sure they will have a doctor or a healer of some kind." I wasn't sure, but I wanted to be.

"The town does not have the medicine I need."

I held his hand more firmly. "I won't simply give up on you."

"It would be better if you did. Do not hold on to me. There is no reason for you to. Your conscience is clear. The Goddess will not hold you responsible for my fate."

"Perhaps She won't, but it is my choice," I explained. "I'm not here out of duty or owing anymore. I'm here because I want to be. That is just as important. I want to know that, whatever the Goddess chooses for you, I have done everything I can to ease you and to restore you to health. Lieutenant Fhurrk, I'm going to the town tomorrow, and I'm bringing you with me."

"You're a foolish woman. This will get you killed," he grumbled.

"If I am being foolish, so be it. Unless you are right, and my choices cause my untimely end, I will bring you to the town to be healed. I won't give up on you."

He looked at me for a long time. It was clear by his expression that, despite having carefully thought about it, he could not understand my reasoning. It didn't matter. He didn't need to understand it. He only needed to accept my company and my assistance.

"We've come this far," I said softly, giving his hair a stroke. By now, it was a familiar gesture to me. "The town won't take long to reach. Tomorrow, we will know whether you are right or I am. For both our sakes, I hope it is me."

"You should have left me when we went our separate ways."

"Possibly, but what's done is done. I'm talking about how we will proceed from here."

"You don't understand. She'll find me. Whether I'm dead or alive, she will track me."

"Who?" I asked, my brow furrowing in confusion. Was he talking about an actual woman hunting him, or could he have been referring to the Goddess?

"A Traveller."

I felt a shiver crawl over my body. "The one we met last night?"

"Her or the other one."

"He is injured," I replied. "He cannot travel until he has had time to heal."

Now it was Lieutenant Fhurrk's turn to look confused. "No..." he started to say but suddenly froze, looking alert.

"What is it?" I asked, my voice dropping to an even quieter whisper.

He didn't reply, but after a brief moment, the scent of him filled the room. It was his familiar smell, only sharper and spicier. It grew more powerful until it stung my eyes.

"I warned you..." he said, looking pained before he drooped, losing consciousness.

For a few seconds, absolutely nothing happened. Nothing changed. I could nearly fool myself into thinking that Lieutenant Fhurrk had been hallucinating from his fever.

The sensation didn't last. Suddenly, I had the distinct feeling that Lieutenant Fhurrk and I were not alone in the room. My eyes darted around until a woman appeared not far from where we were. She wore Kavylak clothing including trousers and a long jacket with wide lapels. Her hair was short, and her expression was intensely focused.

I gripped Lieutenant Fhurrk's hand as though it would bring the unconscious man comfort. It was much more likely that I was in need of the reminder that he was here and that I had sworn to protect him. My oath would bring me courage.

"Get away," I shouted, prepared to protect the Warrior from whatever this woman had planned.

"Irys?" called Sir Fhirell from the loft above.

The woman looked at me, curled her nose in disgust, and I screamed as she placed her hand on the Sefaline's shoulder.

I blinked and when I opened my eyes, I was wincing against bright white lights. I was sitting on a cold tile floor. This was not Gbat Rher.

Chapter 13

Megan

"You are Megan, I am Star Archer," said Captain Uber-Confidence. "Please, come with me."

I nodded and followed him. Like most of the people I had seen in the village, he had rich, deep tan-coloured skin and neatly combed long black hair. He wore brown leather pants and soft leather shoes with leather lacing. Around his waist was a wide decorative belt with beads and carvings of animals. His torso, which wasn't lacking in the muscles department, was bare. On his arms, from about his elbows to his wrists, he wore leather bracelets. Around his neck were cords of beads and ropes of quills. The bracelets almost looked like gauntlets except that they were far too decorative to be gauntlets. Around his neck, he wore a choker of three rows of quills and wooden beads as well as a longer beaded necklace with a fang that hung like a pendant. It was a fascinating outfit, and I'd bet that there was a story behind every piece of it.

We walked just inside the edge of the woods, toward a cliff-like outcropping of land. A low fire burned in the centre of the land. Star Archer walked up to it and gestured for me to sit down on a square piece of smooth leather that was set out on the ground like a picnic blanket. I took a seat. He knelt down on another piece of leather near mine.

I watched him, getting more tense by the second. I was extremely worried about what he'd ask. He reached out with his hands and swooshed some of the smoke from the fire over himself. When he was finished, he looked expectantly at me.

Um. Crap. He must be waiting for me to start talking. What do I say? Keep it simple, Megan, and just say something nice.

"Thank you for your hospitality," I said, inwardly cringing at how lame that sounded.

If my stupid words offended him, he didn't show it. He simply shook his head and held out a hand as though to silence me. I looked at him curiously, having no idea what he wanted from me. Seeing my befuddled expression, he indicated the fire and then performed the same smoke swoosh again, using his arms and hands to waft the smoke over his upper body. When he was done, he looked at me again with his soft brown eyes.

I understood then that he wanted me to perform the same smoke swoosh on myself. I nodded to him and rose to my knees and did my best to copy what he'd done. It didn't bother me to do it, but I held my breath all the same because after running through a burning town, I had to say I wasn't a fan of inhaling smoke of any variety.

When I was finished, it was my turn to look at him expectantly.

"The fire cleans everything. The smoke washes off everything but peace and truth," he told me. "Now we may speak."

Oh, geeze! I just took part in some sort of truth ritual?

This guy had no idea how much I didn't want to lie to him, and how much I felt I didn't have a choice in the matter. I'd try to be as honest with him as possible, but I knew eventually I wouldn't be.

"I am speaking to you here because my woman is near her time to have our child," he explained.

I smiled. "Congratulations! You must be very excited."

Woo! Starting off with honesty!

I was genuinely happy for him. This had to be a good sign.

Star Archer nodded and smiled a little. "Yes. Our first," he said and then asked, "The man, the Dmevjekyan Kavylak soldier, is yours?"

Well, the whole truth thing went downhill fast.

"Yes."

"Did you choose him long ago or is he recently yours?"

"He is recently mine." Yeah, like an hour or so, give or take.

"Are you pregnant?"

"No."

He nodded. "It will happen soon enough," he assured me. "My wife will give you something to help you," he said calmly as if this is what he normally tells every woman who has a man but isn't pregnant.

Wow! That was a very presumptuous and forward thing for him to say. Where did he get off telling me it would happen soon enough? What if I didn't want it to happen soon? What if Mez and I were waiting? What if I got a clue and stopped getting miffed and defensive about a fake relationship?

"Thank you," I said.

Because, honestly Megan, bigger picture. Who cares?

"It will please her to share it."

I nodded.

"Your man and the other soldier are both of Kavylak, but you are not a soldier."

"I'm not," I confirmed.

"Have you heard of the Warriors?"

"I have."

He looked thoughtful for a moment, and I was certain his next question would be to ask me if Mez and Keavren were Warriors. My mind raced as I tried to think up lies.

"Have you heard of a Warrior who looks like he is of the People?"

I looked at him, surprised.

Was he asking me about Amarogq? Does he know him?

I decided not to lie. I nodded.

"Does he live?"

"He might, if the man you're asking about is Lieutenant Ioq'wa."

He raised a brow and looked at me oddly. He hadn't recognized the name I'd given.

"Does he go by another name?"

"Amarogq."

Star Archer looked enlightened. "Ah, so he lives, and his name can be spoken. He was clever to have returned to his childhood name after his death," he said with a mixture of distaste and respect in his tone.

What the heck does he mean?

"I guess you know him then. Is he a relation of yours?"

He nodded. "Before he died, he belonged to Ash Dancer," he said. His face became stern. "Before he died, he was my brother."

My eyes widened in surprise. "Oh. I'm sorry." Even though I didn't know the circumstance I felt the need to apologize. "Does he know you still live?"

"He has no reason to assume otherwise. The village was moved, so his spiritless husk cannot return to it. He knows we live on without him."

Harsh, man! Yeesh, Amarogq! What did you do? Burn down the village?

I wanted to ask a bunch of questions, but I held back. It wasn't my business, and I didn't want to be asked a whole pile of questions in return.

"I'm sorry. I know how difficult it is to lose family that you love," I empathized. That was something I did understand.

He nodded but didn't seem affected by my words. "I no longer suffer the loss. It is Ash Dancer who suffers it. She mourns a man who lives in form but whose spirit has risen above."

"So, he was her man, then?"

"Yes."

I frowned, thinking about Ash Dancer and what Dawn Seer had said to Bediagq about Ash Dancer having mourned enough for the day.

Oh, no! Bediagq and Ehsaig.

"Her children are his?"

"Yes, but they are not his," Star Archer said. "They belonged to his spirit and the bond he had with Ash Dancer. He has no claim to them now."

My food was no longer sitting right. It swirled along with my mind as I tried to make sense of everything Star Archer had said and revealed about Amarogq and his former family.

How long ago had Amarogq left? Why did he leave? Did he know about his children? Did Amorette know about his past? Why was Ash Dancer still mourning for him every day, and why was she mourning a guy who wasn't actually dead? Shouldn't she be moving on?

Even though I didn't know the circumstances I honestly felt that regardless of what happened, if he'd left her and their kids to live another life, then she deserved better.

"I really don't know much about Amarogq or how long he's been gone from your lives but won't Ash Dancer find someone else?"

Star Archer shook his head. "She cannot. Not until Doom Breaker, our Mawkipaw, releases her from her bond. Even though his body remains alive, until it dies as his spirit did, she must mourn him."

Wow! Doom Breaker. That's an intense name. And, what's a Mawkipaw? Is this what they call their leader?

Whatever she was, I thought it was pretty crappy of Doom Breaker not to release Ash Dancer from her bond. I mean, if Amarogq had gone off with the Warriors and was pretty much dead to these people, why were they making Ash Dancer suffer for it? Amarogq certainly didn't seem to have this problem. He was engaged to Amorette! There was so much about the People of the North's culture that I didn't get, but now wasn't the time to boost my understanding of it.

"Do you have loyalties to the Warrior Amarogq? Will you be telling him where our village is located?"

I shook my head. "No. Your business is your own, and his business is his own. It is not for me to tell him anything." I was serious about that. I wanted to stay far away from whatever mess this was.

"Good," Star Archer said and then added: "Doom Breaker has a message to send to Kavylak. She asks if you will carry it back with you to deliver to them. Will you do this in exchange for our hospitality here?"

"A message? Sure, I can do that," I agreed. It sounded simple and fair enough to me to bring a message in return for their generosity. I mean, they could have just let us go so we wouldn't have been here in the first place, but whatever. Bringing a message in exchange for food and rest sounded like a good deal to me.

"Good," Star Archer said with a nod. "Then you may return to Dawn Seer. She will make sure you are rested and cared for, so you are ready for your journey home."

I nodded and stood, glad I would be returning to Mez and Keavren.

"Thank you, Star Archer. I wish you and your wife...woman... every happiness with your new family," I said, genuinely wishing good things for them.

He nodded and stood as well. "Thank you."

I smiled and turned to leave.

"Are both men at my sister's hearth Warriors or only your man?"

His question halted me in my tracks, and I turned to look at him. His arms were crossed, and the expression he wore told me that I needed to take care with how I'd answer him.

Shock and panic took hold as I debated my two options: lie and make up some elaborate story or just come clean. I decided on the second option. I had a feeling that if I lied this time, it would be bad for all of us.

"They both are," I confessed.

He gave a short nod, not looking the least bit surprised.

"Be more honest over the flames of my sister's hearth. It is the fire that feeds you and that will keep you warm at night."

He sounded more like he was delivering a warning than a helpful request.

"You go on ahead, while I put this one out," he said and turned his back to me, using a long-handled tool to crush down what was left of the embers in the fire.

I didn't watch him any further. I turned away and started walking back. As much as I was filled with a growing pit of fear, I also felt anger toward Star Archer for his words about honesty. Even though it wasn't his fault, he had no idea how much I wanted to be honest and how much I couldn't be for my own safety.

He made me feel like I was some sort of criminal, meanwhile it was *his* people who were the ones who hadn't just let us peacefully go on our way. Not to mention, if they clearly already knew Mez was a Warrior, why didn't they just call us out on it? In their own way, they were being just as dishonest as we were and only fed us the information that suited them. I felt more on edge with every step I took.

I glanced up at the sky and noticed the sun was hanging lower. It wouldn't be too long before sunset would begin. I hated the idea of spending the night here.

I briefly looked at the guy who was standing guard in front of Dawn Seer's home. He looked just as stern as before, but he didn't stop me when I pushed past the flap to enter the space.

I nearly let out a sigh of relief when I saw Mez and Keavren. Mez was sitting and watching Keavren, who was busy putting on a show of flexing his arm muscles for the kids, who were laughing and looking at him in wonder.

I noticed that Dawn Seer had left the hearth and was speaking with a pretty, and very pregnant, woman at another fire. I guessed that must be Star Archer's woman.

I reclaimed my seat next to Mez, nodding to him as I sat down. He shifted closer to me and brought his arm around me, kissing the side of my head, like a good fake husband.

"Are you alright?" he asked quietly.

I turned to look Mez in the eyes, smiling as if I were pleased with his attention.

"He knows who you are," I replied softly.

He nodded. "Have we been asked to leave?"

"No, but I think we should. I have a bad feeling," I confessed.

"Do you think we should try to slip away now or should we stay the night and leave first thing in the morning?"

"I think we should do whatever is the safest option, but I don't know what that is." I frowned. "I don't know if it's more dangerous to travel now or more dangerous to stay here."

I glanced over in Keavren's direction, when giggles erupted from Eshaig and Bediagq. Keavren was now lifting the children like weights and had one dangling from each of his arms. I swallowed hard, remembering who their father was.

"We're sitting with Ioq'wa's family," I murmured.

My words surprised Mez. The expression on his face remained tender and loving, but I could see it in his eyes.

"If they have not made an imminent threat, we can wait until the morning and leave right away. That way, we will leave freely, without the risk of having them track us down," Mez reasoned. "They may follow and watch us but at least we leave with their permission. Do you agree?"

It was my turn to be surprised. Mez wasn't humoring me. He was genuinely asking me for my input on the matter. I thought about what he'd said, and his suggestion made the most sense. If we were to try to sneak away before we were permitted to leave, there was a good chance we'd get caught, and if we got caught, I knew our hearth-sharing days would be over. I still couldn't shake the feeling that staying was also a bad idea, but for the time being, it was the more sensible of the two options.

"Yes. I agree," I said finally.

I lifted a hand and stroked the side of Mez' face, to make it look as though our conversation was something romantic and not the escape strategy talk it really was.

His expression softened. "We'll stay together. If things look like they're turning sour, we'll run. Otherwise, we'll walk safely out of here tomorrow."

"That's a good plan," I smiled a little.

In response, he gave me a small hug with the arm that was around me.

"Thank you for representing us and speaking with him. I'm sure you did well."

My lips twisted into a wry smile. "I hope it went alright. It's hard to say. Lately, I feel like I'm the worst judge of character."

"Nah." He chuckled. "You made me your man, didn't you?" he teased.

I laughed a little at his joke. It wasn't that funny, but I was over-tired and over-stressed.

"Were you afraid while you were talking to the man?" he asked with care. "Did he threaten you?"

"No. He didn't threaten me. He seems like a decent enough guy. He's his brother," I added. I knew Mez would know I meant Amarogq.

"Oh, Goddess," he said, looking at me with greater understanding of just how close we were to Amarogq's family.

"He wants me to bring a message back to Kavylak from their Mawkipaw named Doom Breaker," I whispered this last bit. "I don't know what the message is or who she is, but I agreed to do it in exchange for their hospitality."

"If she's their Mawkipaw, then she's their leader," Mez explained. "We can bring a message back," he agreed. "That sounds like a fair enough exchange."

I nodded and yawned, feeling exhausted from the day's events. Mez had to be feeling the same way. Probably even worse with his headache.

"How's your head?" I asked. "Do you want to lie down or try to get some sleep?"

"It's easing a little, but I do need a good rest before I'll be the man you fell in love with again." He grinned. "I'll sleep when you do," he added, dropping the tease. "You can sleep next to me tonight. They'll expect you to. I promise, you'll be safe with me."

I smiled. He'd read my mind. "Thank you. I do feel safe with you and Keavren."

I'd had every intention of sleeping right next to him and Keavren if I could. As much as I was sure Mez could probably use his mind powers on me if he wanted to, I didn't feel threatened by him. I never had. There was something about him that I trusted, in the same way I trusted Keavren, Thayn, and even Aésha. Each of them left me with the feeling that they had my best interests at heart.

He smiled. "I'm glad you do."

"I wouldn't mind lying down and resting now," I said.

He nodded and stood, offering his hand to me. I took it and rose to my feet, not really knowing where he intended to take us.

I followed him to the pallet-style bunkbed. He released my hand, and he lay down first, so he was closest to the wall. Once he was settled, I slid in next to him, turning my back to him. It wasn't because I was trying to ignore him, I just felt better being able to see what was going on around us.

I felt him draw a big animal fur blanket over us. He re-settled, keeping a space between us. I appreciated that he didn't want to crowd me or make me feel uncomfortable but right now, I didn't need space.

I reached behind me and found one of his hands, pulling it over me, so his arm draped over my ribs. Yes, that was forward of me, but I did it so I could always feel where he was. If he moved or if someone tried to take him away, I would know.

I waited to see how he would react. I hoped he'd stay put, but I wouldn't blame him if he didn't want to be that close to me. I didn't actually want to make him uncomfortable, either.

To my relief, he slid his arm further around me and shifted in closer behind me, so we were in more of a snuggle-spoon position.

"Sleep well, Megan. You're safe with me." Mez said softly. A strand of my hair tickled the side of my face when he spoke, and I had to stop myself from physically shivering from the feeling.

"Sleep well," I whispered back.

A strong part of me wanted to look at him, but I didn't dare do it. I might have been bold enough from my fear-stress to initiate the contact, but I was way too chicken to see the expression on his face, and I didn't want him to see I was blushing like an idiot. I shut my eyes imagining that he was Cole or even Keavren; a guy I thought of as only a friend.

Mez was different. I thought of him as a friend but unlike Keavren and Cole, I couldn't deny that I was also attracted to him in a way that I certainly wouldn't classify as platonic. I didn't have the same feelings for him as I did for Thayn, of course, but it occurred to me for the first time that under the right circumstances, maybe I could. I wasn't sure what I felt about that. It was a stupid thought, and Mez probably wasn't attracted to me like that anyway. Sure, he cared for my wellbeing, but if he actually was as great a guy in real life as he was when playing the role of "my man", there was no way he was single.

This was stupid. I had to stop thinking like this. I was being ridiculous. It didn't matter if Mez was single or not. I had already told Thayn that I would be happy to be his girlfriend, and I was serious about that. Besides, who even knew how long any relationship between Thayn and I might last. My ultimate goal was, and continued to be, getting back home as soon as possible. I didn't have any intention of building a life here, and I couldn't let my heart forget that.

I released a small breath, calming down from my silly thoughts, and opened my eyes, focusing my attention on Keavren. He had stopped playing with the children and had returned to sitting at the fire, sipping his tea. Ehsaig was right by his side, talking to him and looking up at him like he was amazing. He looked calm and was nodding to her, but I could tell he was just humouring her. He couldn't understand a word she said. He was tired and completely oblivious to the fact that Ehsaig had a huge crush on him.

Eventually, she left him and made her way over to her mother and Bediagq. Ash Dancer was combing his hair while he sat in her lap. She was talking to him quietly. I couldn't hear what she was saying, but by the dreamy look on his face, and Ehsaig's interested expression as she sat on the floor next to her mom to listen, I guessed she was telling a story. It was both peaceful and heartbreaking to watch them.

Did Amarogq know about his children? Why hadn't Ash Dancer left with him? Amarogq seemed like a decent guy, and Amorette really loved him, but how could he have abandoned his wife and kids? What could possibly have happened?

I blinked, looking away from Ash Dancer and her children. Regardless of what had happened, it wasn't my business, and it wasn't my problem.

Glancing back at Keavren, I noticed he was making his way over to where Mez and I were resting. He nodded to me and gave me a tired smile, which I returned, before he climbed up onto the pallet-style bed that was above us. I watched him until his feet disappeared from view.

Shifting slightly to get a little more comfortable, I was pleased when Mez didn't budge from my careful movements. I could tell from his deep breathing that he'd fallen asleep. I was glad. He needed the rest.

I shut my eyes again, deciding to think about happier things while I tried to get to sleep. I reminded myself that tomorrow we would be leaving here, and I would finally be returning to the military base and finding my way back to Thayn.

Thayn.

I smiled, forcing myself to think of nothing else, letting the sounds of soft conversations and crackling fires lull me into unconsciousness.

Chapter 14

Irys

As far as I could tell, I was in some kind of hospital. Everything looked and smelled sterile. People in crisp uniforms buzzed about me carrying papers and medical implements of various shapes and sizes. The walls were lined with shelves containing vials and complicated-looking instruments. Flasks bubbled with liquids in various colours and consistencies on countertops with burners and other various devices.

There was a warmth in my hand. It took me a brief moment to realize that I was still holding on to Lieutenant Fhurrk. The Traveller stood over us.

"Stupid woman," she huffed at me in Kavylak.

"Where are we?" I demanded, displeased with the tremor in my voice.

"Kavylak. Move away from him."

"No," I replied defiantly. I was terrified that the Traveller would try to take me somewhere else. Somewhere even worse.

"He's over here," she called to the medical staff as she rolled her eyes at me.

Footsteps rushed toward us, and despite my best efforts to cling to Lieutenant Fhurrk, I was pulled away from him. Flailing, I scrambled to reach for the Warrior, if only to remain close to the only person I knew.

"Lieutenant Fhurrk!" I called to him. "Please wake up. Fhurrk, please!"

After all my thrashing, I was no nearer to him. The Traveller approached me, looking me over.

"Release her. I will take care of her," she said, and the grip relaxed on my arms and body.

Before I could attempt an escape, the Traveller's hand darted forward, grabbing my arm. I couldn't even think, let alone move, before we were standing in a metal room with a metal table, and two metal chairs. The furniture was bolted to the floor. There was a door but no windows. I turned to speak to the Traveller, but she merely released my arm and disappeared.

Stepping up to the door, I knew it would be locked – and it was – but I had to try it. Out of options, I pounded on its smooth surface with my fists.

"Hello? Let me out!" I shouted as loudly as I could, considering the deafening echo within the room. I continued for only a minute or two but gave up and chose to reserve my energy and composure when my efforts failed to bring any response. Seating myself on one of the chairs, I waited.

Great Goddess, what is happening? Where am I now? Is this still Kavylak? I cannot become a slave again. Please, I beg of you, do not enslave me again. Nobody knows I'm here. Save me.

To my surprise, it wasn't very long before the door made a loud clicking sound.

"Miss Godeleva, back away from the door," spoke a deep, cold voice in the Sylizan language.

I stood from my chair, backing up against the wall opposite the door, wishing I could move the furniture in front of me.

The door opened, and a man entered, wearing the black leather Warriors' uniform. He had thick, long, black shiny hair with shorter pieces at the front that hung down in his face. His complexion was pale to the point that I would have called anyone else with such pallor sickly, though he appeared anything but frail. Though very little about him brought the military to mind, he suited his flawless uniform perfectly. He was one of *them*.

From the moment he stepped inside the door frame, his dark blue eyes fixed upon me. They remained set on me as he walked up to one of the chairs and calmly took a seat.

"Miss Godeleva, I am Captain Aaro Wintheare," he introduced himself in polite Sylizan words and a strict Kavylak tone. "Please, have a seat." It was not a request.

For an extended moment, I remained frozen where I was. My mind and body could not decide whether they were too afraid to move, to defiant to move, or whether I should do as he commanded. I stared at him, wide-eyed, until I finally willed my feet to budge.

I sat on the hard metal chair and pushed myself as far back into the seat as I could. I didn't want to be any closer to this man than I had to be.

"Why were you with Lieutenant Fhurrk?" he asked, eliminating any suggestion that pleasantries might be a part of our conversation.

"I was helping him to travel east. He was injured. I couldn't just leave him," I replied honestly.

He nodded and continued to talk. "Did you or anyone with you worsen his injuries? Did you give him anything to poison him? Please, speak the truth. You are not in any danger."

"Of course not!" I blurted, surprised and offended that this could be suggested after the lengths to which I'd gone to care for him. "I treated his injuries as best I could under the circumstances. We had nothing to help him. Then, we came across kind people who treated him and gave him medicines to help him sleep. This was what he needed in order to heal."

He nodded once again. If he doubted my truthfulness, it was not revealed in his expression. I was hopeful that he believed me.

"Have you had further communication with the male Traveller?"

"No. He left us. He didn't come back. The Lieutenant and I were stranded alone. The Lieutenant was hurt, and I was lost and blinded by the darkness. We helped each other. Then, the woman Traveller brought us here."

"Do you know why the male Traveller chose to place Lieutenant Fhurrk in harm's way? Did you ask him to do this?"

I shook my head. "I didn't ask him to do that, nor do I know why he did it. I had never met the Traveller before that day. I most certainly didn't want him to take me to Gbat Rher."

"By remaining with Lieutenant Fhurrk and caring for him as you did, you likely saved his life. We are grateful to you for your help and will be returning you home."

Of all the things Captain Wintheare had said until this point, this statement surprised me the most.

"Thank you. I'm glad to have helped him. I was terribly afraid that he wouldn't make it," I replied. "Will I be leaving now? I'd like to be returned to the same place from which I was taken, if you please."

"We will return you to Gbat Rher if that is your wish, but you will not be leaving now. Unfortunately, the Traveller who brought you here has left and is not expected to return for two days. She has another mission, and we did not anticipate your presence here. I apologize for this inconvenience, Miss Godeleva. In two days' time, when the Traveller returns, you will be taken back to your requested location. Until then, you may write a letter to whomever you wish to let them know of your safety and impending return. There is another Traveller among us who can travel with objects, though not people."

"Two days..." I tried to tell myself that this was far better than being a prisoner – or a slave. Shaking my head, I tried to focus on what he was telling me. "Yes, thank you. I would be very appreciative for the opportunity to send a letter. I will require a response from the recipient as this will tell me where I should be returned in two days. Might I request some paper? This must be done right away as I'm certain my traveling companion is fraught with worry."

"Certainly. The sooner, the better," he said, rising from his chair. He stepped over to the door and knocked on it. A soldier on the other side opened the door, and Captain Wintheare spoke to him in Kavylak. "Fetch a pen and paper immediately."

"Yes, Sir," replied the soldier, shutting the door.

Not a minute passed before he had returned, handing the requested items to the captain, who brought them to me. He took a seat and watched me in his eerily calm way. Clearly, I was expected to write my letter right now, and he was going to wait right there, watching me, while I did it.

Suddenly, I had no idea what to write. How could I possibly express to Sir Fhirell what was happening in a way that would ease his concerns? Without any specific plan, I put pen to page, marvelling at the way the Kavylak implement contained its own ink, without the need to dip its nib to refill it. At any other time, I would have taken the opportunity to examine the piece much more closely. Right now, I could only hope that the Goddess would use it to guide my words.

Dear Sir Fhirell,

I am writing to inform you that I am both safe and well. Though I find myself in Kavylak among the Warriors, it was by means of error and not nefarious plans.

I'm most distraught at the thought of the worry this situation must have caused you. I hope this letter brings you some degree of comfort until we see each other again.

I have been informed that a Traveller will become available in two days' time, at which point, I will be returned. Please respond to this letter by way of the Traveller who brought it, informing me of the best location in which to find you.

I hesitated a moment with the pen over the paper before adding:

I miss you.

Cordially,
Irys Godeleva

My eyes scanned the page as I tried to think of something else to say. There was nothing else. Picking up the paper, I waved it around a little to allow the ink to dry and folded it in half before handing it to Captain Wintheare.

"Thank you, Captain," I said.

It shouldn't have surprised me that he opened the letter right in front of me and started to read it. In fact, I should have appreciated the fact that he was being quite direct about his intention to screen everything I'd said. However, all I could think was that I wouldn't have told Sir Fhirell that I missed him, if I'd thought Captain Wintheare would see it.

If he'd had any thoughts on my personal note, however, he did not share them in either his words or the expression on his face. Instead, he said simply, "Thank you for your cooperation, Miss Godeleva."

He stood and walked over to the door, knocking to the soldier on the other side. The door opened nearly immediately.

"Tell Alukka to come here," he said.

"Yes, Sir," replied the soldier, rapidly shutting the door.

Captain Wintheare returned to his seat, still holding my letter.

"While you remain our guest, quarters will be assigned to you. You will be able to move about the public areas of this complex. You will be provided with identification tags," he informed me.

I nodded. "Thank you, Captain Wintheare. If I might ask: where are we?" I assumed we were still in Kavylak.

"You are in the main military compound in Kavylak's Capital City. You will be safe within these walls and on the immediate grounds. You will not be permitted entrance to the city itself. Wear your tags at all times for your own safety and protection. Stay away from restricted zones. They are clearly marked as such," he explained. "You are a guest and we are grateful for the assistance you gave Lieutenant Fhurrk, but breaking our rules will not be tolerated and will have consequences."

I hoped the captain could not see how frightened I felt. From that moment, my intention was to remain within my quarters until I could be returned to Sir Fhirell, possibly with a barricade in front of the door.

"Will my meals be served at proper hours?" I inquired delicately. "Will I be provided with everything I need? Clean clothes and toiletries? Will I have a maid assigned to me?" As long as I had the captain's attention, I would make certain that I would be provided with my basic necessities throughout the duration of my stay.

"Three sufficient meals will be brought to your room each day. You will be provided with appropriate clean clothing. You will not have any servants. A guard will be placed at your door for your added protection. If you need to make any requests, they can be made to your guard," he replied. It was more than evident that these conditions were not up for negotiation.

"I'm sure I will manage for the two days I'm here. Thank you."

"I'm under the impression you are fluent in the Kavylak language. Is this correct?"

"Yes. My accent needs work as I taught myself primarily from books, but I can understand it and express myself well enough."

"While you are here, use this language when you speak."

"I will. I don't imagine I will be speaking to many people," I agreed. "Will I be able to visit Lieutenant Fhurrk?"

The captain opened his mouth to answer, but a woman appeared in the room, before he could say anything. He appeared unfazed, but

I jumped quite dramatically, needing a moment before I could slow my heartbeat.

"You requested my presence, Captain Wintheare," she spoke coldly, resting her gaze upon me after addressing the Warrior. Nearly instantly, I realized that Alukka was the Traveller who had held me hostage in Gbat Rher. She was the one who had forced Rimoth to return Lieutenant Fhurrk from Korth.

"Yes," replied Captain Wintheare. "Take Miss Godeleva's letter to the home where Zayset found Lieutenant Fhurrk in Gbat Rher. Place it in the hands of Sir Dynan Fhirell and wait for his response. Return to this room with his reply and hand it directly to Miss Godeleva." He held the letter out to her without fully extending his arm, requiring her to step closer to him to take it.

Alukka looked put out but took the letter. "Yes, Captain Wintheare," she said before disappearing.

The captain returned his attention to me. "I hope you don't mind if we stay in this room for a little longer. I want you to receive the letter as soon as it is available, and I want you to receive it directly from the Traveller. That way, you will know it has not been intercepted and tampered with."

"Thank you, Captain. I appreciate your precaution and prefer it this way." As cold and emotionless as he was, I couldn't help but recognize the respect he was showing me.

He nodded, his typical response to virtually anything I said that didn't require a specific answer. "To address your earlier question, yes, you may visit Lieutenant Fhurrk. The medical ward is not in a restricted area."

"Thank you. I do look forward to seeing him in recovery. Am I likely to run into many Warriors if I stay where I should?" My intention in asking the question was to ensure I could avoid meeting any Warriors. However, by the time I'd finished asking, I realized that my intention did not apply to Acksil.

"You may. They use the same corridors. I know of your history as Captain Galnar's slave, but he is no longer a threat to you. He will not feel any inclination to address you should he see you, and you should not address him. If you are ever concerned over your safety, tell your guard or inform anyone foolish enough to accost you that you are my guest."

"Thank you," I replied, returning to my earlier plan to remain within my quarters, aside from a possible brief visit to Lieutenant Fhurrk.

"If you had any intentions to visit Miss Megan Wynters, you should know that she is currently out of the city. She has, of her own free choice, become a resident here and is employed. There is no reason to be concerned for her."

I wasn't sure whether or not to believe him. *Why would Megan choose to live here? Were Commander Varda's efforts to rescue her unsuccessful?*

"When is she expected to return?" I asked, shaken.

"She has been hired as a translator and is away on a translation task. I do not know when she will complete it and return. Should I learn more, I will inform you. Should she return while you are still here, I will alert you."

"Yes, please do. Thank you." My mouth tripped over the words. The captain had to be lying. Megan couldn't possibly turn her back on us all. Not after everything we'd all been through. Trying to stretch my imagination around the captain's claims felt next to impossible.

Before we could discuss it further, Alukka returned, looking thoroughly annoyed.

"You have an ill-tempered lover," she said to me with accusation, tossing a piece of paper onto the table in front of me. She turned her attention to Captain Wintheare, crossing her arms. "Anything else?" she asked him with irritation.

"Wait until Miss Godeleva finishes reading this letter, in case a response is required," Captain Wintheare instructed.

Alukka huffed and crossed her arms, watching me as I reached out and picked up the letter. Upon turning it over, I was surprised to see that it was fastened with Sir Fhirell's seal pressed into the wax.

Despite the fact that he had taken care to seal the letter to show me that it was indeed from him, the rest of it was clearly completed in haste.

Dear Miss Godeleva,

Please consider this a confirmation that your letter has been received and that I am relieved to hear that you are safe.

Considering the situation, you may find challenges ahead over the next two days, but you must remain strong. I have seen your inner strength and haven't any doubt that you will manage.

I will remain where you last saw me. When you return in two days, please join me here. If you have not returned after two days, I will make the necessary arrangements to have the Knights fetch you.

Please communicate to the Warriors that I expect to hear from you by daily letter. Should I not receive your letter when it is expected, I will consider this an instruction that I am to send the Knights to bring you home.

May the Goddess walk with you,
Sir Dynan Fhirell

I permitted myself a quick second read of the letter and took in the comfort it brought me. It wasn't until the second reading that I realized Sir Fhirell had not replied to my having told him I missed him.

My cheeks burned with embarrassment at what he must have thought of me when he'd read my letter. I could only pray that this man, who had so romantically kissed my hand and declared his intention to court me, this Knight whose affections I returned so deeply, had assumed our letters would be read by Kavylak representatives and had withheld his true feelings. Sensing the captain's gaze on me, I took a breath and decided to focus on more pressing things.

"Sir Fhirell has confirmed that he would like me returned to his current location," I informed him. "He would like to receive a letter from me every day throughout my time here, in order to confirm that I am well and that the plans have remained the same. May I reply to him to tell him that this is acceptable?"

Alukka huffed and rolled her eyes. "He was quite adamant about those daily letters," she muttered.

Captain Wintheare didn't appear to notice Alukka's discontent.

"Yes. That is acceptable," he agreed, turning his attention to the Traveller. "Once you have delivered Miss Godeleva's message, you are dismissed, Alukka."

I picked up the pen and started a new letter on a fresh piece of paper, determined to sound more formal this time and less like a silly doting girl. At the same time, Captain Wintheare took the opportunity to open Sir Fhirell's letter and read it for himself. I tried not to let it irk me as I once again put the Kavylak pen to page.

Dear Sir Fhirell,

I am writing to thank you for your letter and to confirm that I will be returned to your present location in two days. The Warriors have also agreed to allow us to exchange daily letters.

I will be given my own quarters, which will be guarded for my safety. I am not a prisoner here. I am permitted free rein of the public areas of the building where I am staying. That said, I intend to remain in my quarters the vast majority of the time.

I look forward to rejoining our mission.

Cordially,
Irys Godeleva

"Thank you, Captain Wintheare," I said as I handed him the letter. This time, I kept it open in an acknowledgement that he would read it.

He took it from me and gave it a skim before folding it and handing it to Alukka. The moment it was placed in her hand, she was gone.

"Unless there is anything else you wish to discuss in this room, Miss Godeleva, I will take you to your quarters," the captain said as he stood and walked to the door.

"Thank you. I'd like to see where I will be staying."

After he knocked on the door, it opened and the soldier stepped aside to allow us to pass.

"Follow me," he said, now speaking in Kavylak.

Though I was tempted to run off, I knew that it would be foolish to do so. It was an automatic response to having the doors opened and being given the opportunity to escape from a Warrior. I had to remind myself that I was not a prisoner and that my best way home was with a Traveller in two days. The last thing I wanted to do was delay my return and miss my chance to send letters to Sir Fhirell.

The hallway was stark and institutional. It was artificially lit and was lined with numbered metal doors on either side. I attempted to memorize some of the numbers, so I might get to know where I was in relation to other places I might see along the way. Although I tried to find other noteworthy details to remember, I couldn't spot anything different from one step to the next. Upon my return to Sir Fhirell, anything I would be able to share about this structure would be limited.

The hall came to an end at a large double doorway. Captain Wintheare pushed open the door on the right side, and we exited the hallway into a wider, central-looking area. There was nothing in the large, square space other than more room than there had been in the hallway. Other sets of double doors suggested that it led to other halls aside from the one we'd just exited. The foot of a large, wide staircase was immediately to our right.

Soldiers and what appeared to be civilian workers, walked briskly through this place. Evidently, it was not meant to be used for lingering and socializing. It was simply a junction through which they were required to pass to arrive efficiently at their intended destinations. No one looked up at us, other than for the occasional salute to Captain Wintheare by soldiers taking our path in the opposite direction.

"This is the entrance hall," Captain Wintheare said once we'd reached its centre. His voice startled me out of the intensity of my observation of the place. "You are permitted in this area and in any corridor unguarded by soldiers. Signage on the doors will also tell you whether the area is open to non-military persons."

"I understand," I confirmed, feeling increasingly inclined to stay within my quarters. The thought of making my way to visit with Lieutenant Fhurrk was becoming increasingly daunting.

"Your room is located on the second floor. That floor is open to you. There are certain common spaces you may access. Their doors are not locked, and they are well signed."

"I understand," I replied, not knowing what else to say.

"My office is located on the fifth floor. It is the third door on the right and is clearly marked. If you should need to speak with me, you may go to my office. If I am not there and it is urgent that you speak with me, alert your guard. He will have a soldier find me. If I am still unreachable, Lieutenant Atrix will see to your needs."

"How do I find Lieutenant Atrix?"

"He will find you."

The second floor looked much like the first; doors on either side, each with numbers or other forms of identification. We walked partway down as I read the signs on the doors we passed. Nothing appeared to be all that interesting or useful. Finally, the captain reached out, opened an unlocked door, and gestured for me to enter.

As brave as I'd felt until then, the prospect of entering this room ahead of Captain Wintheare chilled me a little. Still, I didn't want him to know how afraid I was. I stepped forward, sliding my hands along the door frame and holding it momentarily, hoping I would be able to stop myself from being shoved inside if I should change my mind about entering.

I peered into the room, half expecting to see a dark dungeon cell, but it looked to be entirely harmless.

"As I said before, Miss Godeleva, no one is going to harm you. If we had wanted to do that, it would have been far easier to do it upon your first arrival, so we could skip the charade. Your room is perfectly safe," Captain Wintheare assured me.

"Given the nature of our relationship to date, I think I am permitted a certain degree of skepticism and suspicion, at least for a while, Captain Wintheare. I do mean that with all due respect," I replied as gently as I could. Then, I squared my shoulders and stepped into my new temporary quarters.

Captain Wintheare merely nodded to me and stepped into the suite after I had entered.

It was a basic space, but one that would serve me well enough while I was here. The door led into a main sitting area with a small sofa and chair positioned around a low table as well as a café table with two chairs.

"When may I expect clean clothing and my meals?" I asked as I slowly examined the space, hoping I didn't look either too approving or disapproving of these quarters. Certainly they weren't large or luxurious, but perhaps they were the space reserved for the most important dignitaries. I didn't know enough of Kavylak custom to decide.

"I will have fresh clothing brought within the hour. Are you hungry now?"

"I should eat a little something. Is there a menu from which I may select my choices?"

"Your meals will be decided for you. They will be nutritious and adequate."

"I'm sure they will suffice. If not, I know how to reach you or Lieutenant Atrix," I replied. "Is the room already stocked with other items? Toiletries? Paper and ink? Books?"

"Yes," he responded flatly. "Fresh sheets, blankets, towels, soaps, and other basic necessities for washing are in the bathroom. Writing implements and paper are in a drawer in your bedroom."

"Thank you, Captain Wintheare. It seems that I am provisioned well enough."

"You are," he said, stepping toward the door again. "If there is nothing further, Miss Godeleva, I will be leaving. I will send your meal and clothing." Withdrawing a key from his jacket pocket, he handed it to me.

"Thank you," I said as I accepted the key, assuming it was for the door to my quarters. "I will not make a nuisance of myself."

"I will visit you later to make sure your situation has not changed. Good day." He turned and stepped out, closing the door behind him.

"Good day," I replied, though I suspected he would have left regardless of whether or not I had anything else to say.

When I turned to face my quarters in his absence, they suddenly felt small and empty. Claustrophobic. I walked into the bedroom, hoping to improve the sensation by investigating everything my suite had to offer. The bedroom was as basic as the living space. It had an unmade bed with two pillows next to a folded set of sheets and a blanket. The maid must not yet have been through to prepare it.

The nightstand drawer contained everything I would need to write my letters to Sir Fhirell.

The bathroom was tiny, with a small shower stall, a pedestal sink with a mirror above it, and the privy. How I longed for a good bath. The shower would have to do, though I'd never used one in my life. On the edge of the sink basin, there was a little box. I opened it and found that it contained a wrapped bar of soap, a comb, toothbrush, and a pouch of tooth powder.

It was likely best that the bathroom didn't contain a bathtub. It would have been only disappointing with such limited toiletries. Lifting the soap I inhaled the fragrance and involuntarily curled my nose. I wasn't sure what botanical oils were commonplace in Kavylak, but whatever they were, I didn't like them.

Before I could dwell on the matter, there was a knock at the door. Slowly, I stepped into the sitting room, looking at the door as though I expected a monster to appear from the other side. Indeed, I had been told that a delivery of clothing and food would be sent. I was also aware that a guard was supposed to be placed on my door. Still, I felt alone, small, and vulnerable.

"Who's there?" I asked the door.

"Edda," replied a woman's voice. "I have fresh clothes and your meal, Miss Godeleva."

Turning the bolt, I opened the door. "Please come in," I said to the woman who was holding a bundle of clothing under one arm and a tray in her hands. Her brown hair was tied neatly behind her. She was dressed in a charcoal grey jacket, belted at the waist and a shin-length skirt. I tried not to be shocked at the thought that not only were her flat black shoes showing, but also the lower parts of her legs.

Behind her, I glimpsed my door guard. He appeared young, with short, pale blond hair. He was about my height, was dressed in a soldier's uniform, and neither looked at me nor spoke. I stepped out of the way to allow the woman entry and backed into my quarters.

"Thank you, Miss Edda. With whom do I speak about having my bed made?"

Edda smiled at me as though she was about to laugh but suddenly corrected herself and answered with a much more serious expression.

"I can make it for you." Her statement was slow and slightly hesitant as though she was waiting for me to say or do something unexpected.

"Thank you. Please make sure the guard at the door gives you a gratuity. I have not been provided with any money, or I would do so myself."

Again, she looked at me oddly but set her tray down and handed me the folded clothing she had been carrying.

"I don't need a gratuity, Miss Godeleva. You needn't worry about having any money," she said before heading into the bedroom.

I had to assume that they treated their housekeeping differently here than they did in Sylizan inns and hotels. Had I been at home, it would have been mortifying to be a guest at a lodging where I would not leave a gratuity for the staff.

Shrugging it off, I took a moment to look at the clothing Edda had brought for me. There was a plain white blouse with long sleeves and a high neck as well as a brown skirt that was dreadfully short. Holding it up to my waist, I was absolutely certain that its hem would stop just short of my ankles! There was a tiny chemise, short bloomers, and stockings. After examining everything, I returned to the skirt. It simply would not do. It was scandalously short.

I stepped into the bedroom doorway to see Edda making my bed with neat tucks and folds.

"Will better clothing be provided to me later?" I asked as sweetly as I could. "This selection, I'm assuming, is only due to the short notice available for procuring it, is it not?"

Edda paused from her work to look at me with a brow furrowed with confusion.

"Better clothing? What's wrong with the clothes I gave you, Miss Godeleva?"

"It seems that the skirt was selected for a woman who isn't quite as tall as I am. It is far too short. My ankles will be exposed. I'll manage with the underthings, if I must, but there is no shift to speak of. I'm also missing a vest or sweater to wear over my blouse. I'm afraid I wouldn't be able to step a foot outside my quarters in the outfit provided. I appreciate the effort that was made, of course, but you understand." I smiled to her, hoping to form some kind of feminine bond between us.

"That was the longest skirt I could find. I can assure you that the clothing I've brought you is perfectly appropriate whether you're here in the military compound or out in Capital City. I can fetch you a sweater if that will help you to feel more comfortable," she said, making it clear that she was unwilling to find a skirt that would actually fit my height.

"A sweater would be lovely," I replied, understanding that this poor woman knew nothing of what a proper lady should wear. I would have to speak to someone else if I were to be appropriately attired.

Edda simply nodded to me and returned to making the bed.

"Before I go, I should tell you that while you do have a very effective guard at your door, he is mute. He can understand you perfectly, and he is able to pass your requests to the right people, but you will not be able to carry on a conversation with him. Address him as Rolern."

"Thank you. I'm glad to know how to address him and that I should not expect him to speak to me in return."

Edda finished up with the bed, giving its surface a final sweep with her hand.

"I'll get you your sweater, Miss Godeleva. Is there anything else you need?"

"No, thank you, Edda. The sweater will do nicely for now." I walked to the door to see her out.

"When you're done your meal, place the tray outside the door and someone will take it away."

"Thank you. I will," I said as she stepped out into the corridor without ceremony.

I took a moment to look at the meal that was brought to me. It appeared to be scrambled eggs, fried potatoes, brown toast, and a small cup of fruit as well as a glass of milk. Only the fruit appealed, but I resolved to try to eat as much as I could of it.

Before sitting down to my breakfast, however, I decided to address the matter of my clothing. Opening the door again, I stepped inside its frame without actually exiting my quarters.

"Good day, Mr. Rolern. I would like to speak with Captain Wintheare or Lieutenant Atrix with regards to arranging for proper clothing. What has been sent for me simply will not do. I'm sure it was well intended, but I have requirements which have not been met," I said in a pleasant tone.

Rolern smiled at me, and I had to return the expression. He was the sweetest looking guard I'd ever seen. His light blond hair fluttered over his forehead any time he moved his head, and his face was positively angelic. Nodding to my request, he jotted something down on a piece of paper he'd withdrawn from his pocket.

Suddenly, he made a sharp whistling sound with his mouth, and I jumped, but when a young slave man approached, I realized this was a predetermined signal to allow him to have his messages sent to the Warriors. The slave scurried down the hall with the note.

"Thank you," I said to Mr. Rolern, who merely gave me his adorable smile in return. "Have you tried today's breakfast? Do you think I will enjoy it?" I asked with a teasing smile on my face.

Mr. Rolern looked at me while I spoke but merely smiled without a nod or shake of his head.

"I see. It isn't safe to insult the chef," I joked.

To that, he gave a short, silent laugh, but his expression remained joyful. *Such a happy guard!*

"Who do you think will be sent to help me with my request? Captain Wintheare?" I held up one finger to indicate that this was the gesture for Captain Wintheare, "or Lieutenant Atrix?" I held up two fingers to represent the Lieutenant.

Mr. Rolern studied my gestures for a brief moment before holding up two fingers.

"I see. Lieutenant Atrix," I said thoughtfully. "I've met him, though I've yet to form a real opinion of him. Is Lieutenant Acksilivcs in this building?"

To that, Mr. Rolern merely shrugged.

"If I wished to see him, would I be able to?"

He shrugged again. It was clear that he was there only to guard me and to pass my messages to the Warriors. He wasn't given any authority over my situation here.

"I suppose I can only hope to be lucky."

Before Mr. Rolern could do anything but smile in response, Lieutenant Arik Atrix was strolling down the hallway toward us. He was the embodiment of confidence and charisma.

Every rich blue hair on his head was precisely as it should be, a fact that surprised me this time as much as it had in Fort Picogeal, the last time I'd seen him. That said, it was not its perfection that continued to shock me as much as the fact that it was blue, and not the sleek black it had been when he was in disguise at the Godeleva Masquerade ball. Still, its perfection was certainly worth noting every time. The Warrior had a way of tilting his head to cause his hair to tumble down in front of his eyes, only to return precisely to where it should be, once he straightened up again.

He was dressed in the black leather Warriors' uniform, just as Captain Wintheare had been, and yet he somehow made the gear appear chic and roguish. I could only imagine what Lorammel's most prominent clothing designer, F, would do with the chance to dress him.

"Good morning, Miss Godeleva," he said to me with a perfect Sylizan bow. I would have found his greeting much more charming if it had not been followed up with a mussing of Mr. Rolern's hair. "Hey there, Rolern, buddy."

I was about to object on Mr. Rolern's behalf, but Lieutenant Atrix rapidly withdrew his hand from the guard and appeared to knock himself in the chin with his own fist. This looked more than slightly odd to me, but neither the guard nor the Warrior seemed to observe anything strange in the gesture. Mr. Rolern continued to smile in his natural, boyish way, and Lieutenant Atrix grinned at him in return. If something passed between them, I hadn't any idea what it could have been.

Without missing a beat, Lieutenant Atrix turned his magnetic blue eyes on me.

"Shall we go inside?" His words were uncomfortably suggestive but for reasons I could not explain, I didn't feel disinclined to accept his invitation. In fact, I found myself looking forward to spending a little bit of time with this new Warrior.

I nodded quite stupidly to him and stepped into my quarters. With my back to him for a moment, I was able to gather my thoughts again. *Strange. It's as though my mind suddenly cleared.*

"Thank you for coming. The clothing provided to me, though lovely, I'm sure, is not adequate. As a young lady of Syliza, I have certain requirements which must be met."

"Oh? What's wrong with what Edda brought you? Too boring?" he replied, with an amused expression as he took a seat on my sofa. He looked as though he owned the furniture. In fact, he looked as though he owned the entire room, and that I was the one visiting him.

"Not at all," I insisted, only barely able to remember what it was we were discussing. He was frightfully distracting. "It's that the skirt is not the right size. It is far too short to be decent and..." It dawned on me, quite suddenly, that I was speaking to a man. This wasn't the same as telling Edda why each item was inappropriate for me. Leaning toward him, I whispered, "The under things are barely even there!" Resisting the urge to fan myself to cool the heat burning in my cheeks, I added, with greater comfort, "Edda is bringing me a sweater to wear over my blouse, but I would prefer a vest as well if one could be procured."

As he listened, his eyes never left me. It was terribly disconcerting. I perched on the edge of a chair to feel steadier. It wasn't that his expression was at all intimidating or threatening. In fact, it was quite welcoming and perhaps even slightly amused.

"I understand that you may find it challenging to adjust to the fashion here in Kavylak," he said, rebelliously speaking in Sylizan. "But you won't find anything here that is as stuffy as what you wear at home. I could put together an outfit that will be long enough to hide your shoes, but the fact of the matter is that you're just not going to find yourself wearing as many layers here as you do in Syliza."

"I understand," I replied in the Kavylak language. Captain Wintheare told me to speak in Kavylak, and I was determined not to be caught breaking the rules. "Still, I would appreciate something long enough to cover me all the way, please. Will it also be possible to find something to wear over the white blouse? Just one more layer?" I asked him, smiling as sweetly as I could. As much as I was hoping to sway him with my smile, I was pretty certain that all I was managing to do was fall victim to his own.

As he watched me, he visibly pondered my question. "I'll have something new arranged for you. I know you'll feel practically naked in it, but try to remind yourself that it's only the way you feel. You'll be perfectly covered, and no one here will think you're dressed inappropriately. Dressing as you normally do would draw far more attention...the wrong sort of attention."

Fairly certain that my face was defining a new and previously undiscovered shade of red, I nodded and peeped out a quick "thank you." After a brief recovery, I was able to add: "I understand what you mean. I am only hoping to find somewhat of a compromise between your fashions and mine."

"In that case, you've definitely come to the right person." He rose and began strolling about the room, allowing his gaze to slide over every little detail of my suite, until he sighted the tray containing my breakfast. "Chaos, don't eat that. I'll have something better sent."

I was surprised, both by his language and the reason for it.

"Thank you. I'll be sure to wait for whatever meal you send," I agreed.

It was at that quite random moment that I realized I had a new opportunity to inquire about Lieutenant Acksilivcs. Mr. Rolern may not have known the answer, but Lieutenant Atrix was a Warrior. If anyone would know, he would.

"Is Lieutenant Acksilivcs in this building, too?"

"Why do you want to know?" he asked with a sly grin. "Have a crush, do we? Want another kiss?"

I was mortified. If he had not been one of only two Warriors I was permitted to ask for assistance, I would have sent him away and demanded that he be reprimanded by his superiors. Instead, I simply withdrew the request.

"Never mind. Please forget I asked. I will be grateful for the clothes and the meal you've promised," I said quickly with a barely-disguised chill to my tone. I managed to achieve this coolness only by avoiding eye contact with him.

"If that's what you want," he replied casually. "But to answer your question: no. He's not here."

"Thank you." My reply was curt, but I could feel my expression softening the moment I looked at him again. It was as though my reactions were not entirely within my own control. I knew I wanted to be stern with him for having been abrupt with me, but every time I looked at him, I was forced to suppress the urge to smile and possibly giggle!

"Do you intend to stay in your quarters the entire time you're here?"

"Mainly," I nodded. "Particularly as I haven't anything appropriate to wear outside my door."

"Even if you feel the same way about the clothing I give you, don't let your outfit decide for you. I'd hate to think that you'd miss out on our very impressive library."

"Library?" My mouth responded before my mind could have the chance to think better of it.

He nodded slowly, a tantalizing smile gliding over his perfectly symmetrical lips. "Oh, yes. It spans three floors."

"That does sound like something worth seeing while I'm here," I confessed. "If I feel that my attire is adequate to allow me to venture out of my quarters, I shall certainly head there."

"Then I'd better see about those clothes for you. And some real food. I don't want to stand in the way of your explorations."

"Thank you, Lieutenant Atrix." I stood to see him out.

"I'll see you soon," he replied with a lingering look that should have made me feel uncomfortable. Instead, I merely smiled, relieved that was all I'd done. At least I was fairly certain I wasn't drooling.

To that, he turned and stepped out the door, walking down the corridor without a backward glance.

Turning to face the room, I wondered what to do with myself. I washed my hands and face, then took another tour of the space, looking in every drawer and cupboard. Finally, I stared out the window at my balcony, thinking about Sir Fhirell and hoping he was coping better than I was.

I allowed myself to imagine Sir Fhirell. In my mind's eye, I saw him working in the fields with Drudvis while Elika ordered them around. I nearly envied the thought. I wouldn't have minded working with Elika another day if it had meant I would not be here waiting, alone and wondering what to do with myself.

For a moment, I shut my eyes. I imagined myself back in that farmhouse where Dynan had revealed his interest in courting me. He'd held my hand. He'd kissed my fingers. My hand still felt the memory of his warm skin touching mine. I sighed as the memory fizzled away.

Indeed, I was promised a stay of only two days, but when every minute felt like an hour, those days were feeling painfully long.

Great Goddess, you are wise and all-knowing. You are both kind and merciful. I don't doubt that your choice to bring me here is an important part of your plan.

Please, take care of Sir Fhirell. He does not deserve the concern my decisions are certain to have inflicted upon him. Please bring him comfort throughout his wait for me.

Please, also bring me the strength to pass the time with dignity until my return. I wish only to rejoin my mission with Sir Fhirell in Gbat Rher, that I may complete it, in your name...

I was drawn from my meditations by a knock at my door.

"Who is it?" I asked without opening it. I wasn't about to trust that this guest was a welcome one, even if he or she had gained Mr. Rolern's approval.

"It's the man of your dreams, Twinkles. Won't you let me in?" said Lieutenant Atrix.

I was tongue-tied. Instead of making him wait in my attempt to come up with something clever, I unlocked the door and opened it. I hoped my sensation of blankness didn't translate to my face in front of this audacious man. If it did, he gave no indication.

Instead, he stepped into my quarters, and I moved away from him in the hopes of keeping my thoughts straight. In one hand, he carried a paper shopping bag with ribbon handles. The other hand supported a round, domed tray.

As was the case the last time he had visited, he moved through my suite as though it was his. He set the tray on the dining table and rested the bag on one of the chairs. With his gifts sorted out, he turned to face me and smiled.

"As promised: clothing and edible food," he said in Sylizan as I prayed for enough strength in my legs to keep me standing.

"Thank you. That's very kind of you," I replied in Kavylak, eyeing the bag. I'd never worn a single outfit that could have been contained in a bag that size. I had my doubts that whatever he'd selected for me would suffice.

"What do you want first? The clothes or the food?"

"I'd like to dress. The clothes first, please."

His grin suggested I'd chosen the option he'd preferred.

"Everything you need is in there. I selected some shoes for you, too. I guessed your size." It was clear he was confident he'd guessed correctly, though it was terribly embarrassing of him to discuss my shoes, let alone choose them. "Keep an open mind as you dress, Twinkles. Remember, you're in Kavylak now. No one here wears stuffy Sylizan clothes."

"It's very difficult for me to forget that I am in Kavylak, Lieutenant," I replied with a frown. "Even so, despite the fact that I am very aware of where I am, I cannot change my sense of decency or personal modesty."

"Oh, don't frown. It's not the end of the world. You got a new outfit out of it, and you have me as a friend. I'm the best friend you could ever want here."

"Perhaps," I conceded. "You've been generous to me, of course. But you are a Warrior," I said, feeling that statement was self-explanatory.

"I can see why that may seem like a problem. Maybe after spending some time with me, you'll change your opinion, at least of some of us."

"Are you planning to spend more time with me?"

"Did you want me to leave?"

"That wasn't what I was saying. It's only that you sounded like you intended to be around for a while. I plan to change into my new clothes and then eat. You shouldn't need to wait around for me to do those things."

"What will you do once you're dressed and fed?"

"I hadn't entirely decided. I might visit the library. Do you know if I'm permitted to borrow books and bring them here?"

"You may, but you will be restricted as to the number."

"Oh, I'm sure I won't need too many. I'm going home soon."

"Then perhaps I'll see you in the library," he said with a tone that suggested he planned to make a special trip to the library where he would be waiting for me. I wasn't certain whether that thought pleased me or whether it made me want to lock myself in the bathroom.

"If not, I'm sure our paths will cross again before I leave. Thank you for the gifts," I said, very aware of his unwavering gaze on me.

"You're welcome," he said with a grin as he rose, strolling toward the door. "Have a good breakfast," he added, glancing over his shoulder before heading out.

"Thank you," I replied stupidly, staring at the door for an extended moment, even after he had closed it behind him. Shaking myself from my stupor, I locked the door and turned to face the shopping bag and whatever dreadful garments it must contain.

I carried the bag into the bedroom to lay out its contents on the bed. Once I'd done it, I stared at the clothes, not entirely sure that I was pleased with what I saw. There was a white blouse with a black vest to wear overtop as well as a black skirt that was a far more decent length than the original one I'd been given. Still, it wasn't a full skirt as I was accustomed as it was far more form-following. There wouldn't be enough room for even a single petticoat underneath, which was likely best as none were provided to me.

Indeed, it was certainly an improvement over what Edda had brought me, but I was starting to feel that I would never again be comfortable in my clothing.

The footwear I was provided consisted of a pair of black booties in fine leather with a low heel. They were rather unimaginative, but looked adequately comfortable and practical. All things considered, they were likely the piece with which I would feel the most secure.

I resigned myself to washing and dressing without any assistance, taking my time to do so. I felt no inclination to rush as I had two days to spend in this room without any specific plans to fill each hour.

As much as the fashion was not to my taste, I was surprised at how well everything fit, right down to the shoes. I refused to try to imagine how Lieutenant Atrix could have made such accurate selections. My metal identification tags finished the look.

Back in the suite's sitting room, I sat down to take my meal. I was surprised to see a cheese and vegetable omelet, a warm muffin, and a bowl of fresh fruit. It was lovely, flavourful, and satisfying. Even more surprising, was the pot of tea that sat next to the plate. A little sniff revealed that this wasn't just any tea – it was Sylizan! This was far from the type of food I was expecting to eat while living within a Kavylak military building.

I sipped the tea and felt some of my tension melt from my shoulders. It was such a familiar flavour that I could nearly close my eyes and pretend that I was sitting in a shop in Lorammel. *Nearly.*

Giving myself the chance to savour the tea, I fortified myself for leaving my quarters. I was determined to see the library, so I could spend the rest of my stay here reading. I hoped for the chance to visit with Lieutenant Fhurrk as well.

When I finished my meal and tea and could find no further excuse to remain idle in my quarters, I crept up to my door and unlocked it as quietly as I could. Unlatching it, I opened it enough to peek out into the hallway.

I spotted Mr. Rolern standing at his post and when he saw me, he quickly hid a paper and pencil behind his back, giving me a boyish smile as though I'd caught him stealing dessert when his mother wasn't looking.

"Have I disturbed you from writing something?" I asked with a teasing smile as I opened my door enough to step out.

He smiled more and shook his head, bringing the paper around in front of him to reveal that he had been working on some form of word puzzle. Indeed, guarding my door must have been rather boring. I hadn't gone anywhere yet and if anyone were to approach, he would see them coming down the corridor. He raised a finger to his lips without accompanying it with the "shhh" sound the gesture implied.

"Your secret is safe with me," I promised him. "Would you be so good as to point me in the direction of a library entrance?"

His boyish smile never faltered, and he nodded, waving his hand in a beckoning gesture as he stepped away from my door. It seemed that I had a guide in Mr. Rolern, not just a guard.

Shutting my door behind me and locking it, I stepped up to him to walk with him.

"Would you like me to take out a very small book for you as well?" I asked Mr. Rolern quietly. "One you could tuck behind your back with your puzzles?"

He laughed soundlessly and shook his head, but then looked thoughtful. Withdrawing a small pad of paper from his pocket, he wrote a few words before holding it out for me to see.

"Maybe you could read to me through the door," it read. His expression was mischievous, and he broke into another soundless laugh.

It was as though a light had been turned on inside me. "I'd like that very much," I agreed. "I know you were joking but would you mind if I did that? What type of book do you prefer? Adventure novels? History texts? Romance stories?"

The last option had been a tease, but his smile turned bashful as he held up three fingers to suggest the third option on my list. He then closed his hand and held up his "shhh" finger once again.

I couldn't help but giggle. "I'll find us a lovely one."

He looked pleased, and I felt as though we were both rather relieved to have found a friend in each other.

After a bit of a walk, I discovered that it wouldn't have been at all difficult to find the library. The corridor wall was replaced by a floor-to-ceiling glass barrier allowing us to see right into the vast space filled with row upon row of bookshelves.

"What a lovely surprise," I said. Mr. Rolern nodded his agreement as he opened a glass door for me. "Are the fiction novels on this floor?"

Mr. Rolern shook his head, holding up three fingers.

"Then let us proceed to the third floor." I smiled, feeling as though I had finally found a tolerable space in which to lose myself for a while.

As soon as I was inside, I was greeted with the warm and welcoming smell of books – thousands of books. The sight of the organized shelving and softened natural lighting was enough to help me forget that the individuals seated at the various reading stations and study carrels were primarily Kavylak soldiers.

I glanced curiously at the books on the shelves we passed as we made our way toward one of the flights of stairs that would take us up to the third floor.

Every now and again, other people in the library would look up at me with interest and curiosity. It was making me feel very aware of my outfit, so I was glad when Mr. Rolern and I were able to leave that floor and make our way to the next one.

There were far fewer people on the third floor. Perhaps fiction novels weren't a popular choice in the middle of the day in a military compound. That said, this floor wasn't empty. Girlish giggles trilled repeatedly as a couple of young women responded to another person's whispers.

It was an offensive sound, soiling the sacred space among these books. Even if I had wanted to excuse the behavior by saying that it might be a cultural difference and that Kavylak people didn't mind a noisy library, I knew that was not the case. The quiet second floor had already made it clear that libraries here were meant to be just as soundless as the ones I knew back home in Syliza.

Out of the corner of my eye, I saw Mr. Rolern roll his eyes and when I looked over at him, his boyish smile faltered. He shook his head at me in a way that showed he disapproved of what he was hearing as much as I did.

I nodded in agreement with him.

"Ow!" cried out one of the no-longer giggling women, followed by the sound of a thump.

"What's wrong?" asked a voice that could belong to none other than Lieutenant Arik Atrix. No other man's voice was as rich and alluring.

"A book just fell on me!" replied the woman.

If I wasn't mistaken, Mr. Rolern's expression had transformed into a smirk, only momentarily, until it returned to his usual boyishness.

I couldn't fathom what was going on, and I didn't want to.

"Where do we go from here?" I asked Mr. Rolern, wanting to put the giggles behind me.

He nodded in a new direction, and we started walking toward what would hopefully be a much more peaceful time in the library. We turned and walked down a row of shelves before he stopped, gesturing to either side of himself in an indication that I should make my selection here.

Slowly, I strolled down the row, allowing my eyes to make their way through the titles of Kavylak-language books. This was clearly a romance fiction section. I did my best to find a title that looked as though it might be somewhat more reserved than what many of these rather shocking looking headings suggested.

I had only just withdrawn one of the books by its spine when I was sharply interrupted by a voice. I stuffed the book under my arm to hide it.

"I had a feeling I'd find you in this section of the library, Twinkles." Lieutenant Atrix said in Kavylak, not Sylizan as he sauntered down the row toward me with a smile on his face.

Mr. Rolern kept out of the way, simply standing nearby as my guard. His boyishness had entirely disappeared.

"I thought I would choose one book from several sections to improve my chances of finding one that will be to my taste. I haven't read much fiction in Kavylak."

"Makes sense. But who doesn't love a little romance? I certainly do. This is a particular favourite," he said as he ran a finger sensually along the spine of a book before withdrawing it from the shelf and holding it out for me to see. It was, most certainly, among those volumes I had been deliberately trying to avoid.

I glanced at it but did not take it from him. Scandalized, I turned up my nose at him and looked to Mr. Rolern.

"Where might we find historical fiction?" I asked him.

Mr. Rolern nodded his head toward one end of the row and started to head in that direction. I followed.

"I can be your guide if you want someone who actually talks," Lieutenant Atrix called from behind me.

"I'm doing quite well with my guard, thank you," I replied haughtily over my shoulder. "He doesn't try to shock me with pornographic book selections."

A glance at Mr. Rolern revealed that he was more than a little amused with my reply.

"Well, if you ever become bored of your little guard, I won't say 'I told you so'." I could hear the smile on Lieutenant Atrix' lips.

"I'm content with my present company, thank you." I kept my eyes looking forward. I knew that if I had turned to look at Lieutenant Atrix as I spoke, I wouldn't be nearly as able to remain collected.

"Suit yourself. You do look good in Kavylak fashions, by the way." I could feel his gaze sliding over my body as though it produced actual heat.

"Thank you," I replied, not entirely certain I liked receiving that compliment. "Good day, Lieutenant Atrix." I returned to walking with Mr. Rolern in the hopes that we would not be followed.

"Good day, Miss Godeleva," he said in a tone that made my name sound like something naughty. I was glad he couldn't see the pink it brought to my cheeks.

I caught a small shake of Mr. Rolern's head and when I looked over at him, he rolled his eyes. Smiling, I allowed myself to focus on my little outing with him.

"Perhaps one more book before we head back?"

He nodded and gave me a friendly smile, an expression I returned. It was nice to have such a gentle and honest friend as my guard. It was as though I had been given a companion instead of a soldier.

Mr. Rolern directed me toward the historical fiction section of the library. There were a number of fascinating-looking titles available, tempting me to make more than one selection. I had to remind myself that I wasn't going to be staying long and that if I did run out of books, I could always return here to select another. Finally, I made my choice and held it with the romance novel.

"Must I check out the books or do I merely leave with them?" I asked.

Withdrawing his little pad of paper, Mr. Rolern wrote a few quick words and held it out for me to see.

"You're Captain Wintheare's guest. No one will question you. Take them."

"In that case, I believe I'm done here. Shall we?"

We turned and went back downstairs before heading out into the corridor. To my relief, there wasn't any sign of Lieutenant Atrix. The more I saw of him, the less I felt as though I could trust myself. It was an unsettling feeling.

As we approached my quarters, we passed a man in a Warrior's uniform. His long, sleek black hair seemed to be floating around him as though caught in a soft wind that I could not feel. He appeared to be interested in Mr. Rolern and sent him a rather odd expression as he neared us. Saying nothing, he continued on without a backward glance.

"Do you know that Warrior?" I asked Mr. Rolern when we were far enough from the Warrior that he would not hear us.

Mr. Rolern merely shook his head and shrugged, not seeming to know why the Warrior had looked at him as strangely as he did.

The rest of the walk was without incident. I unlocked my door and paused, turning back to Mr. Rolern.

"Are you permitted to come inside to listen to the book or must you stay out here?"

He shook his head and frowned.

"I understand. In that case, I won't invite you in. I will read to you for a while, then perhaps we will go for a walk."

He nodded, looking pleased, then withdrew the pad of paper.

"Let me know when you are hungry. I will make sure Lieutenant Atrix brings you a meal," he wrote.

"Thank you. That's kind of you. I will be sure to tell you," I assured him, placing my hand on the knob without turning it. "Is there anywhere else that we might go where I can read to you in person instead of through the door?"

To that, he looked thoughtful and then his face brightened.

"Yes. Outside," he wrote. "You could sit outside, and I would be required to guard you."

"Lovely. Is the weather nice enough for me to be outside, reading 'to myself'?"

He nodded, smiling happily.

I set the historical fiction novel inside my quarters and relocked my door, then turned to face our new little adventure.

Despite the fact that I carefully watched for other Warriors along the way, there were none to see. Before long, we were outside, walking along a paved area where soldiers trained in formations in response to the commands barked by officers.

Mr. Rolern didn't seem nearly as interested in the soldiers as I was. Men and women marched side by side, a fact I'd known to be true but that still amazed me to see in person. This certainly wasn't the way of the Sylizan military. I had to assume that this wasn't at all the first time Mr. Rolern had seen these drills. In fact, I imagined that as a soldier, he was required to take part in them rather regularly.

Beyond the paved area, we passed rows of identical and wholly unimaginative buildings in various stages of damage and disrepair. Farther along, was a surprising stretch of grassy hills. It was likely another training area that wasn't currently in use but, for the moment, there were several couples and small groups of people taking advantage of the little natural space.

Though hardly a park, I could understand why the people here would gravitate to this space instead of the stark pavement that covered the rest of the ground.

My eyes fell upon a young man in a Warrior's uniform, lounging on the grass. He appeared to be quite youthful – possibly fifteen or sixteen cycles in age – and had pale blue hair cut into many lengths with the longest portions reaching midway down his back. Curled in against him was a woman of about the same age who was covered in Sefaline markings.

It was nearly impossible to resist staring, but I was afraid to draw attention to myself. I didn't want to be rude.

"Are Sefaline commonplace here?" I quietly asked Mr. Rolern, forcing my gaze to remain ahead of me instead of lingering on the fascinatingly unique couple.

Mr. Rolern considered my question, glanced over at the Warrior and the Sefaline, then back at me before shaking his head.

"Is she related to Lieutenant Fhurrk?"

He shrugged, looking more interested in finding a location for us to sit than in the Warrior and Sefaline, who had far greater appeal to me than a place on the lawn.

Soon, I was seated in a nice little spot tucked into one of the hills. It gave the impression of being somewhat secluded, even if we weren't really all that far from other people – or marching soldiers, for that matter. Mr. Rolern stood nearby, watching over me as I read "to myself".

Angling the book so I was reading in his direction, I dived into the prologue. Though Mr. Rolern was certainly watching out for me, I could tell he was listening and was amused by the story. It wasn't quite to my taste, but I did my best to ensure my new friend would enjoy his time with me.

As we entered into the third chapter, I saw Mr. Rolern stiffen a little, and I paused my reading. At first, I thought he was reacting to the sight of the one person I'd hoped not to see while I was here: Captain Galnar. I felt the blood drain from my face, and my hands shook as I watched him cross the grounds and disappear behind a damaged building that appeared to be in a state of reconstruction.

As it turned out, Mr. Rolern hadn't even spotted Captain Galnar. He was watching as the young Warrior and the Sefaline woman were headed toward us. His arm was around her, and she walked as closely to him as a person could without tripping him.

Though I'd expected them to pass us by, they stepped right up to me, and the Warrior addressed me.

"Are you Miss Godeleva?" he asked in a smooth, entrancing voice. He looked upon me with eyes of molten gold that were just as entrancing as his voice. I couldn't have forced myself to look away from him if I'd wanted to.

"Yes," I replied, rising to my feet. "With whom do I have the pleasure?"

The Sefaline woman leaned closer to him and inhaled at his throat, bringing up a hand to rest on his shoulder in a very possessive way.

"Lieutenant Hozis Icender," he replied, causing me to forget all about the woman who was claiming him. "I heard what you did for Lieutenant Fhurrk, and I wanted to thank you."

"I was glad to help him. We both helped each other for a while. Our survival depended on it," I explained. "You're a Warrior?" I asked quickly, before I could lose my nerve.

Lieutenant Icender nodded but didn't elaborate.

"Are there many of you? I've met a few of you now," I asked, nearly getting lost in his eyes.

"There are enough of us," he replied in his hypnotic voice.

"Would you like to join me?" I asked, welcoming them to join me on the grass.

He shook his head, wisps of light blue hair swaying over his forehead.

"No, thank you. It was lovely listening to your story earlier. You have a soothing voice."

"From you, that is quite the compliment, Lieutenant Icender," I replied.

"If you are seeking an audience for your reading, you may want to visit Lieutenant Fhurrk."

"Perhaps I'll do just that. Thank you for the advice."

The Sefaline woman looked up at Lieutenant Icender, purring.

"We should go running," she said as though she was unaware of my presence.

Lieutenant Icender turned his attention to the woman, and it felt as though I had been freed from a trance. He looked at her with deep adoration and smiled at her as though she'd offered him something deeply touching.

"It was good to meet you, Miss Godeleva. Please excuse us," he said, staring into the Sefaline's eyes.

"And you. Pleasant day, Lieutenant Icender."

I watched them as they walked away then turned to glance at Mr. Rolern. He was raising an eyebrow at me as though he thought that entire situation was quite strange.

I grinned in reply. "Are you ready for a break from the book? I wouldn't mind visiting Lieutenant Fhurrk."

He nodded to me and tilted his head to the side, indicating that he would take me.

"Thank you."

We turned toward the building and I felt my heart leap with the prospect of seeing Lieutenant Fhurrk again.

Chapter 15

Megan

The smell of cooking food pulled me from sleep. I slowly opened my eyes and focused on my surroundings. I didn't know what time it was, because I honestly never really knew what time it was on Qarradune. My best guess would have been the early morning, based on how still it was.

After a few more eye blinks to clear my sleep-hazed vision, I saw Ash Dancer was up and moving around. She had rebuilt one of the fire pits and was cooking something in a clay pot. She sat down, tending to it. Bediagq walked over to where she was, still looking half asleep, and sat down next to her, sucking his thumb.

I watched them, still feeling half asleep myself. I shifted, wanting to get a little more comfortable, but I halted my movements immediately when I remembered I wasn't alone. Mez was snuggled in behind me, his arm securely wrapped around me. As I became more aware of his presence, I realized that my back was right up against his chest. We must have shifted closer to one another during our slumber.

I was pretty sure he was sleeping, so I stayed still for a while, not wanting to wake him. Finally, I had to move. My body was growing increasingly uncomfortable, and I really needed to use the bathroom.

As carefully as I could, I slowly moved away from Mez, gently lifting his arm from around me.

"We don't have to get up yet, Glenara," he mumbled in his sleep before drifting off again and shifting to hold me comfortably.

Who the heck is Glenara? Oh, great. He does have a girlfriend, doesn't he?

This time, when I moved to extract myself from his embrace, I was less careful and more determined about it. Being called the name of another woman was just the motivation I needed to get up. I knew Mez and I weren't actually together, and that he wasn't exactly awake when he'd said the name, but I still didn't like being mistaken for another woman.

I sat up and stretched a little. Bediagq saw me, smiled, and waved. I smiled and waved back. Mez stirred behind me.

"Is everything alright?" he asked quietly in a groggy voice.

I turned to look at him and smiled a little. "Yes," I whispered. "I'm just going to find a bathroom. I'll be back."

Mez nodded. "Did you need Keavren or me to come with you?"

"No, I'll be fine. You stay here and try to get some more sleep if you can."

Mez nodded and shut his eyes. I watched him for a moment, then stood up. I glanced at the bed above ours to see if Keavren was awake. He wasn't. He was flopped on his back with one of the blankets loosely draped over him, and one of his boots stuck out and over the end of the pallet bed. I loved how innocent and boyish he looked.

"Did you eat fire to make your hair red?"

I looked down at Bediagq, startled by his question, not having realized he'd approached me.

"No. I was born with it." I grinned at him. "I think if I ate fire, I wouldn't have any hair at all."

He broke into a fit of giggles at my comment and nodded in agreement.

"I didn't eat fire, either," he informed me, his eyes now focused on Mez. "He looks like he ate a lot of ice."

"He does," I agreed, wondering if Mez was listening to our conversation. "Thankfully, he didn't."

Bediagq's attention drifted up to Keavren's sleeping form. "When I grow big, I'm going to get muscles like the hungry one," he said proudly.

"He has very big muscles. The biggest I've seen," I told him. "I bet if you keep eating as well as you do every day, you'll get very big muscles, too."

He nodded and grinned, clearly liking that idea. He then slipped his hand into mine and gave it a tug, wanting me to follow him. I did, walking with him toward the hearth where Ash Dancer sat. I nodded to her, greeting her with a friendly smile. She returned the gesture and indicated I should sit.

"Thank you, I'll be happy to join you. I just want to use the bathroom, first." I explained.

She nodded. "You can wash and relieve yourself outside by the river."

"Thanks," I said. "I'll be back," I added to Bediagq as I released his hand.

I turned and left the house. I was surprised to find the man who had been guarding its entrance was still there, looking as hard as nails and just as unfriendly as the last time I'd seen him. I debated smiling at him and saying "hello" but thought better of it and continued on.

I found my way to the river, which took me to the edge of the village. Keeping a lookout for some type of latrine, it didn't take me long to spot a tent-like structure that I assumed must be the "bathroom" I was seeking. I was right.

While I was glad it was a sheltered space, after days of not seeing a real bathroom, I felt certain that as soon as I returned to the type of civilization I was used to, I would never take a bathroom for granted again.

My business complete, I headed back to the building. As I walked, I had to admit that it was a beautiful day. The weather was warm, the breeze was soft and cool, and the birds were singing. This was going to be a great day for travel, and I smiled thinking about it. Soon, we'd be on our way, and soon, I might finally be finding my way back to Thayn.

Without even glancing at the guard man, I pushed the door flap aside and entered. The first thing I noticed was that Mez and Keavren weren't on their beds. I did a quick scan of the space and didn't see them anywhere, which I immediately found odd and worrisome, considering they'd both been sleeping when I left, and I couldn't have been gone for more than ten minutes at the very most.

Don't jump to conclusions, Megan. There's probably a logical explanation for their absence.

I approached Ash Dancer, who was still sitting at the fire with Bediagq at her side. Eshaig and Dawn Seer had also joined them. They nodded to me, and I returned the gesture in greeting.

"I have your breakfast. You'll want to eat before you travel," Ash Dancer said.

"Thank you," I answered appreciatively. "Do you know where my man and our friend went?"

"Yes," Ash Dancer said easily. "They're speaking with Doom Breaker."

Okay. Wow. Apparently they'd been summoned. I guess that wasn't super-weird.

Star Archer did say that Doom Breaker wanted me to bring a message back to Kavylak for her, which I'd agreed to do. Maybe she was going to give them the message directly instead of relaying it to me, since they knew that Mez and Keavren were Warriors. That would make more sense, after all. Still, something about this made me feel uneasy, and I didn't like being separated from them and not knowing where they were.

"Come sit with us," Ash Dancer encouraged me. She had, no doubt, seen the strained look on my face. "You'll need your strength."

I slowly sat down, hoping that she meant I would need my strength for the journey back to Kavylak and not for something else.

Dawn Seer scooped what looked like oatmeal from a pot into a bowl and then added a fried egg on top. She placed a wooden spoon into the bowl and gave me my breakfast. I accepted it with a nod.

I watched her do the same for everyone else, before looking down at the food. Anxious, I was. Hungry, I was not. My stomach was a ball of nerves, and now, more than ever, I wanted to get out of here.

"You told Star Archer you'd be willing to take a message to the Kavylak soldiers. Doom Breaker is giving it to them."

My gaze flicked up to Dawn Seer when she spoke.

"Oh, right, of course." I said. "That makes sense."

I was glad she'd spoken. It made me feel a little better to hear her voice the words without my having to be the one to ask if this was the reason they were with Doom Breaker. Still, I couldn't shake the worry.

Stop worrying, Megan. Eat.

Ash Dancer was right. I needed my strength, and I had made a promise that I wouldn't forget Rral's lesson. It didn't matter what I might or might not face, I should eat. I had to be smart and energy was important, so I ate.

I finished the entire bowl of food in silence, barely tasting any of it.

"When we're finished eating, I will help to prepare the horses for your journey," Ash Dancer said.

"Thank you," I said to her.

She nodded. "I've put a few things together for you to eat, so you won't need to hunt and forage along the way," she added.

Dawn Seer looked at Ash Dancer, surprised. She wasn't the only one. I was also surprised by her generosity and was even a little touched. That was incredibly kind of her, and based on Dawn Seer's reaction, I assumed her generosity was out of the ordinary.

Out of the ordinary or not, I wasn't about to question it.

"That's very gracious of you, Ash Dancer. I truly appreciate that. Thank you." I nodded to her deeply, hoping to convey my gratitude.

She returned the gesture, and for a moment, I felt like we had an unspoken bond. What that bond was, I couldn't say, but it was the feeling that mattered to me. It made me believe that I could trust her, and I really needed to feel like I could trust someone right now.

"Want me to braid your hair before you go?" Ehsaig asked me.

"Sure," I smiled to her.

She nodded, looking thrilled, and started wolfing down the rest of her food.

"Slow down," Ash Dancer told her with a chuckle.

I laughed a little, too, finding Ehsaig's eagerness to braid my hair both endearing and amusing.

Not a minute after she had swallowed the last bite of her food, she rose from where she'd been seated and stepped up behind me. Immediately, she began to gently work a comb through my hair. It felt nice and calming. A feeling of nostalgia erupted inside me with the sensation. I shut my eyes, remembering when Aunt Vera used to comb my hair when I was a little girl.

What I wouldn't give to see you right now, Aunt Vera. I hope you're okay.

The comb left my hair, and I could feel Ehsaig's tiny fingers expertly weaving my hair into several braids. When she was finished, I opened my eyes and raised my hands to my hair, inspecting her work. She had made six braids, which she'd then braided together to make two larger braids on either side of my head. While I was no stranger to hair braids, I couldn't say that I had ever sported this style before. Without a mirror, I had no way of knowing how it looked but, honestly, all I cared about was that my hair was out of my face.

"This is very nice, Ehsaig," I complemented her. "I've never had my hair styled like this before. You're very good at braiding."

She beamed at my praise, looking proud. "I'm good at it. If you stayed longer, I would teach you."

"I have no doubt you would. I can see that you're a very good teacher. You have a lot of patience."

Ehsaig nodded, looking pleased.

"I'm taking the children to play," Dawn Seer spoke. "You should help Ash Dancer and then find your man," she told me.

"Oh. Yes, alright," I responded, a little taken off guard by her abrupt declaration and instruction. "Thank you for letting us share your fire, Dawn Seer." I said with both appreciation and respect on behalf of the guys and me.

She gave me a respectful nod. "Thank you for sharing it, too."

Without another word, she got up, took the hands of Ehsaig and Bediagq, and headed outside with them. I watched them leave, wondering if that would be the last time I'd see them.

Turning to Ash Dancer, I said, "You have two beautiful children, Ash Dancer."

She smiled. "They are the joy in my life. Ehsaig will be very strong when she is grown. Bediagq will be a keen hunter. He thinks before he acts."

I nodded, genuinely glad that her children brought her joy, especially since she still had to mourn for their father, who wasn't actually dead. I was still fuzzy about the logistics of that one but now wasn't the time or the place to ask questions about Amarogq or their situation. And anyway, it wasn't my business.

Ash Dancer stood, picking up a brown leather sling bag, and carried it over her shoulder. Taking it as the cue that we were leaving, I got to my feet and followed her out of the house.

"Do you know the right direction for leading your men home?"

"No," I replied honestly. "But Mez and Keavren know the way."

This was a good thing, because on top of having a crappy sense of direction at the best of times, I hadn't the foggiest idea where I was.

"You should know, too," she said and strolled over to a tree at the edge of the camp, gesturing toward it. "See the trees like this? Their branches grow only one way. Walk the opposite way. These branches point toward the land of the People."

I watched her and studied the tree, paying close attention to what she was telling me. She had a point. It certainly wouldn't hurt me to know the right direction.

"Thank you. I'll remember that," I told her.

She nodded. "Also, as you travel, use your nose. Smell for water. You'll be able to smell rivers when they are not too far if you pay attention. The water you carry will not last the whole journey. You will need to refill the water bladder."

I nodded. This was also good to know, but again, I was sure that Mez and Keavren would have already known this, since they must be used to going on missions.

Seeming satisfied with the basic instructions she'd given me, she walked up to two horses that were being saddled by Rain Traveller.

Rain Traveller looked up at us when we approached. His expression was grim. I didn't like it. Every uneasy feeling that I had managed to quell came rushing back. Something wasn't right.

"They're ready to go," Rain Traveller told Ash Dancer. "Fed first thing and watered."

"Thank you Rain Traveller," Ash Dancer said. Rain Traveller nodded and left without another look or word.

Ash Dancer began to take things out of her bag and put them into the horses' bags.

"Both horses carry water," she told me. "I will put food in the bags of both horses, too."

Hey! Didn't we have three horses? What happened to Vacant Horse? Meh, I'll let the guys decide if they want to fight that battle.

"Thank you," I responded. "Is he alright?" I asked about Rain Traveller.

"He is," she said simply, continuing to pack the bag. "Your man and the other man's weapons are wrapped in the leather tied to the side of the horses," she added, securing the bags.

She then stepped up to me and held out a bone knife. "Here." She said. "In case you need it along the way home."

I reached out and took the knife from her, observing the simple blade with both interest and dread. I didn't want to imagine any circumstance where I might have to use this as a weapon and not a tool.

"Thank you, Ash Dancer. You've been very kind and patient with me. I truly appreciate all your help. I know that my man and our friend will be grateful, too." I genuinely hoped she knew that I did appreciate her help more than I could ever express to her.

Ash Dancer gave only a slight tilt of her head in response. It was an odd gesture. Maybe it was just my uneasiness and paranoia getting the better of me, but it was as if she had acknowledged my words but didn't feel my thanks was necessary.

"I think it's time you find them. You will want to travel for as much of the day as you can."

I nodded to her. I was fine with finding the guys and getting out of here.

"Where would I find them? Does Doom Breaker have a house?"

"Yes," Ash Dancer confirmed. "It is the first one, there." She gestured with her hand to what was very obviously the largest longhouse-style structure in the camp. "I'll stay with the horses."

I nodded to her with a smile, and tucking the bone dagger into my pocket, I headed over to the house. No one was standing outside guarding the entrance, which was blocked by a curtain of leather. Taking a breath to calm my nerves, I decided to just go in, propelled by the knowledge that I'd be leaving soon.

Pushing aside the flap, I entered and took two steps inside before I stopped and stared at the scene before me.

The woman, who had to be the Mawkipaw, Doom Breaker, was seated at the centre hearth. She was heavily decorated with lots of red, white, and black feathers and beads woven into her long, sleek black hair. Some of her hair was plaited into small braids. There didn't seem to be any particular pattern to her hairstyle, but at the same time, it also seemed very deliberate. The outfit she wore was heavily decorated with beads, quills, and other eye-catching stones and wooden ornaments that likely held some significance I didn't know about. Her eyes were heavily painted with black eyeliner and smoky eye makeup, further adding to her striking appearance.

To say this woman looked intense would be an understatement. Her presence was as serious and frightening as a heart attack.

There were a lot of people around her hearth, mostly large men and women. They were engaged in discussion. By how solemn everyone was and the business-style feel of the atmosphere, I doubted that these people were her family. Maybe they were the village's main hunters, warriors, or her advisers. Whatever the case, it didn't really matter to me. What did matter was that Mez and Keavren weren't among them.

I quickly tore my gaze away from the hearth and did a quick scan of the space that had a similar smoky haze to Dawn Seer and Ash Dancer's house. Mez and Keavren were nowhere to be seen.

Maybe they were done talking to her and had returned to the other house in search of me.

"Do you seek to speak with Doom Breaker?"

I snapped back to attention, looking at the large man who addressed me.

"Yes," I said. My voice sounding an octave higher than normal.

Smooth, Megan.

He nodded and walked up to Doom Breaker, leaning down toward her, speaking quietly. She turned her head sharply to look at me, her outfit clacking with her movement. The Mawkipaw's fierce gaze bore into me with such an intensity, I took a step back.

On second thought, maybe this is a bad idea, and I should just leave.

"I will speak to her." I heard Doom Breaker say, foiling my plans of escape. Her fierce gaze had yet to leave me.

The man nodded in my direction, signaling that I could approach. Willing my feet to move forward, I walked up to the hearth and stood in front of her, the fire pit between us. She didn't move, remaining on her elevated seat composed of a mound of soft furs and leathers. She watched me the whole time. I felt like I was on trial for my life. I suddenly wondered if that was why "Doom" was a part of her name, because I felt like I was heading toward my doom, and she was about to deliver it.

Don't be ridiculous, Megan.

Ignoring everyone else sitting around the hearth, I focused on Doom Breaker, who continued to stare at me, obviously waiting for me to speak first. I opened my mouth to greet her and realized I had no idea how to properly address their Mawkipaw. The last thing I wanted to do was insult or offend her, so I decided to resist my inclination to act like I was in a bad movie and call her "Mighty Doom Breaker" and just kept it simple and polite, hoping that would be respectful enough.

"Hello, Doom Breaker. Thank you for speaking with me."

My greeting was met with silence.

Crap! Did I just say that in Kavylak?

For the second time I debated hightailing it out of there.

"You are the Megan woman," Doom Breaker finally spoke. Her voice was confident and stern. "Mez is your man, and Keavren is his Warrior friend."

It wasn't lost on me that these were statements, not questions. This woman wasn't fooling around, nor was she interested in exchanging pleasantries or small talk.

"Yes," I confirmed. "I am Megan, Mez is my man, and Keavren is our friend."

She gave a single nod. "We are preparing for you to leave. You'll have your Skydashers soon."

I looked at her, confused. "Skydashers?"

Wasn't that Dawn Seer's spirit bird?

She observed me for a moment before she spoke, "Birds that send a message." She didn't hide in her tone or her expression that she was both unimpressed with me and thought that I was slow in the mind.

Um. Okay? So, what? They're giving us some sort of homing pigeon to take back with us to send a message?

Weird. Maybe Mez and Keavren would understand the meaning. Whatever, as long as we get out of here, I couldn't have cared less if they'd given us a monkey to take back.

"Thank you." I said, still remaining polite, even though I felt like this woman was one of the rudest people I'd ever met, especially since it wasn't like we invited ourselves to stay in her village. We were all but forced to! Frightening as she might be, I didn't like her. Oddly, this made me feel a little more confident, and I stood a little taller. "Where are Mez and Keavren?" I asked, firmly, feeling done with this meeting and wanting to escape her presence.

"They are just outside the village."

That still didn't give me much of a clue as to their whereabouts, but I had a feeling Ash Dancer would know, so I'd just ask her.

"Thank you and thank you for your hospitality," I added genuinely.

"Go back to your land and forget about this place. Never come back," she commanded, narrowing her eyes at me. "We don't want your lies to infect our water and air."

Wow! I get the feeling she doesn't like me, either.

My expression hardened, all nervousness evacuated my body, and the politeness left my voice.

"We won't be back," I stated, returning the intensity of her gaze with my own, doing everything in my power to make it clear that we had no interest in coming back to this place for any reason. I was starting to wonder if Amarogq took off because he had such a nasty Mawkipaw!

Doom Breaker nodded and regarded me with one last look that told me that if we tried to return, we'd be shot dead on sight. She then turned in all her outfit-clacking-glory to face one of the women at the hearth and started to speak with her. I ceased to exist to her.

That was fine with me. I took that as my cue to leave and promptly walked out of the house, never looking back.

Motivated by the frustration of being treated so rudely, I sought out Ash Dancer to find out where the guys were, so we could start our journey away from this place. She was still with the horses.

"Doom Breaker said that Mez and Keavren are just outside the village. Do you know what direction that is? Should I bring the horses?"

"Yes," Ash Dancer answered, softly and indicated the direction. "I will bring the horses and what you need to travel."

The softness of her voice reminded me that I wasn't mad at Ash Dancer. She, unlike Doom Breaker, had been very helpful. I gave her a little smile and placed a hand on her shoulder.

"Thank you for all your help."

She rested one of her hands on top of mine. "I think of you in a friendly way, even if you will never return." She curled her fingers around mine for a brief moment and then released my hand. "Go," she implored me. "You shouldn't wait."

I nodded to her. I thought of her in a friendly way, too, but she was right. I had to get a move on.

I jogged off in the direction she had indicated, and slowed to a walk once I reached the woods, starting to wonder if I was heading the right way. There wasn't anyone around, just a lot of tall trees. There wasn't even much noise beyond the distant activity of the village, the gentle wind rustling the leaves, and the sound of my boots thudding on the soft forest floor, with the occasional twigs snapping beneath my feet.

"Mez?" I called out, finally. "Keavren?"

Seriously. Where are you guys? If you're playing some hide-and-seek trick on me, I swear...

I huffed in annoyance as I kept walking, knowing I'd likely have to eventually return to Ash Dancer to ask for her help in tracking them down.

Why does my internal compass have to suck so badly?

I continued on for several more minutes without any luck. Frustrated, I clenched my fists and turned to head back toward Ash Dancer. I took one step and something wet struck my shoulder. It felt like a hard rain drop, but it wasn't accompanied by the sound of more rain hitting leaves. I tensed.

Oh my god! I swear, if one of those Skydasher birds we're supposed to bring back just pooped on me...

Tentatively, I glanced at my shoulder, expecting to see bird droppings and found none. Whatever it was, it wasn't white and I couldn't make out the colour on the black shirt I wore. Curiously, I touched the tip of my finger to the wet substance. I withdrew it and let out a startled gasp when I saw the pad of my finger was bright red.

Oh, god! Please tell me this isn't what I think it is.

Terrified and unable to resist the urge, I slowly tilted my head back to look above me.

All colour drained from my face and a strangled scream erupted from my lips as another drop of blood fell and hit my cheek.

I had found them.

Chapter 16

Irys

The smell of antiseptic greeted me even before I stepped in through the door of the infirmary.

Mr. Rolern walked ahead of me and began writing on his notepad to allow him to communicate with a nurse, who had very little interest in trying to be pleasant with him.

"Through the doors. Second room on the left," was all she said before she returned to her work as though we had ceased to exist.

I smiled at the nurse, though I knew she wouldn't actually see me do it, and turned to head through the door with Mr. Rolern. We entered a narrow corridor painted pale grey and stepped up to the second door, which was open.

Inside, Lieutenant Fhurrk was lying on a narrow bed with his eyes closed. The space was a sparse, cramped one with only a small shelved bedside table next to the bed. I noticed a number of small corked vials and tubes containing different brightly-coloured liquids and wondered what fascinating medicines they contained. I found my mind wondering if any were responsible for the calm, restful sleep the Sefaline appeared to be enjoying.

He was covered to the chest with a white sheet and a dark grey blanket, leaving the Sefaline markings on his arms completely visible. I couldn't imagine ever becoming accustomed to seeing the sharp, winding designs.

Stepping quietly to the bedside, I reached out and gently rested my hand on top of his, with the intention of remaining quiet by his side while he slept.

It startled me when his eyes opened, and he looked directly at me with confusion. I hadn't expected him to wake.

"Lieutenant Fhurrk, it's Irys Godeleva. How are you feeling?" I greeted him in a voice just above a whisper.

His confusion didn't seem to ease, and his gaze darted to Mr. Rolern.

"Sunetar?" he inquired. Now it was Mr. Rolern who looked confused, giving a small shake of his head to Lieutenant Fhurrk's query.

Lieutenant Fhurrk looked as though he had intended to say something else to Mr. Rolern, but the movements of his mouth weren't accompanied by any sound.

"This is Mr. Rolern. He's my guard," I explained to Lieutenant Fhurrk in the hopes of easing some of his confusion.

Lieutenant Fhurrk seemed to accept my explanation and turned his attention back to me.

"Why are you here?" he asked groggily and in a quiet voice.

"A Traveller appeared at the house where we were staying in Gbat Rher. She brought you here and accidentally brought me with you. I will be sent home again, but it could be up to two days before the Traveller returns. For now, I am a guest of Captain Wintheare." Squeezing his hand a little, I smiled at him, glad to see that he was recovering. "I wanted to check on you to see how you were faring."

His brow furrowed in concentration as he listened. Occasionally, he glanced at Mr. Rolern but always returned his attention to me.

"I am healing. I will live now," he said in a tone I'd come to interpret as friendly as he'd made it clear to me that if he was not feeling friendly, he would sound far more aggressive.

"I'm relieved to hear that." I was. Simply knowing that Lieutenant Fhurrk's life was no longer in danger lifted a great weight from my shoulders that I hadn't realized I'd continued to carry.

Thank you, Great Goddess. Thank you.

"You shouldn't be here."

"I have asked if I am permitted to visit the infirmary. Captain Wintheare told me it was acceptable for me to visit you."

"Does the Knight who wants to be your mate know you are here?"

I smiled, amused at Lieutenant Fhurrk's description of Dynan. My cheeks didn't flush, though I knew they likely should have. Perhaps I was becoming accustomed to the Lieutenant's direct speech. Or, perhaps Kavylak was hardening my complexion to such statements.

"I have been granted a daily letter exchange with him. Another Traveller who cannot transport people is carrying the messages back and forth. I have informed Sir Fhirell as to what is happening and have received a letter in reply," I told him.

He nodded, seeming satisfied by my response, and shut his eyes for a moment before opening them to look upon me once more. I didn't imagine that he would be awake for much longer.

"Is there anything I can do to make you more comfortable? Do you have any family? Have they been notified?"

"I have a mate," he said. "She knows."

A mate! How delightful!

"Is she Sefaline, too?"

"She is part Sefaline."

"Does she have markings like you do?" I asked curiously.

I wasn't sure whether or not it was my imagination, but he seemed to soften as he thought on her.

"She has markings. She has spots. She is not of my clan," he explained, holding out his arm to show the sharp twisted lines that composed his own marks.

"How interesting. Those marks are hereditary, and your families share similar marks." I was fascinated.

"Something like that," he confirmed with a small nod of his head.

"I hope you like spots," I said with a bit of a giggle.

"I like her spots," he replied. Though his tone hadn't changed, the statement somehow sounded very romantic to me.

He yawned, and I could see his energy draining. He was forcing himself to stay awake because I was there. Certainly, that couldn't have been good for his healing.

Giving his hand a little squeeze, I started humming until he shut his eyes, looking peaceful. After a moment, I quietly sang a gentle song he'd seemed to respond well to when we were in Gbat Rher. Before long, he'd fallen asleep. Releasing his hand, I kissed his cheek very lightly before turning to Mr. Rolern with a smile.

Mr. Rolern smiled in return and nodded to our unspoken decision to leave the room. As I stood, I allowed my hand to sweep by the shelf of vials, palming two of them, one containing a pale blue liquid, the other containing a bright orange one. I wasn't entirely sure why I did it. It wasn't a completely conscious decision, but I slipped them into my vest pocket on the way out the door.

We didn't waste any time leaving the infirmary and returning to my quarters. I stopped outside the door, sorry that I would have to part company with my companion.

"As much as I loathe to ask him for anything, would you please send for Lieutenant Atrix so that he may bring me my lunch?"

Mr. Rolern nodded and quickly wrote on his notepad, holding it up for me to see.

"I'll have him alerted," it read.

"Thank you. Perhaps, after lunch, I will sit near the door and read more of our book."

Chuckling soundlessly, he nodded and stepped into position to guard my door.

Inside my room, I locked the door, set the book down, and washed up, taking my time as I knew that there was very little there for me to do.

Fortunately, there was a knock at my door after only a short while.

"Who's there?" I queried.

"Edda," came the woman's apathetic voice.

Unlocking the door, I opened it to allow Edda entry.

"Ah, this must be my lunch," I said conversationally as I stepped out of her way and observed the tray Edda was carrying. This time, it was similar to the one Lieutenant Atrix had brought me for breakfast, not the tray she'd brought with the food against which he had cautioned me.

"Yes," she confirmed and set the tray on my table.

"Thank you."

"You're welcome, Miss Godeleva. Is there anything else you require?"

"No, thank you, Edda. I'm well for now."

She nodded and headed out without another word. I locked the door behind her and returned to the table to find out what was under the dome.

To my relief and delight, I'd been served a fresh salad with vegetables and cold chicken. There was a slightly fruity vinaigrette to go with it. For dessert, I had an airy pastry with a touch of jam. The meal was light, filling, and comforting, particularly as it was complemented by another pot of Sylizan tea.

I enjoyed my lunch, set my dishes outside my quarters away from Mr. Rolern, and spent my afternoon reading by the door for him until we'd both had enough of the book. I used more of my day by adding to the letter I was writing to Sir Fhirell, before I practiced several hairstyles in my mirror.

The hours moved sluggishly and when Edda delivered my dinner, I was relieved, not because I was hungry but because eating the meal offered me a new activity to pass the time.

That evening, when there was a knock at my door, I'd been staring out the window. I had been daydreaming about Sir Fhirell, wondering if he had finished another day of work with Drudvis. If so, perhaps he was now watching the same sky, also wishing the time would pass more quickly.

"Who is it?" I asked, rising and approaching the door.

"Captain Wintheare." His voice was flat and emotionless as always.

I opened the door and greeted him. "Good evening, Captain."

"Good evening, Miss Godeleva. May I come in?"

"Yes, of course," I replied, stepping out of his way.

He entered, and I indicated the small sitting area. I made use of the chair while he sat at one end of the sofa.

"I trust your day and treatment have been satisfactory?" He began our conversation.

"More pleasant than I had expected," I admitted. "Lieutenant Atrix' behaviour was rather surprising. However, I feel that we have come to an understanding. He has sent lovely meals and has provided me with a change of clothes but has respected my wish not to be disturbed with regular visits."

"He is a Charmer," Captain Wintheare agreed. "Such behaviours are in his nature."

At first, I believed the statement to be sarcasm, but the captain seemed quite humourless, and I had to assume that Lieutenant Atrix' actions had become expected and accepted among the Warriors.

"Mr. Rolern has been a steady guard and a pleasant companion. He accompanied me when I went to the library, when I took some air outside, and when I went to visit Lieutenant Fhurrk. If there is any way for me to register my satisfaction with his performance, I'd appreciate it if you would do so on my behalf, Captain."

"Good," he replied simply, adding nothing else.

"Edda has also been very accommodating, though the clothing she initially brought me was entirely inappropriate. I don't imagine she is accustomed to dressing Sylizan ladies so that may, of course, be forgiven. Lieutenant Atrix resolved that situation well enough." I felt as though I was required to keep the discussion moving. Captain Wintheare was not at all skilled in the art of conversation.

"Good," he said again, not even bothering to change the inflection in his voice over the last time he'd used the word. "Have you any requests or concerns?"

I started to shake my head when a question rose to the front of my mind, and I stopped the gesture.

"Who is Sunetar?" I asked with innocent curiosity.

"Sunetar is a Warrior," he replied.

I wasn't entirely sure how to process that answer. Instead of pursuing the topic any more, I moved on to another question. I was certain that I would regret not trying to learn more about this name Lieutenant Fhurrk, in his confusion, had directed at Mr. Rolern, but I couldn't think of anything else to ask about it.

"Has there been any word from the Traveller who will bring me home?"

"Zayset is not due back for another day as I have already explained."

"Of course. I wondered if the situation may have changed."

"If the situation changes, Miss Godeleva, you will be advised. We have no wish to keep you here any longer than necessary. If there is nothing else, I will bid you a good evening and will check on you again tomorrow morning."

I rose, and he did the same, heading to the door.

"Pleasant evening, Captain."

With a nod of his head, he left my quarters, and I locked the door behind him.

Deciding to settle in for the night, I brushed out my hair and curled up on one side of the sofa with the book I'd borrowed from the library for myself, not the one I selected for Mr. Rolern. I was starting to feel quite sleepy when I was startled back to alertness by a knock at the door.

"Who's there?" I called from where I was, though I took the opportunity to rise and approach the door to hear the answer.

"Your favourite Warrior Twinkles."

I could hear Lieutenant Atrix' perfect smile in his words. In fact, it was almost as though I could sense his eyebrows waggling.

"What is it?" I queried without opening the door. It was rude of me, but I was hoping that the purpose of Lieutenant Atrix' visit could be shared without forcing me to face him. Regardless of whether or not he could be trusted, I felt uncertain of my own trustworthiness when he was around.

"I've brought you something," he replied, sounding amused. "It's friendly. I promise."

What could I do? Unless I intended to continue interrogating him through the closed door, I would have to open it and see him. Pathetically, I opened the door just enough to peek out to see if I could spot what he had to offer. To my simultaneous horror and delight, he was dressed not in a Warrior's uniform but in a civilian's button-up shirt and trousers, and he was holding a tray with a tea set and a small plate of delicious-looking treats.

"Are you hoping to join me for tea?" I asked, opening the door in the hopes of rescuing at least a portion of my dignity. As I posed the question, I noticed that there were indeed two cups on the tray.

"I am, if you'll allow me to. I'd like to apologize for being unpleasant with you earlier," he replied. He looked sincere, but I couldn't, for the life of me, decide whether or not I believed him.

"Do you think it would be more appropriate for us to take our tea in a common space?" I asked, dreading the thought of how it would look if I were to invite him in, particularly at this hour.

A grin slid across his perfectly symmetrical lips, and it appeared as though he was stifling a laugh.

"No. I assure you, you're quite safe with me, and no one would think you indecent for inviting me in for tea."

Taking the opportunity to glance at Mr. Rolern for his opinion on the matter, I felt greatly reassured when my guard – and friend – smiled at me and nodded to my unspoken question. The little communication between us gave me an idea, and I smiled at the pride I felt in myself for coming up with it.

"May I request the presence of my guard as a chaperone?"

"Certainly, if it will make you feel better," Lieutenant Atrix replied without a moment's hesitation to consider the matter.

I nodded and smiled to both men as I stepped back into my quarters to allow them to enter. While I'm certain that if Lieutenant Atrix had had any dubious intentions, there would likely be little Mr. Rolern could do to stop him, it still made me feel much better to have my guard watching over me inside my quarters while this particular Warrior was visiting.

Lieutenant Atrix set the tray down on the table while Mr. Rolern took his position inside the door, just as he had been in the corridor.

I approached the table and Lieutenant Atrix waited for me to take my seat before he made use of his own chair. It amused me as he poured the tea for us both, offering me the various condiments he had brought with him.

"I hope you've been enjoying the tea I've been adding to your meals," he said as he casually teased a slice of lemon with his spoon, causing the fruit to bob in the water as though it was giggling from the sensation.

"Yes, thank you. I do enjoy tea with or after my meals. It is comforting to me."

"I thought it might be. Lucky for you, Acksil just recently replaced all the coffee in my quarters with tea. Otherwise, I wouldn't have had any to give you." His grin was equally wicked and alluring.

"Oh?" I was forced to grin, and I sipped my tea to give me something to do with my hands. Although I'd later notice that the tea was fine and soothing, and the treats were delicate and flavourful, at that moment I noticed nothing of what I was tasting. At that moment, my attention was entirely absorbed by his grin.

"Is my unfortunate situation humorous to you, Miss Godeleva?" he asked, reflecting my smile.

"Of course not as I don't see it as unfortunate at all."

At that, he laughed outright. I bubbled with pride. The smile grew on my face and became more genuine at the same time.

"Does this mean Lieutenant Acksilivcs has returned?"

"Not to my knowledge. At least, I haven't seen him if he has. If you'd like, I can check tomorrow, and if he is here, I can let him know you'd like him to pay you a visit."

"Thank you. I'd like that," I said appreciatively. "Will I be given fresh clothing tomorrow?"

He nodded. "It will be delivered with your breakfast in the morning. It'll be similar to what you're wearing now."

"Thank you again."

"What is the deal between you and Acksil, anyway?"

I was taken aback. "There is no 'deal' at all. I wish only to thank him for..." I paused, realizing that Mr. Rolern was in the room and that I wasn't sure if I would cause trouble for Lieutenants Acksilivcs and Atrix if I revealed that they'd kept me safe in Fort Picogeal. "...for that time I saw the two of you very briefly. I've come to realize that the intentions then were not ill in nature."

His brow raised as he listened, but it evened out, and he nodded. "If you don't see him during your short stay here, I will pass that on for you if you'd like."

"I would appreciate that, thank you...Provided you don't add any 'deal' to it," I smirked.

"You could write him a note, so he could see it in your own words, if you want," he responded with a chuckle.

"Should I not see him, perhaps I will take you up on your offer," I agreed. "Does he live in this building? Is this where the Warriors live?"

"Yes, in fact, he lives two floors above these quarters," he said, somehow sounding as though he was meddling, even as he merely answered my question.

"Thank you again."

He nodded and finished his tea.

"Lieutenant Atrix, what is a Charmer?" I asked as the word Captain Wintheare had used to explain the roguish behaviors came swimming into my mind.

"It's what I am," he replied as though this short explanation would be enough.

"And, what are you?"

"Irresistible."

I huffed childishly. "What is that supposed to mean in a practical sense?"

"It means that, at any moment I choose, I could make you find me absolutely irresistible."

"By magic?" I asked, trying not to give in to the shiver his words sent up my spine.

"It's not magic. It's a skill. An enhanced skill."

"You had a skill and somehow improved it? Through lessons of some sort?"

"Something like that."

"How do you mean?"

"Something like classified."

I sighed. "Do you plan to use this enhanced skill on me, Lieutenant Atrix?" I wasn't certain that I wanted to know the answer. Moreover, I also wasn't sure if I could trust any answer he did give me.

"No," he said quite simply.

"Should I believe what you say?"

He smiled. "You'll believe what you believe, Twinkles, regardless of what I tell you."

"Why do you call me 'Twinkles'?"

"Because light dances in your eyes in a way that makes them twinkle and sparkle like stars."

A flush rose to my cheeks. "I'm sure they're quite ordinary," I said, stumbling over my words.

"I've seen ordinary. Trust me. You're anything but ordinary."

"Here, perhaps, but that's only because I'm Sylizan."

He chuckled "Being Sylizan has nothing to do with it. You could be from anywhere, and you'd still be extraordinary."

"Lieutenant Atrix, I do believe you are saying these things to show me what it is when you are a Charmer."

"I'm not," he said lightly. "But, as I said before, you'll only believe what you believe."

I took a silent moment to think about his words as I finished my tea.

"Why is it that you have *truly* come here, Lieutenant Atrix. You could have apologized to me through a brief conversation at the door or even through a note. Why the tea?" I asked as delicately as I could.

"I thought it might be nice to have a friendly cup of tea."

"Is there no special woman in your life who would object to this time you are spending with me in my quarters?"

"Oh, I have girlfriends, Twinkles," he grinned wolfishly. "But I have friends, too."

"That's not what I mean. I was referring to someone far more important to you, and who might become jealous if she were to learn that you were here."

"Yes. I have many girlfriends who would be jealous if they were to learn I was here." He grinned. "I'm a Charmer."

I gave up on trying to gain a serious answer from him. We both knew what I was asking, and now we both knew he would never reply with a direct answer.

"Can Charmers love?" I asked, taking the conversation in a slightly new direction.

"Of course."

"Do you?"

"I love, but not in the way you're asking. I don't have that one oh-so special woman in my life who can't wait to marry me and have our six children."

I frowned. "Does that not sadden you?"

"No," he said quite frankly.

"I would find such a life very difficult. I want love in my life."

"Most people do. I'm not like most people."

"What is it that fulfills you, if not the pursuit of love or family?"

"Being a Warrior fulfills me. I love my life."

"Making young women giggle in the library and bringing tea to your Captain's guest fulfills you?" I asked doubtfully.

To that, he laughed. "Not exactly. No more than reading a romance novel fulfills you. It's just a part of my day. I didn't say that every minute was fulfilling."

I felt my cheeks flush again as he pointed to the novel I'd been reading to Mr. Rolern, and I attempted to turn the conversation toward him again.

"In that case, what parts of your day do you find fulfilling?"

"Why do you care?" He asked, looking as though his grin would break into a laugh at any moment.

"I was merely making polite conversation. I've finished my tea. If you'd prefer our discussion come to an end, you have your excuse to leave," I countered, trying to find my way out of the losing end of our talk.

He nodded, accepting my position. "Fair enough. I was simply curious about your motive in asking. The parts of my day that I find the most fulfilling are those I spend with my brothers, especially my other half, Lieutenant Stargrace."

"Your other half? Do you mean you have a special relationship with Lieutenant Stargrace or is he another Charmer?"

"Lieutenant Stargrace is a Charmer, but he is a she," he grinned.

"My apologies, I'd understood you to mean that the other Charmer was your brother."

"She is. She's the female member of our brotherhood. Don't over think it."

I had a feeling that I was already over thinking the issue. *How confusing!*

"Like I said," he chuckled at my befuddled expression, "don't think on it too much. I am going to bid you goodnight, Miss Godeleva. I have a date, and I'd like to be on time."

"Of course. Thank you for the tea."

"It was nice talking with you, Twinkles."

Heading toward the door, he paused, looking over his shoulder toward Mr. Rolern.

"Come along, Little Guard," he said and smiled to me before exiting with Mr. Rolern on his heels.

After giving Lieutenant Atrix enough time to make his way down the corridor, I opened my door and peeked out at Mr. Rolern, who was now standing at his post once again.

"Do you like tea?" I asked him quietly.

He smiled but shook his head.

"What about cookies?"

His smile grew, and he nodded.

Leaving the door as it was, I jogged over to the tea tray, collecting a few of the tea biscuits into a napkin and bringing the bundle back to the door. Peeking out to make sure no one was around, I passed the little package out to him.

Mr. Rolern looked very pleased and opened up the napkin, selecting a cookie, which he stuffed into his mouth and chewed with a happy smile that was warped by his bulging cheek. The rest, he tucked into a pocket, looking boyish.

"Have a good evening. I hope you're relieved for the night soon. Perhaps I shall see you tomorrow," I said, and just in case this was the last I was to see of him, I stepped out and kissed his cheek. I couldn't imagine how I would have survived the day without Mr. Rolern. I wanted him to know it meant something to me.

"Goodnight," I said as I stepped back into my doorway.

"Goodnight," he mouthed in return.

Stepping in, I shut my door and locked it.

I decided to prepare for bed and read for a while as I had nothing better to do. It was a good thing that I'd made that decision as only a quarter of an hour had passed before I started feeling exceptionally tired.

Dressed in my nightgown, I climbed into the bed and rested my head down on the pillow, abandoning the book. I was too tired to shut it and return it to my side table. I was too tired to keep my eyes open. How very suddenly this exhaustion had arrived...

Chapter 17

Megan

I stared in shock at a sight so horrifying it crippled my senses.

Several feet above me, Mez and Keavren hung, alive, suspended from the trees. They had been strung up by their arms, which were tied to ropes that held them open and fully extended on either side of their body. They had been stripped to the waist and large black feathers had been jabbed into their skin all along the backs of their arms and shoulder blades. Blood ran down their skin from where the quills of the feathers had pierced their flesh. They looked like grotesque, mangled birds.

A wave of nausea hit me as I was overcome by the sickening realization that Mez and Keavren were the Skydasher birds of which Doom Breaker spoke. They were the message these cruel and twisted people meant for me to bring back to Kavylak.

Although they made no sound, I knew the men were in excruciating pain. Their eyes were tightly shut, sweat glistened on their faces, and their chests were rising and falling with their staggered breaths, which could barely be heard over the rustling leaves.

"Mez? Keavren?" I hardly recognized the sound of my own voice.

Both of them opened their eyes to look at me when I spoke.

"W--what happened? W--why?" I stammered and shook my head to clear my thoughts. "I--I'll try to get you down." I added, but there was no promise in what I had said. There was no substance behind my words. I had no idea what to think, say, or do.

Keavren shut his eyes again, but Mez kept his gaze fixed on me.

"Leave us. Get away. Run south," Mez rasped between shaky breaths. "Steal a horse if you can. Run," he repeated, shutting his eyes against the pain and clenching his teeth as he tried in vain to adjust his arms to relieve the pressure and strain.

Watching him struggling pushed me over the edge and my fight or flight response kicked in.

Listen to him, Megan. Run!

Overcome by fear that I could end up strung up in a tree, too, I nearly turned and ran. Instinctively, I knew saving myself would likely be the smartest course of action. I also knew there was no way I would be able to live with the guilt of leaving them like this, especially when I owed them both for saving my life. I was their only hope of getting down. I forced my feet to stay put, shut my eyes, inhaled deeply, and slowly let out the breath.

You can do this, Megan. If you could save Irys' life, you can save theirs. This isn't the first monster you've faced on this world. Find. A. Way. Fight!

Thoughts of Galnar and Doom Breaker bubbled up and boiled off my terror. I let this anger consume me. My hesitation transformed into conviction, and I opened my eyes with new focus.

"I'm getting you down," I told Mez and Keavren. "I'm not leaving here without you. I'll…"

The heavy thud of something hitting the forest floor close behind me cut me off. I whirled around sharply, drawing from my pocket the bone knife Ash Dancer had given me, ready to face whomever dared to be in my presence.

Ash Dancer stood, alone, a few feet from me, the bag she had been carrying was at her feet. She held my gaze. Her face was without emotion, but her body language, and the understanding I read from her eyes told me she wasn't here to make the situation worse.

"Can you climb a tree?" she asked, her voice calm and direct.

"Yes."

"Take your knife." She nodded to the weapon in my hand. "We're cutting them down." She turned and began to climb one of the trees to which the men's ropes were attached.

She didn't have to tell me twice. Looking up, I found the other tree with the ropes attached to it and moved up to it. Returning the knife to my pocket, I jumped up to grab onto the tree's lowest branch, hauling myself up. In truth, I wasn't exactly an expert tree climber. The last time I'd climbed one, I had done so with Rral's assistance. The purpose had been to hide from Warriors, not save them. I knew as the bark bit into my hands and the ground grew farther and farther away, that I should have been scared. I wasn't. I was so overcome with determination, that if Ash Dancer had asked me if I could fly, I would have told her I could, and would have found a way to do it.

It was strange, but this feeling was akin to the one I'd had when I'd freed Irys from her cell. I felt propelled by a similar unnatural focus and determination that I didn't even know I possessed. Although with Irys, I had felt desperate to save her, and ready to sacrifice my life for hers, this time, the feeling was something else entirely. I didn't feel that I was sacrificing myself at all. No. I wanted to do it and without knowing why, I knew I could.

I stopped climbing when the rope was within cutting distance and steadied myself. Taking the knife from my pocket, I looking at Ash Dancer, who was in the tree across from me, waiting.

"Cut one of them down," she instructed. "I will stop him when he swings this way. Then, I will cut him down, and we will do the other one."

Turning my attention to the ropes, I quickly sawed through one of them, deciding not to waste the time to find out whom it held. When it released, I saw a terrified wide-eyed Keavren, swing toward Ash Dancer. Reaching out for him, she positioned her body to block him from smashing into the tree trunk. Once she had him, moving swiftly, she secured him to a branch and cut his other arm free. Using the ropes attached to him for extra support, she held him close to her and proceeded to awkwardly lower him to the ground. It wasn't a smooth descent and by the wince that was frozen on Keavren's face the whole time, I didn't imagine it felt nice for him, either. Once she had him on the ground, he rolled onto his stomach and lay there, silently, unmoving, leaving his arms in an outstretched position.

When Ash Dancer started to re-climb the tree, I dared a glimpse at Mez. He was looking directly at me. Unlike before, when I could see the agony etched into his expression, he looked utterly calm as if all fear and pain had left him. He seemed so serene that I wondered if he was close to death and was hallucinating that I was an angel, or something.

"Cut him down," Ash Dancer called.

I glance at her, to make sure she was in position, then immediately sawed through the rope.

Mez continued to watch me as he swung toward Ash Dancer, until he was forced to look away when he turned in mid-air. As she had done with Keavren, she let Mez collide with her body instead of the tree. Once she was ready to begin her descent with him, I put the knife away and climbed down.

I walked up to Keavren, relieved he was breathing. He'd been so still, I hadn't been able to see the rise and falls of his breaths when I was up in the tree.

His head was turned to the side, and his eyes were closed. The skin on his face was filthy, and I could see the tracks tears had left behind. My anger rekindled at the sight and surged even more when I noticed that, in addition to having had feathers jabbed into him, fresh purplish blue bruises were forming along angry red marks on his back. He must have been struck with something hard.

I couldn't possibly understand, or even imagine, what Mez and Keavren could have done to deserve this type of torture and death sentence. This made me question the very sanity of the People of the North and Ash Dancer's role in this.

Why is she helping me?

Ash Dancer returned to the ground with Mez, who promptly collapsed to his knees and lay on his stomach with his arms outstretched as Keavren had done. I saw that Mez, too, had the same bruising marks on his back.

"We have to pluck them," Ash Dancer said, walking over to her bag and opening it.

All the anger I had been feeling fled with the word "pluck", and I nearly lost my breakfast, realizing what she meant.

"I have a salve to stop infection." She pulled from her bag a small wooden container with a fabric cover secured in place by string as well as a thick roll of bound fabric. "We will need to bandage them after we are finished," she added.

Not waiting for my reply, she stepped over to Keavren, set the container and bandages down, and started tearing feathers from his skin by the handful as fast as she could. Keavren howled sharply in pain with her first yank, but fell silent with clenched teeth after that.

I tensed and gagged at the sight and the sound of the quills ripping free from his flesh, until I forced myself to bite down hard on my tongue, to get a hold of myself. The sharp pain and the taste of my blood was enough to snap me out of my downward horror spiral.

Wrenching my eyes from Ash Dancer and Keavren, I looked at Mez. The black feathers I had to face, glistened a dark blue and green from where they caught the sunlight that poked through the canopy of leaves above us. On a bird, I would have found this pretty, on Mez, it was revolting.

Time to pluck, Megan. Mez is depending on you. Pull yourself together and puke later.

I took a steadying breath and knelt beside Mez, gently gathering his thick long hair to move it off his back and up over his right shoulder. His once-sleek silver hair had become a tangled mess of dirt mixed with strands of wet and drying blood.

"I'm sorry," I whispered to him, hating that I was about to cause him even more pain.

He shook his head slightly. "You're saving me," he whispered, still looking as calm as he had before, and shut his eyes.

Hoping in vain that his calm expression was the result of his nerves having shut off, or he had somehow mind-warped himself to a happier plane of existence, I went for it. Grabbing a fistful of the feathers embedded in his right shoulder blade, I rapidly yanked them out. Mez jumped at the sensation but, surprisingly, didn't make a sound. I continued to pluck him as quickly as I could without stopping. He remained silent throughout the entire excruciating process, and I was incredibly grateful to him for that. I wouldn't have blamed him if he had screamed or cried, but I didn't know if I would have had the guts to continue if he had.

Numerous small, blood-seeping holes lined the backs of his arms and shoulders. The holes started at one wrist and followed a path all the way to the other.

I glanced over at Ash Dancer, who had finished plucking Keavren. She was kneeling over him and was applying to the holes on his skin, a butter-coloured paste from the wooden jar she had taken from her bag. When she was finished, she looked at me and held out the container.

"Spread this on him. It will stop his wounds from filling with pus."

I took the container from her and swallowed my gag at the word pus. I was beginning to hate words that started with the letter "P".

Unlike me, none of this seemed to bother Ash Dancer. She proceeded to bandage Keavren, wrapping a thin, beige-coloured, lightly-woven fabric, that reminded me of gauze, around his arms, upper back, and shoulders to cover the salve.

Turning my attention to Mez, I dipped my fingers into the soft-but-sticky cream-like substance and spread it over his wounds. I tried to be as gentle as possible, and I hoped, at the very least, that the salve didn't sting his open wounds. Whatever the case, Mez didn't complain. If I didn't know better, I'd swear I was giving him a spa treatment.

"Wrap the one arm, bring the fabric over his shoulders, across his back, and then do the other arm." Ash Dancer said, holding out the roll of bandage to me and pointing to how she had wrapped Keavren.

I took the roll of bandages from her, and starting with Mez' right arm, I mummy-wrapped him as carefully and quickly as I could. Wrapping his arms was a lot easier than wrapping this shoulder and back area, but I managed to fully cover his wounds. I felt better seeing both he and Keavren bandaged, even though I knew they probably had a long way to go to fully heal.

"I'll get your horses. They're packed, like I promised," she said as she returned the bandage roll and salve to her bag.

I looked uncertainly from her to the men. "Are their arms broken?" I asked Ash Dancer, afraid of her answer.

"No, but they will not be able to use them for a while. They hung there for a long time." She stood, picking up her bag, leaving briskly to get the horses.

I rose to my feet, watching her leave, feeling my anger rebuild. Don't get me wrong, I was grateful their arms weren't broken and even more grateful for her help, but I just couldn't shake the feeling that none of this would have happened if the People of the North had just let us leave. Without knowing the true reason they insisted that we stay, it seemed like their only goal had been to torture Mez and Keavren because they were Warriors. I know that Ash Dancer didn't actively participate in this but at the same time, I also believed that she knew about it, which wasn't comforting in the least.

This wasn't the first time I'd felt like a fool on Qarradune. But, unlike the time when I'd been an idiot and allowed myself to get sucked into Galnar's lies – even kissing him when deep-down I knew better – this time, I felt like the victim of a people who took full advantage of my gullibility. In many ways, this humiliation felt worse. I couldn't believe that not long ago, I was terrified of Doom Breaker. Now, all I wanted to do was friggin' doom-break her face.

I swallowed, getting a hold of my emotions. I had to stay rational and strong for Keavren and Mez. They were in bad shape, and they couldn't use their arms. It was up to me to somehow find a way to get them home.

"Thank you, Megan," Mez spoke in a quiet ragged breath.

I looked at him and nodded, dropping to my knees at his side. "I'm sorry I didn't find you sooner. I didn't know you were in trouble," I promised, needing to express this, because I didn't want him to think, for one moment, I would have abandoned them.

He shook his head, wincing with the movement. "I couldn't be more proud of my 'Woman'." He gave the smallest of smiles to punctuate the point.

I gave a small smile back, although I had no idea if he'd be able to see it beyond the freaked-out expression that must have been permanently plastered on my face.

"Ash Dancer has prepared horses and provisions for us. She told me how to travel and the direction I should take." I could hear that my voice didn't sound half as confident as I'd wanted it to.

"We'll make it back," he said, managing not to sound concerned.

I looked at him before stating more than asking: "You're the message they wanted me to take back, aren't you?"

"Yes. We're the message."

A dozen questions popped into my head with Mez' confirmation but before I could ask him one, the thud of horses' hooves drew my attention to the more pressing matter at hand.

Standing, I marched up to Ash Dancer, who was leading the two horses that were both packed with supplies. Each horse was pulling a frame made of two long wooden poles. I didn't know what those poles were for or what was being dragged but for now, I had only one thing on my mind.

"Why was this done to Mez and Keavren?" I demanded, tired of not understanding what seemed to me like obvious madness.

"To show that we will not tolerate Warriors on our land," she responded evenly. "We have an agreement with the Warriors and with the Kavylak soldiers. You are not allowed here," Ash Dancer explained.

"So, I was spared this...this *punishment,* because I'm not a Warrior?"

"Yes, and because you are the woman. You lead them and will carry their message home."

I stared at her intently, trying to make sense of her words and trying, once again, to figure out her role in all of this.

"Why are you helping us? Helping me?"

Ash Dancer's solid expression softened. "Because I like you, and because you carry my own message with you?"

What in the heck message is she talking about now?

"Your message?" I asked, losing the intensity to my confusion. "Do you want me to say you helped us?" She'd lost me.

She shook her head. "You know the Warriors. You know one of the People. You could speak to him of my children."

My brain was slow to connect the dots at first. Then, I understood. She wanted me to tell Amarogq of her children. *His* children.

He didn't know.

I looked at her in silence. I didn't know what to tell her. She was asking me to stick my nose where it really didn't belong, and I really didn't want to drop this bomb on Amarogq or Amorette. Plus, if I had to choose, I was kind of Team Amorette.

Ash Dancer took one step closer to me, resting her hand on my shoulder in a friendly and meaningful way. I looked from her hand to her eyes.

"I would never ask you to carry such a message and allow you to become a widow," Ash Dancer said. "I know that pain too deeply. Your man and the soldier will make it home with you, my friend."

Any remaining animosity I was harbouring for Ash Dancer melted away. The emotion behind the words she spoke was filled with the raw pain of love lost. Whatever had happened between her and Amarogq had clearly been devastating for her. This wasn't hard to imagine, considering how much the People despised the Warriors and that Amarogq had become one. I wondered if – like Ash Dancer's message – the People's message was also actually meant just for him.

I placed my hand on top of hers and nodded deeply. "Thank you. I won't forget you or what you did for us. What you did for *me*." I meant that. I still didn't know if I would relay her message to Amarogq, but I was no longer confused about my feelings toward Ash Dancer.

She was a friend.

A small not-quite wistful smile graced her lips, and she nodded.

"I will not forget you, strange red-haired woman," she said.

Her words were odd and nearly offensive, but the pleasant, almost affectionate way in which she said them, made it clear that she thought of me as a friend in her own way, too.

"Let us put the men on the sleds. They won't be able to ride," Ash Dancer explained, walking up behind one of the horses and hauling a long piece of leather off the wooden poles it was dragging.

My eyes glanced from her to the poles attached to the horses. Moving around the animals to get a better look, I saw that each one was dragging its diagonally inclined poles. The wooden frame structures were in the shape of an isosceles triangle and, in the center of the frame, was a braided net-style hammock securely tied to the poles. Even though she had called it a sled, to my surprise it looked exactly like a travois. I remembered learning about these historical frame-structures in my Canadian history class. I recalled that they were once used by the indigenous plains peoples of North America, who used them to drag tools and goods over land. It felt a little surreal to see one here in real life and not in a museum.

"Take his other side," Ash Dancer instructed, drawing me out of my old history lesson.

Turning to look at her, I saw that she had pulled the leather tarp over to Keavren and was crouched on his right side, ready to move him onto it. I jogged over to his left, ready to help, understanding now that Ash Dancer intended to load each man on a travois-sled.

As quickly as we could, and securely holding Keavren under his arm pits, we pulled him onto the leather. It was hard and awkward. He wasn't light, and he released a sharp yelp of pain. It took everything in me not to let him go to stop hurting him.

Once he was on the leather, we gently released him, and Ash Dancer grabbed its end.

"Pull with me."

I took hold of the leather and helped her pull Keavren over to the sled, hauling him up and onto it. He was now lying on his stomach on the hammock part of it with his arms outstretched. It took a great deal of effort, and I was huffing, puffing and sweating up a storm by the end of it. I felt ready to take a nap on the forest floor and worried that I might not have enough energy in me to repeat the process with Mez.

Ash Dancer didn't seem to have that problem. She was already dragging the second leather tarp over to Mez. I watched her in amazement, wondering where she found the strength and drive to keep going. Then I remembered she was a mother of twins.

'Nuff said.

I joined her at Mez' side, and we repeated the same steps with him we had done with Keavren. He inhaled sharply from the pain when we moved him onto the leather, but maintained his stoic silence for the remainder of the grueling hauling process.

When both men were loaded and ready to go, Ash Dancer tied the horses together, and handed her bag to me.

"There is more salve and bandages in here. Water and food are on the horses." She nodded over to the saddle bags.

I took the bag from her and ducked under its strap to wear it across my body.

"Thank you, Ash Dancer. Really. Thank you for everything."

She gave a short meaningful nod. "Go quickly and safely."

"I will."

Approaching the horse I intended to ride, the one dragging Mez, I paused. I'd never mounted a horse on my own. The horse seemed a lot taller now that I was expected to ride by myself.

You can do this Megan. If you can climb a tree, you can mount a horse.

Grabbing on to the horse's saddle and placing my foot in the stirrup, I leapt off the ground as hard as I could, and managed to pull myself up. It was entirely ungraceful, and I nearly fell off in the process, but I did it and was glad my embarrassing horse-mounting display was being witnessed only by Ash Dancer. Still, I couldn't bring myself to see her expression, knowing how silly I must have looked.

Once I was settled on the horse, it occurred to me that I had no idea how to make it move. What was the "go" word? Giddy-up?

Geeze, I really, really wish I had a car right now.

Sighing, I looked at Ash Dancer, who by the expression on her face, was clearly wondering why I hadn't started on my way.

"I've never ridden by myself before," I leveled with her. "How do I make the horse move forward?" It was absolutely pointless to hold on to any pride I had left.

Ash Dancer approached and said, "Squeeze your legs into the body of the horse to go forward. Pull back on the reins to stop. Pull left or right to go in the direction you want."

Well, that sounded easy enough.

"Thanks," I said gratefully.

She nodded and backed away. I squeezed my legs into the sides of the horse as she instructed and to my relief, it moved forward and the other horse followed. Giving one last look at Ash Dancer, I waved. She didn't wave back but stood tall and proud, watching me leave.

Facing forward, I released a slow breath, guiding the horses by using the directions Ash Dancer had given me. I kept an eye out for the trees with the branches that grew only one way and made sure that we were always headed in the opposite direction of the branches' growth. This, Ash Dancer had said, would take me out of the land of the People.

I had no idea what direction I would take once we'd left those trees behind, but hopefully Mez and Keavren could guide us from there. For now, I wanted only to leave this place and never look back.

* * * * *

The sound of a distant flowing stream was music to my ears. Without a watch, or even knowing how to properly measure time on Qarradune, I had no idea how much time had passed since we'd left the People of the North behind. The sun was sinking, and I knew sunset wouldn't be far off.

Even though I just wanted to keep going, the increasing ache in my thighs, back, and arms as well as the huffing and puffing of the horses, told me we all needed a break. I also really needed to check on Mez and Keavren. They hadn't said anything since we'd left, but they had to be feeling miserable. While I couldn't do much for their overall comfort, they could probably use some water and a bit of food, which might help a little.

I steered the horses toward the water and pulled back on the reins, easing them to a stop once we'd reached the little creek. Before I even released the reins, both horses began to drink. I took this as my cue to get down. Sliding off the saddle, I landed harder than I'd meant to and nearly fell over. My legs were wobbly and stiff and felt entirely alien under my weight. I took shaking steps toward one of the saddle bags, and I took out the water bladder. I had a long drink, feeling refreshed. Taking a deep breath, I shut my eyes and slowly released it, hoping to relieve some of the tension and stress I felt. It didn't work.

"You're doing wonderfully, Megan."

My eyes opened when Mez spoke. He had turned his head in my direction. His voice was rough and slightly raspy.

"Thanks," I said with the tiniest of smiles and walked toward him, holding up the water bladder. "Drink?"

He gave a slight nod. "I can't hold it," he confessed.

"Don't worry, I promise not to drown you," I teased lightly. We both knew why Mez couldn't hold it. His arms were completely useless to him right now.

Gently tilting the mouth of the water bladder toward his lips, I let a small stream of water flow. He drank steadily, very obviously forcing himself to drink slowly so he wouldn't choke. A pang of guilt hit me as I watched him drink. It hadn't even occurred to me just how dehydrated he and Keavren must have been.

Who knows the last time they had any water? Geeze! I'm so bad at this!

When he'd had enough, I moved the water bladder away from his mouth.

"Will you sit with me for a moment after you've seen to Keavren?"

"Sure. I'll be right back," I told him and made my way over to Keavren, who had been watching Mez and me. I smiled a little at him. "Water?"

"Thanks," he said in a dry, cracked whisper.

I gave him water in the same way I had done for Mez, letting him drink what he wanted. When he was finished, I closed the water bladder.

"You o-kay?" Keavren asked me quietly. I still loved the way he said "okay".

"Not really," I replied honestly, "but we'll get back."

"We will. We're going in the right direction and if anyone dangerous comes around, Mez'll take care of them," he said confidently. "All you have to do is what you're doing. You're really great, Megan."

Tears pricked at the back of my eyes when he said that. I didn't feel like I was great, but Keavren's words touched me, and I was already teetering on the edge of a complete emotional collapse.

"Thanks, Keavren." I forced out the words and forced back the tears. Now wasn't the time to fall apart. "You guys are doing so well, too, even after everything you went through."

"I'm better than he is," Keavren levelled with me. "If you run low on that medicine stuff she gave you, put it on him first. He took most of it. A lot of the time he wouldn't let them get to me. I think he knew we'd be strung up eventually, and I was more likely to come out of that alright. He's probably worse than he's saying."

I glanced at Mez, finding that hard to swallow, then looked back at Keavren.

"I'm not telling you this to scare you," he assured me, "but you should know."

"Yes. Yes, of course. I should know," I agreed with an overly-enthusiastic nod. "Thanks for telling me, Keavren. You really don't need to worry about scaring me. I think I'm about as scared as I can get."

He looked at me with understanding and a weak smile. "When we get back, I owe you some really good chocolate."

"Yeah, you do," I joked and gave his temple a light kiss. He shut his eyes in response. With a single sweep of my fingers, I gently stroked his hair, before returning to Mez. I took a seat on the grass beside his sled. We looked at each other for a moment before he spoke.

"Did they give you all our things?"

"Yes, except the third horse."

He nodded but didn't seem to care about poor missing Vacant Horse. "Next time you get up, would you mind getting me one of those little cubes you've seen me take out of my jacket? The ones wrapped in paper."

"Of course, I'll get it for you now," I said and pushed myself to my feet with a bit of a grunt. "How many did you want?" I asked, searching for his jacket.

"Just one. But if you're sore, you can have one, too."

"Thanks. I'll be alright, though," I promised. That said, in truth, even if I was more than just sore from riding the horse, I wouldn't have taken this medicine. He really needed the painkiller more than I did.

Finding his jacket, I fished one of the wrapped cubes out of a pocket and returned to him, unwrapping it. I held the small, bright blue cube close to his mouth, so he could take it. He did and shut his eyes. Within a matter of ten seconds, the tension in his face visibly eased.

"If you think Keavren needs one, he can have one, too, of course."

I nodded, but after what Keavren had told me about Mez, I had no intention of giving him one of those medicine cubes. They were all going to be for Mez.

"I think he's alright for now," I told Mez honestly. "He seems to be sleeping. I don't want to disturb him,"

"That's best," he agreed.

I stroked Mez' hair in a smooth motion, sweeping my hand from the top of his head to just above his shoulder. The rest of his hair was tucked under him. I hoped the gesture would bring him some comfort, and it seemed to work. He smiled softly at me.

"You're doing everything right, Megan. As long as we keep moving, they'll find us," he assured me. "They're already looking for us by now. You're doing just fine."

"I'll get us there," I vowed. "I won't let anyone else hurt you guys."

"If we run into someone, and you're scared, just make sure I'm awake. We'll be safe."

"I will." And I would. Before, I didn't like to think too much about Mez' skill and what it did to people. Now, I was grateful he had it.

"Tonight, you can sleep near me and Keavren. We'll be the brave ones. You sleep."

Aww, that was so sweet of him, but after today, I'm never going to sleep again.

He attempted to move his arm, bending it at the elbow, trying to reach toward me. Almost immediately, he gave up on whatever he had intended to do, realizing it was a futile effort. His arm returned to its original resting position.

I looked quizzically at Mez.

"I was trying to do something really cool just now," he confessed with a glint in his eye.

I had to laugh at his words and expression. "I believe you, but all I need you to do is rest. Save your cool for later. I'll be alright."

He smiled. "I'll be alright too, Megan. So will Keavren. Honestly. They'll find us, and we'll be fine." He was so confident that I glanced around our surroundings, half expecting to see a pack of Warriors walk out of the trees.

"You know your people better than I do."

"I do." He smiled. "You'll know us soon enough, too. We're not just good looking, you know," he added, his eye-glint returning.

I smiled back, but I had no intention of getting to know them better. My mission was to find Thayn and get out of Kavylak.

"Well, Mr. More-Than-Good-Looking, unless you need something else, I'm going to get us travelling again."

He smiled and shut his eyes, so I took that as my cue to leave. I walked in front of the horses and gave them both a good stroke on their necks, silently thanking them for getting us this far. They both seemed happier having had a drink and a rest.

Hoisting myself back up in my awkward-horse-mounting way, I winced as my inner thighs complained in protest. Ignoring the discomfort, I moved us onwards and had no intention of stopping until it was absolutely necessary. My thighs would just have to deal with it.

*　*　*　*　*

I rode until twilight, finally stopping near another stream. It would be night soon, and I had no intention of traveling in the dark. I slowly eased myself off the horse and collapsed on the ground, landing hard on my butt. If my butt hadn't fallen asleep a million hours ago, I'm sure it would have hurt. I had no doubt I'd feel it later. Sighing, I fell backward onto the cool grass, lying like a starfish and gazing up at the pretty purples, pinks, and blues of the sky.

"Are you alright?" Mez asked with genuine concern in his voice.

"Uh huh," I responded, still not feeling any motivation to move. My body felt like lead.

"Do you need help?" he asked. I heard him shift on his sled, and he gave a sharp exhale. The noise was enough to drive me back to action.

"No. I'm fine. Don't move." I forced myself into a sitting position and slowly pushed myself to my feet. Wincing from the pain it caused me, I bit back a grunt. My entire body was a solid ache, and each movement I made was a punishing reminder of that ache.

I glanced at the horses to make sure they were alright and saw that, like before, they were busy drinking from a stream and eating grass. Unlike me, they knew exactly what they were doing.

Horses – 1,000,000

Megan – 0

"We'll stop here for the evening," I informed Mez and Keavren, taking the water bladder out of a saddle bag and walk-hobbling toward them.

"Good call," Mez agreed.

With a nod to Mez, I glanced from him to Keavren. Keavren was sound asleep. He was even snoring a little bit. A smile tugged at the side of my mouth at the sight of him. With his sleeping face all mushed into the sled, he looked like a little boy. I was really glad he was still sleeping.

"Did you sleep at all?" I asked Mez, stepping closer to him.

"Off and on," he said. "We really need to pave these woods."

I laughed because I had to agree with his comment. Paved woods really would have made travelling a lot easier.

"Water?" I asked, holding up the water bladder.

"Please."

I held it for him as I did the last time and when he'd had his fill, I had some water, too.

"Do you need any of that cube medicine?"

"Not yet, but soon I'll give in," Mez admitted.

"On a scale of one to ten, how much pain are you in?" I asked, hoping he would play along and level with me.

He lifted a brow at the question but then gave it some thought. "A solid seven-and-a-half but a weak eight."

I couldn't help but grin at his response. I really liked that he'd humoured me, and it wasn't the first time he'd done it. Of all the people I'd met, Mez really was the one who seemed to have no trouble embracing my weird.

"What hurts the most?"

"My shoulders and hands are in bad shape."

I gave him a small sympathetic smile. I remember how uncomfortable it felt to hang from the monkey bars for too long when I was a kid. I didn't want to imagine how his shoulders, arms, and hands must have felt after hanging that way for goodness only knows how long. I hoped for his and Keavren's sake that there was some giant medicine cube that could fix them.

"Hungry?" I asked.

"Not really," Mez said, "but I'll chew on something if it's there."

"Alright, I'll get us something to 'chew on'." I wasn't really hungry either, but I knew it would be stupid not to eat if there wasn't anything stopping me from doing it. I tried to honour my promise to Rral whenever I could.

I took out a leather pouch that Ash Dancer had packed for me. It contained some nuts and berries. I brought it to Mez, opened it, and took turns feeding him and myself in no particular hurry. When we'd had enough, I closed the bag and put it away. I didn't bother offering food to Keavren. He was still fast asleep.

Yawning, I returned to Mez. It was officially getting dark, and I could feel exhaustion creeping in.

"Do you want to climb on this thing with me to sleep?" Mez offered. "I swear I'll keep my hands to myself." He grinned because we both knew that in his condition, he couldn't be naughty with his hands if he tried.

Sizing up the sled, I decided that there would be enough room for us both but as tempting as the offer was, it would be too risky in his current condition.

I shook my head. "No. I would be too worried I'd hurt you."

"Don't worry. If you hear me crying like a child, just stop what you're doing," he teased.

I smiled and took a seat on the grass.

"You'll get cold down there if you sleep on the ground."

"Should I stand?" I couldn't hold back the sarcasm.

"If you can sleep standing, yes. That's definitely better."

Gotta respect a guy who answers sarcasm with sarcasm. I playfully stuck my tongue out at him all the same.

He returned the gesture, surprising me. I laughed. He smiled.

My laugh tapered out when I noticed that I could already feel the cold seeping through my pants from the ground. Mez wasn't kidding that I would be cold.

Great.

I half debated joining him on the sled, remembering how nice it had been last night, sleeping next to him with his arms around me. It was a safe and warm feeling. I yearned for it. Instead, I drew my knees up and put my arms around them, remembering something I had been curious about earlier.

"Can I ask you a personal question?"

"I'm not going to run away," Mez replied. "This is the best time to do it." His smile was a borderline smirk.

I snorted a laugh, then asked, "Who is Glenara?"

His otherwise calm expression morphed into genuine surprise, and I was pretty sure if it were possible for his skin to be paler, it would have been.

He stared at me in bewilderment and carefully asked, "How do you know that name?"

"You said it in your sleep this morning."

"I'm sorry..." he said, looking slightly awkward.

I gave a simple shrug and a small head shake to let him know I really didn't think it was a big deal. I was just curious. It wasn't like I was actually his "woman", or anything.

"Glenara was my wife."

Now it was my turn to look like a deer in headlights.

"Oh, uh…I see."

Geeze, Megan! Could you have said anything stupider?

He gave me a gentle smile and shake of his head. "She died nearly five cycles ago. I must have been dreaming."

"Oh. I'm so very sorry." I hoped he could hear the sincerity I wanted to convey over my shock.

His smile turned bittersweet. "I was fortunate to have known her."

I opened my mouth to speak, but quickly shut it before I could risk asking the most inappropriate question.

Now is really not the time to ask him how she died, Megan!

My mind was swimming with so many thoughts and questions.

How young was Mez when he got married? No wonder it was normal for him to ask me if I was married when he first psycho-analyzed me. Was he married since he's been a Warrior? Did he have kids? How many other Warriors were married? Oh my god, Mez is a widower.

"Should I have told you that I had no idea who Glenara is?"

I looked at him, realizing I must have been silent and lost in my head-ramble for way too long.

"No, I'm sorry. I didn't mean to go all quiet on you. I do prefer honesty. I'm just very surprised," I leveled with him. "I wasn't quite sure what you were going to say, but it wasn't that."

He nodded with understanding, his smile returning. "That's alright. She didn't think I'd ever be her husband, either. It took me many tries to get her to even date me for the first time."

My brows rose in amusement. "I hope your first date with her wasn't as bad as ours," I joked, referring to the horrible mess that was our two-day fake relationship.

"Megan, nobody's first date was as bad as ours."

I laughed heartily at that because it was so very true. This was definitely a record-breaking bad date.

"Well, if it's any consolation, at least I'll never forget it."

"I think it would work better for me if you did."

I laughed again and shook my head. "Perhaps it might not be so bad to forget some of the details, but I wouldn't want to forget you."

"Thank you," he said, sounding genuinely touched.

I nodded. "For what it's worth, Mez, I do hope you find love like you had with Glenara again."

"Thank you. I hope so, too. But I was lucky to have it once."

I wondered if I would be lucky enough to have it once, too. Smiling, I lifted my gaze from him to the night sky. The stars were waking up from their daytime nap and were twinkling brightly. I searched for the one bright blue star I had seen from Mez' office while on the ship during the journey to Kavylak. I couldn't find it.

"Is it up there, yet?" he asked, having a good idea what I was looking for.

"No."

"It will be," he promised. "It'll watch over you."

I nodded, but kept my eyes firmly planted on the sea of stars above me. Tears were pricking my eyes, but I didn't want him to see them. For no reason other than my desire to return home and make sense of Qarradune's existence, I had begun to think of the blue star as Earth. It brought me comfort to imagine that home was something I could see, even if I couldn't reach it. I shut my eyes as a wave of homesickness threatened to drown me.

Mez shifted, and the sound drew my attention back to him. He was slowly and carefully reaching out his arm to me.

Understanding his intentions, I lifted my hand and met him the rest of the way, gently holding his.

His grip wasn't firm, but his hand was warm, and it felt good to feel his fingers close around mine. The contact made me feel less alone, and once again, I felt like I could survive this.

"When we get back to the Capital, would you like to have a coffee with me sometime?" It was clear he wasn't asking me out on a date. It sounded like a coffee was something he'd like to share with me because he genuinely wanted to enjoy my company, no strings attached. That felt good.

"I'd like that." It was true, even though I doubted I would be in Kavylak long enough for it to happen.

He smiled, looking pleased. "I think it would, too. I wouldn't mind having a talk with you that was neither an interview nor an afraid-for-our-lives moment."

"That would be a nice change," I smirked.

He nodded and released a long sigh. "I think I need to sleep now."

"Sleep," I agreed and reluctantly released his hand. He adjusted with a light grimace. Once settled, he looked at me.

"You're incredible, Megan. I wish you could see yourself through my eyes."

Heat filled my cheeks. I wasn't expecting him to say that and had no idea how to respond to such a powerful compliment. So I just gave a small tiny nod, wondering if my lame response lost me some "incredible" points in his mind. If it did, he certainly didn't show it. Mez merely shut his eyes and within minutes was asleep. His deep breathing joined Keavren's soft snores.

Resting my arms on the tops of my knees, I returned my gaze to the stars and smiled. Mez was right. The blue star had shown up.

A tear fell and was joined by another.

"Goodnight, Aunt Vera," I whispered.

Chapter 18

Irys

She sighed as she woke to the feeling of a warm, soft hand stroking the side of her face. Slowly, she lazily opened her eyes, not in any hurry to extract herself from her sleep. Still, she had to smile at the sight of him.

The young man before her looked upon her with a knowing softness. His white hair glistened with iridescence where it was caressed by the light. His crystal-clear aqua eyes reminded her of a favourite gemstone, with striking facets across their surface adding immeasurable depth to his gaze.

Though his complexion was as pale as ivory marble, there was a gentle rosy freshness to his cheeks that made him appear nearly ageless; more of a flawless portrait than a mortal man. Vitality and life seemed to radiate from his skin.

"Hello, My Love. Do you remember me?" he asked in a voice brimming with tenderness.

She calmly considered him, not bothered by her confusion or the blur of her memory.

"Yes," she said, looking him over. "Though I don't know how."

He smiled, pleased with her reply. Seated on the edge of her bed, he reached out and took her hand, holding it in an affectionate way.

"It will all become clearer with time. I have been searching for you."

"Why were we parted?"

His smile faded. Clearly, it was not a fond memory.

"Your sister didn't want us to be together. She stopped at nothing to see us separated."

Her heart ached at the sight of his unhappiness, and a frown creased her lips.

"That is in the past. We're together now."

"We are," he agreed. "Soon we will be together again as we were meant to be. No one will part us."

"Who would want to part us now?" she asked, holding his hand a little more tightly. Confusion continued to cloud her thoughts. Her emotions were strong, and she was confident in them, but her memories weren't there to explain what she was feeling.

"Your sister and her allies will try again if they discover I have found you."

"My sister? Is she alive, too? I don't remember her."

"She is. It is not important that you remember her now. I won't let her stop us this time."

"What will we do now? Will I come to know you again?" she asked. She trusted him with every part of her soul, whoever he was.

"You will." He smiled. "For now, you need only focus on growing stronger so you can become your true self again. Right now, the girl is more powerful than you are. That will change."

"How can I grow to be stronger than the girl?"

Leaning his face toward her, he rested his cool forehead against hers.

"Let me in," he replied.

Without understanding, she knew exactly what he meant. Opening her mind to him, she felt her senses fill with him. It was as though their spirits were weaving themselves together. She could smell the soft scent of him. His heartbeat filled her ears. The love he felt for her was wrapping itself around her as though it were a gossamer fabric.

She felt fuller than she had; more complete. She had become more of herself than she formerly had been. The familiarity of him was nearly overwhelming.

She was starting to remember.

"My Love," she said in a breath, only just beginning to know why she was saying it.

At her words, he drew back from her to look upon her with an expression of worship.

"I miss you," she said, meaning the words. Her love for him was inestimable.

"I have missed you, too," he replied after a moment to gather himself. His words carried the weight of his prolonged suffering. The ache and longing he'd endured were plain in his eyes.

"I feel myself remembering you and yet I don't have the memories. I am incomplete and yet I feel as though I am filling with life for the first time. Tell me what to do, My Love," she pleaded.

With his free hand, he stroked her gleaming white hair.

"I will visit you as often as I can, just as we are now. When I know that you are growing strong enough, stronger than her, I will come to you in person, in our physical forms, and free you from her."

"I long to be freed, My Love. I have been trapped in nothingness for too long."

"I will keep the girl close to me, far from what she loves and holds dear. This absence will weaken her. You will feel it. Your closeness to me will strengthen you. Her weakness will strengthen you."

"I will draw strength from you when we are together. I will allow her to wither in her loneliness. When I am strong enough, we will be together again without her, My Love."

"Yes," he said as a broad grin crossed his face. "We will be free to love and to finish what we started. All this time, I have been preparing for your return. Still, there are tasks I must complete. I must leave you so I may finish them."

Her eyes glistened with tears at the thought of parting with him, but she nodded bravely.

"Tell me your name," he said with another stroke to her hair.

She opened her mouth, expecting to be able to respond, but the name would not rise to her lips. She looked at him, lost and desperate.

"Tell me my name," he then said, not appearing upset by her lack of response.

Taking a moment to shut her eyes and consider his request, she opened them again and spoke with confidence.

"Xandon."

Smiling, he leaned in to kiss her.

She was about to touch his lips with her own when a name arrived upon them instead.

"Irys?" she said, looking hopefully at him.

He froze, his eyes opening, and he slowly drew back from her, looking calm.

Confusion swam through her mind. She had been nearly certain that this was her name, but doubt remained.

"I will remember it, My Love."

"You will," he agreed.

"I will not fail you next time."

He nodded. "Do you know who Irys is?"

Humiliation washed over her as the answer came to her.

"The girl."

"The girl." He nodded. Reaching out, he stroked the side of her face. "You will remember soon and then she will be nothing more than a distant memory."

Her senses filled with the softness and warmth of his fingertips on her face.

"I will remember."

He rose and held her hand to encourage her to stand with him. When she did, they walked across the room together. She moved with a grace that felt simultaneously new and familiar.

Bringing her to a full-length mirror, he nodded toward the glass.

"Look," he said.

Peering at their reflection, she stared in fascination at the young woman standing next to Xandon. She was tall, fit, and graceful. Her long, flowing white hair had a silvery sheen where his was iridescent. Her sage-coloured eyes were wise and knowing. She was dressed in a long gown of a fabric so delicate that it fluttered from a breeze in the room too soft for her own skin to detect.

"Who do you see?" he asked.

"I see myself," she replied confidently.

"I see you, too," he agreed.

"I see myself as I truly am."

He smiled and slipped an arm around her waist.

She watched them in the frame of the mirror as though studying a portrait of themselves.

"Remember this when you are in need of comfort. This is your future, My Love," he said, watching her in her reflection.

"I will. We are beautiful this way."

"We are," he agreed. "Close your eyes."

She studied the image for a moment longer before she allowed her eyes to close.

"I see you..."His voice seemed to fade and echo all around her. Without opening her eyes, she knew she was alone.

Chapter 19

Megan

Enadria!

She opened her eyes to starlight. She didn't know this place, but she knew Enadria was in trouble. She was with him.

She could feel Xandon's toxic magic pulling at the strings of her sister's heart, seeping into her spirit to further darken the stain he had long since left there. She could feel Enadria's longing and her pain.

She had to save her. This time she would not fail.

She shut her eyes and concentrated. If Xandon could find her sister, so could she.

A mirror appeared, a glowing beacon of light that illuminated the darkness that surrounded her. She heard their voices as she approached it.

"Who do you see?" Xandon asked.

"I see myself," Enadria replied confidently.

"I see you, too," he agreed.

"I see myself as I truly am."

She reached the mirror and stared achingly at her sister. Enadria's face and features were identical to her own. She was tall, fit, and graceful. Her long, flowing white hair had a silvery sheen. Her sage-coloured eyes were wise and knowing.

Her sister was dressed in a long gown of a fabric so delicate that it fluttered from a breeze in the room where she stood.

Enadria always loved dresses like that.

Her gaze shifted from her sister to Xandon, who smiled and slipped an arm around Enadria's waist.

"Enadria, I'm here!" she called to her sister, who seemed to see only herself and Xandon.

"Remember this when you are in need of comfort. This is your future, My Love," Xandon said, watching Enadria in her reflection.

"No! Enadria!" She pounded her fists against the glass. "Don't you see me?"

"I will. We are beautiful this way," Enadria said lovingly to him.

"We are," he agreed. "Close your eyes."

"No! Enadria! Don't listen to him! Open your eyes! See me, your sister, Elindria! I'm here! You must fight him!" She continued to pound on the glass, desperate to shatter it and break through. The glass was impenetrable.

Enadria studied the image of herself and Xandon for a moment longer before she allowed her eyes to close, and she vanished from view, unaware of her twin desperately trying to reach her from the other side.

Xandon's metal arm shot through the mirror toward Elindria, its cold fingers closing around her throat, stilling her flying fists.

"I see you, Elindria," Xandon said, "but she will never see you, and you will never see her again." Elindria gasped for breath as he squeezed harder. "I may not be able to destroy you this time, but you will not be free to ruin my plans," he seethed. "I am going to set her free. She'll be free of the girl, but you won't be free of yours."

Struggling to breathe and understand this madman's words, she flicked her gaze from Xandon to her reflection in the mirror and saw that it had changed. Starring back at her, with a frightened expression was a girl with red plaited hair wearing strange-looking black clothes. She, too, was struggling in Xandon's unyielding metal grasp.

"Wake up, Megan," were the final words Elindria heard him speak, before her vision went black.

Chapter 20

Irys

I sat straight up in my bed, and a scream ripped its way from my throat. Pain and emptiness filled me to my very soul. I felt as though I had been torn away from everything that mattered to me, everything I loved, and it was agony. After a moment, the feeling subsided, and I looked about my room feeling disoriented.

Suddenly, the door to my quarters was slammed open and heavy footsteps ran into my room. I scrambled to pull the covers over me as Mr. Rolern burst into my bedroom looking wildly around, ready for anything. His sword was drawn.

"Thank the Goddess, Mr. Rolern! I'm glad to see you. Please, would you turn on a light?" I asked breathlessly, surprised at the scratchy sound of my voice.

I watched him move in the dim room, and he sheathed his sword before turning on the light. He turned toward me, writing on his little notepad. When he'd reached my bedside, he held the pad out to me to read what he'd written.

"Are you injured? Do you want Captain Wintheare or Lieutenant Atrix called?" it said.

I shook my head. "Will you just sit with me a moment. I've had a terrible nightmare, I think. I'd just like to be with someone until I shake the sensation. Would you mind?"

He nodded, taking a folded blanket off the foot of my bed and spreading it over my shoulders before sitting on the edge.

"Thank you," I said, moving slightly closer to him. I was desperate to escape the empty and lonely feeling that haunted me. "I hope this day goes by quickly, Mr. Rolern. I want to go home. I'm very frightened."

Looking concerned, he wrote, "Why are you frightened? It was only a nightmare. You are safe."

"I feel safe when I'm talking to you, but there is still something inside me that won't let me forget that this is a very dangerous place for me. I want to return to where I belong."

His expression changed to one of understanding. "I'm sure you'll be going home soon," he wrote.

"Thank you, Mr. Rolern. I'm very glad I have you to talk to," I said, reaching out and taking the hand he wasn't using to write to me. His fingers closed around mine. His hands felt impossibly warm. They were comforting.

"How warm your hands are," I commented.

"Yours are very cold," he wrote in reply.

"Are they?" I asked in surprise. I'd thought I was flush, not chilled.

He nodded.

Before I could ask another question, there was a knock at my door.

"Miss Godeleva, is everything alright?" called Edda's voice from my sitting room. Mr. Rolern must have left my door open.

In the absence of a dressing gown, I drew the blankets further around myself, releasing Mr. Rolern's hand.

"Yes, Edda. I seem to have had a nightmare. Mr. Rolern is here to make certain I am safe. You may enter if you wish."

She stepped into the bedroom, and though she had initially looked calm, her eyes widened when her gaze fell upon me. After a brief second, she seemed to recover from her shock and she looked calm again.

"Goddess, you look like you've had a fright," she said when she finally spoke.

"It was a very upsetting dream," I acknowledged, assuming that I must look quite rumpled.

Edda nodded with a touch of uncertainty. "I'll get you a glass of water and then let Lieutenant Atrix know he can bring you your lunch now."

"Thank you," I started to say, but then realized what she was offering. "Lunch? Will I not be having breakfast today, Miss Edda?"

She shook her head. "No, Miss Godeleva. You slept right through it. You slept right through the morning and into the afternoon."

"I must have been more tired than I had realized. I haven't had a proper sleep in days." I attempted to justify my lengthy rest. I was certain that I'd gone to bed early the night before. It was difficult to imagine that I had remained asleep that long.

Edda stepped up to me and placed her wrist to my forehead. "Yes, it must be exhaustion. You're certainly not running a fever." She took her arm back again. "Once you've had your lunch, I will let Captain Wintheare know that you're ready to receive him."

"Thank you," I said and then out of curiosity, I asked, "Would you happen to know if Lieutenant Acksilivcs is in this building?"

"I will check for you, Miss Godeleva. If he is, I will let him know that you would like to see him."

"Thank you," I replied. I wasn't sure why, but I felt determined to continue checking to see if he was here.

Edda left the room, returning a moment later with a glass of water, which she handed to me.

"You should have something to eat. I'll go get Lieutenant Atrix."

I drank half the glass of water before setting it aside. Though I hadn't felt thirsty, once I started drinking, I realized I was parched.

"I appreciate that. Thank you, Edda. Even the water has refreshed me."

She nodded to me and left the room.

"Do I still look terrible?" I asked Mr. Rolern.

"You look very frightened," he wrote in reply as he smiled a little to me. "You usually look elegant and composed. It's surprising to see you this way."

"Thank you for your honesty," I said appreciatively.

"Are you going to wash up and dress before your lunch arrives?" he wrote.

"Yes, I should."

"I'll be right outside the door." He held the notepad out for me to see, then tucked it into his pocket.

"If I become nervous, I'll call, but I should be fine," I assured him and leaned forward to kiss him on the cheek. "Thank you for being sweet to me."

He smiled boyishly and rose to leave without glancing back.

Once he had left my apartment, I locked the door and stepped into the bathroom to wash up. Glancing in the mirror, I gasped, holding in another scream.

A wide streak at the front of my hair was no longer the rich, vibrant shade of purple that matched the rest. Instead, it was a silvery white from root to tip as though it had always been that way.

Great Goddess, what has happened to me? Is this place truly such a danger to me? Today it is my hair, but I must remain here until tomorrow. Please, Great Goddess, give me the strength to survive this place so it cannot blemish me further.

The image in the mirror blurred before me as I thought I might swoon. What would Lord Imery think of my hair now? What would Sir Fhirell think? I splashed some water on my face and managed to keep the faint at bay. I had to do something. I couldn't be seen like this.

At first, I considered cutting it off, but it was right in the front, which would have made it impossible to cover the shorter hairs. I attempted hairstyle after hairstyle to tuck the white strands under the purple ones, but it was no use. It seemed to stand out no matter what I tried.

Frowning to myself, I finished washing and dressing. I hoped the remainder of my stay here would be brief. Clearly, the strain of this place was taking its toll on me.

I had returned to trying to style my hair, sweeping it to one side and pinning it to adequately cover the uninvited streak, when there was a knock at my door.

"Who is it?" I asked. It was likely Lieutenant Atrix, but I wasn't about to make any assumptions. I couldn't even assume that my reflection would be the same the next time I looked in the mirror.

"It's your favourite Warrior, Twinkles," said Lieutenant Atrix' smiling voice.

I opened the door and had to take a step back to prevent myself from reacting to how attractive he looked. It was humiliating to think of how difficult it was to behave respectably in front of him. I tried to focus on anything but his face.

He stepped into my quarters carrying a domed tray. I nodded to Mr. Rolern, who returned the gesture before I closed the door.

"Lunch?" asked Lieutenant Atrix as he strode across the room, setting the tray down on the table.

"Thank you," I replied and took a seat across from him.

"How are you feeling today? Well rested?" he inquired casually.

"I should be," I said with a weak chuckle. "It seems I slept through the morning." Though I was attempting to be light about the subject, my oversleeping and the change in my appearance were weighing heavily on me as was the continuing fog I could feel sitting over my mind. I doubted I was doing an even moderately decent job at being convincingly jovial.

If my concern was at all apparent, Lieutenant Atrix didn't seem to notice, nor did he seem to see the new streak in my hair. Perhaps I'd done a better job at covering it than I had thought.

He merely lifted the dome on the tray to reveal a teapot, two tea cups, and a light lunch. I was relieved at the clear effort he'd made to choose something appetizing as the first meal of my day.

"May I join you for a cup of tea while you have your lunch or would you prefer to eat without me?" he asked, though he was already seated across from me.

"Please do," I replied, arranging the dishes properly in front of myself and pouring a cup of tea for each of us. As there were two teacups in the set, it was evident that his decision to have tea with me was not a spontaneous one. Interestingly, the only tea condiment on the tray was a single slice of lemon, which I added to his cup, remembering that this was how he took his tea, just as he clearly remembered that I took mine black.

"Do you have any plans for adventures this afternoon?" he asked after taking his first sip.

"I was hoping to check on Lieutenant Fhurrk before possibly going to the library. I don't intend to create a stir. I'm just trying to stay occupied until I can return home again."

"Fhurrk has gone home. If you want to visit him, you'll have to go to his quarters."

"Oh, well that is certainly good news for him. Is he on the fourth floor?"

"He is. He lives with his wife. Technically she's not a wife. He calls her his mate. But to a Sefaline, a mate is the equivalent to what we would call a wife. She may be home, too," he said in a tone that sounded like a warning.

"You say that as though you are cautioning me. Is it unwise for me to visit if his mate is at home?" I asked with uncertainty.

"I'm only cautioning you because most women aren't keen on having other beautiful women call on their husbands." He grinned slyly at me.

"I would only inquire about his health. She may remain the whole time, of course," I said, feeling distressed that any woman would think I would pursue her husband. I found myself hoping I would have more trust in my own husband, one day.

"Oh, I know that, Twinkles. Try not to be so serious all the time. Your intentions are good and anyone with half a brain can see that. But you are very attractive, more so than the average woman, and Fhurrk likes you, which in itself, is interesting. I don't think I've seen him show any interest in interacting with a woman outside of his mate or Aésha."

"I was kind to him, that's all. We were both in danger, and we worked together to survive a difficult night. I didn't do anything special. It's only that other women have not had the same opportunity to prove themselves," I explained.

He smiled in a way that made it clear to me that there was something he wasn't saying. "No. You're special. Trust me. I've been around him long enough to know."

I frowned a little. The topic of my appearance forced my thoughts to return to the changes I'd seen in myself when I woke. They were changes no one else seemed to want to acknowledge. I couldn't be the only one who could see them. That was ridiculous. Reaching up, I took my hair out of the style I'd so carefully created before Lieutenant Atrix had arrived.

"Lieutenant, have you ever seen this happen to a person overnight?"

The expression on his face was of genuine surprise and fascination.

"No. I can't say I have," he replied, leaning forward to more closely study the change.

"Nor have I."

"Are you feeling alright? You don't feel ill at all? Light headed?" he asked, glancing me over.

"I feel perfectly well, aside from being rattled from my change in appearance. It seems that I slept for a very long time last night. Right through into the afternoon. I woke up screaming. I can only assume that I had a nightmare, though I don't remember it," I explained. "I can't imagine such a fright would change my hair, though."

"Would you like me to have a doctor examine you?"

"Not yet. I'm hoping to return home soon. There are nurses where I'm headed." The thought of being examined by a Kavylak doctor in that hospital full of flasks and beakers made me shiver.

"If it makes you feel any better, the change in your hair is a good one," he said in a tone that may or may not have been a tease. I could not tell.

"Thank you, Lieutenant Atrix, but I'd much rather it return to normal, even if it is less pleasing to your eye," I replied, attempting to be as witty as I could, though I could not help the frown from forming at the thought.

"Aww, don't frown, Twinkles," he said sympathetically. "I understand. I'd look into some purple dye for you, but it would be hard to match your gorgeous colour."

"Even if you couldn't find an exact match, do you think you could find something close today?" Even the wrong shade of purple would be easier to hide with the right hairstyle than a stripe of iridescent white."

"I could get it for you today and give you more to bring with you when you leave tomorrow. Consider it my gift to you."

"Thank you. I'd like that very much."

A knock at the door interrupted the topic from advancing any further.

"Shall I get it?" he offered. "My guess is that it is Captain Wintheare."

"Oh, yes, you're most certainly right. Thank you, but I'll answer," I said, rising and approaching the door. "Who's there, please?"

"Captain Wintheare."

I opened the door, hopeful that he was here to give me Sir Fhirell's letter for the day. Captain Wintheare stood in the hall in his flawless black Warrior's uniform, looking as stone-like and emotionless as ever.

"Good afternoon, Captain. Do come in. I was just having my lunch with Lieutenant Atrix."

He nodded to my offer and entered, looking past me with disapproval to the other Warrior.

"I have a letter for you from Sir Fhirell," he said, returning his attention to me as he offered an envelope which bore Sir Fhirell's undisturbed seal.

"Thank you," I said as I received it. "Am I to reply to it right away so the Traveller may bring Sir Fhirell my response?"

"Yes," was his flat reply.

Bringing the envelope to my desk, I took my seat to read it. Now, more than ever, with the streak of white hair visible out of the corner of my eye, I longed for Sir Fhirell's reassurance. I needed to know that he was thinking about me, that he believed in me, and that I would see him again soon. My eyes searched his brief letter for feelings of warmth or fondness. As was the case in his first letter, the words were there, but the feeling was not. My shoulders sank.

Jotting a quick line to close the letter I had been composing throughout the day before, I folded the page, standing and returning to Captain Wintheare. I held out the folded paper to him.

My eyes lingered on the paper, my one link to Sir Fhirell. It sent a sharp stab of pain through my heart to think that he might not be waiting on my letters with the same longing I felt as I waited on his. I wished I could speak with him in person and know what he was truly feeling. We both knew our words would be read by Captain Wintheare before they could reach each other.

"Thank you," I said to Captain Wintheare as he took the letter.

"I will bring you any reply addressed to you. The Traveller, Zayset, will take no longer than expected to return. You will be with us only until tomorrow."

"Thank you. I know you'd already told me how long I would be staying here, but it is reassuring to hear that we remain on schedule. As kind as everyone here has been to me, the strain is causing my hair to turn white." I said, indicating the altered section of my hair. "It will be good to be home again."

Captain Wintheare's eyes flicked to the white streak of my hair as I drew it to his attention, but his gaze rapidly returned to my face.

"I had assumed you had coloured it that way. That is peculiar," he acknowledged.

I nodded in agreement.

"Would you like to see a doctor?" the captain asked me.

"No, thank you. Lieutenant Atrix has already offered the same. There will be nurses where I'm headed when I return home. I'm sure one will be able to have a look. Should I change my mind about seeing a doctor here, I will certainly ask."

"Is there anything else you wish to discuss today?"

I tried to think of anything else I might need to ask before he would leave, but I could think of nothing.

"Not unless you object to my visiting Lieutenant Fhurrk at his home. I'd like to see how he is healing."

"I have no objections."

"Then I will wish you a pleasant afternoon, Captain Wintheare. Thank you for delivering my letter and for your continued hospitality."

"I will return tomorrow when Zayset has arrived."

"Thank you, Captain Wintheare."

After nodding to me, the captain gave Lieutenant Atrix a very deliberate look, telling him to stay out of trouble. For his part, Lieutenant Atrix gave his captain a grin that was far too innocent to be genuine. Still, Captain Wintheare seemed appeased and left my quarters.

"Do you need anything other than the hair dye when I visit next?" Lieutenant Atrix asked once the captain had left. He spoke as though Captain Wintheare had never been in the room, and we were continuing a previous conversation.

"Only for something to wear tomorrow, please," I requested, hoping I wouldn't be there long enough to need anything more.

"I'll get something for you," he said before finishing his tea and setting down his cup.

"Thank you." I hoped that whatever I would be wearing when I was brought back to Sir Fhirell would be something decent in my eyes, not just Lieutenant Atrix'. For a moment, my mind started to wander to thoughts of Sir Fhirell and how happy I would be to see him again. My mouth crawled into a smile at the thought of his surprise upon seeing me in my new Kavylak fashions, which managed to be proper and naughty at the same time; covering just as much as they must without a single extra step.

I was drawn back to reality when Lieutenant Atrix stood up and spoke.

"If you'll excuse me, Twinkles, it seems I've got some errands to run."

"Of course. Thank you for the meal." I rose to see him to the door.

He nodded to me and walked out the door as I opened it for him. "See you at dinner."

I smiled at him. I couldn't have helped it if I'd wanted to. There was something about him that would have made me smile at him, even if he'd told me he was leaving because he couldn't stand the sight of me.

"See you at dinner," I said, stupidly repeating his words.

He flashed a smile at me and turned to walk down the hall. As soon as he stepped in front of Mr. Rolern, he tripped a little, shook his head, grinned, and walked perfectly the rest of the way down the corridor. I wondered how that could have happened. Mr. Rolern hadn't moved a muscle. Why would Lieutenant Atrix have pretended to trip?

Once Lieutenant Atrix was out of sight, I stepped the rest of the way into the hallway, locking my door and turning to Mr. Rolern.

"We're going for a little visit," I informed him with a mischievous smile.

He tilted his head with curiosity but nodded and walked with me down the hall. As we walked, he scratched out a quick note on his little pad of paper.

"Where are we going?"

"The fourth floor," I told him. "We're hoping not to anger a mate while we're there."

"I'll wait outside," he wrote in response with a knowing smile on his face.

I chuckled and climbed the mountain of stairs until we arrived on the fourth floor. The grey metal doors on this floor were identical to my own, only each one featured a small name plate at eye level. As I looked for Lieutenant Fhurrk's name, I watched for Lieutenant Acksilivcs' quarters as well. I didn't spot it on the way, but promised myself not to give up.

When we arrived at Lieutenant Fhurrk's door, I knocked. Barely a moment passed before the Sefaline opened his door looking tired but strikingly better than the last time I'd seen him.

"Lieutenant Fhurrk, how well you look!" I declared happily, keeping my voice down in case his mate was home.

"Irys Godeleva," he greeted me sounding surprised, but neither pleased nor displeased to see me. He looked at me a moment before his nose twitched and curled slightly. "Are you not well?"

This took me entirely off guard. "Oh, you must mean my hair," I said with a frown. "I don't like it either. It turned up while I slept last night. I'd had a nightmare. It must have been awful to have such an effect."

He looked up to my hair and his brow knit as he appeared to notice the streak for the first time.

"You smell different," he informed me. "Not like yourself."

"How so? Could it be that I'm using a different soap than I had when we last met?"

Lieutenant Fhurrk glanced at Mr. Rolern before looking to me again. A low growl in the back of his throat seemed to mutter displeasure. "Maybe," he said with what sounded more like resignation than an honest answer.

"...but that's not what you think?" I prompted.

"No. But sometimes what I think is wrong. I have been unwell. Maybe my senses are not as accurate as they should be," he grumbled.

"I understand. You must be happy to be home with your mate instead of down in the infirmary," I said, hoping to change the subject to something he found more pleasant.

"Yes," he said flatly, to my disappointment. "Why are you here?" he asked bluntly.

"Because I care and wanted to see how you're doing. I don't mean to take much of your time."

His expression softened, lightening my heart. The corners of his mouth lifted a little, and his eyes brightened. It was as though someone had smoothed away the edges in his formerly sharp appearance. It wasn't a smile, but it was the next best thing.

"Thank you," he said, the suspicion gone from his tone. "Would you like some milk?"

The offer surprised me.

"...milk?" I asked, hoping my bewildered tone didn't insult him by questioning some form of important Sefaline custom. "I...certainly. Milk sounds very nice, thank you." I'd never much enjoyed the taste of milk, but the offer felt like a meaningful one, and I wasn't about to decline.

"You can come in," Lieutenant Fhurrk told me. "You stay outside," he added to Rolern.

I glanced to Rolern in case he would object to Lieutenant Fhurrk's instructions, but he merely smiled and stood next to the door where he would await my return.

I smiled at him with a bit of a shrug and headed inside for what would most certainly be the most fascinating glass of milk I'd ever been offered in my life.

Chapter 21

Megan

I abruptly sat up, gasping for air as if I had been underwater for too long. My heart was racing, and I couldn't make sense of what was happening or where I was. All I could remember were feelings, faces, and names: Xandon. Enadria. Elindria.

Who the heck are Enadria and Elindria?

Why am I dreaming about Xandon again?

At least Irys wasn't in my dream this time.

I shook my head violently in an effort to rid myself of my muddled and disturbed thoughts and the odd and foreign feelings they brought. Shivering, I opened my eyes to the darkness. I didn't know what time it was, but there was no hint of dawn in sight. My whole body and my head ached. It was a miserable feeling made even more miserable by the lack of light.

Mez and Keavren were still sleeping. I knew because I could hear their soft snores. I'd be jealous of them, except that I could move my arms without excruciating pain, which still made me the luckiest one of us.

Grumbling quietly, I rose to my feet and found it difficult to stand straight. I took a careful step forward and stopped, suddenly keenly aware that something felt strange. I knew this eerie feeling.

I felt like we were being watched.

Blindly, I crept over to Mez, reaching out toward his sled with the intention of stroking his face to wake him as calmly as I could.

"Don't wake him. He needs his sleep," said a quiet but very, very, very deep voice.

I gasped and whirled around, seeing no one. A shiver crawled up my spine. I had never heard a voice like that before. The tone was definitely male, but the sound was more demon than man.

"Wh-who's there? Who are you?" I managed to squeak out in barley a whisper. My hand went to my pocket for the bone dagger.

"Lieutenant Gabeld Sangoa," answered the demon-voice-man. "I'm a Warrior. You're safe. I'm just watching over you until the others arrive."

Yeah, buddy. I don't feel any safer.

My heart was steadily pounding from the fear that this Warrior's nightmare voice had caused. It was like my six-year-old self had come face to face with the imaginary monster in her closet and now she knew he was real.

"Where are you? How can you see me?" My hand closed more tightly around the dagger's handle as I debated waking Mez.

There was a long silent pause before he answered. "I'm next to a tree on the edge of your little clearing. It's really better that you can't see me. People don't like the way I look. I can see you because I see best within the darkest shadows."

He sees best within the darkest shadows? Whaaaat?

Part of me was feeling relieved that I couldn't see him now, but my imagination had officially gone wild, guessing at and fearing his appearance.

Did he have horns coming out of his head? Did he have fangs? Did he have large red eyes and grotesque features? Did this Warrior look like a fairytale monster?

Then it occurred to me that since I couldn't see him, I couldn't see his uniform.

What if he wasn't really a Warrior? What if he was some freak watching us in the woods who liked scaring people before he ate them?

Deep breaths, Megan. Get. A. Grip.

"You say you are a Warrior," I said, unable to keep my voice steady as I spoke. "If that's true, what are the names of these two men?"

"Mez Basarovka and Keavren Fadeal. They are my brothers," he replied.

Okay. He gets one friend point for that.

"Who am I?

"Megan Wynters."

I gasped and tensed when I heard my name in his promise-of-doom-to-come voice. Still, as much as I was quaking in my boots, I had to give him a second friend point. Obviously, he knew who we were and now I was pretty sure he was a Warrior since he used the term "brothers."

"Aésha says to say, 'Hi Baby'," he tacked on for good measure, and my knees nearly buckled at his words. I never imagined that the word "baby" could sound so haunting.

"Uh. Um. Wow." I said nervously, really not knowing what else to say other than: "Guess you're a Warrior."

He laughed, and it was utterly terrifying to hear. I shrank back in fear, and it took everything in me not to cover my ears and shut my eyes like I was watching a horror movie.

What the hell was *this Warrior?*

I listened to hear if Mez and Keavren were awake, but their breathing hadn't changed. They were still sleeping.

Geeze! They must really be sound sleepers.

I debated waking them again, but didn't and decided to learn more from this new Warrior.

"Is, uh. Is, Aésha coming?" Well, I now knew what my impersonation of a frightened mouse would sound like.

"Yes. She insisted on leading. Amarogq is coming, too, I think, and probably Remms."

I didn't know who those other Warriors were, but I was glad to hear I would be seeing Aésha. I was in desperate need of a friendly face.

"You won't be travelling on your own anymore. They'll come to you," he informed me. "They should be here soon. If not, I will bring them out here, myself, because if they're not here by the time the sun comes up, I won't be of any use to you," he added.

What the...? Is he a vampire? No, Megan. Vampires aren't real. You need sleep. Focus!

"Wait," I said, fully processing his words after my vampire-freak-out, "You can do that? Bring them here? Why didn't you just do that, or take us back to begin with, instead of just watching us?" I asked, slightly exasperated.

"Because my arms get tired," was his logical response. "I might bring Remms, though," he pondered aloud. "He's light enough."

Seriously? What in the heck was he talking about? Does he run with people like Rral had run with me? Is that why his arms get tired? If that's the case, how fast can this guy run?

"Will you be alright for a short while?" He asked, clearly having decided he was going to speed-run, or whatever, to get some light-weight guy named Remms.

"Yeah, I'll be alright. Thanks. I'm just going to change their dressings." I turned toward Mez.

"Don't bother," he said, causing me to jump. "I'm getting Remms."

"Um. Okay." I guessed Remms must be the medic Warrior. I hoped he had more pain-killer drugs for Mez.

"It was nice meeting you, Megan,"

"Yeah. Uh. You, too, Lieutenant Sangoa."

Meh, at least he's a polite scary demon.

He didn't respond. Instinctively, I knew by how un-tense I suddenly felt, that he had already left. He had done it without a sound. That was definitely the most paranormal-like experience I'd had in my life to date.

I sat down, waiting for Lieutenant Sangoa to return, for one of the guys to wake up, or for dawn to break. There was nothing for me to do until one of those things happened, so I chose to admire the stars, particularly the blue one that was still shining brightly.

*   *   *   *   *

"I'm back," the demon Warrior's deep voice greeted me, shocking me back to life and pulling a startled gasp from my lips. I must have fallen asleep because when I opened my eyes, I discovered it wasn't as dark out anymore. False dawn had arrived.

I could now see the shadowed outlines of the trees, the horses, and Mez and Keavren, who appeared to still be sleeping on their sleds. Scrambling to my feet, I looked in the direction of his voice, but saw only the black silhouettes of the trees.

"Sorry. That was my soothing voice," he said with a chuckle. I laughed uneasily. It was the best I could do.

"I'll watch until the light is visible, and then I will see you in the Capital," he informed me.

"Um. Okay. Thanks," I said and tensed when I noticed that someone was walking toward us from the trees. It was still too dark to make out any real details, but from what I could see, it looked like a very slim man with a slightly above average height. As he drew closer, I could see the distinguishing outline of a Warrior uniform. I braced myself, afraid that it was Lieutenant Sangoa and worried that his appearance would frighten me to my core.

"Lieutenant Sangoa?" I queried tentatively.

The approaching man giggled in response. "No."

Wow. Yeah, this guy sounds the exact opposite of a baritone demon.

"I'm Remms Neajet," he responded quietly in a soft and friendly voice.

Woo hoo! The doctor Warrior is here!

He stopped a couple of feet in front of me. I still couldn't make out any of his features in distinct detail, due to the lack of light, but nothing about him seemed overly odd from what I could see.

"I'm Megan. Mez and Keavren are hurt really badly. Lieutenant Sangoa said that you could help them."

"Hi Megan," he said with a nod. "I'll help them as much as I can here so they can travel home more comfortably. Then, I'll really fix them up. I just helped someone else, so I need to take it a little easier than usual," he explained, even though I had no idea what he was talking about.

Wasn't he just going to feed them some cubes and maybe clean their wounds better, or something? Why did the Warriors always have to be so complicated?

"Don't worry. They'll all be here soon enough," he assured me, when I hadn't responded to his earlier statement. "Thank you for taking care of them."

I smiled a little. I couldn't help it. There was something about this guy that I liked and trusted. "No problem. They're good men."

"You're not hurt, right?" he then asked.

"No. I'm fine. Nothing a nice hot bath, a masseuse, and three-thousand hours of sleep won't fix."

He giggled, looking toward Mez and Keavren.

"Mez is worse than Keavren," I supplied.

Lieutenant Neajet nodded. "I'll get to him," he promised, "but I need to heal Keavren, first. Dawn is breaking, and Gabeld will be leaving in a few minutes."

"Nope. Now," corrected the deep voice from the trees. I shuddered from the sound, and a flock of birds took off from a nearby tree. "See you soon guys, and Megan."

"Bye," Neajet said with a giggle.

And, just like that, Lieutenant Sangoa was gone again. I swear I felt the nature all around us give a collective sigh of relief.

Lieutenant Neajet walked over to Keavren, examining the still-sleeping man. I didn't understand why he wanted to help Keavren first, but I also didn't feel it right to question him.

"Is it just what's under the bandage?"

"It's also their arms and shoulders. They were strung up in trees, hanging by their outstretched arms. They were there like that for a while."

He winced at my description. "I'll see what I can do." He sighed with a bit of a frown, extracting a pair of scissors from a pouch he was carrying. "I have a feeling I'm going to be spending a lot of time at home with my cat for the next few days."

Heh? What the heck does that mean? I guess being a doctor stresses this guy out...maybe. Whatever.

I watched as the Warrior very, very carefully and gently cut Keavren's bandages, peeling them off so he could see the damage. Keavren didn't budge.

It was becoming lighter out with each passing minute, and I could see Lieutenant Neajet more clearly. He was maybe my age with a very thin, pale face and long dark hair that had vibrant streaks of possibly red, or maybe even pink, mixed through it.

He put the scissors back in his bag and looked calm for a moment as if he was collecting himself before he carried out the next phase of his healing. I braced myself, expecting to see stitches being performed or some other surgeon-y thing.

That didn't happen.

Instead, I watched, dumfounded as the Warrior leaned over Keavren, inhaled deeply, then exhaled a dark-looking smoke from his mouth. The smoke lingered briefly over Keavren's wounds before wrapping around them, enveloping Keavren's back, shoulders, arms, and hands, like a big smoke hug.

What in the name of...

Lieutenant Neajet drew in his breath, and the smoke disappeared, leaving Keavren's wounds knitted together. He wasn't fully healed, but instead of being only several hours old, his injuries now looked like they were two weeks old!

I had never witnessed anything more cool or amazing in my life. Remms wasn't a doctor. He was a literal healer of wounds. My mouth had fallen open as I stared, numb for words.

Lieutenant Neajet stood on unsteady feet, wobbling a bit as he walked toward Mez. He managed to regain his balance and knelt down, looking exhausted.

"I'll just be a minute before I start," he said, catching his breath.

"Are you alright?" I asked with concern, approaching him. I could hear in my voice the awe I still felt from witnessing his skill. Each time I looked at Keavren's back, I still couldn't believe what I'd just seen. Even though he remained sleeping, Keavren appeared more relaxed and peaceful.

"Oh, yes." He nodded and took a small package out of his pocket, unwrapped it, and took a bite out of the bar it contained. He struggled to swallow it but got it down. "It just takes a lot out of me."

My eyes flicked from Keavren's back to Lieutenant Neajet, amazed.

"How did you do that, Lieutenant Neajet?"

"I use my own energy to heal others," he explained as he worked up to taking another bite of the bar. "And you can call me, Remms."

I nodded to him, but was still having a hard time wrapping my brain around the fact that he could use his energy to heal people.

"I might get weak after I heal, Mez," he added, looking at me seriously. "If I pass out, could you help a bit until everyone gets here? Keavren will be strong enough to guard us," he assured me.

"Yes, of course, Remms. I'll keep watch and do whatever I can. I've got a knife, too." I revealed.

"Thanks, Megan," he said with a smile of appreciation. "You're as neat as they said you were."

Someone said I was "neat?" Cool! Um…I think?

I moved closer to Remms. "I'm right here if you need me."

He nodded to me and wrapped up the rest of the bar, putting it away. I didn't know if he was saving it for later or if he just couldn't stomach it anymore.

Picking up the scissors, he carefully cut through Mez' bandages, and we both grimaced at the skin beneath. The sun was rising now, and the angry flesh of Mez' back could easily be seen.

Remms steadied himself, taking a few deep breaths and then took a long inhale before slowly exhaling the healing cloud of smoke over Mez. Just as it had done with Keavren's wounds, the smoke enveloped Mez' injuries, working its magic. The only difference this time, was that with the additional light, I could see that the smoke Remms had exhaled was a dark grey. As it blanketed Mez' wounds, I watched it change from dark grey to light grey to pink.

Remms' breathing returned to normal and the smoke dissipated, leaving Mez' skin slightly less healed than Keavren's was, but still miles ahead in recovery from where it had been. Like Keavren, Mez remained asleep.

Remms swayed and brought a hand to his eyes. Immediately, I wrapped an arm around his shoulders to help keep him steady.

"I got you," I promised.

Taking me by surprise, he hugged me like he was a little boy and I was his big sister. "Thanks," he whispered.

I held on to him more securely, noticing that he smelled nice; a soft scent somewhere between clean laundry and wild flowers. It made me yearn to take a shower.

"Mind if we just sit like this until the boys wake up or everyone gets here?" he asked. I could tell by his tone that he felt ashamed that he had to ask, but I didn't feel that he had anything to be ashamed about. Honestly, he just healed two people. He should feel he could ask for anything he wanted!

"I don't mind at all, Remms. You can sleep if you want to." I really wanted him to know that whatever he decided was okay with me.

He shook his head. "Thanks. I'll sleep later. For now, we'll watch over them together."

I nodded, and we sat down. Once we were settled, Remms rested his head on my shoulder, and I kept my arm around him.

"I like you, Megan," he said then. "I've just got a feeling, you know?"

"Yeah," I agreed. "I think I do, Remms. I think I have the same feeling about you." I smiled, realizing as I spoke the words that they were true. There was just something about him that I liked and that made me feel completely at ease, and in return, I felt accepted by him. It was a nice feeling and one I had needed for a long time.

"If you're hungry, I have more of those nutrient bars in my bag."

"Thanks, but I'm okay right now. I ate a little earlier, and I don't have much of an appetite at the moment," I confessed.

He nodded with understanding. "I don't usually eat for a while after I heal people. It all just comes back up."

"It's really amazing what you can do," I said, wanting to change the subject, because between feeling scared for so long and massive lack of sleep, the thought of food was starting to make me feel nauseated.

"Thank you, I think I'm pretty unique. I don't know anyone else who can do it," he said without sounding full of himself.

"You really are. I've seen what some of the other Warriors can do, but you're really one-of-a-kind."

"Yeah. They're really crisp, and they don't have to spend a ton of time in their quarters healing on their own."

"It sucks that you have to spend so much time recuperating after you use your skill," I empathized. "But your skill really is cooler, uh, I mean crisp-uh-er."

Wow. Smooth, Megan.

He giggled, amused. "Oh, yeah, my cat tells me my skill is crisp, too," he joked. "Well, I like to imagine that she would tell me that."

"I have a cat, too, or at least I did. I hope I still do. I lost her the night that I was captured by the rebels," I explained, frowning at the memory of losing Pounce and still hoping beyond hope that I'd find her, by some miracle, once I returned to the military compound.

"I'm sorry to hear that." Remms frowned. "I just got mine, since I've been very lonely from healing people a lot lately. Most of the time, she's my only company."

I nodded, curiously looking at Remms as something occurred to me.

"Healing a lot of people?" I queried. "Wait, was Mez one of the people you healed? I mean, after the battle where Syliza invaded the compound?"

He nodded. "Yes. I healed him and some of the other guys a few days ago. That's why I got the cat. Now that I've healed these two again, I'll be in my quarters for a while."

Ah-ha! Healed-Mez mystery solved.

"Was Mez badly injured?"

"He got hit in the head and back with a chunk of shrapnel. He'd lost some blood. Head wounds always bleed a lot."

Ah-ha again! I knew he'd been injured badly, and I wasn't crazy for being surprised when I'd discovered he was a part of the rescue party. This was all starting to make more sense...okay, as much sense as can be made of a world with people who possess super-human powers.

"His head likely saved my life," I told Remms, feeling I owed him a bit of an explanation as to why I was suddenly randomly asking him about the specifics regarding previously-injured Mez.

He nodded against my shoulder. "He's lucky he didn't get a concussion. I can't heal those."

"Oh? How come?"

"I can do things like broken bones, torn tissue, cuts, that kind of thing. I can't do brain damage, heart failure, and that sort of thing."

Interesting.

"What about disease?"

"Nope. Your stuffy nose is your problem...and please don't share it with me," he tacked on with a giggle.

I laughed and nodded toward Mez and Keavren, who still slept soundly.

"How fast will they heal on their own now?"

"Pretty fast," Remms said with confidence. "They'll be sore, but it's all put back together. The itching is what'll bug them the most for the next couple of days."

"I'm glad to hear it. I was really worried. We were lucky to get out of there alive."

"The Northerners are dangerous." Remms nodded.

"They really are, and they don't like you guys very much."

"No. But we have a kind of deal with them. We're supposed to pretty much leave each other alone, if I understand it right."

"I think you understand it right. I know I certainly do now. Got the message loud and clear."

He frowned. "I'm sorry you went through all that. It had to be scary."

He lifted his head from my shoulder and looked at me with tired eyes that I could now see were a funky shade of burgundy. The sky above us grew brighter and brighter.

"Thank you for bringing my brothers home."

I nodded seriously. "I wouldn't have left them there. I couldn't. Besides, I owed them both."

Remms shook his head, "You didn't owe them anything. You're just a very good person for bringing them back. We're all grateful to you for that. Well, most of us."

Without even saying his name, I knew exactly who he was omitting from "most of us": Galnar. Definitely wasn't going to be getting a thank-you card from that guy. That being said, now that Remms had helped me solve one mystery, I wondered if he'd shed a little light on another.

Remms rested his head back down on my shoulder and sighed.

"Remms?"

"Hmm?" Remms asked, sounding sleepier.

"When I was outside in the battle on the compound, I could have sworn that I saw Galnar light himself on fire."

"That's his skill."

"His skill is lighting himself on fire?"

"Yes. Well, not exactly, he..." Remms stopped talking abruptly as if he suddenly realized in his sleepy state that he'd said too much. "We're not supposed to talk about Captain Galnar," he concluded.

I didn't pester him further. I filed away the new piece of information I had learned about Galnar and decided I'd learn the rest of it later. That being said, more and more, I was starting to think that he might actually be pyrokinetic, which was a frightening thought.

"What's your cat's name?" Remms asked, drawing me out of my thoughts.

"Pounce."

"Pounce is a good name."

I could hear the smile in his voice.

"Mez got her for me. She has bright blue eyes, and she's all black except for white on her paws and a bit on her chest."

"Mine, too," he said happily. "Her name's Killer."

Hmm. Guess that's a popular cat colouring on this planet.

"Killer?" I laughed a little. "That's an interesting name."

"Yeah. She kills fluffs."

"Oh, yeah? That's funny, mine does that, too." I was finding the coincidences between our two cats rather curious.

"Mine's a Fairwilde," I said, wondering if his was the same breed.

"I don't know what mine is. I got her from a scrounger, not a breeder. Did yours have cute horns?"

My brows raised at his genuine question.

Uh…Okay. So here's where the similarities stop.

"Um, no."

"Maybe they just hadn't come in yet," he said with a little shrug, and he still wasn't kidding.

"Yeah, maybe," I agreed, really not knowing what else to say there, because, seriously…what?

"I don't think I'm ever going to find her again, though," I confessed, feeling a clench of sadness in my chest as I voiced my fear out loud for the first time. "I dropped her in the battle right after Mez saved me."

"I'm really sorry. Maybe we can ask around when we get back and see if anyone has seen a cat like yours."

"Thanks, Remms," I said.

"Sure."

"Oh, and I've been meaning to ask, do you know if Amorette and Fiffine made it back alright?"

"Yes. They're home. They arrived and sent us out to look for you when you didn't turn up, too."

"That's good. I'm glad to hear that."

I had to admit that as much as I was still on the fence about the Warriors, they were very efficient at completing their missions and returning people to Kavylak.

The sound of feet speeding toward us on the ground made me jump and I tightened my hold on Remms, who abruptly lifted his head from my shoulder. We both turned toward the sound.

A wolf materialized mid-run, and I knew we had been found. I never thought I'd feel relief from seeing Amarogq's spirit wolves.

A second wolf joined the first, and they ran up to us, sniffed us, and then proceeded to check out Keavren and Mez, sniffing their wounds.

The approaching thunder of galloping horses' hooves pulled my attention from the wolves. Turning, I eagerly scanned the tree line in anticipation of the approaching riders.

I heard her before I saw her.

"Baby!" Aésha cried, and a moment later, she rode into view on her horse. Pulling back on the reins she brought the horse to an abrupt halt and dropped to the ground, running toward me.

Her pet name for me, that I had once found irritating and then tolerable at best, was now music to my ears. Abandoning Remms, I jumped to my feet, taking off toward her, flinging my arms around her when we met. She held me back just as tightly.

God, I was glad to see her.

"I'm so glad to see you," I said to her, still not letting her go, while doing my best not to break into tears from the relief.

"Are you hurt? Did Remms fix you up?" she asked me quietly in a protective tone that was not unfamiliar to me or even unwelcome at the moment.

"I'm not hurt. He didn't need to heal me. I'm just really tired and sore from riding the horse."

Aésha drew away from our hug, but kept her hands gently resting on my shoulders.

"I'll take you home, Baby. We'll get you all fixed up." Her eyes traveled up and down my form, and she gave me one of her best sultry grins. "And I can massage those legs for you," she purred.

I gaped at her before catching myself and cracking a smile. I could never tell if she was just playing with me or if she was serious, or both. I think she liked it that way. It was probably the heart of being a Charmer after all.

Amarogq arrived and got off his horse. I turned from Aésha and watched him. He nodded to me before heading over to Mez and

Keavren, where one of his wolves stood guard. Keavren had woken at some point while I was wrapped up in Aésha and was already on his feet. I was glad but still surprised to see him looking so well, after I had become accustomed to seeing him injured and immobile for so long.

Amarogq nodded at Keavren, but made his way to Mez, bending down and quietly speaking to him. He helped him to get to his feet. Unlike Keavren, Mez appeared sore, stiff, and exhausted. He definitely had more healing ahead of him than Keavren, but looked so much better. After a few more words with Mez, Amarogq made quick work of unhooking the two sleds from the horses and tossed them aside.

I hope they're going to recycle those.

"Thanks for getting these two fools out of that mess, Megs," Amarogq said, smiling at me.

I looked back at him and gave a little tense nod. I suddenly felt awkward in his presence after having spent time with his family, the children he didn't know about, and after having been saved by his ex-wife. I feared if I spoke I'd reveal everything to him.

"You good to ride with Aésha or would you rather *snuggle* with me," Keavren asked me with a grin, knowing full well I had every intention of riding back with Aésha.

"I think we both know I'm riding back with Aésha," I said to him, grateful for the distraction from Amarogq.

Keavren chuckled and walked up to Remms, reaching down to help him up. I gave a small smile to Remms, and he returned it with a tired expression.

Glancing at Mez, who wasn't looking so steady on his feet, I asked, "Are you going to be alright to ride?"

"I'll be riding with Keavren," he told me. "Thank you, Megan. You were great. I hope to see you for that coffee."

"Looking forward to it," I said, and I was, even if it would never happen.

Mez held my gaze, his eyes saying more than his words ever could. I hope mine said just as much back to him, because in that moment, I knew that something had changed between Mez and me. He was important to me now, in a way that he wasn't before.

I liked him.

"Take care of Mez," I all but ordered Keavren, my directness and tone surprising me.

"I will," Keavren promised. "My turn now. You two have already done your parts." He smiled at me. "See you back there, Megan, and thanks."

I smiled. "See you."

"Come on, Baby," Aésha said, draping her arm around my shoulder and guiding me over to her horse.

Releasing me, she mounted her horse and then helped me climb on behind her. I wrapped my arms around her waist like a loose belt and pressed the side of my face to her shoulder, careful not to lock her long braided ponytail between us. Shutting my eyes, I inhaled the soft and sweet scent of her dark brown hair and perfect sun-kissed skin, which pleasantly mingled with the mild leather smell of her black uniform jacket. The familiar scent of her brought me infinite comfort, and I was already drifting off before the horses took their first steps.

Chapter 22
Irys

I followed Lieutenant Fhurrk into his quarters and, when I realized he was headed into the kitchen, I waited patiently in the living room. Never having been invited into anyone's kitchen before, it seemed inappropriate for me to follow him there now.

Before I could have the time to question my decision, Lieutenant Fhurrk had returned, holding two glasses of milk. He offered one to me, and I took it, a little surprised that it was indeed a glass of milk.

"Sit," he instructed me, and I took my place on a chair in the small living space. "Tyrasar, come and meet Irys Godeleva," he called back toward the kitchen.

I felt tense at the thought of actually meeting his mate and set my glass down on an end table next to me so my trembling hands wouldn't spill milk on my clothes. I braced myself for what I was expecting would be the female version of the Sefaline in front of me.

A smiling woman appeared in the kitchen doorway, dressed in a blouse and trousers. She had long, vibrant, orange-red hair and happy light brown eyes. Though she was likely my height, she gave the impression of being taller because of her smooth, graceful movements and confident manner.

"Hello, Irys Godeleva," she greeted me pleasantly, stepping up to Fhurrk who leaned down and inhaled at her neck. She returned the gesture.

In any other circumstance, this exchange would have been quite awkward for me, but Mrs. Fhurrk's gesture was quick and natural enough to make it easy to comfortably watch. That it changed Lieutenant Fhurrk's entire demeanor only made it more fascinating. Suddenly, Lieutenant Fhurrk seemed content and pleased to have me there.

"This is my mate," he proudly told me.

"It's very nice to meet you, Mrs. Fhurrk," I smiled to her.

This seemed to amuse Lieutenant Fhurrk, whose face broke into a wide grin, exposing the fangs among his upper teeth.

"Thank you for helping Fhurrk to come home again," Mrs. Fhurrk replied, looking nearly as amused as her husband.

"He helped me, too. I'm glad to have made a friend at a time when we were both in need of someone," I replied, hoping this response would be as well received as my greeting.

They took a seat together on the sofa, sitting so close together that light wouldn't have found its way between them.

"Yes. I will always be grateful to you for your help, Irys Godeleva. You did save my life," he said quite seriously, but his former tension had tapered off with his mate's presence. The softening effect she had on him was striking.

"I will always be thankful to you for helping me to find my way through the darkness. We were both fortunate that day," I replied.

Lieutenant Fhurrk nodded and sipped his milk. I decided that I couldn't put off drinking my own beverage any longer, so I picked up my glass and had a sip. It tasted just as I remembered it from my childhood, though I hadn't liked it much then, either. I returned the glass to the table hoping I'd had enough of it to avoid showing my distaste for it.

"You need to return home to that Knight and tell him you want to be his mate. He wants you, too," he informed me quite matter-of-factly.

I was grateful that I'd already swallowed my sip of milk and put down the glass. The flush immediately crawled over my cheeks.

"I do look forward to returning to him very soon, once the Traveller returns," I replied as noncommittally as I could. Still, I felt as though I had been caught in a lie.

The lieutenant nodded, accepting my response. He looked as though he might pursue the topic further, but his mate raised her hand and scratched him gently under his hair. A low purr rumbled from the base of his throat, and he looked tenderly at her. For that instant, it was clear that she was the only thing that existed to him. Mrs. Fhurrk purred to him in return.

It was a touching and yet equally uncomfortable moment to watch. Though I didn't want to interrupt their happiness, there was only so long that I could pretend to be a part of the furniture.

"Have you seen Lieutenant Acksilivcs since you've been home?" I queried as though continuing a civilized conversation and not watching the couple rapidly forget that I was present. "I've been hoping to say 'hello' to him before I leave."

"His name is Lieutenant Acksilivcs Fhir," Lieutenant Fhurrk informed me.

"Fhir?"

"That is his name. We usually call him Acksil, but his last name is Fhir," he said bluntly.

"I had no idea. I'd thought Acksilivcs was his family name."

"No." He shook his head. "You were wrong."

"In that case, have you seen Lieutenant Fhir?" I asked with a smile. It struck me as odd that no one had brought up this detail before as I had inquired about Lieutenant Fhir to many different people since my arrival.

"I don't know if he is here. I have not seen him since we arrived, but I have not yet returned to duty."

"Thank you. I thought I'd asked in case you'd seen him in the hall or if, perhaps, he had visited you in the infirmary."

"He lives next door. You can always knock there."

"I will. Thank you for the advice."

We both sipped our glasses of milk and though I was willing to continue our conversation, Lieutenant Fhurrk seemed to be far more interested in his mate than he was in me. He turned to her, bringing both arms around her to hold her closely. She sank into him, purring as she tucked her face in against the side of his neck with her head on his shoulder. He purred in response, shutting his eyes.

I rose abruptly from my chair, heading for the door.

"Thank you very kindly for the milk, Lieutenant Fhurrk. I'm very glad to see you're feeling much better. It was lovely to meet you, Mrs. Fhurrk. I must be going as I have other visits I must make this afternoon." I hoped that if it sounded like my afternoon was pressing, I might not appear rude by leaving abruptly.

Lieutenant Fhurrk's eyes opened and moved to me before he nodded.

"Thank you for coming to see me. I hope I will see you again before you go. I like you."

It was the friendliest thing he had ever said to me. It was a genuine compliment.

"That would be lovely," I replied just as genuinely. "I look forward to it."

Neither Sefaline made a move to see me out, so I stepped into the hall and shut the door behind me, leaving the happy couple behind.

In the corridor, Mr. Rolern was leaning casually against the wall, but he stood up straighter when I turned to face him. He looked at me expectantly, and I smiled.

"That was an adventure." I giggled a little. "It was actually quite nice to see him. I met his mate."

He made a silly spooked face, and I chuckled, turning to head to the door next to Lieutenant Fhurrk's. I took a breath and stopped, looking at the name "Fhir" stamped into the name plate. Raising my hand, I knocked before I could lose my nerve.

I'd felt certain Acksil would be home, and I'd finally be able to speak with him. Something deep within me wanted to tell him what was happening and have him assure me that everything would be well. He'd helped me twice before. I craved his encouragement.

Mr. Rolern stepped up next to me. I'd been standing and waiting too long. No one was home.

"May I have one of your papers and borrow your pencil so I may slip a note under his door?" I asked my silent guard.

He nodded and tore a tiny paper from his pad, handing me his pencil with it.

I thanked him and took the items. Coming up with something to say suddenly seemed more difficult than I had anticipated. *What would I write to him? It's not as though we were close friends. He wasn't expecting me to visit. What if someone else were to see my note first?* I decided to write a short note. Simple seemed to be the best route.

Lieutenant Acksilivcs Fhir,
Just a little note in greeting to wish you well.
I stopped by while I was here, but you had not yet returned.
Cordially,
Irys Godeleva

Sliding the note under the door, I returned the pencil to Mr. Rolern.

"I think I'd like to return to my room and read to my guard for a while if you wouldn't mind," I told him, feeling as though a bit of the wind had been taken from my sails.

Mr. Rolern looked at me kindly and smiled. Though he hadn't used any words, I knew he was telling me he'd like that, too.

We walked back down the stairs to my door, and I unlocked it. Before turning the knob, I looked down the hall in both directions to make sure there wasn't anyone else there. When I was certain we were unobserved, I approached him and kissed him on the cheek. Without Mr. Rolern, I would have felt entirely alone. He wasn't just a guard to me. He was there for me not only to make me feel safe, but he'd also become a companion I never expected to have. It meant a lot, and I hoped he knew it.

"Give a little knock if anyone comes near. Until then, I'll read to you," I said and stepped into my quarters. Settling in next to the door with the book, I read until I heard a light tapping on the door.

Not long after, there was a knock.

"Who's there?" I asked.

"Your dinner date," replied Lieutenant Atrix.

Chapter 23
Megan

"We're here, Baby." Aésha's soothing voice woke me from my mild slumber. I had fallen in and out of sleep throughout our journey but was glad to learn that we had arrived.

I perked up a bit, fully opening my eyes to take in the Kavylak Capital. We moved at a slow trot through the city. People naturally moved out of our way, and I swear it was more because they didn't want to block Aésha's route than it was to avoid being trampled by a moving horse.

Once again I felt like I was riding a horse with a celebrity. This time, though, I wasn't sitting in front of Thayn and riding proudly through the pretty cobblestone and colourful city streets of Lorammel. Instead, I was holding on to Aésha as we rode through the crowded, orderly streets of Capital City. They held about as much colour and "pretty" as the browns, blacks, and greys of the industrial revolution. A hazy layer of pollution hung over our heads to complete the city's overall smoggy atmosphere.

We rode up to the massive and unwelcoming gates of the military compound. The otherwise stony-faced guards saw her and smiled before saluting and opening the gates to let us pass. Aésha returned the salute as she entered. I might as well not have existed.

She guided the horse to the stables, woah-ed it to a halt, and easily slid to the ground, passing the reins to a waiting stable boy. He had dark copper-coloured hair and couldn't have been older than thirteen or fourteen.

"Thanks, Tshul," she said, kissing his cheek. I thought the boy's head was going to explode it went so red.

Turning her smiling face to me, she reached up to offer me a hand. I took her help and got down but was surprised when my legs gave out as soon as my feet touched the ground. I would have fallen had Aésha not caught me.

Wrapping a secure arm around my lower back and waist, she helped steady me.

"Let's get you home and in bed, Baby," she grinned at me.

I didn't argue, falling asleep forever in a bed was all I wanted to do right now. I was emotionally, mentally, and physically spent.

We walked toward the residences as fast as my legs would carry me. I tried to keep my eyes peeled for Pounce. I knew it was unlikely I would see her, but I had to at least try.

"Aésha, do you know if there has been any word about Pounce? I dropped her during the attack and haven't seen her since."

She frowned sadly at me and shook her head. "No, Baby, but I can ask around for you."

"Thanks." I managed a tired but appreciative smile at her and continued my all but hopeless search. There were all sorts of people moving about the compound. There were soldiers, a couple of Warriors I didn't recognize, and regular civilians. There were also people that I guessed were probably slaves based on the dingy clothes they wore and the unsettling way they walked; shoulders slumped and heads bowed low. Instantly my mind shot to Thayn.

"Hey, uh, Aésha? Do you know if Balo is alright?"

"Balo is currently being kept out of trouble," she replied.

"Out of trouble?"

Uh-oh.

"Yes. Your slave fought for the wrong side during the attack," she explained. If she knew that Balo was actually Thayn, she didn't reveal it to me through either words or expression.

Still, I felt quite confident that she knew.

Crap. He's probably in a prison somewhere on the compound. How am I going to find him without getting caught?

"Have your key?" Aésha asked, startling me from my thoughts. I was so tired and worried about Thayn that I hadn't even realized we'd stopped walking.

"Um, no."

She nodded and shrugged like it wasn't a big deal. "We'll get you a new one, but for now..." She trailed off, grinning, and drew away from me, slipping something out of her jacket pocket. She stepped up to the door and used whatever small tool she was holding to quickly and expertly pick the lock. Within ten seconds, the door was open. I was equally impressed and disturbed. Impressed, because she made that look simple. Disturbed, because I now felt like the lock on my door wasn't very secure.

The first thing I noticed when I entered the space was that there was a lot more colour in the room. Well, a lot more pink, to be accurate. Aésha had clearly added some touches to the apartment while I was gone. The bed had a fluffy duvet, pillows with shams, and there was a circular shag rug on the floor. All of it was pink.

"Shall we have a nice shower?" Aésha asked as if she had every intention of joining me.

I laughed a little. "I think I've taken up enough of your time."

She pouted at me. "You shower. I'll go find out if you have a cat, then I'll come back so you don't miss me too much."

I nodded to her, kissed her cheek, and hugged her tightly. "Thanks for everything, Aésha." I really, really meant it.

She returned the hug just as tightly. "Glad to have you back."

We released one another, and she turned to walk out the door but paused to look back over her shoulder, shooting me a wink before she left. I laughed, knowing why she did it. It was impossible not to watch her or the other Charmer, Arik, walk away. It was magnetic attraction.

Making sure the door was locked behind her, I immediately checked out the entire space to make sure I was alone and that my door to the joined kitchen was locked. I pulled off my ruined boots that had once been so attractive when I had first worn them for my Masque costume. As sad as I was to see them in this worn-out state, I couldn't say I would miss wearing them. I would have to enquire about new practical shoes the next time I saw Aésha.

I walked to my nightstand, barely feeling the floor beneath my numb feet. Opening the drawer, I placed the bone knife Ash Dancer had given me into it. I also removed Rral's ring from the dog-tag necklace around my neck and Irys' handkerchief from my bra. I placed these items in the drawer as well, shutting it.

Heading to the bathroom, I stripped out of the rest of my dirty clothes and hopped into the shower.

The hot water that poured over me felt divine.

I stood under it for a long time, shutting my eyes and letting the heat sink into all my aching muscles. I was so tired that it wasn't until I reached up to wash my hair that I realized it was still in the braids

Ehsaig had given me. The tears came and this time I didn't stop them. I couldn't.

Sinking to my knees onto the floor of the shower, I wept uncontrollably and started to unravel my hair from the braids. Each time I freed my hair from a braid, I wished I could free myself from memories that I feared would haunt me for life. I had seen things I couldn't unseen, learned things I couldn't unlearn, and felt things I couldn't un-feel.

My mind was swirling with the events of the past two days. It was all too much: Fiffine pregnant and sick; Sabear crying, screaming, and lying motionless on the ground; Amarogq's other family; and Ash Dancer asking me to tell him about the children he didn't even know existed; Mez and Keavren tortured, bleeding, hanging from trees and left to die; and Mez...was good...

Mez.

I pushed away the rest of the bad thoughts and focused on only my memories of him. The only good feelings that came out of this whole ordeal were from him. He made me laugh when I was scared. He held me to keep me safe. He looked at me like I mattered, like I was important. He thanked me for saving his life. He wanted to have coffee with me...

Mez.

Holding on to those feelings, I worked the last braid out of my hair, climbed to my feet, and finished washing, taking it one step at a time.

I shut off the shower and stepped out. Grabbing one towel, I gently dried myself. I then snatched a second towel to wrap up my wet hair. Poking my head out of the bathroom, I made sure Aésha – or anyone else – wasn't in my apartment before padding over to my small dresser, hoping I would find fresh clothes. I did.

I slipped some underwear and a black t-shirt on, but instead of putting on pants and socks, I took out a folded pair of each and set them on top of my nightstand. I knew I would need them later for whenever Aésha returned, or if I wanted to get something to eat, or when I would investigate Thayn's whereabouts. For now, however, food and investigation had to wait. As much as I did want to find Thayn, the bed with the pink fluffy duvet was calling to me, and I couldn't say no. I was just too exhausted and being this exhausted wouldn't do me or anyone else any good. I needed to sleep.

Mind made up, I pulled back the covers, crawled into the bed, which felt one-hundred times more comfortable than it did the last time I'd slept in it, and cocooned myself into the sheet and duvet. I felt cozy and comfortable wrapped up in the soft fabrics that were courtesy of my super-hot gal-pal Aésha. I really did need to find a way to thank her better.

She was the last thought on my mind before sleep blissfully carried me away into sweet, deep, dark, nothingness.

Chapter 24
Irys

I readied myself to face the Charmer. Determined "not to be so serious all the time," as per Lieutenant Atrix' recent accusation, I replied playfully: "I'm sorry, but my date has a deeper voice."

There was a pause in which I could practically hear the surprised smile.

"Your dinner date," he said again, only in a deeper voice. I couldn't help but laugh.

I opened the door and stood back to allow him entry. He stepped in, holding a bag and a domed tray. I smiled to Rolern before shutting the door.

"I've brought you dinner and a gift," Lieutenant Atrix said as he set the tray on the table.

"A gift?" I asked with curiosity I couldn't help, wondering if it would be my new clothes and the hair dye I'd requested.

"You can look if you want," he replied, holding the bag out to me.

I took it and looked inside, smiling when it was indeed what I'd guessed.

"Thank you. It's just what I wanted," I said jokingly as though he was a gentleman who had brought me jewellery or a bottle of my favourite scent.

Lieutenant Atrix grinned and sat down at the table, removing the dome from its tray.

Tonight's meal was a pink fish with rice and vegetables. It was precisely what I would have chosen for myself.

A small box tied with a ribbon sat next to my plate as did a teapot and teacup. I reached out and tugged the end of the ribbon, untying it. Inside the box were two little chocolate cubes. I couldn't help but smile.

"This looks wonderful. Thank you. You always seem to know just what will appeal to me."

"I've paid close attention to what you like," he replied smoothly then nodded toward the little box with the chocolates. "Those are from the best chocolatier in the city. I thought you might like to give them a try. Syliza may have the best tea, but we have the best chocolate."

"I will try them, but only if you haven't brought them with the expectation of a dinner date," I said as an attempted joke, still determined not to be too "serious."

"Of course I have!" He laughed. "Why else would I bring them?"

I found myself out of my league and could only giggle as I shook my head at him in playful scolding.

With a victorious expression on his face, he sipped his tea.

"Did you have an eventful day?" he asked conversationally.

"Only at its start. I visited with Lieutenant Fhurrk, who is doing well. I had milk with him and his mate."

His nose crinkled. "He really does like you. I'm sorry," he said apologetically as though being liked by the Sefaline Warrior was a genuine shame.

"I'm glad to know he does. I value the friendship I seem to be building with him," I said after a chuckle to what I hoped was indeed a joke.

"What did you think of his mate?"

"She seemed friendly. Quite pretty." I was grasping for ways to describe the woman who was fused to her husband the entire time they were in the room together.

"Did they peel themselves apart from each other at all during your visit?" he asked knowingly.

"No," I replied after a hesitation. It was difficult not to laugh so I focused on taking a bite of my dinner instead.

He, on the other hand, gave a very genuine laugh.

"Social etiquette isn't one of Fhurrk's strengths."

"I'm sure he meant well," I replied with a grin, wanting to say something kind about my new friend who had tried, in his own way, to make me feel welcome in his home.

"He did. He invited you in, gave you his favourite drink, and introduced you to his mate. That's saying a lot for Fhurrk. He's a Sefaline. They don't care about the same social customs we do."

"In that case, I'm quite flattered." I smiled to myself at the thought that all the strangeness I had endured during my visit with Lieutenant Fhurrk was in fact his best effort to be welcoming.

We shared a quiet moment before his eyes moved back over me again.

"I don't see any new streaks in your hair. That must be a good sign."

"I'm hoping there won't be any more of them and that this one will fade away somehow."

"Stranger things have happened." The confident, casual way in which he made the statement told me that he meant it and that he had seen stranger things with his own eyes.

"What of your day? Was it pleasant?" I asked, hoping to turn the conversation in a more positive direction.

"Oh, yes. My days are always pleasant. Especially when I have lunch and dinner dates with you."

"Oh, stop trying to flirt," I said with a huff, though my eyes were smiling uncontrollably.

"Don't you like it?" He grinned in that way that was uniquely his own and that he knew, without a shadow of a doubt, was irresistible.

"Is there no woman whose attention you favour?" I'd tried the question before, but it was worth another effort to see if I could pry an honest answer from him.

With a chuckle, he replied. "We're back to this again, are we?"

I nodded with a guiltless smile. I wanted to know the truth and was no longer interested in subtleties. There had to be someone in the life of a man such as this one. I had nothing better to do with my time than to try to learn more.

"Nothing has changed since you asked me this earlier. The answer remains 'no'. The span of a few hours has not thrown romance into my life."

"Perhaps the answer would be different, if I were to ask you again tomorrow."

"Perhaps if you were to ask me tomorrow, *you* would be my answer."

I shook my head. "No. That certainly wouldn't be the case."

"I guess we'll have to wait and see." His face was the picture of amusement.

We chatted throughout the remainder of my meal. It was all teases, flirts, and tiny flatteries, but nothing of any substance. Any effort I made to get to know him was consistently overturned.

"Is there anything else you will want this evening?" he asked after I had finished my meal, and we'd enjoyed a cup of tea together; my first, his second.

"I don't think so, thank you. I'm quite tired, despite all the sleep I had last night."

"You look tired," he agreed. It wasn't a criticism of my appearance. It was a sincere observation.

"I do look forward to your company tomorrow morning. I'm eager to hear about the woman you'll have met and fallen for."

He laughed at my joke as he stood, collecting the tray. "When I do meet her, I'll make sure I have your approval before I decide she's the one for me."

I stood as well, with the intention of seeing him out. "Good. I have excellent taste."

He smiled, but afterward his flirtatious act seemed to slide away a little. "Get some rest, Twinkles." His voice sounded truly caring.

"I will. Thank you, Lieutenant Atrix," I replied warmly.

His smile to me was kind and very real but only for a moment. Soon, it had transformed into that alluring expression from which one was powerless to look away.

Without another word, he left my quarters, and I stood gaping at him obtusely. After a few blinks, I returned to my senses and looked over at Mr. Rolern with a smile. To my surprise, the guard at my door wasn't Mr. Rolern at all. Instead, a man in a Warrior's uniform looked at me pleasantly.

Chapter 25

Megan

I woke up, stretched, sat up, and was startled when something fell from my head.

My eyes sprang open, and I looked behind me to see that the towel wrapped around my hair had tumbled onto the pillow behind me.

Yawning and stretching, I vaguely noticed that the outside light seeping through my curtained window seemed to be dimmer than when I had shut my eyes for my nap. I rubbed the sleep from my eyes, wondering what time it was. Instinctively, I looked to my nightstand, stupidly expecting to see my alarm clock where it would have been if I were in my room back home. My *real* home.

Of course, there was no clock. All that greeted me was the folded pants and socks I had left there.

No, wait...

There was something else there, too. Beside my clothes, a key rested on the table, and on top of my pants lay a small pink envelope. I assumed the key must be the new one for my apartment, and based on the colour of the envelope, both the envelope and the key must have been left by Aésha. I reached over and snagged it, plucking out the paper from the envelope to read its contents:

> *Baby,*
>
> *I didn't have the heart to wake you, but the boys need me, so I couldn't stay.*
>
> *Wanted you to know I worked my magic, and you're off the hook at work for the next couple of days.*
>
> *I've stocked you with some clothes. It was fun picturing how you'd look in your new skirts, tops, and workout*

clothes...of course it's what I bought you to wear underneath that really got my imagination running.

I've asked around about Pounce. Nobody's seen the little fur ball, but I'll keep asking. I'm sure if I call her enough times, she'll come right to me. My big kitty, Fhurrk, always does.

Dreaming of you while you're dreaming of me,
Aésha

Whoa! How long have I been asleep?

Whipping off the duvet, I launched myself out of bed and went directly to the small square window, pulling aside the stiff beige curtains to look out. The sun was setting.

Gosh! Wasn't it still morning when I took my nap. Yikes! I must have really needed to sleep.

I re-read Aésha's letter to better absorb the information and clued in on the fact that she had mentioned getting me off work for a couple of days.

Oh, yeah! I have a job...

I had completely forgotten about the ultra-intense perfect blond military woman who had hired me for translation and had given me my special tags so I wouldn't be kicked out of the compound. Thank goodness I didn't have to worry about that for a couple of days. With the extra time Aésha bought me, maybe I would be lucky enough to avoid it all together if I were to manage to find Thayn and get out of here.

Aésha, you're a saint!

It was also super-sweet of her to tell me that she had asked around about Pounce. I'd be lying if I said I wasn't curious about who Fhurrk was. I hoped she was actually being facetious and there wasn't a big cat-man wandering around this place.

Although, at this point, after everything I've seen so far, would I really be all that surprised if I saw a cat-man? Who am I kidding? Yes. Yes I would.

With images of large cat-men on the brain, I went over to my dresser to inspect the new clothes Aésha brought me.

True to her word she had stocked my dresser with a couple of long skirts, tops, workout clothes, and very sexy underwear. I picked up a hot pink lace thong and had to shake my head in amusement. Workout clothes and sexy lingerie. Aésha really was one of a kind.

I was tempted to put on a skirt, a blouse, and pumps after spending days feeling grubby and rather unattractive, but I opted for a practical dark purple athletic outfit and running-style shoes. My body and my feet needed comfy.

Picking up one of the running shoes, I examined it closer, noting that it had a cushioned insole. I turned it over to check out the treads and to see if there was any indication of size, noticing that a bright pink kiss mark had been placed right in the middle of the clean sole. I grinned, wondering if this was the trademark of whoever had made these shoes or if Aésha had freshly kissed them before she gave them to me.

The shoes were easy to slip into, were comfortable, and fit me like a glove.

Yup. Aésha was definitely a saint.

All dressed, I checked myself out in the small mirror in the bathroom. My hair was a disaster! It had dried completely crazy and was flipped up everywhere from being wrapped up in the towel. Running a brush through it didn't do much to improve it, so I pulled it up into a ponytail to at least get it out of my face. That would have to do.

As I finished washing my face and brushing my teeth, I could hear the unmistakeable "Doo-dum-dum-dee's" sound of someone humming. Stepping out into the main space, I discovered it was coming from behind the door that lead to the kitchen. The hummer must have been my neighbour. Based on the pitch of the hum, I guessed she was female.

Oh, well, no time like the present to introduce myself, right?

Unlocking the door, I knocked lightly before opening it to greet the person on the other side.

"Hi. I hope I'm not intruding," I said to the woman who was busy preparing a sandwich at the kitchen counter. Her medium-dark brown hair was wrapped neatly in a bun at the back of her head. She was wearing a black tank top and the closest thing to jeans I had seen on Qarradune.

Oh my god! I want those pants!

She turned to look at me with a friendly smile. "Hi! Not at all. You don't have to knock, it's your kitchen, too."

I returned her smile, instantly liking her. "I just didn't want to scare you if you were using a knife or something."

"Thanks." She chuckled. "I'm Asimara by the way."

"Nice to meet you. I'm Megan."

Now that we were face to face, I got a better look at my new neighbour. She had a very classic girl-next-door appearance with honey-brown eyes and soft features that gave her a very pleasant and welcoming look. We were about the same height and maybe even the same age. However, unlike me, Asimara was clearly physically fit. That fact, coupled with her hair bun, made me wonder if she was in the military.

She glanced back at the food she was making and then looked at me. "Did you want some of this? I have more."

As if on cue, my stomach growled, and I realized I couldn't remember the last time I'd eaten something that could be classified as a meal.

Blushing a little at the sound, I nodded and she chuckled. "Yes, thank you. I mean as long as you have enough, and it's not too much trouble."

"It's no trouble," she replied easily and picked up a bun and cut into it, making a second sandwich for me. She put a white thick sauce on the bun, along with lettuce, tomato, and a white meat that I would guess was probably chicken. Except, I was on another world. I really couldn't assume I knew what I'd be eating, regardless of how close it might have looked to something I thought I recognized.

"As much as I can, I try not to eat at the mess hall. I don't think that stuff is actually food." She laughs.

I wondered what she meant about the mess hall food, and at the same time, hoped I would never have to find out.

"Want some vegetables, too?" she asked, removing the lid of a square pot that was on a hotplate.

"Sure, please."

She nodded and scooped out some crispy-looking yellow, orange, and dark purple-pink vegetables shaped like fries. She added them to her metal plate and then to the one meant for me. It felt strange to stand back and watch her make my food, but I figured this awkwardness was better than offering to help and getting in the way. Asimara definitely had her own groove going on.

"I thought you'd quit the day after you arrived," she said. "I've never had a neighbour show up for one night and then leave for a number of days." She grinned in amusement and took down two metal mugs from an open wall shelf, filling them with water at the sink.

"Oh, yeah, well, this time you just happen to have a neighbour who has a lot of bad luck." I gave her a "what-are-you-going-to-do" smile.

She chuckled lightly. "Well, that's no good. Tell you what, some evening when we're both here, I'll open up a bottle of wine, and you can tell me the whole thing."

Wow. She's got wine.

"Thanks, that sounds nice." And it honestly did.

She smiled, holding out a metal plate and mug for me. "Here you go. Did you want to come over to eat?" she offered, adding: "It's alright if you want your space, too."

I took them from her. "Actually, I'd love the company." It felt so good to talk to someone who seemed normal.

She nodded happily, and picking up her own plate and mug of water, she walked through the open door that led to her room. I followed.

Her space was just as small as mine but had a more settled-in look. A braided rug lay in the middle of the floor and a country patchwork quilt covered her bed, on top of which sat a slumped, well-loved stuffed toy that looked like no monkey I'd ever seen before. At the foot of the bed was a small trunk, on top of which she had rested a couple pairs of shoes, including shiny black military boots and a pair of expensive-looking, fashionable low-heeled black pumps.

The room also contained the identical small nightstand, dresser, desk and chair that mine had. On her desk there were opened letters, envelopes, and writing paper as well as an intricately carved wooden horse. She had covered the top of the dresser with a decorative towel, on top of which lay a hair brush, two clean pristine wine glasses, and a simple corkscrew device.

I also noticed that, in addition to the drab beige curtains, she had added bright blue gingham curtains to her window. This helped to make the place even more cheery. As a finishing touch to her country home-style, she had hung a wooden picture frame on the back of her door that contained an embroidered image of the word "Family" with a cluster of colourful wild flowers surrounding it.

I grinned as I took it all in, loving how she had decorated. I liked her even more. In her room, I could almost imagine I was on Earth.

Almost.

"I like your place."

"Thanks. Bits and pieces of home." She smiled. "Have a seat." She gestured to the chair at the desk.

I sat on the chair, setting my metal mug on the desk and resting my plate in my lap.

Asimara sat on her bed, crossing her legs. She set her mug down on her nightstand and rested her plate in the "bowl" of her crossed legs, starting to eat. I joined her, first trying one of the crispy vegetables that reminded me of sweet potato fries, before taking a nice sized bite of the sandwich. It was sweet, tangy, and savory. I enjoyed every bite of it.

"This is really good!"

She grinned at my compliment, looking bright as she happily munched on her own food and then swallowed.

"So, are you from Kavylak? Capital City, I mean," I asked her.

"No. I'm from about four hours south of here, if you're a good rider. My family owns a vineyard there."

"Oh, cool! What's it like working on a vineyard?"

"I love it." She smiled with a warm fondness. "My parents adore it. We're the eleventh generation in our family," she said with a swell of pride.

"That's really great. Is that where the wine you mentioned earlier is from?"

She nodded. "It'll be nice to share it with you. I'm glad I have a neighbour again. It's creepy when you are in these shared places and the other unit is empty."

"Have you had many other neighbours?"

"A couple. They were both men. The first one, I didn't see much. I have no idea what happened to him." She shrugged at the memory. "I think the last guy got promoted and moved to a bigger place. He was a decent enough neighbour, but he never did the dishes." She scrunched her nose.

I mimicked her nose scrunch.

What a lazy dude!

"I'll do our dishes," I told her then. "It's the least I can do after you've been so nice to share your dinner with me."

"Thanks," she beamed, continuing to eat her dinner. "I already like you more than the last guy."

I laughed and asked, "Are you a soldier?"

"Yup. Just a private for now, but I'm hoping to make corporal soon. I'm up for the promotion, and I've earned it," she said confidently without sounding full of herself. There wasn't anything cocky about Asimara. She was simply sure of herself. I respected that and envied it, too.

"I hope you get it," I said with sincerity, taking a sip of my water.

"Thanks. You're a civilian, right?"

"Yes." At least I was pretty sure that's what I was. "I've got a job as a translator," I added.

"Oh, hey, crisp!" She seemed impressed with that, which made me feel a little important. "How many languages do you speak?"

Uh...boy, do I wish I knew the answer to that one.

"A few: Kavylak, Sylizan, Northern, Gbat Rher-uh-rian?"

She chuckled. "Interesting. I don't even know that last one. Say something in Gbatrur or whatever."

I stared at her blankly for a moment. Due to my complete lack of understanding of how I was able to speak and understand the different languages on this planet, I had no idea how to randomly say something in Gbat without some sort of written word or voice prompt. Put on the spot, all I could call to mind was Rral saying "Kavylak Pigs", which had been the first words I'd heard in his language. I didn't imagine Asimara would be wild about me saying that.

"Actually, I don't know if I'll be able to say anything in that language right now," I leveled with her. "As weird as it sounds, I'm much better at hearing and reading the language than speaking it straight out of my head. I, uh, just seem to pick up languages as I hear them." I looked at her, waiting for her deer-in-headlights expression to happen. It never did. Instead, she looked thoughtful.

"I guess that make sense."

Wait. What? It does?

"You're somewhat like Ildois in that way, I suppose."

"Ildois?"

Was that a French word?

"The Warrior, Lieutenant Etiaid Ildois." She nodded. "He knows a pack of languages and how to be a part of all those cultures from other places." She shrugged. "I thought you might be like that."

Whoa! There is a Warrior who has a knack for knowing languages like I do?

I wondered how similar our language abilities were and was also slightly disturbed that I had a skill that wasn't unlike a Warrior's; a skill that never existed prior to my being on Qarradune.

Does this ability have something to do with why I was brought here?

"Then again," she added, startling me out of my reverie, "if all you can do is read in the languages, I guess it's not the same, unless the Warriors need an international librarian." She chuckled.

I had to laugh at that. "You know, I think I like that title better than 'translator'. I'm the new International Librarian," I joked and she laughed. "I'm even a librarian with a cat," I added without thinking. I was too wrapped up in the librarian stereotype image to remember that my cat ownership was currently past tense. I frowned. "I mean, I had a cat. She's actually missing."

Asimara frowned. "Oh, I'm sorry to hear that."

"Actually, by any chance, have you happened to have seen a small black kitten with bright blue eyes and white paws wandering around anywhere?"

"Outside you mean?"

"Yeah. I lost my kitten during the attack on the compound."

Her frown deepened. "No, but I'll keep my eyes peeled for him."

"Thanks. Her name is Pounce, and she's a Fairwilde breed," I added, in case that information would somehow help her.

"Aww. I like the ones with the horns."

Aw, geeze. Here we go again with the cat horns.

"Horns?"

"Yeah." She nodded. "You said she's a Fairwilde, right?"

Seriously, Mez. What the frig kind of devil-cat did you get me?

"Yes," I confirmed. "That's what Mez said she is."

Asimara looked at me in stunned surprise. If it were humanly possible, her eyebrows would have shot above her hairline.

"Mez Basarovka?"

I nodded carefully, wondering if I just made a huge mistake saying his name.

"Hoo! You have some important friends...unless he's not a friend...in which case, it's been nice knowing you," she joked.

"Just friends," I confirmed, noting that Mez' mind-bending skill must have had quite the reputation for Asimara to make that joke.

"Crisp."

Okay, clearly she didn't think it was crazy to be friends with him, at least.

"So a Fairwilde cat has horns on its head?"

She nodded, looking curiously at me as if she found it strange that I wouldn't know this. Still, she answered. "Yup, little short ones. They're the only breed that does as far as I know."

"Oh, I didn't realize. She didn't have horns the last time I saw her. I didn't know that cats could have horns."

She chuckled. "Well, regular farm cats don't, but the expensive snooty city cats do."

"Wow! I had no idea he got me an 'expensive snooty city cat'." I chuckled.

She looked shocked again. "Oh my Goddess! Basarovka actually *bought* you a cat?" She grinned from ear to ear like she had just been given the juiciest piece of gossip.

I had to laugh at her reaction. "Well, yes. But he was just being nice when I was going through a bit of a rough time. It was a friendly gesture."

She nodded but was wearing a playful expression as if she were imagining Mez and me with hearts and stars in our eyes for each other.

"Hey! It's really not like that!" I protested, calling her out on her obvious unspoken thoughts, even though I was pretty sure she was just being a goof.

"Suuuuuure it's not." She laughed. "That's why I have twelve cats in here that he gave me. He just hands those things out like mints."

I cracked up at what she said and how she said it. If I had been holding something soft and not a metal plate, I would have thrown it at her in playful response.

"I'm sure he's given gifts to other people before. If not, then maybe I'm just the biggest pity case he's come across."

"Oh, yeah. I'm sure that's it." She nodded unconvinced. "He's known for running a charity where he hands out pets to sad people." She smirked.

I laughed more, shaking my head. "Honestly! We're only friends."

"Alright, alright," she said, holding up her hands in mock surrender. "If you insist. But if I find out you're secretly his wife, I'm never giving you another free sandwich," she teased.

"Nope. I swear. I'm not his secret wife. I'm not even his secret girlfriend. We haven't even gone to coffee, yet."

She arched a brow with interest at my coffee comment. "Well, maybe you'll go tomorrow." She smiled. "You have to start somewhere."

I knew she was kidding…mostly.

"What about you?" I asked her, trying to get out of the hot-seat. "Do you have a boyfriend or a secret husband?"

Asimara shook her head, polishing off the rest of what was on her plate and drinking her water. "No. I never have the time for that sort of thing. The Major works us too early in the morning. When you need to get up that early, your social life is dead." She chuckled good naturedly.

"Well, if that should ever change, I know this guy who gives good cat presents. Maybe I could hook you up."

She laughed. "If I ever feel that I'm sad enough to earn one of them, I'll be sure to ask you to introduce us."

"Deal," I said and polished off the last bite of my sandwich with a smile on my face. I was genuinely enjoying Asimara's company. After so many unhappy moments, it was such a nice feeling to be carefree and have a normal and playful conversation with another person. I really didn't want it to end, but I also didn't want to overstay my welcome.

"I guess I should go and clean up these dishes. I imagine you're busy," I said.

She smiled and sighed. "Thanks. I do have to start getting ready for bed. Early shift." She scrunched her nose again at me, and I mimicked it back at her.

Yeah. Work sucks.

We both stood, and I picked up my empty plate and mug and collected hers.

"It was good to meet you, Asimara. Thanks for dinner."

"You, too, Megan. I look forward to sharing that bottle of wine with you."

I nodded and smiled at her, heading into the kitchen to clean up the dishes. I made quick work of washing them and dried them before returning them to their shelves. I was just setting the last dish on its shelf when I heard someone knock on Asimara's door.

"Coming," she called to the knocker and walked to her front door, opening it. I was surprised I was hearing everything so clearly from where I was. Glancing at the kitchen door that led to her apartment, I saw that I hadn't shut it when I had entered with the dishes.

Oops!

I tip-toed over to the door to quietly close it so I wouldn't invade her privacy.

"How's my favourite private today?" I heard her visitor ask in a sensual male voice that sounded all-too familiar.

I know that voice. Why do I know that voice?

"You're here," she responded. "How could I be anything but perfect?"

Whoever it was entered, and the front door to her apartment shut. A moment later, I heard a new sound and realized that what I was hearing was kissing.

Kissing! Didn't Asimara just say she didn't have a boyfriend?

Unable to resist catching a glimpse of who her "secret" boyfriend might be, and to put a face to the voice, I dared a peek and saw Asimara lip-locked with the male Warrior Charmer: Lieutenant Arik Atrix.

What the...?

Before either of them could see me, I whipped my head back into the kitchen, desperately trying to make sense of what I had seen.

This is too weird! Aren't Arik and Aésha in a relationship? Why is he kissing Asimara if he's with Aésha? Asimara said she didn't have time for a boyfriend, but here she is kissing Arik! She didn't even sound surprised to see him. Why would she be secretive about their relationship? Are they not supposed to be together? Is Aésha not supposed to know?

"I thought you were coming for dinner," I heard Asimara say quietly. "Is everything alright?"

I snapped back to attention when she spoke and remembered that I was supposed to be shutting the door, not snooping. I rested my hand on the door's lever to push it closed but stopped before I could.

What if the door creaks or it makes a loud noise once it's shut?

I didn't want to risk being caught and having to face the Charmer. I couldn't keep my head on straight around him. One look in his eyes, and I became a star-struck ditz.

"Yes, everything is fine," Arik answered. "I got tied up. I've been busy with a new little project."

Asimara gave a resigned sigh.

"Oh, it's nothing like that," Arik answered her sigh. "This one's an actual assignment, not a personal conquest. It's a delicate situation and she's...tough."

What?

"Tough?" Asimara queried. "What is she? Military?"

Arik laughed. "No. She's about as far away from military as you can get. She's Sylizan."

"Sylizan?" Asimara sounded like she ate a bug. "Here? Why?"

Um? What? His mission is a Sylizan woman?

I leaned in farther to hear more.

"It's a long story," Arik said. "A boring one. I'd rather not waste my few precious moments with you, talking about it."

"Aww, poor Arik," Asimara said with mock sympathy. "Thank you," she added with genuine warmth. "Do you want me to make you something? I could probably get another dinner out of what's in the fridge?"

Oh, crap! No! Don't be hungry, Arik!

"No, thank you."

Phew!

"I'm hungry but not for food," he said with a deepening voice.

Aw, geeze!

Asimara laughed lightly. "Shhhh! I have a new neighbour. A nice girl, actually. Civilian."

Awww! She likes me!

"Yes," Arik said knowingly. "I know the one. I know everything."

Aw, geeze!

"I don't know if that makes me feel more comfortable or less." Asimara chuckled.

Yeah. You and me both, Asimara.

Arik laughed. "Don't worry. As fun as she might be for me, she's off limits to *poor* Arik. She's Ésha's project."

"Now I like her even more," Asimara said, and I could hear the grin in her voice.

What? I'm Ésha's project? Did he mean Aésha? What did he mean by project? Why was Asimara happy with that?

"Maybe the four of us should have a party together," Arik teased.

What? A party? Oh...ewwww.

"I would if I trusted any part of how that would go. You can't rope me into your scheme, Charmer," Asimara said with both play and affection in her voice.

He chuckled in response. "Me? Scheme? With you? Never. You know that you're different, Mara," he answered with equal play and affection.

He calls her Mara?

She scoffed. "Terrible."

Arik laughed but this time it sounded different. Lighter, softer, adoring. Genuine.

I heard the distinct sound of clothing sliding over clothing. I didn't dare look this time, but I guessed they were hugging.

They really seemed to like one another.

"I think I'll be able to take a leave again soon," Arik said softly, all play and allure gone from his voice. "I hope your mom and dad won't mind that I'll be back so soon."

Wha-a? He knows her parents?

"Oh, that's wonderful!" Asimara exclaimed sounding over-the-moon thrilled. "Of course they won't! They'd have you over before they'd have me there." She laughed merrily. "My mom can probably sense that you said that and already has a pot of coffee on."

Arik laughed. "No one makes coffee like your mother."

"It's true," Asimara agreed, ecstatic. "I hope we can get at least two full days out there this time!"

This time? My gosh? Is this something they do regularly? Does Aésha know?

"I hope we can, too" Arik agreed sincerely. "I'll probably be able to swing it in a week. My current assignment shouldn't last longer than that."

"I'll talk to the Major. We're only training right now. She's usually more lenient at times like this."

"Let me know if you need me to talk to her, if she needs some convincing," Arik said, the Charmer side of him with which I was familiar, seeped back into his tone.

"Terrible," Asimara responded, chuckling.

Arik laughed again in the same way he had the first time she had called him that. As if it was a term of endearment.

Weird.

They were silent for a long moment but then I could hear they were kissing again. I frowned, feeling disappointed in myself for spying on them like I was. This wasn't my business, and I knew it. I made a promise to myself that I wouldn't do this again. This time, I had to ride it out. I was in too deep to risk exposing myself now.

"I've really got to get some sleep, Arik," Asimara said, when they drew away from their second heated kiss. "I have an early shift again."

"We can be fast," Arik said in a voice so tempting I almost felt like revealing my presence and joining them.

"Don't!" Asimara laughed. "You know I can't stay up late," she scolded, weakly, clearly affected by how alluring he was.

He laughed. "Fine," he said as if he was being merciful. "I'll let you off the hook tonight, but only because I want you full of energy tomorrow."

"So I can knock tomorrow?" Asimara asked hopefully.

"Yes."

"I will," she promised.

They kissed again, and I took a step away from the door, prepared to return to my own apartment.

"Love you," Asimara said, freezing me in my tracks.

"I love you, too," he answered with deep adoration.

I had officially heard more than I could handle. Without another thought, I quietly crossed the kitchen to my apartment and slipped inside, shutting the door to my room as soundlessly as possible and locking it. I leaned against it, having no idea what to think about what I had just overheard.

They love each other?

There was a knock at my own front door, and I jumped, staring at it like it was the enemy.

"Who is it?" I managed to call out from where I stood, hoping to god a Charmer wasn't waiting on the other side to pay their "project" a visit.

Chapter 26
Irys

I'd seen this Warrior before, having passed him in the hallway. Like the first time I'd seen him, his long black hair seemed to float lightly around him as though lifted by a small breeze that only he could feel.

As I watched the locks of hair drift around him, I realized that they weren't all the midnight black I'd thought they were. Some were a surprising tan shade which, when combined with the fact that it appeared that no two locks of his hair were the same length, made the floating effect of his hair all the more dramatic.

When I finally looked past the hair, I noticed that his topaz-coloured eyes were fixed on me.

"Has Mr. Rolern gone home for the night?" I asked the Warrior. "I knew he couldn't possibly have been here all day and all night, but I've never seen anyone else on my door."

"Yes," replied the Warrior. He seemed pleasant, but he was a Warrior. I wasn't about to simply assume he had my best intentions at heart. "Do you need anything, Miss Godeleva?"

I shook my head, intending to return to my room but thought better of it. "Yes. I think I'll go for a short walk to get some air before bed. I won't be long."

"I'll accompany you," he said easily, to my chagrin. I was hoping to walk alone, not with a new Warrior. He offered his arm, but as comfortably and smoothly as he did it, I didn't take it. I was going home the next day. The last thing I wanted to concern myself with was whether or not to trust yet another Warrior.

"Thank you, but I'm sure I can walk safely outside. I won't be going far. I'll follow the same path I took with Mr. Rolern. I know my way," I said and smiled, hoping to convince him.

"Then lead the way, please," he said, withdrawing his offered arm. "I'm Lieutenant Jadusyr Odurog. Call me Jadusyr, if that suits you, Miss Godeleva."

I looked at him, biting my lip. "I needn't disturb you from your post. I can walk alone without any problems or dangers," I insisted.

"I'm certain you can walk on your own, but being who you are, it would be much safer for you if I were to accompany you. If you'd prefer to feel as though you are walking alone, I'll trail behind and keep my distance as I watch over the situation."

I didn't like the idea of being observed that way. "I'd rather walk with you and imagine I have company than feel as though I'm being supervised." Moving the rest of the way into the hall, I locked my door.

He stepped up next to me and when I started walking down the hall, he kept pace with me. We had nearly reached the stairs when a man crossed our path, walking up the steps at a comfortable pace. The sight of him alone brought me to an abrupt halt.

He was unlike anyone else I had ever seen. He was tall and remarkable in his flawlessness. His white hair was nearly iridescent. I imagined it was his original shade and not one that had turned with age. He was robust without being athletic looking, with the type of form a sculptor would favour for his masterpiece.

These handsome features were perfect to such an extent that one could nearly fail to notice his right arm. It was made entirely of polished silver metal, but he moved it as though it was a natural part of his body. Each joint slid smoothly for effortless-looking motions.

As much as I would have wanted to continue to focus on the intriguing mechanical limb, his eyes were far too captivating to allow it. I saw Lieutenant Odurog salute out of the corner of my vision, but I was fixated on those indescribable eyes.

They were aquamarine and caught the light as though they were faceted gemstones. Though he nodded to Lieutenant Odurog's salute, his gaze was settled directly on me, never breaking. The look he gave me made me want to run back to my quarters and lock myself inside. At the same time, it also drew me to him as though I were falling under a magician's spell. I knew this man, though I'd never met him before. Merely standing in his presence was causing my heart to break.

"Are you quite alright, Miss Godeleva?" Lieutenant Odurog asked. "Would you like to return to your room?"

I turned to face the Warrior, blinking a few times to shake myself from the spell.

"No. Thank you. I'd much rather go outside. I need the air," I replied. When I looked back to the stairs, the man was gone.

It took an extra second, but I started walking.

"Who was that man we just saw, Lieutenant Odurog?"

"Xandon," he replied.

"That was Xandon?" I wasn't sure why, but that answer disturbed me.

"Yes." He grinned as he added: "He has quite the commanding presence."

"To say the very least," I replied, making my way directly toward the door Mr. Rolern had used when we'd previously gone outside for our walk together. Lieutenant Odurog kept pace with me and held the door for me, removing the final barrier to my exit.

Once outside, I took a deep breath of the cool air. It didn't smell entirely fresh, but at least it wasn't the same stale air I'd been sharing with hundreds of Kavylak military members inside the building.

"I imagine you have lovely gardens at home, Miss Godeleva. Much nicer than what you're seeing here," said Lieutenant Odurog.

I strolled along one of the paths until I'd had enough of the pavement and left it in favour of the grass. "Yes. Though I'd imagine it isn't uncommon for a home to have finer grounds than this military compound."

"Indeed," he said with a chuckle. "The home I grew up in certainly did."

"Do you ever visit your childhood home?"

"Sadly, that home no longer exists. I'm originally from Sorcheena."

Sorcheena. It was once a country with an ancient history. Its culture deeply valued its traditions, including many beautiful art forms. They produced some of the most delicate fabrics in the world, and their pottery painting techniques were unparalleled. Six or seven cycles ago – I would need to confirm my dates upon returning home – Kavylak's military walked in and took it over. The newly-taken state was devastated.

Many of the people fled. Among those who didn't, some fought back. Of them, most were killed. Those who did not flee and were not killed by the military were taken or killed by the Tarvak Raiders who took their chance to step in and take everything that was left in the shattered nation.

"I'm sorry to hear that," I said softly before adding, "and for your loss."

"Thank you. It was a long time ago," he responded without emotion.

I'd intended to find the place where Mr. Rolern and I had spent some time together reading, but I noticed that there were damaged buildings still under construction, even at this hour. I decided that it would be more interesting to watch the well-lit rebuilding than to see nothing at all in the growing darkness.

"That's where the attack happened," Lieutenant Odurog informed me as he realized where I was taking him. The walls of the building were smashed and burned.

"Attack?" I asked, surprised. "You were attacked? By whom?" *Who could have been foolish enough to attack a military base right here in Capital City?*

"Syliza," he replied to my great surprise. "It wasn't a large battle, and they were quickly overwhelmed. Whatever they were after, their mission failed."

"I had no idea..." I said, amidst the thoughts flooding my mind. "Great Goddess...are we at war?"

"No," he said in a sheepish way that suggested he'd realized he should not have told me what he had. "I imagine they came looking for your friend, Miss Wynters."

"Did they rescue her?" I asked, hoping the Knights were already bringing Megan home and that everything else I'd heard had been lies.

"On the contrary. They managed to put her in greater danger. Because of their 'rescue attempt', they gave rebels the chance to capture Miss Wynters and a few other civilians," he said, sounding unimpressed.

"Rebels captured her?" I asked in horror. "Has she been rescued? Was she hurt?" I felt like my heart had stopped.

"She has been rescued," he said, restarting my heart. "I'm not sure if she has returned yet, but she has been located and should be on her way back to Capital City."

Thank you, Great Goddess.

"That's a relief at least. Perhaps I will be able to see her before I'm brought back home again." Somehow, I would find a way to bring Megan with me. I was sure of it.

"I'm sure Captain Wintheare will tell you whether or not that will be permitted. Between you and me, I don't see why you shouldn't be able to see her. She's not a prisoner. She's a resident here and has been granted employment."

"Thank you for telling me what you know," I said appreciatively. I did appreciate his honesty. That said, I was determined to speak with Megan or, at the very least, write her a letter.

"You're welcome."

My mouth had already opened to pose another question when I caught sight of a man working among those who were cleaning up the damaged buildings. He had disheveled, pale blond hair that fluttered in the breeze, which occasionally lifted it off his forehead to reveal a circlet with a blue gem in its centre. He was dressed in a Warrior's uniform, though this was far from what had drawn my eye. Although, any hint of his boyishness was gone, Mr. Rolern was the Warrior before me. There was still a distance between us, but we were close enough that I was positive.

"Is that Mr. Rolern?" I asked, trying to sound casual in my tone, though I thought I might have heard a tremble in my voice.

"Who?" Lieutenant Jadusyr asked, following my gaze to the Warrior. Once he spotted him, he shook his head. "No, that's Sunetar Stryke."

Taken aback, I started to walk toward this "Sunetar Stryke" to see for myself. I'd been certain it was Rolern. *Could it have been a relative of some kind?*

A loud crack halted me in my tracks.

"Look out!" bellowed a nearby soldier as a few large chunks of bricks held together with mortar fell toward another soldier working below.

I gave a bit of a shriek, my hands rising to cover my mouth as I was sure I was about to witness the soldier's demise. I was wrong.

The large piece of debris suddenly stopped, mid-air, suspended well above the soldier's head. Glancing around to see if anyone else was witnessing this same miracle, my eyes fell upon Sunetar Stryke. His gaze was focused steadily on the floating chunk of wall. Taking a step forward, he raised his arm, and as though the bricks were somehow tethered to his hand, he made a quick throwing motion, sending the debris safely to the ground.

Had I just imagined that scene? Did that Warrior who looked like Mr. Rolern just use his mind to move a piece of a building through the air?

"Lieutenant Odurog, might I ask if you just saw...what I just saw?" I asked nervously.

At that moment, another Warrior, this one looking younger and with brown hair, came running over to the scene.

"Nice catch," he grinned at Sunetar Stryke. My question, it seemed, was answered.

"I saw it," Lieutenant Odurog replied, confirming things further. "Still gives me nightmares that he can do that," he said with a chuckle.

"Indeed," was all I could say.

Sunetar Stryke grinned to the other Warrior's compliment but turned his head and looked directly at me. Any doubt that this Sunetar Stryke was my Mr. Rolern was dashed in less than a second. This was exactly the length of time it took for the man to send a playful wink in my direction.

The Great Goddess must have reached down from Paradise and held me up, because there was no other way for me to have remained standing after that wink.

"I think we should continue our walk somewhere a little less treacherous," Lieutenant Odurog said lightheartedly, snapping me out of my stupor – somewhat, at least.

"Yes," I said, without moving. "Can Sunetar Stryke talk?" I asked as though the two topics were related.

"No," Lieutenant Odurog answered with a shake of his head. "He's mute."

"I see." After a brief moment of thought, I nodded to Lieutenant Odurog. "Yes. I think we should leave here." I had every intention of taking this walk directly back to my suite.

"I'm curious about something, Miss Godeleva." Clearly, Lieutenant Odurog felt nothing of my tension from the scene we'd just witnessed. "What is it that you Sylizan high-born ladies do all day long? What I mean is: do you have any specific job or responsibility, or do you live a life of purely leisure?"

"Ladies do many things. It depends on the lady," I replied as I walked stiffly back toward the building. I couldn't stop my thoughts from replaying all the time I'd spent with Mr. Rolern, thinking he was a sweet, shy, kind young man. All along, he was a Warrior who was no more honest than any of the others. "Many ladies entertain or develop artistic skills. I enjoy reading and helping Lord Godeleva with his research. I also sing and play the harp. Recently, I've become involved in certain charitable causes. I'd been on my way to Gbat Rher on a mission of mercy when I was brought here by mistake."

"A mission of mercy?" repeated Lieutenant Odurog. "I had no idea. That's very impressive, Miss Godeleva."

"Thank you. It is a cause I hold close to my heart."

"I heard about what happened to Gbat Rher. Truly unfortunate." He frowned.

"I discovered their plight only recently. I was hoping to make a difference there."

"Hopefully you will be able to continue with your mission there soon."

"Thank you. I will be returning to it tomorrow, according to Captain Wintheare."

"He told me the same thing. I know you're not staying here any longer than necessary."

It comforted me to know that this Warrior had heard the same thing about my departure as I had. Then again, he could be lying to me as Mr. Rolern – Sunetar Stryke – had been doing the whole time. Or, perhaps he was telling the truth, and Captain Wintheare was lying to us both. I had become far too complacent since I'd been here. A few small kindnesses were all it took to make me think I could trust the Kavylak military – and the Warriors, no doubt – which was well known for its sneaky, underhanded, and devious schemes.

"Do you have any siblings or is it just you and Lord Godeleva?" he asked. Though my first instinct was to believe that he was trying to be kind by filling the silence with comfortable conversation, I didn't trust those instincts any more than I trusted the Warriors.

"Lord Godeleva is my only family. We were raised together," I replied, attempting to sound friendly, not curt.

He smiled crookedly at my response. "Did you enjoy growing up in that massive estate? I've seen few that could rival your home. I grew up in a home that could definitely be considered a mansion, but nothing of that size."

He sounded genuinely friendly, relatable and interested. *Was he truly as he seemed?*

"I love my home. I had a pleasant upbringing there. I miss it very much."

"You'll see it again soon, no doubt."

"Thank you," I said as I stepped up to the door of the massive central military building, which he opened for me.

"Anywhere else you might like to go while we're walking? We have a gym and a pool if you feel like more exercise." It took me a moment to realize he was teasing.

"I've had enough adventures for this evening," I said but decided I sounded a little too stern after he had been playful with me. I needed to try to sound at least as lighthearted as he did. "Perhaps I'll try that gym tomorrow, instead."

He laughed quite merrily as we turned to walk up the stairs.

"By the way, I like what you've done to your hair. That little white streak in the front is crisp. Pretty rebellious for a Sylizan lady. Is it a new fashion?"

He was smiling as he asked the question, but I could feel the blood draining from my face as I was reminded of how visible the blemish was in my hair.

"It was the result of a nightmare I had last night," I replied without adding any more detail.

At first, Lieutenant Odurog laughed, clearly thinking I was joking with him, but he stopped abruptly as he realized I was not laughing, too.

"You're...serious?" he asked hesitantly.

"Yes. I had a nightmare and woke with this streak in my hair. I only hope it will grow out and that it will do so quickly."

"Goddess. That must have been some nightmare."

"I don't remember it, but I woke up screaming."

"I'm sorry to hear that." He was frowning again.

I was keen to change the subject. "Will you be the guard at my door all night?"

"That's the plan." He was, it seemed, just as happy to have something new to discuss.

"I'll do my best to make it a calm one for you."

"If you aren't calm, please alert me. I don't mind coming between you and your nightmares, Miss Godeleva." His smile was like that of a big brother, but I couldn't trust it as genuine as it seemed.

I smiled to him in return. "Thank you, Lieutenant Odurog." Stopping in front of my door, I withdrew my key and unlocked the knob. "It was a lovely walk. Goodnight."

Lieutenant Odurog took up his post next to my door and nodded to me. "It was a lovely walk. Thank you for being understanding, Miss Godeleva. I know it's not easy being around others you'd really rather not see when all you want is your home."

"I am fortunate to have been in good company, this time." I hoped my statement was true.

"If I don't see you before you depart, have a safe journey and good luck on your mission of mercy."

"May the Goddess walk with you," I replied sincerely. I wasn't about to wish him luck on his missions. Warrior missions were far too often in direct opposition to my happiness. Still, if the Goddess was with him, perhaps she could steer him away from such darkness.

He bowed to me in a very tidy way, giving me what I assumed was the sign of the Goddess, though not in a fashion I had ever seen before. Perhaps it was the style of Sorcheena, where he'd once called home. That gesture – that one – I felt I could trust.

I returned the sign in my Sylizan style and stepped into my room, shutting the door, locking it, and letting out a breath I felt I'd been holding for far longer than I had.

It was time to dye my hair.

Chapter 27
Megan

"It's the military police. I'm here to arrest you!" replied a woman playfully, in a mock-male voice.

I smirked, recognizing the owner of the voice and opened the door to see a grinning Amorette on the other side.

"Hi-oomph!" Amorette attacked me with a tight hug before I could get out any other words.

"I'm so glad you're alright!" she gushed.

"Thanks. I'm glad I'm alright, too." I laughed a little, returning her hug. "Are you alright?"

She drew away from me and nodded. "Oh, I'm perfectly fine. I would have come to see you sooner, but Amarogq *just* told me that you were back. He took *this* long!" She huffed, not hiding the fact that she thought he was an idiot for keeping it from her.

I cracked a smile, entertained by her flare for the dramatic. "I'm glad you're fine. Is Fiffine alright, too?"

Amorette nodded. "She's been checked out and everything."

"That's good." I was glad to hear she was okay. "Did you want to come in for a little bit?"

"Sure, unless you want to head out for a walk," she offered.

"Actually, yeah. I wouldn't mind getting out for a bit."

"Great." she grinned and stepped out of my apartment.

"I'm just going to grab my key." Turning, I quickly snatched it from my nightstand. I also double checked to make sure I was wearing my identification tags and made the snap decision to add Rral's ring and Irys' handkerchief to my pants pocket. These days, I never knew if, once I left a place, I would see it again, so I'd made a habit of keeping what was precious to me on my person at all times. That being said, I left the bone knife Ash Dancer had given me in the drawer for two reasons. The first was that I didn't know if it was illegal here to carry around an undeclared weapon and the second –

and most important – was that I couldn't, in good conscience, carry around something that had been given to me by Amarogq's ex-wife in the presence of Amorette.

Joining Amorette outside, I shut the door to my apartment, locked it, and dropped the key in my pocket.

"Lead the way." I smiled to Amorette. "This place is still a giant mystery-maze to me."

She started to walk, and I followed, keeping pace with her.

"Can I ask you a question about the Charmers?" I asked Amorette as we passed Asimara's door.

She looked at me like I just handed her a loaded gun. "Oh, Goddess. What happened?"

I shook my head with a smile. Only someone with previous Charmer experience would have that sort of reaction.

"Nothing. I was just wondering if they're in a relationship with each other, like a romantic relationship."

"No," she said without hesitation. "I can see why you'd think that based on how they act around each other, but they're solitary creatures. Nothing that beautiful could ever be locked down to one person." She laughed.

"Oh. So, you wouldn't say that they're the 'I love you'-saying type?"

She shook her head. "Not the 'I love you' as in 'I'm in love with you' type. They love each other, sure, but I don't know, they're Charmers!"

Oookay.

"So, if they aren't romantically involved, does this mean that they could be in a romantic relationship with someone else?"

She looked at me like I had ten heads. "No way. It's just not them."

Hmm. Either Amorette's right and Arik is messing with Asimara's head or Amorette doesn't know about their relationship.

I really wanted her opinion. I wanted to reveal what I had overheard from the kitchen, but I thought better of it.

One: This wasn't either of our businesses.

Two: I liked Asimara, and it didn't feel right blabbing her secrets to other people. I just hoped that Arik's "I love you" to her was the real deal. I would hate to think someone could be so openly cruel to another person.

"Don't let yourself get swept up in them," Amorette advised me after I'd gone silent on her for too long. I looked at her and she was smiling. "Even if they love you, they'll never fall for you. It's just not what they do."

For Asimara's sake, I hope that isn't true.

"Don't worry. I plan on keeping my distance," I assured her.

"They're good people. Kinder than they get credit for. You just have to know how to take them," Amorette explained, sounding like she was speaking from experience. "I've gone into town with Arik a few times. He can be a lot of fun."

My eyebrows lifted in surprise. "You're friends with Arik?"

She nodded. I smiled.

"I do understand what you mean," I said then. "I'm friends with Aésha. She's been wonderful to me. She even brought me this outfit."

Amorette nodded. "Aésha's got this weird maternal side. She hides it, but it pops out sometimes."

"Yeah. She really does," I agreed, thinking about all the times Aésha had acted like my mother bear. "I was so glad to see her when she arrived at our rescue."

"Was it terrifying?" Amorette asked.

"Yes." I knew she was asking about the experience I'd been through and not the rescue.

"I'm sorry to hear that. Were the People kind to you?"

"To me, specifically, yes. Especially one person in particular. Without her help, I doubt I would have been able to save Mez and Keavren."

"You all would have made it," she said with a certainty she believed. "There's an agreement between us and them. They couldn't have killed you."

I shook my head, in firm disagreement. "No. I might have made it, but Mez and Keavren wouldn't have. It was bad, Amorette. The things they did to them…" I trailed off shaking my head in an effort to clear the memory. "They meant for them to die." I couldn't stop my voice from shaking with the harsh truth.

Her hand took mine and gave it a gentle squeeze. I looked at her, and the frown she wore transformed into a reassuring smile.

"They're alright now, Megan. The Warriors don't stay down long. I even saw Mez on his way to his office when I was coming here."

I blinked, surprised. "You did? How did he look?"

"Just fine. I wouldn't have known anything happened to him."

"Oh, good. I'm glad to hear that. I guess Remms must have finished healing him," I said more to myself than Amorette.

She smiled. "Oh! You've met Remms? Isn't he the cutest?"

"Yes. He's really nice. I was so grateful he was there, especially after they sent this other scary-sounding guy, um, Gabeld San-something."

"Gabeld Sangoa." She nodded with understanding. "Our resident demon." She laughed but was clearly joking.

"Well, he does sound like one, although I never did actually see him."

"He likely didn't step out of the shadow so he wouldn't scare you. He looks as dark as he sounds, but he's one of the nicest guys you'd ever meet."

I quirked a brow up at her, not bothering to hide my skepticism. "If you say so." I was officially imagining a large red demon with giant horns, fangs, and a forked tail.

She giggled, amused at my expression.

She was heading us toward the main building, the massive structure that looked like the last place you'd want to enter. There was something ominous about its appearance, like if I were to go inside it, I might never come out again. I wondered how I was ever going to find Thayn in there.

"I guess there must be a lot of things in the main building," I said, trying to sound as nonchalant and conversational as possible. "I think that's where I'll be working in a couple of days."

"Probably," Amorette agreed. "Everything from officers' quarters to an officers' lounge, offices, and services are in there. There's even a hospital, swimming pool, and library."

"Wow. It sounds like a city."

She nodded with a light shrug.

"Is there, like, a prison in there, too?"

Smooth, Megan.

"Yes. It's the only prison in Capital City."

"I guess that makes sense, since this must be the most secure place in the city."

She nodded and gave me a reassuring smile. "Don't worry, you won't be in any danger working in the main building. The prison is in a different part of the building and is heavily guarded. No one can sneak in and out of there without getting noticed."

My heart sank, and I could feel anxiety breaking through the thin walls of hope I'd been building for somehow reaching Thayn on my own. Trying to find a way into the prison was going to be a lot trickier than I'd thought.

How would I ever pull that off?

"Thanks, Amorette," I said, trying to sound as appreciative as I could, knowing she thought she was helping to calm my fears about working in a building that housed a prison.

"Sure. You know, I don't mind showing you around a bit. I was thinking of bringing Remms a bit of soup since he doesn't cook for himself yet. We all pitch in to take care of him when he's been healing a lot. I can walk you through the building to show you some of the sights before I head over there."

"Thanks. That's really nice of you. I mean, both offering to show me around a bit and being there for Remms. He really is a good guy, and I saw how weak he was after he healed the guys."

She nodded and steered us toward the main entrance.

Grinning, she asked, "So, are you best friends with Keavren and Mez now that you've been through all that with them?"

I laughed. "Well, I definitely think of Keavren as a good friend, especially since he was kind of my first friend here."

"He's such a sweetheart."

"He really is."

We neared the building's main entrance. There were two soldiers standing guard, one on either side of its large double doors.

"You'll need to show your identification," she said quietly to me.

I was glad for that piece of information and watched Amorette come to a halt before the woman soldier. She lifted her tag so the woman could visibly scan it. I followed suit and suppressed my instinct to smile at the soldier who looked at my tag with one of the stoniest expressions I'd ever seen. Without saying a word to either one of us, she opened the closest door, allowing us entrance.

Immediately, I was reminded of how important it was for me to be wearing my identification tag at all times. I had a bad feeling that getting caught without it would be akin to getting pulled over by a cop while driving without your driver's license, or something worse.

Who am I kidding? This place allows slavery. It's worse.

The wide entrance hallway was a busy space. There were people moving every-which-way, and most moved with purpose. Some people were dressed in civilian clothes like Amorette and me, a small few wore slave clothes, but most were sporting uniforms and not all the uniforms looked the same. There were those dressed in the standard soldier uniforms, there were a few Warriors I didn't recognize, and the rest all wore the same style of what looked like non-military uniforms. They were in different muted colours of green, grey, blue, and brown. I wondered if this last uniform group was worn by service employees.

Oh, geeze! Does this mean I'm going to have to wear one of those drab, itchy-looking uniforms if I can't find Thayn and get out of here in time? Bleh! Hopefully the translation service category didn't fall into the realm of brown uniforms.

"This floor has a lot of facilities on it." Amorette's voice interrupted my thoughts. "Pool, gym, mail room, admin, and a lot of other things like that. That's the pool," she added, nodding toward an open door we were approaching.

I looked inside and saw a tall man pulling on a Warrior uniform jacket. He was standing several feet away from us, and I could see a large pool behind him.

"Oh, there's Dendeon," Amorette said. "Do you know him?"

"No," I said, watching as the Warrior, Dendeon, pulled his sleek long black hair out from beneath his jacket. The movement caused the light in the room to reflect off his hair, and for a moment, it shone a bluey-green that reminded me of iridescent fish scales. He looked in our direction and nodded. Unless my eyes were playing tricks on me, I could have sworn his irises were an intense orange colour.

Did any Warrior not look weird in some way? Why did I get the feeling this guy's skill had something to do with water.

Amorette waved at him and turned to me as we kept walking. I noticed she was taking us toward the stairs.

"If you ever get the chance to officially meet him, or if you need to see him for whatever reason, the pool is where you'll usually find him. Just head all the way into the room because he's at the bottom of the pool a lot." She chuckled.

"Okay," I responded, not knowing why I'd ever need to see this guy. Then her words registered with me. "Um. Why would he be at the bottom of the pool?"

Did I really want to know the answer?

"He meditates there," she answered simply.

Of course he does. Who doesn't like meditating while holding their breath?

"He's calmer there than in the water in his quarters, probably because it's deeper. I guess you really don't know Dendeon."

"Nope. What's his Warrior skill? Holding his breath for a really long time under water?" I guessed sarcastically.

She laughed, amused as we climbed the stairs to the second floor. "No. He's from the Water People."

Of course he is. Silly Megan!

"So...he can breathe underwater?" I guessed again, my sarcasm transforming to disbelief.

"Of course he does!" Amorette exclaimed, without hiding the fact that she thought I was being ridiculous. "He's from the Water People."

Sure. Why not? I've already met the Charmers, a pyrokinetic madman, a man who can heal people with smoke he exhales on them, a man who can walk on water, a man with ghost wolves, a shadow-demon man, and another man who can manipulate minds. Bring on the merman Warrior! Oh, boy! I wonder if I'll meet Aésha's cat-man Warrior next...how has this become my life?

"This is the second floor," Amorette announced. "It's got a lot of offices, one of the library floors, more services, and well, more offices." She laughed. "If you work in the building, you're probably somewhere on this floor."

"Good to know, thanks." I smiled. I glanced around quickly, but didn't really see much other than a bunch of closed labeled doors and the large glass windows that belonged to the library, before we began our ascent to the third floor.

"You'll never guess what's here," she said when we reached the third floor. "Offices!" We both laughed. "There's also another floor of the library and certain quarters."

I smiled, finding it pretty neat that the library had multiple floors. The glass window-theme continued even on the library's next floor. At a quick glance, it actually looked nice. Maybe Kavylak saved all its "pretty" for the library. Maybe they were a big fan of books. I'd have to ask Irys if she'd known this existed. I remembered the Godeleva Estate had quite the large library of its own, though nothing of this magnitude, for sure.

"How many floors does this place have?" I asked as we climbed to the fourth floor.

"Five, plus the roof, which has a patio and restaurant."

Now that roof sounds interesting!

"This is fourth." Instead of continuing up the next flight of stairs, she turned to walk down the hall, and I followed.

"Intelligence Warriors to the right. Fighters to the left."

I nodded, glad that I knew what she was talking about when she said "Intelligence Warriors" and "Fighters". I had learned that the Warriors were split up into two factions. Fighters were those Warriors with skills that were more physical, like Keavren and Taye. Intelligence were those Warriors with skills that had more to do with powers of the mind, like Mez and Aésha.

"Upstairs on fifth," Amorette continued, "are the really important people. Xandon, the Warrior captains, the army generals, Mez' office, that sort of thing."

I froze mid-step when she mentioned Xandon's name. It hadn't even occurred to me that he would be here, let alone live in this building. A chill invaded my body at the thought of him and the eerie dream I had experienced. It took everything in me not to flee from the building at that moment.

"Hey, are you alright?" Amorette asked gently. I blinked, looking at her, realizing I had stopped walking.

"Oh. Yeah. I'm fine. Just got a bit dizzy," I lied. "Still haven't caught up on sleep."

She nodded with sympathy.

"So, uh, even though Mez' office is on the fifth floor, he lives on this one, I guess?" I asked.

Amorette nodded. "Yes, right between our quarters and Aésha's." She took my hand and led me down the hall, stopping in front of Mez' door, which was marked "Basarovka" in bold steel letters. The door to the left was marked "Ioq'wa" and the one to the right was marked "Stargrace". All the doors were made of a cold grey metal.

"Do you mind if I knock to see if Mez is home?"

She looked a little surprised but shook her head.

I released her hand and knocked.

No one answered.

"He's probably still in his office if you want to see him," she said, looking at me with a slightly worried expression. I could tell she was wondering if I was alright.

The truth was, I was far from alright. Knowing Xandon was here combined with my growing anxiety from having no idea how I'd get to Thayn, was starting to overwhelm me. I had to talk frankly with someone whom I felt would listen to me without judgment.

I have to talk to Mez.

"Actually, yeah. I think I do want to say, 'hi'. I just remembered there was something I wanted to ask him."

"Uh. Sure." Amorette said, her voice didn't mask how odd she found my sudden urgent need to see Mez. Still, she asked, "Did you want me to show you where it is?"

"Oh, no, that's alright," I blurted. "I mean, I know it's on fifth, and I know you wanted to get that soup to Remms. He shouldn't have to wait because of me," I babbled.

"Alright..."

Yup. Pretty sure she thinks I'm crazy now. I don't blame her.

"Thanks for showing me around, Amorette. Maybe we can get together again tomorrow?" I tried to sound more light and casual.

"Yeah, sure. You can always come to Remms' after you finish talking to Mez if you want," she offered.

"Thanks." She was so sweet. I really did like Amorette.

She nodded. "Take care, Megan." I didn't miss the emphasis she injected in her words, and I smiled to her before turning back toward the stairs to head up to fifth.

When I was halfway up the stairs, I stopped mid-step, shocked to see Galnar heading down in the opposite direction. He looked as pristine, colourless, and unnatural as-ever, with his paper-white skin and white hair standing out in sharp contrast against his black uniform. He walked down the stairs with a purposeful grace that would almost seem charming if there wasn't such a dark and dangerous aura about him. I could feel its invisible intensity as he neared me. For the briefest moment, we shared the same stair and his eyes locked on mine. They were grey, but a spark of red flickered in them for an instant, causing me to grip the railing tighter in fear and revulsion, wondering if something was about to happen. Nothing did.

As fast as his gaze had flicked to mine, it flicked forward again as he continued his descent. I was left with the light breeze of his movements, which annoyingly tickled my face in such a way that I would have sworn he'd done it on purpose. I stared after him, horrifyingly amazed at how someone like him could exist.

He had brought me and Irys nothing but torment, and we had done nothing to deserve it. How could he be so heartless when the other Warriors I had met had been kind? Why was he so hateful? What had happened to him?

I shook my head to free my thoughts of Galnar and quickly resumed my climb, no longer looking back. It didn't matter "how" or "why". What mattered was that I *had* to get out of here.

I *had* to see Mez.

Chapter 28

Irys

The hair dye appeared to be a relatively close match to my natural colour. It wasn't exact, but at least it was far closer than the silvery-white streak it was intended to cover.

It was an odd, foul smelling paste that was difficult to apply with any accuracy. I made sure the offending streak of hair was coated, and I waited around with the hair pinned to my head in an odd little bunch. To pass the time, I scrubbed at my hands to remove the purple splotches that stubbornly stained my skin.

After waiting for a painful length of time, in which the odor from the product had permeated my entire apartment, and my scalp had started to sting in the places where the dye had made contact, I rinsed the product out of my hair. Before my eyes, I could see the thick purple slime coming away from my hair without leaving even the slightest trace behind.

Nearly in tears, I started again, determined to wait longer this time. I recited poems I'd memorized and tried to focus on reading one of my library books in the hopes of taking my mind off the growing discomfort the dye was causing my head.

When I couldn't stand it anymore, I returned to the bathroom to wash the dye away.

The relief I felt from removing the product from my scalp was short-lived when I saw that the second application was no more successful than the first.

Giving up, I gave my hands a final scrub and prepared for bed.

I climbed under the blankets, sliding my hand under my pillow where I could feel the cool glass of the vials I'd pilfered from the infirmary when I'd visited Lieutenant Fhurrk.

Great Goddess, give me strength. I don't even know what these medicines are. I want them. I need them. Save me from them.

Withdrawing my hand from the pillow, leaving the vials where they were, I made the sign of the Goddess in the air above me and lay my arm at my side.

I turned out my light and lay there with my damp hair, not caring that I was soaking the bedding, only hoping for a dreamless sleep.

As I began to drift off, a strong hand pressed itself over my mouth, and an urgent voice whispered close to my ear.

"Irys, it's Acksil. Please be quiet. I'm not here to harm you."

I gasped but listened, eyes wide and searching through the darkness. As I realized who it was, I relaxed a little and nodded against his hand, hoping he would release me.

He did. I turned my head to look in his direction, seeing only a shadow moving through the darkness of the room.

There was a scratching sound, and a small flame burst into life on the end of a match in his hand. He lit a candle on my bedside table that had not been there when I'd turned out my light.

I sat up, pulling up the sheet to cover me. He was standing next to my bed, dressed all in black though not in the Warrior uniform. A hood had been covering his head, but he pulled it down so I could see his face more easily.

"Acksil, what's going on?" I asked in a whisper.

"Irys, I need you to listen very carefully, and I need you to trust me. I don't have time to explain everything right now, but you are in danger."

"What am I to do?" I asked, trying to focus on action rather than allowing the fear to flow through me.

"I'm going to get you out of here."

"I'm already leaving tomorrow. A Traveller is going to bring me back to Gbat," I told him, hoping he had misunderstood the situation and that this peril that threatened me had been in his imagination.

"They've been lying to you," he said with certainty and a shake of his head. "The Traveller has been here all along."

I wasn't sure what to say or even what to think.

"Why would they do this? They've let me exchange letters with Sir Fhirell. They've upheld their side of the agreement so far. Why would they want to keep me here? All I've been doing is reading library books."

"You haven't exchanged a single word with him. You've been communicating with me," he informed me gravely.

A lump formed in my throat. It stayed there for a long moment before it made a slow descent into my stomach.

Watching me for a moment, he left the room very briefly, returning with a paper and pencil and, before my eyes, wrote a sentence in Sir Fhirell's handwriting.

My hands came to my mouth in shock and to stop myself from screaming.

"I know this is hard to hear. Please trust me." He spoke with such sincerity that I could not help but believe him.

"I..." The words stuck in my throat, but I forced them out. "I believe you. I trust you. You have helped me before. I see no reason for you to choose to lie to me now."

"I am going to help you again." He looked into my eyes and reached out a hand as if without thinking, and touched my white streak of hair, looking deeply concerned.

I tensed a little as he did it but did not draw back. Instead, I merely watched him in return.

"It changed on its own," I explained quietly.

He nodded slowly. "You noticed it this morning?"

"Yes."

"You had a nightmare?"

"Yes."

"We need to get you out of here."

Chapter 29

Megan

Reaching the fifth floor, I instantly noticed that it was different from all the others. The hallway was empty and freaky-quiet. There was a definite no-loitering vibe on this level. I walked down the hallway, feeling more unnerved with each step I took. My shoes squeaked with a mercilessly loud basketball court echo.

Why didn't I just bring a drum set with me to announce my presence all the way down the hall?

I found the one that had "Office - Basarovka" on the door. Taking a breath to steady my nerves – which didn't work at all after my surprise stairway encounter with Galnar – I reached out and knocked on the door.

"You just missed him," Mez replied from the other side.

Uh?

"Mez…it's, Megan. Are you busy? I, uh…I can come back if you are," I answered, having no idea how to interpret what he had just said.

Instead of a verbal response, I could hear footsteps approaching the door. It opened, revealing Mez, who smiled upon seeing me.

"Megan, it's good to see you. Would you like to come in?" he asked.

I nodded, grateful that this was an option, especially because I wanted out of this echoey hallway.

He opened the door farther, and I walked in, pausing after I had taken a few steps inside. I looked in awe around his office. It was stunning. He hadn't been kidding when he'd told me that his office here was far superior to the one I had seen on the ship. The room was a large open space with a very high ceiling. Two storeys of books lined the walls, and a two-storey window provided a view of the city and the ocean.

"Wow!" I exclaimed. "You weren't kidding about your office. It's amazing. I really, really like it."

He chuckled, amused by my reaction. "Thank you," he said and shut the door. "It's taken me forever to make it perfect. Coffee?" he asked me.

"Yes, please." I nodded, turning in his direction.

He smiled and headed over to an odd-looking square machine, which sat on the surface of what looked like a small kitchen cart. The cart had small shelves below its counter-like surface. On one shelf, were small dark grey coffee mugs with saucers that were somewhere between the size of a standard office mug and a demitasse. To my surprise, they looked ceramic and not stainless steel like the mugs in my shared kitchen. On another shelf, there were a few small packages and containers. At the very bottom of the cart was a small drawer.

The machine made a light whirring sound, which was followed by a few pops and gurgles. Shortly afterward, I could smell the aroma of coffee brewing, and I loved it. Mez' office was easily my favourite place in the building, so far.

"How are you feeling?" I asked him.

"Still a little tired but otherwise good."

Mez was dressed exactly as I was accustomed to seeing him from our office sessions when I had first met him on the ship that bought us to Capital City. He was wearing his uniform without the jacket, which was currently resting across the back of his black leather office chair. The standard fitted black t-shirt he wore, allowed me to see his bare arms from his biceps down. There was no sign of healing wounds, marks, or scars on the skin that I could see. It was like nothing had happened to him.

"Remms finished healing me," he supplied, in response to my perusing gaze.

I nodded with a smile. "I'm glad. I figured as much when Amorette said she was going to bring Remms some soup while he healed."

Mez nodded. "How are you feeling?"

"I'm alright, but I need to talk. Are you feeling good enough for a serious conversation?" I decided to get right to the point.

"Sure," he said with a more sober expression. "Sit wherever you'd like. I'll just get our coffees. Do you want anything to eat?"

"No, thank you. I had a big dinner."

He took two mugs from the kitchen cart shelf and filled them with coffee. Taking this opportunity to debate my sitting options, I decided on one of the two large leather chairs in front of his desk instead of the long black shrink-couch that was also in the room.

Mez brought us a small tray carrying the coffee mugs, a bowl of white sugar cubes, and a small bowl containing an off-white substance that I guessed was powdered milk or cream. He set the tray down on his large dark cherry wood-coloured desk and took a seat in his chair behind it.

"Do you want anything in your coffee or shall I brace myself?"

"Sugar and whatever this is," I said, scooping the powder with a spoon and adding some to the coffee. I didn't care what it was, I just couldn't drink black coffee.

"Powdered milk," he said with a slight grimace to his face. "I have real milk in my quarters, but I don't keep an ice box in here"

"This is fine," I assured him, adding two sugar cubes to my coffee and stirring it. Mez watched what I added to my coffee but added nothing to his. This didn't surprise me. He seemed like a black coffee kind of guy.

"Thanks," I said, lifting the coffee to my lips and taking a small sip. It tasted great. It had the right amount of kick without being bitter.

Mez took a sip of his own coffee and waited patiently for me to speak.

"Are you aware that I got a slave from the port town we visited?"

"Yes, and I am aware of who he is and where he is."

Gotta love Mez' honesty, even if I now feel like throwing up my coffee.

Still, I appreciated that he didn't make me say what we both knew, and it made me trust him more.

I nodded. "Is he hurt?"

"No. He's been checked. He was a part of the fighting and received a few bumps and scratches but nothing more. I looked into it."

I felt my eyes well up, finding it difficult to swallow.

Thayn is okay.

"I want to return to Syliza with him," I confessed. "But if I go back, will you or the Warriors keep coming after me?"

He studied me for a long moment with a very steady gaze. "If I am ordered to, if any of us are ordered to, we will."

A tear escaped my eye. Deep down, I knew that would be his answer. What other answer could he logically give?

"Are you certain your life here will be less fulfilling to you than the one you could have in Syliza?" he asked me without judgment. It was clear that he was asking because he wanted to know my answer.

"I don't know. I want to believe that I could go back there and be happy with him and with Irys," I explained honestly. "I know I don't know Syliza any more than I know Kavylak, but I had a happier experience there."

He nodded. "You have friends here, too, and a chance for your own life."

I looked at him for a long moment. It wasn't that I didn't believe what he was saying. He was right. I did have friends here, and it did seem that I could begin somewhat of a life here. But this isn't where I wanted to be. In truth, I didn't want to be in Syliza either. I wanted to go home.

Another tear fell.

"I believe that you're honest with me, Mez, so I want to ask you a question, and I want your honest answer."

"Of course," he said without hesitation.

"Do you believe me when I say I'm from another world?"

"Yes," he answered easily.

"You don't just believe I believe it, but you actually believe it's true?" I clarified.

"I think you're from a world that is not this one but that is not entirely unlike this one," he said. "I believe that you lived your whole life there until you were here one day for a reason we have yet to learn."

I nodded, more tears falling. I had no reason to believe that he was lying to me, and it felt so good to hear someone say they believed me.

"The real truth is, Mez, I want to go home, back to where I'm from. I don't belong in Kavylak any more than I belong in Syliza, but

I have no idea how to get back there." My voice broke, and I couldn't continue speaking.

"I need to be honest with you, Megan," Mez said, rising and walking over to the chair next to mine, taking a seat and facing me. "I have no idea how you'd get there, either, but if anyone were to be able to help you, it would not be someone in Syliza." He withdrew a very expensive-looking white handkerchief with a white satin border and handed it to me.

I took it from him, seeing his initials embroidered in the same satin thread in the corner of the soft handkerchief. I dabbed at my eyes and face. Even as upset as I was, there was no way I was blowing my nose into the nicest and most expensive handkerchief I had ever seen.

I let his words sink in and nodded. "Xandon."

"Yes." Mez nodded. "If it can be done, he would be the one to find out how."

"Thank you for being honest," I said. "It really means a lot to me that you believe me. You're the only person I've told about Earth, and who truly believes me and wants to help me find a way back home. You have no idea how much that means to me."

It was true. No one else believed me like Mez did. Not even Thayn. Although I never had this type of heart-to-heart discussion with Thayn, instinctively I knew I couldn't. He would do what he could to help me and keep me safe, but he wouldn't believe me about Earth. Not really.

I was sure it was hard for Mez to accept what I was saying, and he couldn't possibly fully understand, but I knew he believed me, and he genuinely cared about what I believed. That was enough. It was everything.

He reached out and took my hand. "Thank you for trusting me. I will prove to you that your trust isn't misplaced."

I held his hand back. "I know it isn't."

He gave me a small smile and stroked the back of my hand with his thumb a few times before releasing it.

"I do understand that you're a Warrior and sometimes that means missions come before friendships but that doesn't mean you're my enemy," I told him, remembering what Aésha had once said to me.

He considered my words, looking at me thoughtfully, and took my hand again.

"It's my turn to show that I trust you," he said quietly, surprising me. "Missions or not, you will never be deliberately placed in danger by my hand. You will never be my enemy because you won't have to be. You're safe with me, Megan."

I was speechless, genuinely surprised by his statement because no one I'd met here had ever said anything like that to me. At least, they hadn't said it so openly and plainly.

I'm pretty sure Mez just told me that he would defy an order if it meant keeping me safe.

"This is only for us to know," he said, making it more than obvious that if it came down to either keeping me safe or following a direct order, he would choose me first.

"I can keep a secret," I vowed. I would most certainly keep this one. "I won't forget your trust in me, and I won't betray it."

He nodded. "I believe you. You're a good person, Megan. The finest alien I've ever met."

I laughed. In spite of the somber mood, his words touched that silly side of me.

"Well, you're a mighty fine alien yourself."

"I'm not an alien," Mez insisted with a playful grin. "I'm a local." He then looked more serious. "Would you trust me to speak with Xandon about how we might be able to return you home?"

I tensed all over when he spoke Xandon's name. "I...I don't know. I guess."

"I know you want to run, Megan," he spoke softly. "I know you want to find a way to get Varda out of his cell and make your way back to Syliza. If you do that, I won't have enough time to talk to Xandon, that is, if you give me permission. Is there any way to convince you to stay, at least a while?"

I thought about what he said. I thought about the fact that he believed me. I thought about the fact that if I were to leave with Thayn there was no guarantee that Kavylak wouldn't come after me. I didn't want anyone to get hurt. I didn't want Thayn to get hurt.

"Will you let Thayn go?"

"If you stay?"

I nodded.

"I will see to it that he finds his way to a path that will bring him home."

Nodding, I felt my face sinking with sadness as the harsh reality struck me. If I wanted Thayn to be happy and safe, there would be no romance for us. There would be no Syliza for me, no courtship, no Thayntasy. I had to let him go.

"I'm sorry. I know it's hard," Mez said with raw understanding. "You're very brave."

I took a breath, a shaky breath, and nodded, looking at him.

"Help him escape, and I'll stay."

"Would you want to see him before he goes?"

"Yes. If I can say goodbye, I should. I want to." Fresh tears fell from my eyes, and I just let them fall.

Mez reached out and gently stroked my damp cheek with the backs of his fingers. "I thought you might."

I nodded, and he withdrew his hand, and I dabbed at my eyes and face with his handkerchief.

"It will need to be later tonight," he told me, leaning back in his chair.

"Okay," I said. "I'll be ready to go whenever it is. Thank you."

"You don't need to thank me, Megan. I like you, and you just saved my life. This is the very least I can do." He leaned forward in his seat again. "I will need to insist that it stays between us. This will be completely forbidden and very dangerous," he admitted quietly, "But I swear to you that he will arrive home safely."

"I won't say a word, for his sake or yours. This stays between us. Always."

"Not even to him," Mez urged. "Don't tell him I'm involved."

"I won't," I promised. "He'll never know. No one will."

"I trust you," he said.

"I trust you," I replied.

We held each other's gaze for a long moment as if we were each other's lifeline. It was an intense feeling. A powerful feeling. A good feeling.

"I won't speak to Xandon until you give me permission," Mez said finally. "You have time. Just go about your days until you are ready."

My stomach clenched into a tight knot at the idea of staying here instead of returning to Syliza with Thayn. I felt overwhelmed with panic and the urge to cry again, but I blinked back the tears. I had to get a grip. Now was the time to be practical. It was time to do everything I could to find my way home. Xandon *had* to be the key to finding my way back.

Maybe that's why I've been dreaming about him. Maybe I've known all along.

I looked at Mez, who had been quietly observing me, waiting for me to speak.

"I should go," I told him, though in truth I didn't have anywhere I had to be. I just couldn't stay in his office anymore. My thoughts were suffocating, and I needed air.

"Of course," he said, not questioning my abrupt announcement.

I stood. "Thank you for the coffee."

He rose to his feet and nodded.

We looked at each other for several long moments until Mez leaned forward with the clear intention to hug me. I was surprised at first, but the contact was not unwanted. He'd moved so deliberately I could have stopped him if I'd wanted to. I didn't.

His embrace was warm and tender until I held him back tightly, and he matched my pressure, which made me feel even better. It had been so long since I had hugged someone this tightly, and with all the terror I had been through, the security of it felt amazing. It was exactly what I needed.

Finally, I drew away, and he released his hold, looking at me with understanding.

"Thanks," I whispered.

"You're welcome, Megan. Try to have a restful evening."

"You, too."

He took a step back. "Goodnight."

I left his office, quietly shutting the door behind me. As I walked down the echoey hall toward the stairs, I wondered how I had managed to befriend someone as quick-witted, lazer-sharp, and cool as Mez Basarovka and why he would be willing to stick his neck out to help me: some nobody alien.

Maybe I would live to regret the decision to trust Mez.

Maybe I was putting Thayn in more danger by trusting him.

Maybe Mez was telling the truth.

It didn't matter now though, did it? I had made my choice, and I had to see it through. Only time would reveal the truth.

Chapter 30

Irys

"I need you to do exactly as I say."

I nodded. Following Acksil was the right thing to do. Everything I'd trusted here was a lie. Acksil had risked his life to save me before. If he said the Traveller would not be bringing me home, I believed him. I had no idea what I was trying to escape. I didn't know where he would take me. Whatever the case, I knew with certainty that my best hope was with Acksil guiding me.

Great Goddess, I'm scared.

"Arik is going to return. When he does, I want you to remain here as if you are sleeping. There won't be any need for you to react. Just stay quiet with your eyes closed and try to appear unconscious," he instructed.

A shiver washed over me. "How soon?"

"Soon. His purpose is to make sure you're asleep."

"Why?" I asked as another shiver threatened me.

"Because he needs to tell another Warrior that you're sleeping so that other Warrior can enter your dreams."

The shiver was visible this time. Questions flooded my mind, but I knew they had to wait. Everything had to wait.

"I will pretend to be asleep," I confirmed. "Please come back soon."

"I won't leave you, Irys. I promise."

I reached out and took his hand, giving it a solid squeeze in the hopes of expressing even the tiniest fragment of the gratitude I felt toward him. His fingers curled around mine, squeezing gently but firmly in return.

I jumped at the sound of a click from my apartment door. The bolt had been turned.

"Sleep," Acksil whispered quickly. "No matter what." He blew out the candle.

I nodded and lay down, covering myself with the sheet, attempting to look relaxed, comfortable, and thoroughly unconscious. It couldn't have been further from the way I actually felt. Focusing on every muscle from my head to my toes, I released each one as quiet voices exchanged words in the next room.

"Good, you're here," said Acksil.

"Yes, but you shouldn't be. You know your orders, Acksil. Leave quietly. I don't want to have to report you."

"I'm not leaving without her, Arik. I need your help."

There was a long pause, during which I assumed there was an exchange of facial expressions instead of words.

"Acksil, this girl really has caused you to take leave of your senses if you think I'm just going to help you walk out of here with her."

"If I don't do this, he'll kill her. I know he will."

"If you do this, he'll kill you."

"It's a risk I'm willing to take."

"It's not a risk I'm willing to take," Lieutenant Atrix' voice sounded different somehow. Appealing. Very appealing. I felt inclined to agree with him, even though I knew what he was saying was wrong and was apparently threatening my life.

"Please, my brother," spoke Acksil's rapid words. "I need to save her. If this were Asimara, wouldn't you do the same?"

Another pause. Acksil had found a chink in Lieutenant Atrix' armour.

"Arik, this is important to me. It's everything to me," Acksil went on.

"More important than your brothers? Think about Keavren," Lieutenant Atrix replied. The alluring quality was gone. These were his words – stern and direct.

"I am thinking about Keavren. I'm thinking about all of you just as much as I'm thinking about her and me. Whatever he's doing to her, Arik, it's unnatural. It's wrong. She's not just some nobody we picked off the street. She's from an important Sylizan family. He stole her from her home and her people and now he and Fynx are causing physical changes in her. He's inviting war with Syliza for one girl? Why? He has never been this aggressive, this careless."

"It's not our place to question why, Acksil."

"You would question why if he were after Asimara, and you'd want to get as far away from him as possible."

"Stop bringing her into this," Lieutenant Atrix snapped in a sharp whisper. I started and was relieved they weren't in the room to see it. If I hadn't heard it, I wouldn't have believed that Lieutenant Atrix could sound so harsh and rumpled.

"Then stop being a fool and help me to help Irys," Acksil countered. "I'm leaving, Arik, and we both know I'm dead whether you report me or not. He won't just make small changes to me this time. If his alterations don't kill my body, he will have killed who I am. There will be nothing left of me. I'll be nothing more than a weapon, just like Galnar and Aaro."

Another silent pause.

"Fine," said Lieutenant Atrix in resignation. "Aésha and I will help you get out so you'll have a fighting chance. I hope you've thought this through because you know it won't be long before we come for you. We won't be on the same side."

"I know," Acksil agreed grimly.

"Get her ready and take her to the stables. I'll meet you there with Zayset."

"Thank you, my brother." Though still whispering, the gratitude in Acksil's voice was profound.

Footsteps approached my room but paused when Lieutenant Atrix spoke again.

"Acksil," he said. His voice was even quieter than it had been before. "I'll never forgive you for this. None of us will."

Only silence followed. Perhaps Acksil had nodded. Perhaps he had done nothing at all. There was a long moment before the door to my quarters quietly opened with Lieutenant Atrix' exit.

After a breath, Acksil was in the room with me again.

I remained in my "sleeping" position despite his presence, until he lit the candle and rested a hand on my arm very briefly.

"We've got to move quickly now, Irys. I've brought clothes for you, and I need you to put them on. They will help you to hide in the shadows and allow you to move fast. They're not what you usually wear." His words were rapid but clear.

I wondered what I was about to see. My imagination spiralled with images of what he could be asking me to wear. I forced myself to push those thoughts aside to focus on the matter at hand. It was far too easy to try to pretend that none of this was happening and to distract myself with fashion concerns.

I watched as Acksil seemed to produce a bag out of thin air. Likely, he had withdrawn it from where it had been hidden behind a piece of furniture or under the bed, but in the dim light of the single candle, the bag seemed to simply materialize.

I sat with the covers pulled up over myself as I watched him withdraw the various parts of what were to be my outfit. Despite my best efforts to concentrate on the greater threat, the long black tunic and thin leather-like leggings didn't look like nearly enough fabric to even approach decency.

"Is there any more to it?" I couldn't help but ask.

"Irys, I really need you to look past the clothes right now. We don't have time for you to worry about fashions. Your life is at stake. These will help you to hide and will help you to move," he repeated bluntly to me, though he was probably remaining more patient than the situation warranted.

"I'm sorry. I just wanted to be certain. You're right," I said, picking up the clothes and dashing into the bathroom. It was difficult enough for me to go that far in my nightgown. I certainly wasn't about to dress in front of him.

The leggings were easier to pull on than I had expected. While they looked like black leather, they were made from a much thinner and yet surprisingly strong material I'd never before encountered. To my dismay, the tunic was form following and covered me only as far as my mid-thigh. With a glance at myself in the mirror, I felt the flush rise to my cheeks. It felt little better than if I'd been entirely bare.

Returning to the bedroom, I refused to make eye contact with Acksil, trying to pay attention to what I was doing.

"Put those boots on. They should fit you," he instructed me, indicating a pair of high, black suede boots that came nearly to my knees. Their soles were soft, likely chosen for the silent tread they would permit me. Nothing like the boots I typically wore, I had to admit to myself that they were surprisingly comfortable. At least they provided another layer of coverage over the lower part of my leg.

Quickly, I pulled my hair into a braid, deftly tying the end.

Relief swam over me when I was handed a black, hooded cloak. It was long enough that its hem nearly dusted the top of my boot. It had a clever slash in either side which could allow me to slide my arms through or keep them hidden inside the fabric. It was a highly practical piece. Above all, I appreciated that I was covered by more cloth.

Pulling up the hood, I looked to Acksil for his approval. He nodded and indicated the bag he'd used to bring me the outfit.

"If you have anything to take with you, put it in this bag," he said.

Quickly, I added my nightie, my clothing for the next day, a few toiletries and a pencil and paper. I was thrifty with my choices as the bag wasn't very big and there were already a few items inside. He picked it up as soon as I was finished.

"I'm going to take you out the window. We'll never make it if we leave through the building." He pointed toward the window as I tried to decide whether or not he was serious. *He was serious.*

Stepping up to the window I looked out to the ground below. We were only on the second floor, but we may as well have been on the top floor. Should we fall, the drop wouldn't kill us, but there would be little chance we would land uninjured. Suddenly, I was glad to be wearing the leggings instead of my skirt.

"Whatever you do, don't scream. If they find us out, Irys, I won't be able to help you. We will never get out of here alive," he warned.

"I'll be quiet. I'll do what you say," I whispered.

To that, he grabbed my cloak, bunched up its length and handed it to me. I held it, baffled as he deftly folded a length of rope in half.

Before I could tell what he was doing, he was reaching around me, bringing the rope about my waist and tying it twice, drawing it snugly around me. I watched as he dropped the two ends so they hung loosely in front of me and made a small squeak as he reached between my knees from behind me and drew up the two ends of rope, tucking them under the rope belt he'd made for me earlier. He brought the ends around me as a second belt, tying it securely and slightly too tightly for my preference.

As I was about to protest, I realized that I was now wearing a fascinating and yet very uncomfortable harness. A metal loop was clipped around the rope belts at my waist, and he looped another rope through that. I forced myself to pay attention to every move he was making as the alternative was to think about the fact that I would soon be leaving my quarters out the window.

My cloak was pulled out of my hands and allowed to fall behind me. He looked out the window, tossed the bag down to the ground, and lowered himself by a rope before waving his hand and signalling that I should climb out.

It was as though I'd never moved my own arms and legs before. I climbed backward out the window, holding on to the ledge for as long as I could before he began to slowly lower me to the ground. I reached out my feet to stop me from bumping into the building as I was lowered. As much as I would have loved to have made a graceful landing, the first part of me to make contact with the ground was my leggings-clad bottom.

Immediately, Acksil was by my side, helping me to my feet. He untied me from the rope and pulled the knots open on my harness, slipping it off me to tuck both that rope and the metal loop into the bag.

"Stay with me," he whispered into my ear. "Don't speak to anyone. Not Arik. Not the Traveller."

I nodded, afraid to reply out loud.

Taking my hand, he walked me quickly through the compound, keeping near to building walls and avoiding anyone out walking or patrolling. I lost all sense of direction. I could barely see through the darkness and would likely have walked directly into the side of a building if Acksil had not been guiding my every step.

Soon, my nose was assaulted with the smell of the stables, and we slipped stealthily inside. I clutched tightly to Acksil's hand, more afraid of losing him than of what could happen to us if his plan should fail.

The stables were completely empty. We stood in silence, pressed against a shadowed corner, waiting.

The entire time, I didn't move. I didn't speak. I barely thought. I focused on breathing as soundlessly as I could, on watching for any unexpected movement in the darkness, and on the secure feeling of Acksil's hand in mine.

I had no way of knowing how much time had passed. It could have been a handful of minutes. It felt like closer to an hour. Regardless, nothing could have stopped me from starting and gasping sharply when Lieutenant Atrix and the Traveller who brought me to Kavylak, Zayset, appeared close by.

Acksil stepped out of the shadows, bringing me with him, making us easily visible to the two newcomers. I kept the hood to my cloak pulled up, and I bowed my head, turning my face slightly away from the Warrior and the Traveller. Certainly, they both knew who I was, but my hope was to discourage them from addressing me.

Glancing at the pair out of the corner of my eye, I was surprised to see how happy the Traveller looked. While Arik appeared somewhat stern, Zayset was staring at him as though she was intoxicated with the sight of him. After a brief moment, he returned her gaze and leaned in to kiss her with startling passion.

I knew I should look away, but I was compelled to watch them. Even through my sideways glance, I knew I was gaping, and I prayed silently for the Goddess to forgive me.

The kiss broke, and Zayset stared up at Lieutenant Atrix, completely entranced. For his part, Lieutenant Atrix looked more amused than taken with her, and yet he still managed to appear completely alluring.

"Can't we go to your place now?" she asked him with a sigh.

"Soon, my darling. You know there's nothing I want more, but remember, I want you to help Lieutenant Fhir first. Take him and the civilian to wherever it is he wants to go, then come to my quarters where I'll be waiting for you." It was awful to watch. She was smitten with him, and it was more than clear that he did not feel the same. She was being used. "Do it for me, Zayset."

She nodded slowly to him and with a visible effort, dragged her gaze from him to look at Acksil and me.

"Let's make this fast," she said. All the tenderness from her voice had vanished. "Where are we going?"

Acksil leaned toward her and whispered something. She nodded in reply and took hold of my arm and his. I didn't even have time to glance again at Lieutenant Atrix before we were standing in a clearing in the woods with only moonlight to illuminate the space.

She released my arm and did the same for Acksil, but quite abruptly, his hand shot out and he grabbed hold of her arm. Faster than I could see, he had drawn a knife from somewhere, possibly his belt, I couldn't be certain. In a flash, he drove the blade into her chest.

Zayset stared down at the blade and then up at Acksil before slumping to her knees. Acksil helped her onto her side on the ground. Without a word or even an audible exhalation of her last breath, she stopped moving. Her unseeing eyes remained open.

I could barely comprehend what I was seeing. *Did my mind make it all up? Had the fear and desperation I was feeling driven me to madness? Surely Acksil hadn't just murdered someone right in front of me. It was a trick of the moonlight in this ghastly forest.*

I slammed a hand over my mouth as though to hold in a scream, though I did not feel one imprisoned by my palm. Letting my arm drop back down to my side, I began stepping away from Acksil. My legs were shaking and my steps were unsteady.

"You just..." I didn't want to say the words. It was as though giving the situation definition would seal it into reality. "Why would you?" I asked him nonsensically.

"So we wouldn't be caught. It was unfortunate but necessary to keep us safe," he replied emotionlessly.

"This is because of me?" I asked in a whispered horror, taking another step away but stopping as my heel butted up against a piece of fallen log.

I could see his head shake as he turned to face me. "No. Don't put this on yourself. Her death is Xandon's fault, not yours. I had to do it because of him."

There was nothing I could say in response. His words didn't make any sense. Nothing did. All I could think about was the sight of the blade pushing between her ribs and into her heart before the light behind Zayset's eyes went out.

"I need to hide her. I can't let her be found. The last thing we can afford is Alukka's wrath," he said in a stern tone – one that meant business.

His words wouldn't process. I could barely remember the name of the other Traveller, let alone try to understand what he meant.

"Where are we?" I asked, trying to concern myself with something that might help me.

"Sorcheena," he replied. "Near the border of Sefaline. It's a dangerous place but we won't stay here long. You'll need to stay close to me. We're in Raider country."

His last statement repeated itself in my head.

"Tarvak Raiders?" I asked as the words took my breath away.

"Yes," he answered gravely. "There is a river nearby where we can hide the body. Come with me."

If he had not mentioned his intention to hide Zayset's body in a river, I may have been paralyzed with fear at the thought of running into the Raiders. The Tarvak Raiders were a terrifying group of marauders who stalked, pillaged, and killed with or without reason throughout the unstable regions of the world. They were rampant in areas recently taken over by another country.

Raider territory was to be avoided at all costs. If you met the Raiders, you would be fortunate if you escaped with your life, but even if you were that lucky, you were unlikely to have anything left in your possession and would probably be injured in some way. They were, according to the books I'd read on the subject, unmerciful about collecting their toll for travelling through what they felt was their land.

Slinging the bag over one shoulder, Acksil reached out and took my hand. I held his in return. I was too afraid not to. With his free hand, he pointed a light at the ground ahead of us. It wasn't bright, but it was enough to light the ground before our feet. I couldn't see the source of the light. I'd never seen anything quite like it.

"Listen for water," he instructed. His voice broke through the eerie quiet of the night around us. Though I knew why he wanted me to do it, the direction was still welcome.

"Yes," I agreed, and I listened for any sound of a river.

To my relief, we didn't have to continue for long. The sound of the water and its musty smell seemed to arrive at the same time.

"I hear it," I told him.

"I hear it, too. It will be just over there." He indicated the direction with the light in his hand. "I want you to take the bag. I'm going to get her."

"Do I just wait here?" I asked as the leather bag handles rested into my hands. "What do I do?"

"Just wait here," he confirmed. "I'll be right back."

"I won't move," I replied, though when he was gone, I dropped to my knees in prayer.

Great Goddess, have I made the wrong decision? When I thought I was following your Light, did I take the path to Darkness? Is Zayset's blood on my hands? On my soul? Will you ever forgive me?

I looked up to the sky. Above me, the stars twinkled down, effortlessly carving their way through the endless blackness. Brighter than them all was the blue star. Its steady light felt calming as though it approved of me.

I made the right choice. It was a hard choice. There were sacrifices. Those sacrifices will not be forgotten. Great Goddess, I kneel before you, but I'm standing on my own feet. I won't be a victim anymore. I trust Lieutenant Fhir. Acksil. His heart is good and while he has sided with Chaos, he has left it to keep me in your Light. I'm going home.

I stood quickly when I heard footsteps approaching. Acksil carried Zayset as though the woman was only sleeping. Passing me, he brought her to the edge of the river, and I followed. It likely wasn't his intention to have me there with him, but at this point, it hardly seemed to matter whether or not my company was welcome.

"May I say a prayer for her?" I asked him.

"Pray with me," he said, withdrawing a small pendant from a chain around his neck. It had been tucked under his clothing. It was a Goddess figure. I was glad to see it. It felt as though it might draw Her gaze upon us to see what we've done. Perhaps she might choose to understand what had happened and forgive us.

Simultaneously, we made the sign of the Goddess with our fingers. It was the same sign. It was Sylizan. He placed a hand over his heart in preparation for prayer, resting his pendant down on Zayset's chest and laying his hand on top. I tried not to think about the blood soaking her shirt under his palm. I crossed my hands over my own heart and shut my eyes.

"Please forgive me, Great Goddess, and take this woman into your safe keeping. Forgive her for her faults," he said.

He shifted slightly as though to end the prayer, so I withdrew one of my hands from my chest and placed it over his that remained over his heart.

I felt bold and confident as I spoke. "Great Goddess, find it in your wisdom to understand what was done with the intention of goodness, despite its evil means. Please take this woman as an innocent who was used as a part of a greater plan to escape Chaos. Please see the truth of what this man has done in the name of our protection and guide us along your path as we move ahead." I withdrew my hand from him, and our fingers swept through the air to make the sign and complete our prayer.

Acksil remained silent for an extra moment once I had finished speaking. Afterward, he stood without ceremony, leaving the pendant with Zayset.

"Do you want your pendant back?" I asked him delicately.

"No. It is not the first pendant I have given, and it won't be my last," he replied, the emotion drained from his tone.

I nodded. There was nothing else to be said on the matter.

Carefully, as though attempting not to disturb her, he lifted her body and turned, crouching at the water's edge and laying her gently into it.

I couldn't help but watch but was grateful that the darkness obscured the scene for me. I was glad not to know whether she'd sunk beneath the surface or remained afloat and swept downriver.

He took the opportunity to wash, and I chose to focus on those sounds to stop my imagination from running wild.

Soon enough, Acksil returned to my side and took the bag from me.

"We need to find shelter and wait out the night. At first light, we'll start travelling. We won't be able to stay here for too long," he informed me, taking my hand with one of his and shining the light with the other.

Throughout our walk, I listened carefully for any indications that we might be falling victim to Raiders, predatory animals, or Alukka, if she had somehow managed to track us down already. There was, to my relief, nothing at all to be noticed. The night was a silent one.

After a while, we reached a dirt road in poor condition. We followed it to a town. At first, it seemed to be no different from any other town at night.

However, as we approached the buildings, it was clear that these weren't structures that housed a vibrant community. They were the rubble left behind by families, friends, and neighbours who were forced to abandon their homes, or worse, who were killed during invasions and raids.

As we continued walking, it surprised me to find that this was not the small town I'd originally expected it to be. It was the remains of a city. An entire city left in ruin with broken windows and doors, and crumbling walls. Plants appeared to be taking up residence where people no longer lived.

We walked along in the darkness, trying not to stumble over the amputated pieces of homes, shops, offices, and temples, until Acksil selected a building for us to enter. Though it appeared to me as though he had chosen it at random, I was certain that it had met some standard by which he was measuring our shelter for the night.

Stepping through the open doorway – its door actually missing, not just left unlatched – we found our way to an inner room. Only there did he release my hand.

"I'm going to build a fire for light and warmth. It's pretty quiet around here so we should be safe until morning," he said softly, breaking the silence that had stretched on for long enough that I jumped at the unexpected sound of his voice.

"Yes," I said as though I was agreeing to an offer. Without Acksil's hand, I felt unbalanced and uncertain. I took a moment to step about the room to become more confident in it. It was ridiculous to think I would be able to hold Acksil's hand all the way to Syliza. It was time to be strong.

I listened as Acksil moved about the nearby rooms, and I used my feet to clear debris from a large patch on the floor. He soon returned and built a fire directly on the tile floor.

Once the light filled the room, I could see that the space was larger than I had imagined in the darkness without Acksil's hand-light. This must have been some type of public building. We were in a large hall or gathering room. A gaping hole in one of the walls made it appear even larger than it actually was. Through the hole, I could see a broken staircase leading to a second floor I had no intention of visiting.

Here and there, rested pieces of furniture in various states of filth and disrepair. It was more than evident that this place had been abandoned for a long time.

"I'm sorry you had to see what I did, Irys," Acksil said as he settled in near the fire. "Please know that I saw no other way to keep you safe. It was my only choice. Arik's charm was wearing off, and I had to stop her before she could travel away. She would have gone directly to Xandon." His hazel eyes were soft in the firelight. They were pleading with me to understand and, perhaps, to forgive.

I took a seat next to him to allow us to have a conversation without having to speak up. This place made me want to keep my voice at a level below the crackling of the fire.

"I'm grateful to you for saving my life in the only way you knew how." My tone was as genuine as my words. "I know you have done everything you can to keep us from harm. I also know this isn't the first time you have rescued me, placing your own life in danger." I was not outwardly forgiving him for the murder I'd seen earlier. I'd been working hard to forget the dreadful sight. I believed him when he said he felt it was his only choice. It was not a decision he'd made easily.

Wonder and gratitude washed over his face. "I had to save you," he said with conviction.

"You didn't have to save me, but you did it anyway."

A smile touched his lips only briefly before fading away. "They're going to come after us. They likely already know you're gone. They'll send the trackers. Alukka isn't in Capital City right now, but she will return soon. She'll be able to track Zayset's last travel, and she'll learn that we were here."

"She's unable to travel anyone here with her. Even if she reports our location, you have still given us a significant lead over our pursuers," I surmised as best I understood our situation.

"That's right," he confirmed, to my relief. "I chose this place because it borders on Sefaline, which means they won't send Fhurrk. He's their best tracker, but he fears the Sefaline. Their presence would throw him off our scent."

"Who will they send?" I asked, trying to better understand the way the Warriors were dispatched. It was as fascinating as it was valuable to know.

"They will likely send Amarogq Ioq'wa, and he'll use his wolves to track us down. They could also send one of the newer Warriors, such as Rakven Terredge."

The thought of having a Warrior with wolves tracking us was anything but comforting to me.

"We had best be smart and quick," I said with determination.

"Precisely," he agreed. "That was why I didn't take us directly back to Gbat Rher. That will be one of the first places Alukka will look for you, and she would have most certainly found you there. I highly doubt that your Knight is still waiting for you there anyway. Right now, the safest place for you to be is with me. Not in Gbat Rher and not at home. Xandon wants you, Irys. I don't know why he does, but he will try to take you again."

"Acksil, I understand that you're doing everything you can to keep us safe, but my goal must be to return home. I don't belong anywhere else."

"You need to be where you can be kept away from Xandon. I am going to take you somewhere safe. From there, we will find a way to contact the Knights and Lord Godeleva through secure channels. You'll only return to Lorammel again if it can be done without getting you captured."

My heart sank. It was going to take far longer to return home than I had expected. It could take seasons. I was still on the other side of the world without any resources or modes of travel other than my own two feet. No one at home had any idea where I was. Lord Imery must have been informed that I was missing by now.

I thought of Sir Fhirell and how hard he had tried to keep me safe. I remembered the lengths to which he had gone to respect what was important to me, even at a time in which we needed to travel on foot across Gbat Rher to rejoin our group. Despite what may have been his better judgment, he helped Lieutenant Fhurrk at my request. He and I were to open a courtship together if Lord Imery would allow it.

Now, I couldn't imagine that he would be willing to continue his pursuit of me. *How could any man want to be burdened with a woman who was continually targeted by an elite military force from an enemy country? Or who would seek to send herself toward that force to rescue a friend even after having only recently been freed from those soldiers?*

Sir Fhirell's open mind was one of the things I appreciated the most about him, but even the most open-minded man could not be expected to put up with this. I owed it to him to return safely home and show him that I would not hold any grudge against him for withdrawing from his romantic interests in me. Nonetheless, I would forever admire him.

"I trust you," I said to Acksil as much to inform him as it was to reassure myself.

"Thank you. I can only give you my word that I'm not trying to keep you away from the people you love, Irys. I know how the Warriors work."

"I know you're not. I believe you. What you have said makes sense. You lost your entire family today. You would not have done that for something as foolish as to keep me away from my home."

"The people we're now seeking were once my family, too," he said in a confessional tone. "I'm going to take you to the man who was once my teacher, Storr Dimog. He won't be happy to see me, but it won't take much convincing for him to want to help save you."

"I will do my part. I will do what you ask me to. If you trust Mr. Dimog to help us to remain safe, so will I." I tried to sound confident, despite the bout of nausea that was swirling in my stomach.

"How are you feeling?" he asked in a concerned tone as though he could read my mind.

"In shock, I believe."

Reaching out, he brought an arm around me, rubbing my opposite arm. It was a gesture that was clearly meant to be comforting, and I permitted it to have that effect on me. I wanted to be warmed and comforted. Indeed, this would not be considered proper for a young lady such as myself, but I could hardly imagine that these circumstances were what my etiquette guide had in mind when it came to propriety in socializing.

Leaning toward him, I rested my head on his shoulder. I hadn't expected it to be as comfortable as it was. For reasons beyond my understanding, the sensation overwhelmed me, and I burst into a fountain of tears, covering my face with my hands.

"I swear on my life, Irys, I will keep you safe or die trying. I won't let him get you," he whispered into my hair as he brought his second arm around me.

It took a few minutes before I could gather myself, but he sat very patiently with me as I did. Looking up at him, the firelight danced across his face through the veil of tears in my eyes.

"I swear on my soul, Acksil, I will be good. The Goddess will see what you have done and the good person you have saved, and She will welcome you to Paradise one day."

A smile creased the corners of his lips. "I think you're the only person who could say that to me and have me believe it."

"Perhaps it is because I mean it." I was determined to live up to my promise.

He nodded, the smile still playing over his mouth as he released me from his embrace, keeping the one arm around me for warmth.

"Do you know much about the rebels or the rebellion?"

"Not very much," I admitted.

"My teacher, the one I mentioned, is their leader."

"You're taking us to stay with the leader of the rebels?"

"Yes. He is a fighter. He fights for what he believes in."

"Is he dangerous?" I asked, both out of curiosity and because I wanted to know what Acksil's answer would be.

"Everyone is dangerous, Irys. But no, he is not dangerous in the way you mean. He is a good man. One of the best I have ever met."

"Not everyone is dangerous, Acksil. I'm not dangerous."

"You are dangerous, Irys. You're dangerous because Xandon wants you and that means people who stand between him and you are at risk. People could be hurt, and they could die."

"That doesn't make me dangerous. It makes him dangerous."

He nodded as though accepting that we would not agree on the matter.

"I don't want to be dangerous," I said.

"Not many of us want to be that way. I wish I had kinder words to offer you, but you have been lied to enough."

"I don't think I need kind words right now. I need honest ones," I told him, knowing I meant it. I needed words upon which I could rely without having to question them. I needed certainty.

"As dangerous as it may be to be around you, it is worth every minute to me. You're a good person, Irys. You deserve a happy life."

Leaning toward him, I kissed the rich brown skin of his cheek. It struck me at that moment that I felt more free than I had in many days. Here, hiding in an abandoned building in an abandoned city from an abandoned country, I was sitting by firelight with a rogue Warrior who was once tasked with capturing me, and I was free.

"Are you tired?" Acksil's words forced me to blink back to reality.

"I'm exhausted and yet I don't know if I will ever sleep again."

"Try to shut your eyes and see if you can get some rest, even if you don't sleep."

"Do you need to sleep tonight, Acksil?"

"Not tonight. I slept through most of the day. I'll be fine. I promise I'll keep you safe."

I chose not to question him. I'd told him I would trust him, and I was not about to change my mind now.

Tonight, I would end my life as a victim. Tomorrow, I would rise strong and ready to face the path ahead of me as Acksil's equal. I was determined to use my strengths to our advantage. Certainly, he was a trained Warrior, but I had read a library's worth of books and had already travelled across oceans and continents, and lived quite comfortably in an enemy military base.

Today, Acksil led me through our escape. Tomorrow, he and I were travellers together.

He turned to look at the fire, and I followed his gaze to the low flames that fluttered and crackled, sharing their warmth and light in this forgotten space.

Without even knowing my eyes had closed, I slipped into an unexpected sleep.

A cool hand rested on her pale face.

Slowly, she opened her eyes from the depths of sleep to the welcome sight of Xandon.

"Enadria, I will find you, my love."

Chapter 31

Megan

After leaving Mez' office, I debated finding Xandon's to confront him about what he knew of Earth. I chickened out, worried that I might get Mez in trouble or somehow make this bad situation a lot worse.

Instead, I made my way back to my tiny apartment, deciding not to seek out Amorette at Remms' place, either. I was too rattled from my conversation with Mez, and I wanted to be ready whenever he knocked.

I was so lost in miserable thought that I barely observed anyone or anything on my trek back to my place. Once inside, I locked the door, flicked on the light, kicked off my shoes, and collapsed onto the bed, hugging the bright pink heart-shaped pillow.

I didn't move for a long time. Thoughts and emotions swarmed around and around in my head as I desperately tried to make sense of what I had decided to do and why I was doing it.

I still wasn't entirely convinced that I was making the right choice by cutting ties with Thayn and remaining in Kavylak. It felt wrong to say goodbye and to tell him to leave me behind. All this time I had wanted nothing more than to reunite with him and leave. Replaying my conversation with Mez over and over again, I tried in vain to feel the confidence I craved to assure me that I had made the right choice. The feeling would not come. Nothing seemed to ease my fear or my heartache, so I decided to think about home instead. I thought about Cole.

I wondered what he was doing at this moment.

Is he thinking about me? Has he forgotten about me? Has he already moved away to university? Would he have some new crazy story to tell me the next time I saw him?

I smirked to myself, knowing there was no way any story he had to tell me would out-crazy the one I had to tell him, even though he was always the one between us to have the far more weird and exciting life.

I could imagine it now:

Cole: "Hey Meg! You'll never guess who I met this summer?"
Me: "Oh, yeah? Who?"
Cole: "The Dalai Lama."
Me: "No way! That's awesome. You'll never guess who I met."
Cole: "Who?"
Me: "Aliens with super-human powers."

I would finally have a nuttier story to tell than Cole. Of course, he'd never believe me, but that was beside the point.

A light knock at the door startled me back to reality. Springing from the bed, I took the few small steps to the door and asked softly: "Who is it?"

"It's Mez. Are you ready? It's time."

"Yes," I whispered.

Grabbing my key, I slipped on my shoes, flicked off the light, and opened the door. Mez was in full uniform, and greeted me with a light and friendly smile. I stepped out into the cool night air to join him.

I locked the door, sliding the key into my pants pocket, and turned to him, ready. He nodded to me, and without a word, began to walk at a brisk pace. I followed him, easily keeping up with his stride in my athletic pants and shoes.

Yup. Definitely made the right wardrobe choice.

"Do you want me to stay with you or step away so you can speak privately?" he asked.

"I'd rather speak to him privately." I didn't even need to think about that one. I wanted my goodbye to him to be as private as possible. Plus, I couldn't imagine that Thayn seeing me in the company of Mez would be in any way positive or beneficial to what I had to say to him and what I hoped he would understand.

"I will do what I can," Mez promised. "I may check in on you, but I will make my presence known to you if I do."

"Thank you. How long will I have? Will I know when I must go?"

"I don't know how long," he confessed, "but I will do my best to give you as much time as possible, and I will warn you when it's time."

"Okay."

"It's important for you to stay quiet until I say otherwise," he informed me, speaking in a tone just slightly above a whisper.

"Okay," I responded, matching his tone to show that I'd both heard him and understood that being quiet was important.

We reached the main building, and I saw the two guards standing watch at the doors. Remembering from earlier that I would have to show my ID to gain entry, I lifted my hand to hold the tag ready. I was surprised when Mez suddenly reached over and captured my hand in his. I looked at him questioningly, but he didn't return my gaze. His was locked on the guards. He gave my hand a gentle, reassuring squeeze, and continuing to hold it, walked us right past the soldiers, who didn't appear to notice we were there.

Uh...what just happened? Do they just not care because Mez is a Warrior?

Mez pulled the door open and drew me inside after him.

Unlike earlier in the day when I had been with Amorette, the building's foyer was not nearly as busy, but there were still enough people that you had to watch where you were going. The moderate people traffic didn't bother Mez. He walked us at the same brisk purposeful pace toward our intended direction. I kept up, doing my best not to get in anyone's way, but soon realized that this wasn't necessary.

Although there were enough people around that our presence should have been noticed, no one looked in our direction. In fact, not only did they not seem to notice us, but we never had to maneuver around anyone, and no one ever stepped in our way in spite of the rapid pace at which we still moved. It was as though Mez and I were invisible and travelling a path that only we knew existed.

I glanced at Mez, wondering if he found this to be weird, too, but he didn't pay any attention to me. His expression was one of intense focus.

Oh my god! Was he making us invisible? Don't be stupid Megan, you're not invisible. Everyone here just has better things to do and think about than you wandering around with a Warrior.

We approached a large metal door with two soldiers standing guard. The sign on the door read "Restricted Area. Level Six Clearance Required."

Mez slowed our pace and my heart sped up, knowing that this had to be the prison where Thayn was being held. I assumed Mez had clearance and braced myself, ready to do whatever he asked when we stopped to talk to the guards.

He didn't stop.

He reached out and opened the door, and we walked through it. The guards didn't even blink. They didn't show any signs of seeing us, and we were *right* there. I could have easily touched one.

Oh. My. God. He did make us invisible!

I stared dumbfounded at Mez, who quietly shut the door before leading me down a flight of stairs where another pair of soldiers waited. Like the other soldiers we had encountered, they didn't appear to notice us, or Mez opening the door they were guarding.

Once we were inside, and he had quietly shut the door, he turned and leaned toward me, whispering into my ear, "He's at the end. I will wait here but will come to get you if it's time to go or if I need to check on things."

And, just like that, my amazement over Mez' ability was crushed by the anxiety and dread of seeing the man I had wanted to find since the battle had separated us.

"I won't break my promise," I managed to whisper back.

He gave me a meaningful look of trust, squeezed my hand, and released it.

I attempted to swallow but was unsuccessful. I forced myself to make my way down the long hall lined with floor-to-ceiling barred cells. Fear gripped me at the memory of walking through the brig on the ship where I had first found Irys. The only small comfort was that there were no putrid smells of rot and death in this place as there had been in the brig. This told me the prisoners who were kept here had to have at least been treated better than Irys had. Most of the barred cells were empty, and I didn't dare look in the ones where I'd caught movement out of the corner of my eye. It was blessedly and horribly quiet.

By the time I had reached his cell, I had broken into a cold sweat. I stepped up to the metal bars and looked inside. Thayn was lying on a cot that looked more like a metal table than a bed. His eyes were closed. His long hair had returned to its original golden shade from the dyed brown it had been when he was disguised as Balo the slave. It stood out in sharp contrast against the dark outfit he wore, an all-black jumpsuit with two rings of white around the wrists and ankles, which made it appear as though he were wearing shackles.

I tried to swallow again, unsuccessfully.

"Thayn," I whispered.

His eyes opened, and he turned his head to look at me. His blue eyes widened with recognition, and he immediately rose to his feet and approached the bars.

"Megan...are you alright?" he asked in both surprise and concern.

"I'm fine. Are you?"

"Yes."

I exhaled a sigh of relief. "Good. I'm glad. I'm sorry you're here. Once I found out, I did what I could to get to you as soon as I was able."

He shook his head. "I wouldn't want you to place yourself in danger." He reached through the bars and took my hands in his. I held his back. "Are you still in the same situation as before? The same quarters? The Knights will return, and I will help them look for you."

"Thayn," I started, suddenly finding it impossible to make my lips, tongue, and teeth work together to finish the sentence.

He looked at me patiently, expectantly, adoringly, waiting for me to continue.

My face grew hot as I fought the urge to cry. I stared at the beautiful and honourable man in front of me. Any woman would kill to have this man, who liked me enough to risk his own safety and still wanted to be my boyfriend.

I didn't want to let him down. I didn't want to break his heart. But he deserved no less than the truth. He deserved someone from Qarradune who would make him happy in a way that I knew I never could. My heart could never truly be his when deep down I would always pine for a home he would never believe existed.

"Thayn, when the Knights return, or whenever you might get the chance, I want you to leave, and I want you to leave without me." I spoke quietly, but my voice remained steady.

"Of course I can't do that, Megan. Don't be concerned. We will all find our way safely back to Syliza. We would never leave you here. I would never." He raised one of my hands to his lips and kissed the back of it. "I meant what I said to you," he added gently.

I couldn't help but smile, even though I was finding it harder and harder to breathe as the pain of regret, longing, and sadness swelled inside me.

He was absolutely perfect, a fairytale hero brought to life. I was the mad, stupid princess in that fairytale, who was about to crush the hero, and a life of true happiness with him. The princess who would sacrifice it all for the sliver of hope that a villain who had already betrayed her might help her to return home.

It seemed crazy but as long as I believed that sliver of hope existed, I couldn't give up. I had to play the role of the mad, stupid princess.

I hated it.

I shook my head. "Thayn. You don't understand. I want you to leave me here. I'm choosing to stay here."

"I don't understand. Why ever would you want this, Megan?" Confusion and concern crept into his otherwise happy expression. I could tell his mind hadn't yet fully processed or believed what I was saying.

I took a breath, deciding to be as honest as I could. "Because I don't belong in Syliza any more than I belong in Kavylak. You're a wonderful man, Thayn, but I can't be with you. I can't be with anyone. I need to find my way back to the home I remember, and I have a better chance of doing that here than in Syliza."

Thayn shook his head. "Of course you belong in Syliza," he said adamantly. "You have friends there. You have a future there. If you wish for assistance to find your home, I would give you every resource I have at my disposal." He looked at me with a gentle and caring expression, running the pad of his thumb in a soft caress over the top of the hand he had kissed. "You are loved there, Megan. You belong."

I couldn't fight the tears this time, and they spilled from my eyes. I knew it was going to be difficult to say goodbye, but I never dreamed it would be this hard. Still, I thought of Cole, I thought of

Aunt Vera, I thought of my life back on Earth, and I held tightly to my resolve.

"I know you would," I assured him, believing everything he said to be true. "But I don't belong there, and I don't belong here. You can't help me. When I first opened my eyes on Qarradune, I wasn't in Syliza. I was with Xandon. He's my way back home, Thayn."

"No. Don't be enchanted by him, Megan," he implored, whispering and stepping as close as he could to the bars. He brought our hands up to rest against chest. "He is an evil man. He uses his magic to deceive."

"I know he's not a good man. I know he can't be trusted, and I am not enchanted by him," I promised. "But that doesn't mean he isn't my way home."

"Megan, whatever help he could offer you would be a lie or would come with a very great cost, one you may not be able to pay. Please don't make this choice. Come back with me when the Knights arrive. We will find another way for you."

Oh, how I wished I could tell him how much I wanted to do that, but this wasn't a time for wishing and wanting. It was a time to face facts, and all the facts – and even my dreams - pointed to Xandon, not Syliza and not Thayn.

"If I should fail to help in bringing you home," Thayn continued, "you have my word that I would spend my life making sure you could be happy in Syliza. You would know you belong, and you would want for nothing."

I drew one of my hands away from his so that I could rest it against his cheek. He smiled and more of my tears fell.

"I believe you, Thayn. I do, I swear I do. And I would never be able to express to you in words how grateful I am for everything you've done for me, for the risks you've taken to keep me safe. You have always made me feel important and have made me feel like I belong. I will never forget that, ever. But I can't go back."

Disbelief slowly crept into his expression, and for the first time, I could see my words were sinking in and the walls of his hope were cracking.

"Megan…I will beg of you if I must, if that is what it takes to have you hear reason. Think of Miss Godeleva and everyone who is waiting for your return."

"I know it's hard to believe, but I am thinking of her, and of you, and of everyone I care about. I promise you I am. I don't make this decision lightly. I have given it a lot of thought, and I truly believe that you and Irys will be better off without me in Syliza. I know that if I go back with you, Thayn, they'll come after me again, and I don't want to live like that. I don't want to put you through that or Irys through that. You both deserve better."

"I would defend you for all my days. I would stop them, Megan. If you would only give me the chance to show you. It would not be a burden. It would be an honour. Please, give me the chance to love you, Megan."

This was torture, and I was the cause of it. I couldn't stand it. It had to end now.

"I can't, Thayn," I said softly through the tears. "Give your chance of love to another who is worthy of it. I am not the one for you."

He looked at me for a long time, clearly trying to think of anything to say that would change my mind. I held his gaze until, finally, his shoulders sank a little, and he gently released my hand.

I drew my hands back, never having felt more alone in my life.

"I'm sorry," I said softly, wishing I could take his pain and disappointment away, wishing I wasn't the cause of it. "I meant what I said. I will forever be grateful for everything you've done for me."

He watched me with a sad expression and nodded. "If you should ever change your mind, I would never turn my back on you."

I gave him a deep understanding nod, once again wishing I could take everything back and tell him I'd changed my mind. I bit my inner lip hard to prevent myself from giving in. I tasted blood.

Thayn stood taller and said, "Be safe, Megan. Live a long and beautiful life at home."

"You, too, Thayn. I wish you all the happiness in the world. Safe journey home, my friend."

"Safe journey home, my friend," he repeated.

I looked at him one final time and tried to smile but found that I couldn't. I turned and quickly walked down the hall, not daring a glance back in his direction. I knew if I did, I would run back to him and beg him to forgive me for everything I had said, and tell him how much I thought he was perfect and how I truly did want a life with him.

Out of respect for my choice, and equally to my dismay, Thayn never tried to call me back, which only made me cry harder. I slapped my hand over my mouth to stifle my sobs. By the time I reached Mez, I could barely make out his profile through the tears.

He stepped up to me and placed a protective arm around me, guiding me quietly out past the first two guards and up the stairs to the door that would lead us into the main hall.

Once we were passed the second set of guards and a fair distance away from them, Mez suddenly stopped, crouched slightly, and scooped me up into his arms, carrying me out of the building. I didn't stop him. I just hung on and quietly cried, feeling like a total monster.

Have I ruined every shot of happiness I could ever have by throwing in my lot with Xandon? This is a man who has only ever betrayed me, and I've chosen him over Thayn, a man who has only ever been kind and good to me.

Eventually, Mez set me on my feet.

"Can you get the door open?" He asked softly and with sympathy. I opened my eyes and could see through my blurred vision that we had arrived at my apartment.

I nodded and fumbled for the key I had placed in my pocket. Withdrawing it, I inserted it into the lock, after a few tries, and opened the door.

"Thank you," I croaked to him.

"Aésha's here," he responded quietly.

"What?" I asked, sobering a little at his words. I wiped my eyes and looked at him and then over to where he'd nodded, seeing a pair of boots near the door.

"Have some water tonight and rest. I will see you later. I'm sorry, I can't stay," Mez said regrettably.

I nodded to him, knowing that he had other things to do. I had lived up to my end of the bargain, and now it was his turn. I gave his arm a light squeeze of thanks.

He took my hand in response and squeezed it back. "Goodnight, Megan."

"Goodnight."

He released my hand and left. I entered my apartment, shutting the door behind me, and locking it.

Slipping off my shoes and shedding the track suit jacket, I made my way over to the bed and climbed in beside Aésha, still sniffling.

She shifted and turned, putting her arms around me, holding me close. I held her back and let myself cry it out, feeling comforted by the embrace, especially because it was Aésha, and I felt safe with her.

"Why are you here?" I asked curiously when my tears slowed.

She stroked my hair and answered softly and caringly: "Mez told me what happened. I know Balo was technically a slave, but I know you were secretly friends with him, Megan. You didn't hide that well. I'm sorry you lost your friend."

For a moment, I thought Mez had betrayed me, but as she continued to speak, I knew that he hadn't told Aésha the whole truth. He must have told her enough to bring her here because he knew I'd be upset.

I nodded and sniffed. "Thanks for being here, Aésha."

"I'll stay the night, Baby. You shouldn't be alone after a loss. If you need to talk I'm here and if you want to sleep, I won't leave."

"Okay. Thanks," I whispered, grateful she was staying. I didn't know what she thought happened to my slave friend Balo, but I wasn't about to question it. It didn't matter anyway, because it was a loss; my loss.

She gently stroked my face. "I'll take care of you, Baby. A friend of mine helped to take care of him for you, I heard. If you feel the need to pray, WhiteRobe Ihleah met your Balo and brought him his meals. She will know the man you're grieving for."

The word "WhiteRobe" and the name "Ihleah" sounded vaguely familiar, and I slowly recalled that this was the woman who had been in the bunker with Amorette, Fiffine, and I before we were captured by the rebels. It occurred to me that she must be some sort of religious figure, like a nun or a priest or something. The way Aésha spoke of her, she sounded nice. It made me feel a little better knowing that someone had cared enough to bring Thayn some comfort while he had been in prison.

"Thank you, Aésha. I'll remember that," I said, and I would.

She nodded against me, and we both stayed quiet for a long time. I grew calmer in her embrace. Although the tears stopped, a pit of sadness remained, and I knew without question that I could have easily loved Thayn. I had wanted to.

"Aésha...I think I could have loved him," I suddenly confessed, unable to keep this to myself any longer, even if she didn't entirely understand the situation and that I was talking about Thayn.

She held me tighter. "I'm sorry, Baby. It's a lot of hurt when you love someone you can't have." Her words were not empty. She sounded as though she was speaking from experience and it made me think of Asimara and Arik. I wondered if Asimara was someone Arik couldn't have and if he was someone she couldn't have.

Maybe that's why they're secretive about their relationship. Maybe he does love her, but it's against the rules for some reason.

"Aésha? Have you ever been in love with someone, or thought that you could love someone you couldn't have?"

"I have, Baby. I understand what you're going through. It's why I got married."

What? Did she just say she was married?

"Married?"

She kissed my head in response. "Go to sleep. Start fresh in the morning. Whatever we have for breakfast, I'll melt chocolate on it."

She settled in to sleep, leaving me wondering if she was kidding or if she was telling the truth. Since this was Aésha, anything could be possible. I was too exhausted to question her further and engage in an Aésha-banter, but I definitely had plans to figure out what she meant about her "I got married" statement tomorrow.

I shut my eyes, deciding that sleep was what I needed, too.

I let my mind wander to Thayn, and I thought about what I had done for him, and as much as it had hurt to say goodbye, a small part of me felt good and a little proud of myself that I'd had the courage to do what was ultimately the right thing for him. Thayn would be free. He would get over me, and he could live his life without me interrupting it, and without ever carrying around the responsibility of knowing how much I had wanted and still wanted to be with him.

I only wished I was as certain that the choice I had made for me was as right as the one I had made for Thayn. At the very least, now with Thayn out of the picture, there was nothing keeping me here or taking away my focus to get back home.

Somehow, I would find a way home with or without Xandon's help. I just hoped that by choosing to stay in Kavylak, I hadn't put myself in even more danger than I had already experienced. Fear crawled up my spine as I remembered the horror I had seen over the past few weeks, and I reflexively gripped Aésha tighter, desperate to get the memories of blood, torture, and death out of my mind.

Her arms immediately tightened around me to match the intensity of my hold, easing my uncertainties and fears. Her silent response soothed me and assured me in a way that no words ever could.

Situations were not always what they seemed. People were not always who you assumed them to be. Friends could be enemies and enemies could be friends.

Aésha, Mez, and Keavren, people I would have once thought of as enemies, had all proven themselves to be my friends.

I may have lost Thayn, Irys, and Syliza, but whatever awaited me in Kavylak, I wouldn't face it alone.

About the Authors

The Perspective book series was written by two authors: Amanda Giasson and Julie B. Campbell. After having met by chance in the lineup at their university bookstore on their first day of classes, Amanda and Julie became fast friends. They credit their survival of many of their 3-hour long lectures to their ability to escape to the world of Qarradune. The truth is that Megan and Irys were born of note-passing in the form of creative writing. While neither author condones this behavior in-class, as it likely does nothing for a student's grades, it did happen to work out, in their case. It also helped to define the unique writing style shared by the authors in the creation of the story. The two authors have been steadily working on the Perspective book series, ever since.

Made in the USA
Monee, IL
20 April 2021